Everliving

CHRISTINA DUDLEY

Bella
VITA

Bellevue, Washington

Everliving

Published by Bellavita Press
Bellevue, Washington 98004
www.bellavitapress.com

Author photo: www.Platinum-Multimedia.com
Cover design: Kathy Campbell

Printed and bound in the United States of America

ISBN 978-0-9830721-1-9

For the Beauty of the Earth,

for the Glory of the Skies

Scottie: What are you thinking?

Madeleine: Of all the people who have been born and
              have died while the trees went on living.

Scottie: Their true name is *Sequoia sempervirens*.
              Always green. Ever-living.

—*Vertigo*, 1958

Barely had her prayer ended when a deep languor took hold
of her limbs—a filmy bark enfolded her tender breast, her hair
grew into leaves, her arms into branches; dull roots arrested
her feet that were, of late, so swift, while her head became the
crown. Nothing of her remained, except her radiant loveliness.

—Ovid

1895

Albert stood, hat in hand, feeding the brim round and round through his fingers.

Rising, Lindstrom threw his *Humboldt Standard* on the desk. "For God's sake—what now?"

The boy took in the man's unshaven condition and red eyes. He had never seen him like this but Mam said that was what grief did to you—made you hollow and sick and wondering why the world went on like it did.

"Sir," said Albert. He didn't know if the news would make Mr. Lindstrom wild, and, with him pacing back and forth like that, he already put Albert in mind of the caged circus tiger that passed through Eureka last spring.

"Well?" The man prompted. "Is that log bucker Derwent making trouble again?"

"No, sir." Unless you counted that Derwent was sodden drunk behind Miz Etta's and had been for days. Albert's hat brim made another orbit, and he shifted his weight from one muddy, sawdust-crusted boot to the other, taking care to stay on the mat. "No, sir... I'm come to tell you that they found her things."

Lindstrom made a small choking sound. Turning his back on Albert, he stalked to the window where the greenish panes sagged in their glazing bars. The boy knew well there wasn't a thing new to see out there. He waited while Lindstrom got out his handkerchief. Pressed it to his eyes, his forehead. Replaced it. "Which...things...of Mrs. Lindstrom's? And where were they discovered?"

Around went Albert's hat again. Seeing Lindstrom halt and fix his eyes on it, the boy made an effort to hold still. "By the Overhang, sir. You know, downstream from where the footbridge washed out and there's the big drop. Sir, it was her hat. The one with the ribbons wide as my hands. And then her basket, what she used to gather things in. There was still some dried-up ginger and bark in it." Albert delivered this information with his gaze circumspectly on Mr. Lindstrom's knee-caps, but he could tell the man was trembling, and the boy found this so unsettling that his hat slipped completely through his fingers, rolling some feet away—a dreadful scrape. If he chased it, he would get mud on the floor, and Mr. Lindstrom liked everything just so. But he couldn't just let it be and go away because it was Albert's only hat, and, truth to tell, it wasn't that much cleaner than his boots. Not to mention what Mam would say if he returned home hatless. Some prankster had thieved Albert's only other shirt and pair of trousers off the line last month, and Mam swung between accusing Albert's friends and Mr. Kee the Chinaman.

"Nothing else?"

Albert wasn't sure if Mr. Lindstrom noticed the hat problem, even though the man's red eyes were burning a hole in him. Mam said the worst part about the man's grief was that he had no place to hang it. "Without a body or even knowing what became of her—what good will the headstone be, when he knows she's not under it? If you can't be sad over something or feel sad every time you go a certain some-where, well then it just haunts you. All the time and everywhere." Mam clucked when she said this, and all the women she said it to clucked back. Mrs. Holloway said in her sly voice, "Looking haunted is noth-ing new for Pall Lindstrom—it was indecent the way his eyes would follow her around when she was alive! Like he wanted to eat her up!"

All the women clucked again—excited this time—and leaned their heads together.

"Boy?" Lindstrom snapped Albert from his reverie. "I said, did they find anything else?"

"No, sir," he replied at once. He meant, No, sir, nobody found *her*.

Another silence fell, if you could call it that, considering the constant whine of the mill's gang saw. Eighteen months without an accident, Albert's father the foreman said. This was a point of family pride because Albert's grandfather had lost his arm twenty years prior on that very mill floor. "Pa was on the platform running the logs past the saw. Chain gets wrapped around his arm—yanks it clean off."

In a move so fast Albert lost track of it, Pall Lindstrom stooped for the runaway felt hat and shoved it back at him. "All right, then. You've said your news. You make sure those...items...get delivered to my house and get on outta here."

"Yes, sir. Thank you, sir."

But the manager had already forgotten him, running one hand through his unkempt hair (hair Albert had never seen but neatly pomaded) and taking a seat again at the desk. There lay the newspaper, and, with a grunt, Lindstrom swept it off into the waste basket.

Red Gap Woman Continues Missing, Believed Dead.

Albert hurried down the wooden steps.

With a scream, the gang saw broke another log into cants, the dark red heartwood sheared in rough planks.

CHAPTER 1

Wreck

It was hard to say if he hit the deer or the deer hit him.

Not that it much mattered—the end result was the same. Ben surveyed the damage: crumpled hood—a frozen wave of blue, paint-flaking steel—smashed headlight, leaking radiator. He had already tried to force the hood back down, but the latch no longer lined up. A quick check in the back of the borrowed car revealed only the manu-facturer's spare tire and jack. No rope to tie car parts shut, and given the plunging temperature and ominous grating sound from the engine, Ben had no intention of shredding any of his clothing to fashion one.

Damn it all! Now he owed Lance for a wrecked car, on top of ev-erything else.

How far was he from Highway 101? California had upwards of 35 million people, but he looked to be the only one of them on this road, if it could even be called that. The map had it marked as a logging trail—pure dotted line.

Ben powered up his cell phone, more to cover his bases than from any hope it would prove useful. The welcome screen hardly flashed before the Low Battery indicator appeared. No bars anyhow.

What was it that couple had done a few winters ago, when they broke down on a logging road in Oregon? Burned the tires—that was it. Hoping the smoke would catch someone's eye. It didn't, and in the end they froze to death. Or was it starved to death? All Ben knew was that, whatever reasons for survival that couple had, he had better ones. He was already in disgrace and on the run. If this flight now cost him his life—hell, if it even cost him a couple frostbitten toes!—he would be damned if he gave his advisor or his girlfriend that satisfaction. Make that his *ex*-advisor and *ex*-girlfriend.

Ben checked the map again in the fading light. If he didn't know any better, he would say it felt like snow, but this was freaking early October, and he might be at 2000 feet, but he couldn't be more than ten miles from the coast. Still, he rummaged through the duffel bag in the back seat and pulled out his fleece and Gore-Tex. He had let Courtney keep his wool cap, so he was out of luck there.

He remembered her pleading expression as she took it from him. "Come on, Ben. Stay. You can't just drive out of here by yourself."

"Watch me."

"It's dangerous! What if you run out of gas or break down or something?"

"Then a mountain lion will eat me, and wouldn't that be convenient for you?"

"You're being childish."

"It looks that way, since you clearly prefer older men."

She stomped one booted foot then. "You know what—just shut up, Ben. I've already said I'm sorry you had to find us like that. That sucked, I know. I'm not proud of going behind your back. It just... happened."

"'Happened'? What the hell, Courtney? You just 'happened' to crawl out of our tent and into Wilson's? And—what—I know it was dark, but you didn't clue in when he got on top of you and you felt his freaking *beard*?"

Furious tears sprang to her eyes. "That's not what I meant, Ben. I meant that I knew things weren't great with us—"

"Who said things weren't great with us?" Ben shouted. "Because it wasn't me! If you thought things weren't great with us, you think maybe you could've brought it up? Given us a shot at working through whatever the hell you thought wasn't right?"

"Ben—"

He was beyond listening. "Just what the hell did you think it would fix—screwing a second guy who—wait—just happened to be your boyfriend's *boss*?"

"Because that's what this is about, isn't it?" Courtney retorted. Panting, she got right in his face. "You say this is about me 'betraying' you or some b.s. like that, when what really fries you is that I did it with your advisor. This is about your career."

Ben recoiled as if she had punched him in the gut. He would have sat down to ride out the shock, if not for the rampant poison-oak vines curling close by. *Toxicodendron diversilobum.* This time of year the leaves were brilliant orange. Objectively beautiful. If you didn't mind the toxin.

It took a minute, but when he spoke again he was relieved to find his voice steady. "Courtney. I'd be lying if I said career didn't enter my mind. I mean, Wilson's one of, like, four professors on the entire planet doing canopy work and the only one doing coast redwoods. If you had to stab me in the back, you couldn't have picked a better way to do it. But no matter who you did it with, it still would've hurt."

"Oh," she said. Her gaze dropped. "So now you wanna say you're in love with me?"

"I was. In love with you." He unsnapped the pocket on his thigh to fish out Lance's car keys, ignoring her muttered curse. "You tell me, Courtney: if this was about career, are you 100% sure it wasn't about yours?" He thought of her behavior around Wilson since joining the team: enthusiastic, helpful, soaking up the botany professor's knowledge as if he were the Dalai Lama expounding on secrets of the universe. It had almost embarrassed Ben, especially since he suspected his own behavior bore striking similarities. He took a deep breath, finding sick enjoyment in the sight of her clenched fists. "Sleeping with the boss doesn't exactly hurt you, does it?"

She made a strangling noise. For an instant he thought she might even hit him.

"You shut up, Ben," hissed his former girlfriend. "Shut up and get out of here. Do everyone a favor and run away, like you always do. We don't need you. The project doesn't need you. Lance can do your job in the canopy—"

"—And Wilson can do my job in the sack."

"Go to *hell*!" Courtney screeched. She kicked impotently at the soggy forest floor and turned on her heel.

"Hey, Silent Spring," he called after her, "watch the *Polystichum munitum*. You're a botanist, remember? You can screw everything but the ecosystem."

What Courtney thought of Ben and botany and the whole entire ecosystem echoed to the outer limits of the North Coast Range, and with her malediction ringing in his ears, Ben jumped in Lance's Corolla and drove away.

He leaned against the passenger side door to regroup. Okay. Ten miles to the coast, say, which meant fifteen miles to 101. It might be October, but there still had to be a few tourists driving up and down this remote stretch of the Golden State. It would be dark as sin before he was even halfway there, however, assuming the map wasn't out of date and that the logging road actually still connected. In the pitch black he'd certainly get lost, die of exposure, and be devoured by the local fauna, to Courtney and Ed Wilson's delight, Ben was sure. No, the walk would have to wait for first light.

Which meant he was going to spend tonight here. Even as he

thought this, the first flake drifted down, alighting on his shoulder. A fluke, he thought. A fluke flake. But then another followed, and another. Ben groaned at his bad luck. Freezing temperatures meant he would have to sleep in the car and run the engine from time to time, the warped, grating, rumbling engine that would blow up or give out before long. The forest gods hated him.

"I tried to protect you," he said aloud. "It was Courtney who kicked the sword fern—why are you coming after me?" Of course, this could be about the deer. Involuntary deerslaughter was probably worth a year's bad karma, give or take a few months, depending on how much the deer resembled Bambi. This roused him. If it were still alive, he could at least put it out of its misery. How, he didn't know, since there was only the cheap jack in the trunk and his own Swiss army knife. Trying not to picture whether he would have to corkscrew or tweezer it to death, Ben made his way back along the road. A good, fist-sized rock could do the trick—bludgeon it into oblivion—but all he saw were ineffectual stones not much bigger than gravel. Maybe strangle it with poison-oak vines?

The snowflakes were falling faster now and beginning to stick, but after a hundred yards or so he was able to pick out the bloody smear on the surface where the deer landed after impact. Holding his breath, Ben peered into the ditch alongside, but no carcass lay there. He could picture the animal struggling up the farther bank, through that area where the huckleberries were trampled, on into the forest.

He hesitated. If the creature could scramble into and out of a ditch and slog through a tangle of huckleberry and *Rosa gymnocarpa*, maybe it was well on the road to recovery and he could get back to ensuring his own survival. But this smacked of cowardice on his part—Courtney would certainly call it that—and there *was* the blood, after all. "I'll give you another hundred yards," Ben said. "If you're not dead or down in the next hundred yards, we're calling it even." He considered getting his headlamp out of the car, but its batteries were nearly dead, and coming at the deer like a glowing Cyclops would only make its last moments more terrifying. "Man up," he told himself. "And get it over with."

Once among the trees, the snow stopped like magic, none of it able to reach the ground through the thick canopy of branches overhead. Second-growth redwoods, Douglas firs, the occasional hemlock. What light remained of the day came only in a few oblique slants, fingers clawing their way inward. And there was the silence. Even the birds had left off, and his footfalls made no sound in the spongy mulch of plant debris. Had Ben not spent the last couple months in an even denser pocket of redwoods, he might have felt fear, but as it was, the woods acted as a balm. The faint lemony smell of redwood enveloped him. His crises assumed their proper proportions beneath the towering growth. Before post-doctorates, before academic backbiting and machinating, before Ed Wilson's betrayal, before Courtney, even, there had been the forest. The forest and his love for it. He found his attention divided between the spectacular overhead views and the rich flowering of fungi at the roots, humble parishioners in a Gothic cathedral. There was no sign of the deer, and he was easily 150 yards in. He should go back before he got lost. Definitely. Or maybe after getting just one sample of that cream-colored Indian pipe because he'd never seen one so huge—

"H-h-h-help me."

Ben rocketed to his feet, the *Monotropa uniflora* tumbling from his hand.

The voice could have come from any direction, and he spun in place, his heart racing. Who could be out here?

"Hello?" he called. He was glad he had his knife out, inadequate as the blade seemed.

Movement through the trees caught his eye, and he winged up an instant prayer that what he glimpsed would not be human. Better a bobcat, even, than a human owner to that pitiful cry.

It was the deer.

Above him, where the forest floor angled sharply upward, it took another limping step and sagged against the nearest trunk. Ben could see the sheen of blood on its right hind leg, the one that was dragging at an unnatural angle.

"Jeez," he breathed in relief, shaking his head. He was hearing things, obviously. A combination of anxiety and anger and deerslaughter-guilt were doing things to his brain. He would end the animal's suffering, get back to the car, down a granola bar, and sleep it off.

The deer was too spent to flee, but it took a few more stumbling steps as Ben clambered toward it. He debated the most merciful way to kill it. Cut its throat, most likely. But with only his three-inch army knife, he was likely to get kicked while he sawed away at the jugular. Maybe if he kept to the deer's damaged side he could avoid this.

Even as he drew closer, breathing harder with the effort, the deer sank down, its good legs giving way beneath it. Its head drooped, and the heaving of its flanks mirrored his own shortness of breath. Death was coming. The creature had no need of further help from him, then.

When he reached the peak of the slope, Ben sighed deeply and crouched beside the corpse. God, what a crappy day. Crappier for the deer than for him, he had to admit. He felt he ought to say something, since he had killed it. Apologize, at least. "Hey," Ben murmured. "Deer. I'm... sorry. For the collision, I mean. Bet you don't see too many cars up here. Can't blame you for not looking both ways, and I was driving angry..."

That was it for inspiration, such as it was. He fell silent. What was the point? The staring eyes were indifferent to his remorse.

After another minute Ben snapped his knife shut and rose to his feet. Only then did he look around. The North Coast Ranges were no Himalayas—King Peak only cleared 4000 feet—but what drama they lacked in elevation they made up for in weather and vegetation. Ben found himself on a nameless summit, the ground falling steeply away to the south. Although that downward slope was forested, his trained eye easily detected a recovering timber field. You could see it in the scattering of mossed and lichened stumps, the relative uniformity of the new trees' sizes and ages, the gap through them winding southeast where the skid road had passed. The logging must have been done many decades ago. Between the trees curled shreds of fog, precursors to the blanket the North Coast Range pulled up to its ears nearly every night.

Curiosity stabbed him. He ran his fingers lightly over the Douglas fir the deer had collapsed against. Although 95% of the coast redwoods had been logged before conservation efforts kicked in, the remaining 5% were not fully charted, usually hiding in remote pockets of the mountains where it was too laborious and therefore too expensive to log. Every redwood botanist dreamed of finding undiscovered trees. Every redwood botanist and every *wannabe* redwood botanist, Ben corrected himself. Absolutely there wouldn't be any around here—not so close to where loggers had passed—but he couldn't help wanting to make sure. He would just get a little higher and take a quick look before heading back to the car.

Stowing his knife in his pocket, Ben studied the tree for climbing routes. It was relatively young—he estimated distance to first limb at a merciful eight feet or so. Still it was no cakewalk. He had no ropes, no gear, no helmet. All back with Ed Wilson's crew. Long ago he used to free-climb, but as he grew older and the trees he tackled grew higher and higher, he had lost that easy confidence. If he fell now to his death, he could picture Ed Wilson and Courtney shaking their heads over the *Eureka Times Standard* headline. "Ironic," Courtney would say. "Wonder why he was climbing without his gear." "Trying to prove something," would be Wilson's comment.

Ben hunkered down, took a couple running steps and leaped for the lowest limb, cursing as he swung himself up, trying to gain purchase with his soft-soled boots on the trunk and running a long splinter up his palm. But he got up and wrangled into a sitting position. Locking his thighs around the branch, Ben pincered the end of the splinter and extricated it. Then he tucked his feet under him, rose to a stand on the limb and worked out the next step in his ascent.

It was glorious. Risky. Free. When he was thirty feet up, he cast one look down. The deer's broken body lay far below, already part of the past. The branches were getting skinnier at this height; he couldn't go much further and expect them to carry his weight. At forty feet up he knew better than to look down—the descent was a problem to be dealt with later. Instead he balanced himself in the crotch of the branch, wrapping his legs around it. He took a deep breath and looked out.

From this altitude the treetops below formed a seemingly unbroken sea of green and he could look across that sea to where the ground rose again. Trees, trees and more trees. He was right—whatever logging happened in this area happened long ago. In fact the slope immediately below him might be the youngest second-growth as far as the eye could see.

And the eye could see far, thought Ben. His gaze traced the contour of the narrow valley, winding west and south and then rising again abruptly a couple miles away. Even in the time it had taken him to free-climb the tree, the coastal fog had crept further in and begun to swallow the forest. Not all of it. The lowest-lying parts of the valley first. The taller trees and those over the slope had the appearance of rising from clouds. That one tree for example—

He did a double-take. Blinked. Squinted. Patted his chest for the binoculars he wasn't wearing.

There shouldn't be any old-growth coast redwoods for miles around. Not with the timber companies so busy in here. So what was that honking-big thing sticking up even past the trees on the summit? A monster—head and shoulders above its nearest companions, although it leaned a good ten or fifteen degrees off vertical. No way could they have missed that one. 500,000 board-feet of good solid redwood, if it was an inch. Huge like the Dyerville Giant that crashed to earth in 1994. The Giant had been a leaner as well, though at what angle he couldn't remember.

"*Sequoia sempervirens*," he murmured. "The Ever-Living Tree. You really are. You ought to be long gone, but there you stand."

Ben tried to estimate his location. Without money or car, compass or rope, he couldn't go explore this now. It would have to wait until he'd returned to civilization and cleaned up the mess that was his life. But return he would.

A wave of excitement washed over him, the first positive emotion he'd felt since coming upon Ed Wilson and Courtney going at it, and he felt kind of tipsy with it. Which possibly explained what happened next.

"I'm coming for you, big guy!" Ben cheered. Lying along the branch, he hitched his leg back over and, getting a firm grip with both hands, swung himself down. He had to rock himself over to the limb beneath, but he managed, his right foot skidding across it at first enough to make his heart leap to his throat. When he reached it safely, he gave another whoop. Hell, this was awesome! Why did he let stupid academics tame him into using gear? "Screw belays!" Ben hollered to the forest at large.

The next step in the descent looked easy enough. With reckless joy still thrilling along his veins, Ben almost laughed as he swung down, dangling until his toe made contact. No problem. Or, it would not have been, had not two things happened at once: first, in all the swinging and kicking and dangling, his army knife worked its way from his pocket. It tumbled out, and, instinctively, Ben let go with one hand in an attempt to catch it. When he realized his idiocy, he scrabbled again at the branch above, feeling his toe lose contact with the limb below. He might yet have recovered, but the forest had one more thing for him.

It echoed from every direction—louder this time—rushing up to his ears with almost physical breath.

"H-h-h-help me."

With a cry of shock, Ben's hands released their hold, and he hurtled through the twilight. Ricocheting against the branches with painful impacts on his right leg, then left hip, then left shoulder on the way down—collisions which probably saved his life—he finally landed shoulder first on the cooling carcass of the deer, his head rocking back to smack on the tree roots. Pinpoints of light exploded across his field of vision. Then everything went black.

CHAPTER 2

Limbo

His head was cracking open. Someone was pounding on it—thuds with a rubber mallet—trying to break it apart to get at the goods inside.

Ben groaned, his hand flailing at the unseen attacker. This made pain shoot through his shoulder. He felt air on his bare skin.

"Whoa, there. Lie still. This is going to feel cold, okay?"

Cold rocks laid across his head and shoulder. Rocks? *Ice.* His mind labored to find the word. He passed out again.

"Yeah, I agree with Clyde: concussion. Wake him up from time to time. Have Clyde look in on him. Other than that I'd say nothing looks broken."

"His shoulder's pretty banged up," said the woman. "And he's got a scrape on his hip."

"My wife checked him out pretty thoroughly," came another man's voice. "Don't think she would've been this concerned if he hadn't been so young and good-looking."

"Oh, be quiet, you. He's at least graduated from college, though, because he has his class ring—see? 'UC San Diego. 1997.'"

Ben felt hands prodding him again.

"Nah," said the first man. "That's all it is—bangs and scrapes. The important part is the concussion. So like I said, wake him up from time—oh, hey—there—his eyes are opening a little. Son—what's your name, Son?"

Effort. A memory of hiding behind his mother's legs and the pre-school teacher making exaggerated mouths at him: "Ben-ja-min. Well, hell-o, Ben-ja-min!"

"B-b—"

"Yes, Son. Your name is…"

"H-hello Benjamin."

"—Fine where it is. Got his stuff outta the back seat, including his wallet. Looks like Hello Benjamin's name really is Benjamin Platt. So at least he hasn't knocked all his brains clean out."

"Of course he hasn't."

"What do you think he was doing out there, Bea? His duffel bag had a couple carabiners and a few of these—" A clinking sound.

"Hmm…wonder what those are. We'll just have to ask him later. But in the meantime, you have to move his car, Charlie. Or the snow will get in with the hood like that. At least take it to Rube and let him try to hammer it out."

Ben didn't want anyone named Rube hammering on Lance's car, but that seemed impossible to express. He let out a moan of protest.

"Oh!" said the woman, and Ben heard her quick step across the room.

"—Make him muffins or scones?"

"He's not a guest, Bea. He's a convalescent. And convalescing on our dime, I might add. Don't be making him any special foods. Save it for the real guests. Did you call Alice? Can she take him? We're gonna have a full house tomorrow, and we can't have *him* laying around."

"I thought maybe we could move him to the Green Room," said Bea.

Gasping sound and then Charlie choking on his coffee. "What? Green Room? Keep that door locked, Bea."

Clunk of something solid. Bea slamming the coffee pot on the table? Ben tried to pry his eyes open, but the light shot bolts through his head, and he quickly screwed them shut again.

"The Green Room," insisted Bea. "He already has a head injury. He's not going to say anything. And why don't you plow the drive and let me run this place? If no one can get up the road because of snow, we won't have any guests period, and then it doesn't matter if I fill every room with sick people."

His first dream was cold and it might have been wind and it might have been rain but there was a Tap   tap   tap.

A tree swaying, brushing the window.

But no.

The sound again.

And when he looked over, a pale hand with a wide gold ring sliding across the wet pane.

Fingernails on glass.

Tap

tap

tap.

CHAPTER 3

Vision

Ben awoke to the smell of bacon and coffee and the muted sounds of conversation and dishes clinking below him.

Slowly he opened his eyes and found that he could without pain. Equally slowly he turned his head on the pillow. There was a twinge and a throb, but they were bearable. He waited for the two-of-everything to resolve into one-of-everything.

He was in a green room. Brownish-red and green. Redwood wainscoting fenced him in, above which wallpapered ivy climbed. The redwood floorboards peeked between moss-and-forest braided rugs. A lifted corner of the bed coverlet showed him embroidered pine cones and needles. Even the light filtering through the sheers was greenish, as if Ben lay in a forest. Air from an unseen vent rippled them then, sending watery shadows across the ivy.

Speaking of water.

He had to pee like crazy. God—what day was it? How long had he been wherever he was? Vague, embarrassing memories flickered: being spoon-fed and then throwing up; something about a bedpan; Bea and Charlie arguing about him.

He became aware of a tightness and ache in his left shoulder.

Similar tender spots on hip and leg. Bangs and scrapes, that one man had called them. Nothing to freak out about.

With a motion of ages, Ben pushed the coverlet back and heaved himself to a sitting position. Once, twice, the forest room circled him, but when it jerked to a stop, he placed his palms flat on the mattress. Up and at 'em.

Easier said than done. However long he had been in bed, either his body had forgotten how to obey mental commands or his brain had forgotten how to issue them. Ben could only get what he wanted done—crossing the room to the dresser—with intense concentration, and he felt the tightness of headache branching from the base of his skull. Another ripple of the sheers made the room sway, seaweed in an unseen current, and he caught a glimpse of his face in the mirror over the dresser—hand to mouth so he wouldn't throw up. God, he thought again—he must have been out of it at least a couple days, judging by the facial hair. Courtney liked a good five-o'clock shadow, but this would scare her. His brown hair, short and prematurely pep-pered with gray, stood up at all angles, away from his dark, stunned eyes. "I look … like the nutty professor," Ben mumbled, to try out his voice. It worked, even if he had to string the words together visually before they emerged. The hand went from his mouth to his temples, rubbing. That's right—a professor was the one thing he would never actually be now. Once Wilson and the crew packed up and left the canopy in a few weeks, the first text back to the U would probably include something about deleting Ben's name from the project write-up. Hell, why stop there? Why not go ahead and kick him out of the U altogether?

The green room had no bathroom attached. Ben shuffled to the door pinball-style: dresser to hat rack (he knocked this over and a wave of nausea prevented him from righting it) to door. Once that was open, and he wavered in the jamb, he found himself looking down a dim hallway of closed doors, a braided runner traveling its length.

Ben had not managed to try more than two of the locked doors before he heard hasty footsteps, and a woman appeared halfway along.

"Look at you!" she cried, and Ben recognized her voice as Bea. He had pictured her older, but she only appeared around fifty, mostly-brunette, trim and quick. "You probably shouldn't be up!"

Ben arranged the words. "I...probably shouldn't. Bathroom."

"Of course." Quite naturally she took his arm. "This way. I'm afraid it's at the end of the hall. Bed-and-breakfast, you know. Only two of the suites have their own bathrooms. And all the rooms are occupied, so we couldn't put you any closer."

He tried to nod, but it made him dizzy. He knew this. He knew Charlie didn't want him on the couch or in the place at all. Bed-and-breakfast-and-concussed-wildman-wandering-the-halls. A bed-and-breakfast. He really was on vacation. This would have to go on the tab with Lance's car.

"Can you manage?" Bea asked, opening the door for him.

"Yes."

"Take as long as you like. The guests are just finishing up breakfast, and there's another bathroom they can use downstairs before they head out on their hikes and such."

Another glimpse of his crazy lumberjack-professor face in the bathroom mirror alarmed him. "Bath..?"

"Absolutely. Take a bath. I'll get your things and put them outside the door. Charlie went and fetched them from your car. I'm afraid— well—lots of the clothes looked like they could use a wash, so I went ahead and did that."

The headache had wrapped completely around by this point. Ben had a thousand questions, but more urgently he wanted to relieve himself and then lie on the cool tile floor until someone stopped the merry-go-round. "...Thank you...Bea."

Her face lit up. "You did catch my name, then! I knew you hadn't knocked your brains clear out like Charlie feared. Another couple days and you'll be good as new. You get yourself set and then go back to bed if you want, or come downstairs if you rather. Call me or…knock something over again…if you need help." She grinned at him. "I'll be in the kitchen working on the afternoon treats."

He must have fallen asleep in the tub. All he knew was that one minute he was sinking into comfort as the mirror steamed up, and the next his eyes flickered open and he was shivering against the lukewarm water. With a groan, Ben yanked the drain plug and reached for one of the towels. His sudden movements had predictable results on his head, and he clutched the curved rim of the claw-foot tub until the dizziness passed.

A timid knock on the door. "Benjamin?" It was Bea. "Are you all right in there? It's been a good forty-five minutes—"

"I'm good, I'm good," he called. "Just fell asleep. I'll be out shortly."

He hadn't counted on how long it took him to manage simple tasks like dressing and shaving, however, nor the breaks he took in between, stretched out on the floor. He would have to ask Bea for some Advil.

It was during his second stint on the tiles that he made his discovery.

He was running one hand behind the bathroom vanity and the other along the toilet base so he could pull himself up again, when a jagged edge met his fingertips, neatly slicing the skin on his index finger. Detachedly, Ben inspected the blood welling up. Wait till Charlie caught wind of this injury. Now the concussed invalid was gonna bleed all over the antique furniture.

He rolled onto his back to reach behind the vanity with his uninjured hand, and, with a little jiggling to coax it free, Ben pulled out a gilt frame. Perhaps from its fall, the glazing had broken on it—hence his cut—but what it held appeared undamaged. It was a—what were those things called?—piece of needlework. A verse, hemmed in on all sides by painstakingly-stitched trees, firs and redwoods and a California bay:

> My life is like a faded leaf,
> My harvest dwindled to a husk:
> Truly my life is void and brief
> And tedious in the barren dusk;
> My life is like a frozen thing,
> No bud nor greenness can I see:
> Yet rise it shall—the sap of spring;
> O Jesus, rise in me.

What was it? A hymn? Ben frowned. And who would go to all the trouble of stitching such a depressing verse and then framing it and hanging it on the wall? No matter. He would see what Bea wanted to do with it.

~~~

She was bustling about, setting out lemon bars and chocolate-chip cookies beside a coffee urn and tea caddy.

"Nice place you have here," said Ben. He had worked on the bland phrase as he toiled down the stairs, clutching the handrail and resting on the landing. He almost dropped the needlework several times and ended up stuffing it in his waistband. Honestly, the place was a little antique-y for him—spindly chairs with upright backs, dark upholsteries and carpets, fussy lamps, rickety side tables. Plenty of china knickknacks and gewgaws for the unwitting to knock over. More to his taste was the thick stand of conifers he glimpsed from the bay window, barely held off by a flower-bordered lawn. The unseasonable snow had melted away, it appeared.

Bea smiled up at him. "You think so? I do. Charlie isn't so sure. He says he hates all the namby-pamby, grandma stuff. Always afraid he'll break something. But I tell him no one wants to visit a ghost logging town and stay in a place that's all chrome and glass. It's got to fit the period. Not that we could change the Dryad much even if we wanted to, now. They added it to the Historic Register last year, you know."

Her rapid speech left him struggling to keep up, but he gave one nod. Gestured vaguely with one arm at the parlor. "It's like stepping back in time."

"Exactly! Which is what people want. And it should look like that because many of the furnishings are original to the house. But what have you done to your hand?" She inspected his sliced finger. He had applied pressure, but when she pushed his thumb away, a bead of blood emerged nonetheless. "I'll get you a towel for that. Why don't you have a cookie and sit in the armchair? You won't do any harm there. Some coffee or tea?"

Ben obeyed. He extricated the framed sampler from his waistband and sagged into the chair, shutting his eyes. After some minutes he heard the clink of a teacup and saucer on the table beside him and felt a washcloth thrust into his injured hand. "I put some aspirin there for you, too, in case you want it. We had Dr. Stevens from Eureka check you out at first. He said you might have headaches and spells for a while afterward, and if you do, just to call Clyde. Clyde's his brother-in-law. He's not exactly a doctor himself—more of a veterinarian neighbor—but, well, people are just animals after all."

"Thank you." Add doctor's (and vet?) bills to the running total.

He heard the creak of springs as Bea dropped into the wingback opposite. "Oof! This is my little time to put my feet up. Hope you don't mind."

She commenced humming to herself, but Ben had the sense she was merely waiting to see if he would prove more sociable. She was like a kettle on the back burner, set at simmer but easily coaxed to a rolling boil. Because of all she was doing for him and despite his troublesome head, he felt willing enough to comply.

"Bea...I cut my hand when I reached behind the vanity," he began. "...Long story." He cracked an eyelid and saw his guess was right—she had thrust aside her own needlework and sat forward eagerly. "There was...some glass back there. I found this." He handed it over.

"Good heavens." Bea looked dumbstruck.

Ben waited, but she didn't seem inclined to add more. "What is it?" he prompted. "Do you think it's original to the house?"

Ignoring him, she turned the frame over and began prying the backing loose. When it sprung free, Bea gingerly separated it from the sampler, frame and broken glass, laying the last on some newspaper. She ran her finger over the stitches, her lips pursed. "It's original, all right," she said at last. "Look at the date and these initials."

In tiny lettering, hardly distinguishable from the stitched under-growth of the trees: D. L. 1892.

"D. L.?" said Ben.

"Daphne Lindstrom. At that date, she would have been Mrs. Pall Lindstrom for a year already." Bea sighed. "A tragic story. The Dryad is the old Lindstrom home, you know."

"Dryad."

Her quick smile. "This place. This is the Dryad."

His tea had cooled off enough that he could swig it to swallow the aspirin. Ahh...placebo effect, here I come, he thought. "No, actually," said Ben. "It's not...amnesia...or anything, but I don't even know where I am. What town, I mean."

Bea blinked at him. "Oh, yes, of course. I forgot that. You're in Red Gap. The Gap used to be a big, bustling logging town, say, more than a century ago. Its own post office and library and dance hall and everything. And back then it was Mr. Pall Lindstrom who ran the place. He didn't own the lumber company, but he was management, and since everyone in the Gap worked for the lumber company, that meant everyone in the Gap answered to Pall Lindstrom." She smoothed the sampler and fitted it back into the glassless frame. Ben felt like she was avoiding meeting his eyes. "You don't happen to be a lumber scout, do you, Benjamin? Charlie found some carabiners and things in your car and he said that was what you were. And you know the Gap isn't part of the protected woodlands, but it borders on them, and people don't take very kindly to lumber companies scouting around here, for all that Red Gap got its start that way."

Ben started to laugh, but it brought on a wave of nausea and he choked it back. "No, Bea. I'm no lumber scout. I'm the opposite—a graduate student. I study trees." Or he used to, at any rate. Not that Bea needed to hear the Ed-Wilson-Courtney saga. "I thought I would take a … shortcut … to 101, but I hit a deer. How did you ever find me?"

"That was Charlie," said Bea simply. "He drives all the back roads here. Now that the Gap is a … kind of … tourist destination Charlie keeps the hiking trails in shipshape. Someone reported a tree across one of the trails from Big Diamond, so he went to clean it up. When he saw the condition of your car and no *you* in it, he followed where you went into the woods and found you all collapsed. He brought you back here. So it's Charlie you have to thank," she added, on a slight defensive note. Perhaps she knew he'd overheard some of Charlie's complaints about him.

"I do thank him," said Ben. He felt she expected more explanation. "I only went into the woods because the deer wasn't all the way dead. I was going to finish it off."

"Well, you succeeded in that. Charlie found you sprawled on top of the thing. He couldn't figure out if you tried to wrestle it to death or what! You won, but Charlie wondered if that crippled thing managed to kick you senseless before it passed on."

"Right," said Ben. "First you think I'm a lumber scout and then that I got licked by a deer with one hoof in the grave."

She giggled. "I told him that was nonsense. But then, what did happen?"

Not feeling that the truth was much more dignified, Ben described free-climbing the fir to take a look around. Bea sucked in her cheeks when he mentioned how high he got, but said nothing. "I—uh—got in a little trouble on the descent," said Ben. He left out the bits about spotting the mysterious giant redwood, as well as hearing the voice, naturally. "Fell about thirty-five feet or so. I'm no threat to your woods," he finished. "No threat, but maybe not that great of a protector, either."

Bea patted the back of his hand. "I don't know about that. To think you study trees! I bet you would have all sorts of things to teach us. Some of the guests have questions about the trees here that I can't answer." She considered the sampler again. "Though Daphne Lindstrom probably could have. Look at the detail of this work."

"Uh-huh." Until the headache receded, Ben had no interest in examining some depressed woman's hundred-year-old needlework. Not that he would, even in the best of health. "Bummer of a verse she picked, though."

Bea frowned at him. "I told you it was a tragic story. This just proves it. She was a sad case. Local legend has it Daphne Lindstrom was the first child born in Red Gap…" (Ben settled back in his armchair. If Bea was going to start with Daphne Lindstrom's birth, he could be in for a long listen.) "She was Daphne Chase then, and a strange girl, they say. Always out in the woods, making up games for herself. There was one particular grove of redwoods not far from here that was her special haunt. Well, the lumber company decided that grove would do more good sawed up into boards and when Daphne heard about that, she got so upset her family had to send her away."

"Away where?" Ben asked, more out of politeness than interest.

"Oh, you know—back in those days, if a great-aunt couldn't shape you up, you went to a sanatorium somewhere. In any case, she didn't come back to the Gap until she was sixteen, and by then most of her redwood grove was ancient history, and she was ready for a different kind of love. Pall Lindstrom took one look at Daphne Chase and fell head over heels. Here he was, chasing after a girl just sixteen, and him the big manager man and handsomest fellow in Red Gap. Maybe even the county."

"Well, she didn't get her redwoods, but she got the most eligible bachelor, right?" said Ben. "Good 19th-century consolation prize. Mrs. Pall Lindstrom."

Bea shook her head. "Yes and no. It was after they got married that Daphne Lindstrom started going downhill again. Keeping to herself. Wandering in the woods for hours, just like when she was a child. Fighting with her husband whenever he so much as looked at another woman—"

"Oh—and don't forget: stitching gloomy samplers," Ben interjected.

"You men! You're so unromantic," said Bea. "I guess it was all over a hundred years ago, but I must say that living in her house keeps her alive for me."

"I'm sorry," said Ben, grimacing. Bea wasn't the first woman to call him unromantic. "So where does the tragedy come in…? I take it Pall Lindstrom looked at too many other women?"

"No, no! He was a model husband. Worshiped the ground she walked on and such. But Daphne just turned in on herself. Devoured herself, in the end. One day she went for her usual walk in the forest, and that was the last time anyone saw her alive. In fact, that was the last time anyone ever saw her again *period*. Her hat and foraging basket were found a couple weeks later where the trees overhang the Yoak River ravine about a mile down from town. People think she leapt to her death and her body was carried out to sea."

"That's terrible," he said automatically. If he hadn't felt so lousy, he might have asked how Bea knew so many details of the dead woman's story. Or embellishments, as the case probably was.

"I told you it was sad." Bea twiddled with her reading-glasses chain absently. "I'll have to get a new frame for this and hang it up again. Though, like you say, the verse is kind of a downer. I'll put it in the

Green Room. It belongs there."

"My room?" exclaimed Ben. "I mean, the room I'm staying in?"

"Uh-huh." Another pause. Bea collected his cup and saucer, stacking them with hers. "The Green Room…was Daphne's private sitting room when she was alive. I think she liked it because the trees grow almost right up to the window there. There was no bed in there, of course, or dresser, but everything else is original. Do you like it?"

"Sure," said Ben. "It's a great room. And Bea—I really do appreciate you and Charlie rescuing me like this. I'm sorry to be taking up space when you two have a business to run, and you'll have to let me know what I owe you—"

Before he was halfway through this trying speech, Bea was waving her hand at him. "Don't bother your scrambled head about that, young man. When you're feeling a little better we'll find some use for you. Now tell me—is there anyone you need me to contact? Let 'em know you're alive and almost well—just stopping in Red Gap for some R&R?"

He hesitated. Let Bea think he was trying to get his head together. "Uh…I was kind of at the end of a project. No one is expecting me anywhere, anytime soon. Thank you, though."

"No thanks necessary." She pushed herself briskly up from the wingback. "I'd better get busy again, but I don't feel comfortable leaving someone with no entertainment. We have plenty of books and games and puzzles for the guests, of course, for when the weather is bad, but I don't think your head would be up to it."

"It wouldn't," Ben agreed. "I think I'll just rest here a while and look out the windows, if you don't mind."

"Not a bit. But I could at least find you the book on Red Gap that our local historical society put together. Lots of pictures, hardly any words. You can flip through it if you like, if I can remember where I saw it last…"

Diffidently, Ben turned the pages. The black-and-white photographs of Red Gap in its heyday might have been any logging town in the Coast Ranges near the turn of the century. Wooden buildings clustered in the shadow of encroaching evergreens: mill, company houses, general store. A river ran below the town to float logs to the mill when winter freshets allowed. He lingered over the trees. The size of them! Some of them easily twenty, thirty feet in diameter. Fallers posed on springboards, one or two boards up, to clear the tree's base and work clear of the root system. One shot even had a logger lolling in the spacious undercut he and his fellows made in the mammoth trunk of a coast redwood. Nowadays such behemoths drew researchers, worshipers almost, they were so rare and sequestered.

When the sound came again, Ben barely heard it, lost as he was in thought.

Tap.
Tap.

With an angry movement, he flipped a handful of the book's pages. No use mourning over what was past. Those trees were gone. Fallen. Sawed up into houses and furniture.

Tap.
Tap. Fingernails on glass.
The sound stirred a memory. Oh, yes—the dream. The hand on the window.

He raised his eyes to the bay window. There was the postage-stamp lawn, outlined in asters and Gloriosa daisies that had shriveled in the untimely snowfall. Sparrows hopped and preened at a bird bath in the corner nearest the house. Stepping stones made of tree rounds marked several paths away: to the road, around the back, into the woods.

Feeling his headache now only as a dull throb at the base of his skull, Ben's gaze followed the path into the woods, round by round.

And then he saw her.

She stood, hesitating, just where the path disappeared in shadow, a muted glow cast by her long ivory dress. Her back was to the house but her head half turned as if she had just remembered something.

Ben wondered if the Dryad did weddings. It was a picturesque enough spot, although, if there were a wedding being held there today, Bea didn't seem overly concerned about it. But what was with the dress, then? Of course, Bea had said the Dryad was full up right now— maybe there was something going on with the historical society—an excuse for people to tromp around in period clothing.

The woman turned then. Took a step toward him. Ben couldn't see her face, but he got an impression of flowing hair pinned back, pale skin, a pointed chin set at a defiant angle. Her hands, which had been lifting her skirts off the ground, released the yards of material, and she raised them slightly, palms upward. He saw her mouth move.

"…Bea…?" His voice came out rather hoarse. "…Bea! There's someone out here who needs help, I think…*Bea!*"

The room spun again when he tried to sit forward, but he sank back at the sound of Bea's rapid footsteps. Laying a firm hand on his shoulder to keep him in place, she hurried to the window to peer out. "Is it one of the guests? Did someone hurt himself hiking?"

"The woman," he said. Moving wouldn't be so bad, if not for the spinning, and the spinning wouldn't be so bad, if not for the wave of nausea that followed.

"Woman?" echoed Bea. Opening the front door, she marched onto the verandah, the better to have a look around and halloo a few times. A few moments later, he heard the clack of her shoes returning and the door closing. "I don't see her now, at any rate. Was she injured? What did she look like?"

He swallowed carefully. "I don't know if she was injured. She... was back by the trees—no, I see she's gone now. She had a long white dress on—"

"Long white dress!" Bea exclaimed. "Whatever for?"

Ben gave a bark of a laugh. "I was going to ask you. A long white dress. And big, curly hair tied up. And her hands. They were pale. There might have been a ring on one of her hands." He sat up straighter. Why had he said that? He didn't know if there had been a ring or not. Not at that distance. The ring he remembered was from the dream, the long white hand sliding across the pane.

Bea was frowning at him again, her head cocked to one side.

"What?" he demanded.

She bit her lip. "It's all right, Ben. Clyde said you might have some confusion."

"Clyde—what? Clyde the veterinarian?" Ben protested. "He said I might have some confusion about what?"

"Oh, nothing to worry about," she reassured him, coming to pat his arm. "It'll pass."

He resisted the urge to fling her off. "I'm not confused, Bea. Dizzy, yes. Head hurting, yes. Slow, yes. But I'm not confused."

"You might have fallen asleep."

Ben glared at her. "I was not asleep—you've only been out of the room five or ten minutes. And I was not confused! I saw what I saw. A lady, right where the path enters the woods, and she was wearing a long white dress and had her hair pulled back and held up her hands to me. I don't know about the ring," he admitted. "I may not have seen that."

Bea sighed. "You saw a lady outside in a long white dress with wavy hair."

"Curly hair. More curly than wavy."

"And she might or might not have been wearing a ring. Is that right?"

He nodded. He didn't have to rule it out—plenty of women wore rings.

"You think maybe she looked a little something like this, Ben?" Bea pushed his hands away, where they were clutching the historical-society book. He looked down at the open page. There he found a three-quarter portrait of a young woman seated in an arbor, her long white gown spread around her, her light-colored, wavy hair pinned up and back. A slender *Sequoia sempervirens* branch lay in her lap, over which her hands rested protectively. On her left hand she wore a wide wedding band.

The caption read:

Mrs. Pall Lindstrom, née Daphne Chase, 1893.

CHAPTER 4

Charlie

Ben hardly knew what to say.

He stared from the picture to the window, back to the picture. *Had* he imagined it? Dozed off with the book open to Daphne Lindstrom's portrait, hers the last image burned into his retinas and the first when he came to?

"But I heard the ... tapping ... again," he muttered. He felt heat wash his neck and face when he remembered that, the first time he heard the tapping, he had most certainly been asleep. Or on the verge of sleep. In that limbo between waking and sleeping.

"Tapping," Bea repeated, as if he'd admitted to hearing aliens address him over a spaceship PA system.

"Like someone clicking their fingernails on the window. Never mind, Bea. Maybe you're right. I don't know what just happened."

She made a waving motion with both hands. "Don't you worry about it. It's a noisy old house. There are always squirrels running across the roof and birds hitting the window when they misjudge the feeder. And the wind! It just blows through the Gap sometimes, picking up pine needles and twigs and pine cones and just *pelting* the Dryad with them. All kinds of tapping."

He nodded, to show that she was completely right and he was completely mistaken, but when she had returned to the kitchen, he struggled up from the chair, taking the book with him.

It was unexpectedly mild outside. Ben avoided the cushioned porch swing—the less motion, the better—choosing instead a painted wicker chair that groaned so ominously as he lowered himself into it that he wondered if it was meant only for decorative purposes. Not that more decoration was needed. Bea's zeal spilled over from inside, and joining him on the porch were wreaths, statuary, birdhouses, lacy cushions, painted signs.

As he had seen from inside, the Dryad carved out a neat niche in the surrounding woods. If there were neighboring houses, they weren't visible from where he sat. And lucky for them, if trees blocked their view of the Dryad, because the house was painted an aggressive purple, trimmed in white. Were the paint and bric-a-brac all part of the "original furnishings" Bea referred to? If so, Ben thought, Pall Lindstrom's sufferings began long before his wife's death.

A semicircular drive curved away from the house down to the road, which curved downward in turn and was lost in the trees. He could just make out rooftops and a spire or two through the thick cover. The Lindstroms clearly treasured their privacy. Maybe it went with the mill-manager territory—build your house above and away from your workers and their doings to maintain an Olympian distance. Or maybe it was the moody Daphne who insisted on remoteness.

Ben opened the book again, not without a self-conscious glance toward the woods. There was the picture. Without Bea over his shoulder, he had the leisure to study it. Mrs. Pall Lindstrom, née Daphne Chase. She was lovely, he supposed, in that turn-of-the-century way. Meaning she had way too much hair and looked cinched-up and fussed in her impractical clothing. And there was the demure pose. The folded hands. She could be anybody's great-grandmother. And yet—

Something about her face rebelled against this easy classification.

She wasn't smiling, though that wasn't unusual in an era when photographic subjects had to hold still for so long. But neither was her mouth relaxed. There was an air of tension in the compression of her lips, as if she were holding back words. And her eyes, rather than being downcast or focused to the side, stared directly at the viewer. They were dark. He might almost have said angry.

Ben tapped his finger on the page. He wondered who had taken the picture and what Mrs. Lindstrom's state of mind had been that morning. He also wondered how, when he first imagined(?) her in the woods, before she beckoned to him, he saw her from the back. He knew nothing of women's period fashions, yet there was the memory of a short train dragging behind her. Pleated material. If she went walking in the woods in that get-up, she must have come home trailing enough needles and pinecones to risk spontaneous combustion.

The eyes reproached him for these thoughts. They were brown, he supposed. Brown like the thick lashes draping them and her mass of waving hair. If, as her needlework declared, Daphne Lindstrom's life was like a faded leaf, like a frozen thing, you wouldn't know it from this picture. On the contrary: she was burning up inside.

Almost against his will, Ben turned the page. He wanted to study it longer, but he also found himself driven on by curiosity. If she and her husband were such prominent citizens, there would be more about them, he was certain.

A picture of a class gathered before the one-room schoolhouse. *Early 1880s*, read the caption. Only two of the children had been identified: Daphne Chase, chubby and braided and…yes…*gleeful*, and an older boy in the row behind her, lanky and tow-headed, grubby hand on one hip—one Shane Derwent. It must have escaped the photographer's notice, but Shane Derwent's other hand had a hold of Daphne's braid.

The historian had a paragraph here: "The original Red Gap schoolhouse stood from 1878-1913. Unfortunately, few of the teachers or students can be identified with any certainty. This photograph was kindly donated by the Derwent family and features an inscription on the back: 'Me and Daph.'"

Pall Lindstrom first appeared in what must have been a company postcard. It had *Red Gap Lumber Company* printed across the collage of images in flourishing script. The sawmill in the largest picture; logs sliding down a skid road; an early donkey engine with horizontal drum; and the mill manager himself. Handsome, all right. He stood proudly beside a desk in his dark suit, smooth light hair combed neatly back. With his clean-shaven face, Pall Lindstrom escaped the vaudevillian air clinging to some of his moustachioed contemporaries. From his pocket hung a watch chain and he rested the knuckles of his right hand on some papers, his middle finger adorned with a heavy signet ring. A young man at the top of his game. The postcard was undated, but surely Pall Lindstrom looked like this when Daphne Chase caught his eye. And however unhappy she might have been afterward, his attentions must have been flattering.

Ben's eye drifted to the page opposite, and were it not for the signet ring on the subject's right hand, he would have been hard-put to identify the man in the photograph. *Pall Lindstrom, 1905.* Gone was the young Apollo. In his place stood a shrunken man, cheeks hollowed out, hairline receded, flowing moustache and whiskers so pale that Ben suspected they were gray. How old was he, in this shot? Was this wasting-away attributable to some wicked turn-of-the-century disease, or was Pall Lindstrom still reeling from his wife's death, so many years later? The historian Gladys Harrington was no help. She merely noted, "Pall Lindstrom resigned as manager from the Red Gap Lumber Company some time after this photo was taken and returned to San Francisco."

Those were the days, thought Ben, shutting the book. Life got you down? Leave town. Walk off the pages of history into some neverland where no one paid attention to you or even knew what happened to you.

God. What a mess he was in. He was at least going to have to call Lance's girlfriend and let her know he had totaled the car. Reimbursing them—not to mention whatever bills he was racking up here at the Dryad—would take care of this semester's stipend. As for next semester—well, chances were his days as a postdoc were finished. Suddenly the living he had been eking from those miserly checks struck him as secure and relatively luxurious. There was no telling how quickly Wilson would cut him off, but Ben suspected the grace period wouldn't be overlong. With a groan he let his head fall back against the seat cushion, only to feel a twinge when it contacted his injury.

There was the apartment sublet, his mind ran on. With luck, he could just get the tenant to take over the lease—and then what? Move back in with his parents? Work as an arborist and spend the rest of his life climbing fifty-foot trees in the suburbs?

Damn Courtney and damn Ed Wilson. Damn finishing his postdoc and getting a professorship and marrying Courtney and raising three nature-loving, tree-climbing children. Damn *everything*.

∽

"You look like that head's still bothering you."

Ben's eyes flicked open.

It was a heavyset man in coveralls with a shock of white hair springing from his ruddy scalp. How he managed to come up the gravel walk so silently was a mystery, but here he was. Ben straightened up to contradict this assessment. His movement knocked one of the lacy cushions to the porch, but Charlie reached for it and spared him the effort of reclaiming it.

"It's improving by the minute," Ben lied.

"Uh-huh." Navigating a path through the knick-knacks and fripperies with a grace that belied his size, Charlie lowered himself in the porch swing. Perhaps as a concession to Ben's dizziness, he only rocked back and forth a couple times before stopping it with his foot. "I've gone and towed your car to Rube's." As if Ben had any idea who or where that was.

"Um...thanks. I don't suppose it can be fixed?"

"Not for cheap enough that it would be worth it. Rube said he could probably pull some parts off but that it's generally no good for anything but a planter box now. For a fee he can get it to Eureka, let the dealer dispose of it, if you want."

Ben grimaced. "Sounds like a plan. And...Charlie...I want you to know I appreciate all the help. I apologize for the trouble, and I'll certainly be reimbursing you and Bea."

Charlie nodded once. Ben could tell he was satisfied to learn he hadn't nursed a freeloader. Then there was a wheezy laugh. "Just what in tom fool were you doing out there? I figured the deer and the car bit out, but not what you were doing on that road in the first place, or why you went on into the woods."

Feeling like an idiot didn't help his head any, but Ben gave the edited version of his adventure for the second time. He suspected there would be at least another few recountings—to the bed-and-breakfast guests, most likely—so best to get it polished.

Charlie was shaking his head by the end, accompanied by more of those wheezy laughs. With difficulty, Ben resisted the urge to launch one of the lacy cushions at him. "Oh, yeah!" said Charlie. "Bea was right—I had you pegged wrong. Figured you were a timber thief or one of those crazy environmental terrorists. We had one of those a while back—almost got to Grand Daddy but had a few too many down at Etta's the night before and gave up the game."

"—Grand Daddy?" said Ben. "He tried to kill someone?"

His host slapped both hands on the swing seat. "Some*one*? Ben, I thought you were a scholar of trees! If Daphne Lindstrom's grove hadn't been logged, it would have been Red Gap's canopy you and your professor-types scrambled around in. Grand Daddy's all that's left of it. It's the one that wild girl chained herself to and got herself sent away for."

"She what?" Ben leaned forward, sending another frothy pillow toppling to the porch. His heart was hammering. Grand Daddy must be—could *only* be—the behemoth he had spotted from atop the Douglas fir. So it wasn't exactly undiscovered.

"Let me see that," said Charlie. He whisked the historical society book from Ben's lap. Leafing through it, he found the page he wanted and stabbed a finger at it. "There's the Grove, and there's Grand Daddy."

Charlie was right. Daphne Lindstrom's grove would have been crawling with researchers, if it still stood. Though only the trunks could be seen in the picture, Ben saw a stand of enormous trees, amazing in themselves, radiating from one massive redwood. This tree stood straight as an arrow. A Lilliputian logger posed in front of it, for scale.

"Grand Daddy," said Ben. It could only be. Although the tree leaned now, that clearly must be a result of the felling of the rest of the Grove. Holes had been torn in the canopy, leaving the survivor alone and exposed to storm and wind, not to mention any damage done to the root structure.

"Yep. Named by Daphne Lindstrom herself. Though, if you don't know Grand Daddy you don't know who she is either. Seems she had names for every tree in her grove, but that's all that's left for the most part."

"I do know who she is," said Ben. "Bea told me." He related the discovery of the sampler. "Bea didn't mention the part about Daphne chaining herself to Grand Daddy, but maybe that was because she was more worried about me being crazy." He paused. It was better, he decided, that he confess his sighting. Bea was sure to tell her husband anyhow, and it would reassure them both to know that Ben was not going to insist on the reality of any hallucinations.

To his surprise, the news that his unwanted guest was hearing and seeing things filled Charlie with a strange animation. He sprang to his feet, looking sharply at Ben, before backing into the statuette of what Ben took to be a forest sprite. The thing thunked over, rolling onto its grinning snub nose, but Charlie didn't notice. He turned to stare for a long moment into the woods where Ben had pointed.

"You don't—" Ben began cautiously, "—you don't think I actually saw someone, do you?" Charlie neither turned nor answered. "I mean, Bea says that…Clyde…says the concussion might leave me confused. And I did happen to have the book open to Daphne Lindstrom's portrait. Let me show you—"

"I know what she looks like," Charlie cut him off.

All right then, thought Ben, his eyebrows raised. A stiff silence fell like a fog over the porch. Ben waited.

At last, Charlie gave himself a visible shake and resumed his seat, crossing his arms over his substantial belly. "Yeah," he said, as if there had been no break in the conversation, "people see crazy things up here, even without falling out of fir trees and cracking their heads like eggs. It's all the fog and forest and history. We've had sasquatch reports and people swearing on hikes that something was following them. Someone even for a few years took to dressing up like a headless lumberjack on Halloweens and scaring the bejesus out of tourists." Charlie set the porch swing to rocking as he got into his monologue, and Ben was forced to look elsewhere. "And then there's the Come On Inn," Charlie went on. "Joyce puts in her brochures and website that her place is haunted, and that just packs 'em in. No use telling anyone that her folks built the place in 1962, and if anything's haunting it, it's that husband she nagged to death."

"So then…you're telling me people have had Daphne-Lindstrom hallucinations before."

"Huh?"

"If people are always being chased through the woods by Bigfoot and headless lumberjacks, and the Come On Inn has its own pet ghost—has anyone said they've seen Daphne Lindstrom?"

The swing stopped again and Ben saw Charlie square his heavy boots beneath him. "She's—uh—come up from time to time. Makes sense you know. She's a colorful spot in Red Gap history. People can't resist. And environmentalists like to make a hero out of her because of the whole Grand Daddy incident. People see her because they *want* to see her."

Charlie delivered this last declaration as if Ben were among these wishful thinkers, and Ben couldn't help defending himself. "Well, *I* certainly didn't want to see her. I didn't know she existed before this morning. And I'm really not thrilled to find out I'm seeing things." He gave a dry laugh. "Just my luck—I start having hallucinations and I can't even have the one I want. I'd be way more interested in Bigfoot, myself."

"Uh-huh." The downed elf statue finally registered with Charlie, and the proprietor leaned over to right it. "I bet with your broken head, he'll turn up soon enough. Meanwhile, it's lunch time. You think you can keep down a sandwich?"

"Wow," Ben said, grinning. "From the paranormal to the really normal. Smooth, Charlie. Yeah—a sandwich sounds good. Give me whatever you're having."

Charlie paused with his hand on the screen door. "I wouldn't be surprised if you changed your mind, though."

Ben stared at him. "About the sandwich?"

"About Daphne Lindstrom. You say you'd rather see Bigfoot. But…Daphne has a way of getting to you. Getting inside your head." A breeze caught Charlie's shock of white hair, standing it up, and Ben thought he looked like a mad Santa Claus.

"Okay," said Ben. "Now you're freaking me out. I'm an accidental tourist, remember? You don't have to give me the Red Gap routine. Which means the headless lumberjack outfit can stay in the closet."

The screen door swung shut, but Charlie's voice carried out to him. "Just remember. You can't help her. You think you can, but you can't."

CHAPTER 5

Fact and Fiction

Ben studied his sandwich as if it held the answer to all life's questions. Tuna salad on multi-grain bread, mustard, lettuce, tomato. It tasted ordinary enough, and it had certainly done the trick for Charlie. His host was now helping himself to more chips, complaining loudly to Bea about the increase of litter on the trails, while she murmured soothing responses and refilled his iced tea.

Had Charlie really just gone all eerie on him, out there on the porch, or had Ben only imagined the discomfiture and suspicion and warning? He was getting rather sick of asking himself what was inside his head and what out. Besides, with the aspirin keeping the headache in check and something solid in his stomach, he felt remarkably lucid.

He took another bite. It didn't matter, ultimately. It didn't matter if Ben was confused or Charlie was nutty or Red Gap visitors might or might not have hallucinations about Daphne Lindstrom that then got under their skin. Ben's job was to make a full recovery and be on his way. Maybe hitch a ride to Eureka or even Redding with one of the Dryad's guests. Put this misadventure on the credit card to be reckoned with at a later date.

You can't help her was a weird thing to say, though.

Considering that Ben hadn't told Charlie about the voice in the woods—the voice that predated any concussive confusion. The voice that caused his accident and waylaying in Red Gap in the first place.

H-h-h-help me.

"Why would Daphne Lindstrom need help?"

Bea and Charlie's conversation stopped as if a door had shut on it. Ben smiled uncertainly at them—he hadn't meant to say that out loud. Bea looked from Ben to her husband, her expression unreadable.

"She doesn't," she said gently. "Whatever happened to her—whether she threw herself in the river or fell—it all happened years ago. Years and years. She rests in peace." For his part, Charlie was suddenly enthralled by the potato chip in his hand. Either he was avoiding Ben's gaze, or he was picking out the features of the Virgin Mary in the chip's discolorations.

"Of course," said Ben. He had no wish to get Charlie in trouble with his wife. He took an enormous bite of his sandwich and resolved to keep his mouth shut.

Wiping her hands finger by finger on her napkin, Bea gave a long-suffering sigh. "Funny, the effect that woman has on people. Especially on men. You never even heard Daphne Lindstrom's name until this morning, Ben."

"And I never need to hear it again," he said quickly, forgetting his resolve. "That just came out … my confusion, remember? Let's not talk about her. I am not the least bit interested in Daphne Lindstrom."

Bea reached across the table and laid her hand on Charlie's. "Well, we are. Charlie and me, Gladys from the historical society, the whole town—even the tourists. Especially the tourists. Obsession with Daphne Lindstrom is what put Red Gap on the map again."

"You're kidding."

"Not a bit! Just last week Gladys said some *movie producer* even called who heard about her book at a paranormal conference—"

"Her historical society book?" Ben interrupted. "Why would anyone read that at a paranormal conference?"

"No, no—her novel."

"Novel? You lost me."

"*Bury Me Not*, it's called—inspired by all her Red Gap research—"

"Inspired by her own overheated imagination," said Charlie, looking up for the first time from his potato chip. "Just like those conferences. A load of bull—"

"Charlie," said Bea.

"Whoa whoa whoa!" Ben held up both hands in self-defense. "We need to back up here. If I'm not totally imagining this conversation because of my brain damage—and I'm not saying I'm not—then can we start from the beginning?"

"Bea," said Charlie. He extricated his hand and folded his arms over his belly in a way Ben was beginning to recognize. His wife raised her eyebrows at him.

"Okay, then," said Ben, when it looked like neither one of them was going to speak. "I'll give it a try. Here's what I'm piecing together: a long time ago Red Gap was this thriving logging town, doing its part to wipe out the coastal redwoods. Native daughter Daphne Lindstrom marries the mill manager, goes downhill emotionally and then disappears. The mill shuts down; the town declines; Red Gap becomes another one of hundreds of ghost logging towns. A few citizens hang on through the intervening decades, re-inventing the Gap as a tourist destination. Then Gladys the town historian takes all the fruitful material she finds in her research, adds a dash of her own…imagination… and writes a *novel* about it. About Daphne's disappearance. Have I gotten it right so far?"

"That's right," said Charlie. "If you could call that piece of sappy, troublemaking trash a nov—"

"Gladys writes a *bad* novel," Ben amended hastily. "A controversial one, even. So what's the bit about the paranormal conference?"

Bea folded her napkin in precise eighths. "Well, *Bury Me Not* is a ghost story. Daphne—or Justine, Gladys calls her—Justine is murdered by her husband the mill manager and, to keep their jobs, the whole town participates in the cover-up. Then Justine's ghost haunts them and curses every last male descendent. The book's been real popular. I think it even spent a few weeks on some bestseller lists and Gladys got interviewed for some shows. *Bay Area Backroads*—that kind of thing. And then she started getting invited to speak at these conferences. I didn't even know there *was* such a thing, but people get together and talk about haunted this and poltergeist that and go on ghost walks and things."

"Been crazy around here since that damned book took off," Charlie put in. "Swamped with these weekend looky-loos. They tear up the woods and want to strip bark off Grand Daddy and throw love notes off the Overhang where this 'Justine' was strangled."

"Not that it's bad for business," added Bea. "In fact, it's never been so good. Especially for the Dryad, since we're the Lindstroms' own home. Other folks who keep places in town have seen how we're booked solid for the next eighteen months, and they've been trying to come up with ghosts of their own."

"That's what Charlie said." Charlie of the thunderous expression. "Is it the extra litter or the lousy writing that ticks you off most?" Ben asked him.

Before he could answer, Bea jumped in. "It's everybody not knowing the difference between fact and fiction. Daphne just out-and-out disappeared. That's the fact. And there's no evidence to tie Pall Lindstrom to it. That's another fact. Charlie gets a little tired of having to explain."

"And don't forget there's no such thing as ghosts," Ben said. "That's a third fact, and one that ought to make readers take the book with a grain of salt."

"Exactly," said Bea. She sprang up and began stacking their now-empty plates. "I don't say it so definitely, usually, because it's bad for business. But just amongst ourselves I'll say, yes: there's no such thing as ghosts." This last remark she delivered with a jerk of her chin that seemed aimed at Charlie. "No such thing as ghosts, and no such thing as a curse on the town. And especially—" the dishes rang with emphasis "—no curse on the Derwents!"

With that, Bea swept from the dining room.

Silence fell at the table. Charlie was staring at the wall opposite now, on which flowers, baskets, fruit, and birds burst in Victorian profusion all over the red-on-white wallpaper. Ben felt the stirrings of the dull ache beginning again at the base of his skull. He considered Charlie's profile: wary, yes, but not necessarily hostile.

"What did—uh—Bea mean about the Derwents? I saw a Shane Derwent in the history book…does that family come in for special punishment in Gladys' novel?"

At first Ben thought Charlie was not going to answer at all, the pause dragged on so. Really, Ben couldn't explain even to himself why he was pursuing the topic, when it was evidently so touchy. The words were spoken, however, so let Charlie toss him in the road if he'd had enough.

Charlie stirred, dragging his eyes finally from the wallpaper. They glistened suspiciously, and Ben wondered with horror if the big man were about to cry.

"Shane Derwent. He was a childhood friend of Daphne's. Few years older." Here Charlie gave a gigantic sniff, which Ben decided he would pretend not to notice. "Gladys calls him Shep Davenant in the book. Justine blames Shep for not rescuing her from her murdering husband, and then her ghost tortures every Davenant boy—son, grandson, great-grandson—until they go crazy or destroy themselves."

"Sounds like a great book," said Ben wryly. "Justine makes the real Daphne look like a well-adjusted young woman, at least." Frowning, he rubbed the back of his neck, willing the ache away. "What happened to the real Derwents?"

"They went crazy or destroyed themselves—Shane Derwent, son, grandson."

"Oh," said Ben. He managed an awkward laugh. "Well, at least they didn't live to see themselves served up as pulp fiction. A few less people to hate on Gladys."

Charlie cleared his throat. "Oh—they're not all gone."

"You mean there's a current generation? How's the latest Derwent boy holding up? Daphne hounding him to death yet?"

Charlie's lips curled. Folding both hands behind his head, he shifted in his caned chair to face Ben, the accompanying creak and groan reminding Ben of the strength of fragile things. "I dunno. You tell me."

"What?"

The chair protested again as Charlie leaned forward to dig his wallet out of a back pocket. Flipping it open, he teased a business card from one of the leather slots and pushed it across the table to Ben.

Ben had a sinking feeling even before he took in the illustration of a house and "The Dryad" in looping calligraphy. Sure enough, at the bottom: *Charles and Beatrice Derwent, Proprietors.*

"God—I'm an ass," said Ben. "Head injury or no head injury, I keep sticking my foot in my mouth. Sorry. For the comments about your family. My family tree gets pretty mysterious pretty fast, so you could crack all kinds of jokes about my forbears with no harm done."

"You had no way of knowing," spoke up Bea from the doorway. She leaned against the jamb, drying a coffee mug with a dish towel. "And Charlie's good at forgiving people. He's forgiven Gladys, mostly."

Charlie grunted.

"I told him that, so far as anyone knows, Gladys made up all that stuff about the Derwents, just like she made it up that Pall was a murderer."

"Of course," said Ben. He nodded at Charlie. "Your family's…

turbulent…history just got her creative juices flowing."

Another grunt.

Despite his recent embarrassments, Ben found his curiosity piqued. He wanted to know more. Like why the Derwent men went crazy or destroyed themselves. Did any of their cases have something to do with Daphne, or was that just Gladys' fertile imagination? He gave himself a shake. How on earth *could* their lives and deaths have anything to do with Daphne? Whatever really happened to the woman, she was stone dead by now. Of course Charlie was just über-sensitive because *Bury Me Not* aired dirty family laundry and got people thinking exactly the kind of nonsense Ben was thinking.

That was it, he told himself. For the tenth time, *forget it.*

Charlie was determined to. With finality, he scraped his chair back. "Gonna go down to Rube's," he announced. "Tell him Ben here doesn't want to try to fix the thing."

"Should I come?" Ben asked.

To his relief, both Charlie and Bea shot this idea down. "Don't push yourself," said Bea. "I'm glad you're feeling a little better, but that doesn't mean you should go gallivanting around."

"Well, I don't want to get in the way here."

"You're not the least in the way," Bea insisted. "You can explore the house or take a nap or whatever. Some of the guests might come back because we serve up the afternoon treats, and I have a meeting here myself, but we'll be in the kitchen."

"Thanks, Bea," he said, with relief. "I think if I lay low today, by tomorrow I might feel up to a hike in your woods—check out the local flora—"

He didn't mean to pick it up. But there it lay on the spindly occasional table in the Dryad's library, alongside a fanned-out stack of "Historic Red Gap" brochures: *Bury Me Not.* Shadowy trees crowded the greenish-black cover, the sole source of light an indistinct glowing figure half-hidden among them. The title was embossed in forest green two shades lighter while a review in small red letters blared, "A chilling tale of tortured love … !"

Ben turned his back on it, affecting interest in the rows and rows of paperbacks lining the wall shelves. Nicholas Sparks, Debbie Macomber, Tom Clancy. The typical stuff people packed on vacation and left behind when they had finished. Almost at random, he selected one of the Tom Clancy novels. One of those ones with a Special Ops guy on the cover, on his way to blowing the lid off a conspiracy or saving the world from certain destruction.

He was aware of the pulse in his throat and dull roar in his ears which he suspected was his own blood. Glancing over his shoulder, he rested his fingers on the occasional table. Then he took the copy of *Bury Me Not*.

Slipping it under the Clancy volume, he made his slow way back upstairs to Daphne's room.

CHAPTER 6

Bury Me Not

SHE CLUNG TO THE MIGHTY PILLAR OF THE WOODS, her source of life. Her flowing golden-brown hair tangled against the rough bark as she dug her nails into it. "I'll never let them take you."

"Justine."

Shep tried to keep the pleading note from his voice. He would have hated her for her alien passions, her wild behavior. But he was like that one tree his Pa talked about, the one that broke the teeth of the mill saw because it hid, buried in its heart, a horseshoe someone nailed to it decades earlier. Justine was strange, foreign now, but she had too long been a part of him to be rooted out. Yes, Shep would have hated her—except he could not remember a time when he did not love her.

"Justine—people are talking about you."

"Let them! And you get away from me, Shepherd Davenant—you and your whole family. You get away from me. I wish to God I'd never see any of you again! That the whole lumber mill would burn down over everyone's heads—"

"You can't act like this, Justine," Shep said, low, as close to her ear as he dared get. "My ma said she heard your aunt talk about sending you away. 'Till you could act like a proper young lady,' is what she said."

Her eyes flashed at him, and he took a step back. "They're not sending me anywhere." She was shaking. "I won't go. This is my grove. That mill already ate up so much of what's beautiful. They can't have my trees. I'm their protector."

Shep held up a hand and, when she did not object, he rested his fingertips on the covered buttons at her wrist. "Listen, Justine. I know you love this place. But there are other beautiful places in the world. The mill's got control of High Redwood, but, you and I, we could get our own piece of the woods. Homestead it. I'll be eighteen next year." He nearly choked on the words, so scared was he of her possible reaction. He had never spoken of this dream before.

The wild light was fading from her face. She released her hold on Grand Daddy, shaking off Shep's fingers almost absently. "You going to be a farmer, Shep?" The color this brought to his face seemed to amuse her. She hitched her skirt up in back with one hand, the other trailing along the redwood trunk, and retreated from him. "Daddy says nothing grows in these mountains but redwoods and moss."

"Not here, I don't mean," he said. "Not California. I thought maybe Idaho." Shep watched her, to see if the thought of leaving High Redwood appealed. "There's logging in the Bitterroots—not that I'd do that for long—just maybe till I could get a job in one of the mines. And I could—you could—" His throat was closing on him. "There could be a log cabin and a stream and woods for...us..."

She turned on her heel. He had a glimpse of her black boots before she dropped her skirts to the forest floor again.

"You know there aren't any redwoods in Idaho. Even if there were, this is where I belong. If I went with you, what would happen to Grand Daddy? And the Prince? Leviathan? Good Witch?" She tilted her head back as she recited their names, gazing far, far up into the branches of each in turn while Shep stared at the smooth column of her throat, the spill of that hair, rioting from its pins and running down her back. "Or Demigod? Empress? The Court?"

"Justine." His voice was firmer this time. Stumbling over one of Grand Daddy's massive roots, he caught at her again. She had to know the truth. She had to come out of her dream world. "Listen to me. There's nothing you can do to protect them anymore. Any of them. It's gone past just talk with the lumber men. The negotiations are over. Your pa sold your grove. Sold it. These trees—when they finish up over on the east slope—these ones are next."

"You lie!" she shrieked. She yanked her arm from his grasp, the better to strike out at him. "Daddy would never sell my trees. He promised me. How dare you try to make me believe such a thing?"

Her fingernails clawed at his flannel shirt, but Shep managed to seize her by the shoulders. He could feel her bones through the ridiculous puffed sleeves. The anger rose in him, and he began to shake her. "You wildcat! You are crazy like they say! Haven't I always been your friend and tried to help you? I'm trying to help you now. Everyone in town already knows what I'm telling you—I even heard some of the fallers laying bets about what you would do when you found out—"

He shook her till her teeth were knocking together. Until she stopped twisting and fighting him and they both panted with the effort.

At last Justine fell quiet, her head drooping. But Shep knew better than to let go. She had many weapons in her arsenal, and this one he dreaded most. Sure enough, when she raised her eyes, tears brimmed in them. "Shep—what will I do? No one will listen to a girl. You're the only one who can help me. If my own parents betray me, you won't let me down, will you..?"

What could he do? She reached up, removed his suddenly limp hands from her shoulders and, closing the distance between them, placed them at her waist. "You'll help me, Shep. Because no one else can."

A stray breeze lifted one of her curls and he smelled the lavender water, she was so close to him. The gray-green eyes, wet-lashed, searched his.

His rough hands rested exactly where she had placed them, trembling, catching on the machined lace. They convulsed. "What do you want me to do, Justine?" He had a foolish, impossible vision of himself, brandishing an axe to keep the fallers at bay. "I don't know how one boy can stop a whole lumber company."

"One boy—no," she murmured. "But one girl—I could."

He felt the warm current of her breath touch his face and he could not tell if the heat scorching his hands came from her waist or from somewhere inside himself.

"What do you want me to do?"

Her mouth was so close now. The eyelashes fluttered downward. She pressed herself to him. Wrapped around him, almost. When she whispered, the sound might have been his own voice.

"We'll need chains."

Ben let the book drop to the floor as he fell back against the pillows, the headache having returned full force.

However disturbing the factual Daphne Lindstrom might be—unbalanced, unhappy, and possibly undead—he was certain he would prefer her to the fictional Justine Sauvee. Gladys Harrington's creation was all those qualities and more. Manipulative, for starters. Ben was only fifty pages in, and Justine had already hoodwinked her nursemaid, school teacher, parents, and classmates, and what she'd gotten poor Shep Davenant to do for her was infuriating, progressing from carrying her lunch pail to pinning the braids of a girl she didn't like to stealing the loggers' springboards and steel wedges. All for the paltry rewards of furtive hand-holding or a lock of hair or a glimpse of her from her bedroom window before she turned down the lamp.

No wonder Charlie hates the book, Ben thought. If Gladys makes his great-grandfather such a wuss, God only knows how the rest of the family comes off. And if the character Justine was this annoying *alive*, Ben didn't imagine things would improve once she was dead. But they must—otherwise why would tourists seek her out, unless it was to wring her ghostly neck?

In any case, he could read no further with his head like this. The very shadows on the wall seemed to warp and tremble, now crowding his field of vision, now shrinking to invisibility. He massaged the back of his neck, taking care to avoid tender spots. Sounds, too, jumbled together. There were voices downstairs, vibrating the dark redwood paneling of the Green Room, but below—above?—through?—the voices he discerned a faint thudding. It could be his own pulse; he wasn't certain.

He needed more aspirin. One tiny tablet was not up to the demands. Of course, another aspirin required another trip up and downstairs—ten minutes, minimum. Maybe if no one was in sight, he could bump down, one step at a time, on his backside. Moreover, if Charlie weren't among the voices, Ben could ask Bea if the Dryad had an audio book version of the dreadful-yet-fascinating *Bury Me Not*.

When he rested a hand against the redwood paneling to steady himself, Ben felt the thudding. Slow. Muted. It unnerved him and he transferred his hand to the washstand. He had probably pushed himself too far and ought to lie down. Bea would certainly bring him the damned aspirin if he called to her, but she'd already nursed him enough the past couple days.

～

The fussy parlor was deserted, as was the dining room. Ben followed the voices through the swinging door into the kitchen, and sure enough, there he found Bea clustered with two other women and one ancient man around a square pine table. So intent were they that no one noticed him come in. Over the table's surface a map unfurled, and the man stabbed it with a gnarled finger. "We end at Grand Daddy. It's the climax."

"You can't end a walk by abandoning everyone in the middle of the woods," protested the large, blockish-shaped woman opposite him. The sunglasses propped atop her blunt-cut hair slid off the back of her head, and she tossed them impatiently on the table.

"Yes," said Bea. "Wouldn't it make more sense, Ray, to take people from the Grove and end at the Dryad? They could hear some house history, maybe see the Green Room, and then have a cup of cider."

"I think you start at the Dryad, go through the Grove and then end at the Come On Inn," said the block lady. "You know—a history of ghosts in Red Gap—from past to present."

Ray rapped his knuckles on the map. "Aww…face it, Joyce. No one wants to hear about your ghost. They all want Gladys' ghost. They want Justine."

Joyce's lips pursed. "It's a ghost walk, Ray. Sure people want to hear about my ghost—because my ghost is real! Not a figment of someone's imagination. Not 'inspired by true events.' My ghost *is* a true event."

"That's up for debate," retorted Ray. "But even if your ghost was 100% scientifically-proven and Gladys' was 100% made up, that doesn't change the fact that it's the made-up ghost people care about."

"And," broke in the other woman in a honeyed voice, "we all know that Justine Sauvee isn't 100% made-up. Not even close."

Bea drew herself up. "Well, Gladys, neither is she 100% God's-honest-truth, as Charlie and I always have to be explaining to people."

"She's more true than any of you Derwents will admit," was the smooth reply. "I don't know why you don't embrace it. You think business is good now—if you did a little more to exploit it, things would go through the roof. You and Charlie could buy a vacation home somewhere like Maui. You could buy your *girls* vacation places in Maui."

"I'm letting people see the Green Room, aren't I?" demanded Bea. "Charlie didn't even want that, unless they were guests at the Dryad—"

"It's a start," said Gladys, unperturbed. "Although how you're going to show it on the ghost walks when you've got that invalid young man in there is a mystery to me."

Ben figured this was his cue. He knocked on the kitchen cabinet beside him, unable to smother his grin when the four of them jumped. "Not only am I semi-incapacitated," he said, "but I'm needy, too. Bea— could I bother you for some more aspirin?"

"Oh! Of course." She was up in a flash, shooting Gladys a dirty look, which Gladys bore with equanimity. The notorious author tucked an escaped strand back into her chignon and smiled at Ben. Now that he looked at her, he was amazed to find her so young—early 30s, maybe. With a name like Gladys, he had pictured someone grandmotherly, not this whip-thin brunette with cat eyes and a Hermès scarf.

"Everyone," said Bea, "this is Ben. He's a botanist and forester who was working on a university project in the redwood canopy. Ben, this is Ray—Red Gap's mayor—and Joyce who owns the Come On Inn down in town, and then Gladys, the town historian and famous novelist."

"A legend in my own mind," said Gladys. She extended a slim hand to shake. Joyce gave him a curt nod and Ray merely squinted, his fluffy, Muppet-worthy eyebrows caterpillaring together.

"What's this about a ghost walk?" asked Ben.

"It's our latest idea," said Joyce, cutting across Ray. "Ever since *Bury Me Not* was on Good Morning America, we've been overrun with tourists. But other than a few signs on things, we haven't been organized to take advantage of it. If we start offering these ghost walks to go along with Gladys' book readings at the Blind Bard, it'll give people more to do. With the hiking trails and good restaurants, they might stay a week instead of a night or two."

"Sounds great. When does it kick off?"

"Before Halloween, we're hoping," said Bea. She handed him two aspirin and a glass of water. "We just need to hammer out a route and a guide, and then Gladys will take care of publicity."

"That's a few weeks from now," said Ben. "Should give my head plenty of time to recover so I can clear out of your Green Room."

Bea frowned again at Gladys. "There's no rush. Even if you aren't all the way recovered, we can just set you in the parlor when we need to take a group through. It's not like it takes a long time to see."

"Ah...but we want them to go in in small groups," pointed out Gladys. "So they can experience the vibrations."

"The what?" said Ben.

She turned her dark gaze on him. "The vibrations. The ghostly vibrations. Haven't you felt them?"

Ben ventured a glance at Bea—was Gladys serious, or pulling his leg? He saw his hostess swallow, but she said nothing. Had she told them about his confusion this morning? The woman in the woods?

"I'm not very...sensitive...to the paranormal," he said at last, as diplomatically as possible. As soon as the words left his mouth, he thought of the odd pulsing he'd felt in the redwood paneling. Who knew what that was anyhow—but ghostly "vibrations" it was not.

"You mean you have no prior experience of it," corrected Gladys.

"You could say that. I—uh—tend to approach life from a scientific point of view."

Silence greeted this comment of his. Apart from Gladys, the others seemed to be avoiding his gaze. Ray began folding up the map and Joyce perched her sunglasses atop her head again.

"But don't worry," added Ben hastily, "I can keep that to myself. I certainly won't go shouting that from any rooftops." He clapped his hands together. "Red Gap feels like the perfect place for ghost walks. Lots of history and second-growth forest to wander around in."

"I was thinking," said Bea, coming to stand beside him, "that when Ben felt up to it, I'd love him to explore our woods. He might have some good nuggets about the trees and environment to tell us. We could add it to the brochures."

"I'd love to."

Gladys slid out from the table. "Well, why couldn't he take a look now? He'd be the perfect guinea pig for our ghost walk route. Especially since he approaches life from a 'scientific' point of view. Devil's advocate, you know?"

"Oh, no," said Bea. She put an arm in front of Ben. "He's dizzy and tired and has headaches. I don't think he should be walking in the woods."

"It's not exactly a challenging hike," responded Gladys. "And he'd probably like to get out of the house after so many days. But if he's feeling…" she surveyed him coolly—"weak in the knees…I'll get my aunt's wheelchair and push him myself. Then you don't have to worry about him collapsing somewhere, Bea."

"I'd like that," said Ben. He ignored Bea's raised eyebrows. "If it wouldn't be too much work for you, Gladys. I could probably walk some of it—not very fast, though."

"That settles it," said Gladys. "My car's right outside because I had to be in Eureka this morning. We'll drive down and start at the Come

On Inn. Joyce, are you coming?"

The proprietress of the Come On Inn harrumphed. "I don't know that we decided for sure the walk should start in town. Shouldn't it end in town, so that people go to the stores and restaurants afterward?"

"They still can," grumbled Ray. "It's a four-minute walk back down. You've been outvoted, Joyce."

"You coming?" Gladys asked again.

Joyce hauled herself up, whisking the map from Ray's fingers and cramming it in her purse. "Only for the ride down," she huffed. "And to show Ben the Come On Inn. I have no intention of going on the entire walk and retracing the footsteps of Gladys' book character."

"No worries," said Gladys. "I'm sure Daphne will keep us company."

CHAPTER 7

Spiritually-Attuned

Joyce would have a hard row to hoe, Ben thought.

The Come On Inn was a nice enough little motel. Joyce didn't try to work against the 1960s architecture, and Ben preferred the clean lines and lack of clutter to the Dryad's Victorian overload. Apparently the Come On Inn was the straw that broke the city council's back, however—the last modern building approved before Red Gap decided the future lay in promoting its past. After the motel was built, everything that followed had to pass muster with the historical society, which meant that all the newer buildings in town had the earnest charm and period uniformity of Disneyland's Main Street USA. Because she was too late to jump on the nostalgia bandwagon, Joyce affixed a plaque to the front of her motel: *This was the original site of the Red Gap Lumber Company office which burned to the ground in 1926.*

"So who haunts it?" asked Ben, when Joyce led him into the Most Haunted Chamber. Queen bed, two vinyl armchairs, laminate end tables and tv stand, wrapped Dial soap, torchière. It was clearly occupied at present, an overnight bag spilling its contents across the industrial carpet. "A sawyer who couldn't get Pall Lindstrom to unionize?"

"It's somebody angry," answered Joyce, oblivious to any teasing in

Ben's voice. "Sometimes he wakes guests up by shaking the bed. Nothing else in the room will shake, just the bed. Shaking so hard that the headboard bangs against the wall."

There was a pause. Ben studied the motionless headboard. "Are you sure it's not just the guests...er...enjoying themselves?"

Joyce's watery blue eyes fixed on the neckline of his shirt. "I can tell the difference."

Another pause. He resisted the urge to do up his top button.

"Do you have a hard time renting the room?"

"Of course not," Joyce rapped back. "It's the most popular one. Everyone likes a good scare. I only wish it happened more often. People feel gypped if Albert doesn't shake things up."

"Albert?"

To Ben's amazement, a dark red flush washed over Joyce's cheeks. "He was the last mill manager after Pall Lindstrom went away. You know who Pall Lindstrom is, right?"

Ben nodded.

"Albert started as an errand boy for Lindstrom. But after Daphne's disappearance, Pall came to depend on him more and more."

Ben made "hmmm" sounds, to show he was taking it all in. "So this ghost Albert...why would he be angry?"

She licked her lips. "Well. It's just a theory I have. I don't call him Albert to the hotel guests. I just say The Ghost. I mean Gladys is the big spinner of stories in Red Gap, but—" She broke off. Pressed on an air bubble in the carpet with her shoe.

"But—" prompted Ben.

Joyce took a step toward him, invading his personal space. She was nearly as tall as his 6'1" and twice his width, and she smelled of Dial and Pine-Sol.

Ben made a conscious effort to hold his ground.

"—But my theory," she whispered, "is that the ghost is Albert Turner. And that he knows what happened to Daphne Lindstrom.

He's angry the truth has been covered up all this time."

"Truth?" Ben whispered back. "Do you mean you think Pall Lindstrom killed her?"

She made a disgusted sound and moved away, disappointment in him clearly etched on her face. "If that was it," Joyce rejoined at a normal volume, "why would Albert be angry? Gladys' book already trumpeted *that* theory all over the New York Times Bestseller List. No secret there."

"What, then? I take it you don't think like Bea does—that she just fell in the river."

"Fell in the river," snorted Joyce. "That girl grew up in the woods. Climbed trees like a monkey. No way did she just slip off the Overhang one day."

Ben wondered, not for the first time, how everyone seemed to know so much about people who had died long before. Daphne Lindstrom, Shane Derwent, Pall Lindstrom, this Albert person—you would think they were close personal friends! Bowling mates. What would Joyce know about Daphne's tree-climbing talents?

He took a deep breath. "So what's your theory, Joyce?"

Before she could answer, an electronic bell chirp indicated someone had entered the motel lobby. "Excuse me," Joyce said. She quickly smoothed her tunic over her hips and pushed past him.

It was Gladys, returned with the wheelchair, a rickety metal thing that she was shaking like an automatic umbrella in order to open it. Ben suspected it was last used by FDR. By the time he shuffled over to help, she was already plopping it into lock position. "Ready, Guinea Pig? Has Joyce finished hitting the paranormal highlights of the Come On Inn?"

"For now," said Joyce with finality. Clearly she had no intention of sharing her theory with the competition. Turning her back on Ben and Gladys, she switched on the television set behind the counter and began sorting the day's mail. "See you later, Ben. Nice to meet you."

Once Gladys got the foot plates down, Ben was both relieved and embarrassed to sink into the thing. "Sorry to be such a weakling. I could stand the headaches, but the dizziness—"

She gave a dismissive cluck. "That's what all the gimps say. It's a toss-up, who's getting the short end of the stick—me for having to push you around town and up to the Grove, or you for having to go in the first place. All set?"

Red Gap was a compact place, at least. The main drag ran alongside the Yoak River, although calling it a "river" was a stretch this time of year, before the heavy rains began in November. Without having to be prompted, Gladys set a slow pace. "Lucky it's not too foggy today. That's the post office. Library over there. Wave back—that's Alice who owns Etta's. Etta's is the bar—been around in some form since Day One of Red Gap. That across the way is the Market. Since the closest big box stores are in Eureka, Andy and Regan are free to price gouge."

"This isn't the ghost walk spiel, is it?" Ben asked. "Not very frightening."

"Oh—you want the full show, do you?"

"If I'm the guinea pig."

The wind caught the ends of Gladys' Hermès scarf and fluttered it past Ben's cheek. "Sorry," said his guide. She caught at it and stuffed it down her neckline. "Look—I haven't really written the spiel yet. You can help me formulate it. If you were a tourist and not a head case, what would you want to know?"

She had stopped the wheelchair where the sidewalk ended. They were facing the old mill. Unlike the other historic buildings in town, this one didn't seem to have benefitted from a financial facelift. Paint flaked off sagging boards. Grass and weeds sprouted between steps. Dust frosted the windows. A sign was nailed across the door: *Keep Out. Trespassers will be prosecuted.*

Setting the brake on the chair, Gladys sunk on the curb beside him, squinting up against the October sunlight. Her long hair was down now, and she ran a hand through it, teasing out a tangle with her fingers.

"I'd want to know why you're named Gladys," said Ben abruptly. "I expected someone older."

"Expected?" she laughed. "Bea said you never heard of any of us before this morning. But, yeah, it's an old lady name. I'm named for my great-aunt. I'd go by my middle name Pearl, but do I look like a Pearl to you?"

More Pearl than Gladys, he thought.

"Do you buy any of this ghost business?" he asked. "Or is this just good publicity for your book?"

She picked a twig out of the gutter. Started tracing lines in the dirt with it. "Sure I believe it. Not that it isn't good publicity. But I believe it."

"Don't tell me," said Ben. "You're related to one of them. You're a Chase or a Lindstrom or a Derwent."

"No relation at all." Gladys tilted her head to the side, inspecting her handiwork. "I'm fairly new to town—only seven years. But if you're this interested in the whole saga after only a few hours, imagine what a few years will do to you." She leaned back and flung the twig away.

"Look—you're the science type, so everything we say is going to sound crazy to you. But I'm just going to lay it out: I buy the ghost business. Hook, line and sinker."

He remembered Bea's comment. "Because it's good for business?"

"It doesn't hurt. But no. I buy it because I've met her." The cat eyes regarded him. Saw the question form on his lips. "Met Daphne, that is."

"*What*?"

The unsettling gaze slid away. "Uh-huh. Though maybe 'met' isn't the right word. I've ... *encountered* her."

With an effort, Ben maintained a straight face. "Oh. Wow. So ...

what happened?"

"I've encountered her in the Grove. Or what's left of it. Multiple times." Rising from the curb, Gladys brushed off her backside and started pacing in front of him. She had a nice backside, Ben noticed. And her front wasn't too bad either. Too bad she was out of her mind.

"I don't know why I'm telling you this," she continued. "Maybe because you're brain-damaged and I'm hoping you'll forget it all by dinner time. Maybe because you're an outsider like me and don't have any preconceptions. Most people who come here think they know me already because of my books. Or maybe it's just because I like hand-some young men. But in any case, I'm—what would you call it—I'm spiritually-attuned."

Still recovering from her comment that she thought him hand-some, Ben pinned on what he hoped was a respectful expression and waited. "Spiritually-attuned," his ass! He would bet a thousand dollars Gladys Harrington was a transplant from Marin County—Ground Zero for the "spiritually-attuned."

She paced away from him. Stared at the crudded-up mill windows, her hands on her hips. When she turned and marched back, Ben was reminded of a model strutting the catwalk. "Several times in my life I've had visions of people," she began. "Usually they couldn't speak, but they would sign at me—communicate things. The first was a young girl in my neighborhood who disappeared. We used to play together. A couple years after she went missing she…showed herself to me. I helped the police find the body." Gladys raised one penciled eyebrow at Ben, challenging him. He couldn't imagine his face was blank, nor could he muster a follow-up question, but she went on. "Then there was my maternal grandfather. He and my mother were estranged, so I think I only saw him once or twice growing up, and then he died when I was fifteen. But he came to me then. One afternoon when I was over helping my mother clean out his house."

Ben shifted in the wobbly chair. Man, she was laying it on thick. He rather wished he hadn't committed to spending the afternoon with the woman, attractive as she was. "Uh—I wasn't very close to my grandfather either," he said, trying to strike a balance between sympathy and shutting her up.

Her gaze whipped back to him. "He led me to the latest copy of his will. All her life, my mother thought her brother was the family favorite—and then here was this will, dated in the last year of my grandfather's life. It cut my uncle out completely 'because of his own choices.' There wasn't much of an inheritance, but it all went to my mother."

Convenient, thought Ben. Though, if there wasn't much money to gain, it hardly seemed worth a 15-year-old's trouble to invent. As for the other instance, the missing friend—hell—maybe Gladys had killed her herself.

He rubbed his jaw with one hand to hide a grin. Unbelievable. A few days breathing the atmosphere here and he was already turning into a first-rate conspiracy theorist.

Gladys didn't seem to notice his response. She lowered herself to the curb beside him again, clasping a knee to her chest. "And then there was my mother. She died right before I moved to Red Gap. She's the *reason* I moved to Red Gap. I needed a break with my former life."

A break from all the ghost-hounding, thought Ben. Got it.

He knew he was being insensitive, but inappropriate intimacy was really not his thing. Why did he have to be the handsome gimpy outsider who opened the floodgates of this woman's confidences? He should've gone with Bea's gut and stayed home.

Aloud he only said, "Did she—ah—need your help as well?"

"Sort of. Not really," Gladys murmured. "Personal stuff we needed to straighten out."

"Oh," said Ben, trying not to sound overly relieved that the secret-dump was over. He hoped.

They sat in silence another minute. Ben read the mill sign again. Stole a glance at his watch. If they didn't get a move on soon, Bea was going to think Ben was the next victim tossed off the Overhang.

"That's good, I guess," he managed at last. "You—er—help them. The dead come visit you, and you tie up any loose ends. I don't read a lot of ghost stories, but at least in the movies that's pretty much par for the course, haunting-wise."

The next thing Ben knew, Gladys was behind him, shoving the chair into motion. And not at the gentle snail's pace she adopted earlier. They bumped and rattled over kinks in the sidewalk that sent electric shocks straight to his pain center. "Hey!" he protested. "What's the rush?"

"No rush." A hint of a snarl beneath the smooth tone. "But I was done casting my pearls before swine, and we have other things on the to-do list."

What the hell? He'd listened to her, hadn't he, sort of? Ben tried to swivel around to read her face, but that brought on such a wave of vertigo that he nearly pitched out of the chair, and Gladys grabbed his shoulder to keep him from falling. His bad shoulder. When he let out a shout of pain, she immediately released it, and he collapsed against the armrest.

"Sorry," snapped Gladys. Ben had no idea if she was apologizing for her wild mood swing or for the jolting ride or for making him yell in pain. All he knew was that he had offended her and she must be thinking he was not only a boor but a feeble one, besides.

"I'm sorry, too," he said. A vague answer for a vague apology.

It did the trick, apparently. Gladys took hold of the wheelchair handgrips again. "No, it's okay," she said. "I mean—you were being flip when I was trying to tell you something I already said I never told anyone else, but I know it's hard to get your mind around it, and you're a science guy, like you said."

Not only a science guy, but whatever sensitivity he had before smacking his head, it had abandoned him. His filter was missing. Like how he kept saying all the wrong things at lunch. Still, the woman was nuts, and he didn't want to show up as the Tactless Cripple in her next book.

"Gladys—" Ben tried again, "I would look at you if I thought I could turn around without throwing up—" Oh, God. Worse and worse. "That came out wrong," he fumbled. "I mean my head is messed up. There's nothing wrong with looking at you. That is, I mean—*crap*—You know what I mean, I hope. And I'm sorry if I sounded like I wasn't taking you seriously. Your experience is…your experience. And I appreciate you taking time to show me around."

By this time she was laughing. She set the brake on the chair and came to stand in front of him. "Thank you, Ben."

Her chest was right at eye level. Feeling like Joyce at the Come On Inn, his eyes rested for one instant on the triangle of skin bordered by the neckline of her white blouse and the silk scarf.

"Tell me," Ben said, flustered. "In your experience—what does Daphne want from you? Why do you…see…her?"

"Hmm…" Gladys laid light fingers on his injured shoulder before resuming her place behind the chair. This time she set a decorous pace. "Can't you guess?"

They rolled past the Market. Through the plate-glass window, a man looked up from where he sat whittling. He nodded at them.

"My guess would be, she wanted you to tell her story," said Ben. "What happened to her, I mean. And now you have in your book—" mentally he crossed his fingers and hoped Charlie wouldn't overhear "—so that means she can enjoy a peaceful afterlife. You don't 'encounter' her still, do you?"

"Do you know what happens in the book?"

"Well, I hear the husband kills Justine and the town covers it up, so she haunts them." To put it mildly. "Especially the Derw—uh—Davenants. She really has it in for the Davenants."

"You could say so. I do wish people wouldn't give out all the plot spoilers."

"But do you think that's what really happened?" Ben couldn't keep the dubious note from his voice.

"It's a version of what happened."

"Is that what you think—is that what you think she *told you* happened?"

"Let's just say it's what I've pieced together. Some historic accounts, some *encounters*, some guesswork and imagination." Her tone didn't invite further questions. Ben suspected he was still on probation, and he let the subject drop. Privately he thought the mishmash of "guesswork" and "encounters" and whatever Gladys meant by "historic accounts" had clearly not filled the bill. Otherwise, why would Daphne still not be satisfied? Why, he wondered, would she want his help?

Except she didn't, of course. Being *dead* and all. Ben exhaled in disgust. Gladys Harrington wasn't the only crazy one in Red Gap. They should probably put up a sign off the highway exit: Abandon reason, all ye who enter here.

"That's Etta's coming up." Her hand pointed past his face to a free-standing square building, nondescript but for a mural of rigid, turn-of-the-century folk on the parking lot side: a logger, a Victorian lady pushing a pram, a girl licking one of those spiral lollipops.

"You're kidding me," Ben burst out, relieved to have something new to talk about. "That's the bar?" As soon as he said it he winced. Gladys had probably painted the thing.

But she only laughed. "Awful, isn't it? I think it's actually a marketing ploy. People see that thing and suddenly feel the need for a good, stiff drink. But keep your voice down because that's Ray's masterpiece—yes, Mayor Ray. He's got quite the sentimental streak. Etta's has always been the center of town, but there's nothing ghostly about it, so it's not a stop on the tour."

They turned up one of the residential streets, one that dead-ended in woods. A few preschool-age children stared at them over a picket fence. Ben waved at a face peering through the drapes.

"Why isn't the mill a stop on the tour?" he asked.

"The building's been condemned," she said. "If we took any tourists in there, the floor would probably collapse, and we'd have to add those victims to the Red Gap ghost collection."

"Not to mention they might start bugging you. Need your help to check out of the hotel or to post their pictures online." Ben clutched the armrests and groaned. "God—I've done it again—stuck my foot in my mouth."

There was no hitch in their pace. "No, you're exactly right. My plate's full. The Red Gap Historical Society wants to raise money to restore the mill, though. It's pivotal to the town's history."

They had reached the sidewalk's end and faced a small hand-carved sign affixed to a post: *Grove Trail. Half-mile loop.* Underneath someone had tacked a piece of cardboard. Written in Sharpie it read, "Grand Daddy."

"Pathetic, isn't it?" sighed Gladys. "That definitely needs to be re-placed before the inaugural ghost walk."

"Is this going to work?" asked Ben, eyeing the packed dirt trail. Al-though the incline wasn't steep, he wasn't sure the ancient wheelchair was built for off-roading.

In answer, she tightened her grip and shoved him into motion.

"Leave it to me."

The chair gave a petulant squeak and they entered the woods.

CHAPTER 8

Ghost Walk

Despite the lousy signage, the trail was popular. Several times Gladys was forced to pull over and let fellow hikers pass, although at this hour, most were headed back to town. They largely ignored Ben, aside from polite nods, but more than a few of them recognized Gladys. One teenager in particular waved her copy of *Bury Me Not* and shrieked to make his ears ring. "Oh my God! Oh my God—it's you! I so love this book, Gladys—can I call you Gladys? We were just up at Grand Daddy and you could totally *feel* the—the—like, the ghostly *emanations*. It's like she's *there*. And we're gonna check out the Overhang except that takes longer to get to, I think. Could you sign my book? My friends are not gonna *believe*..!"

Things got quieter after that. Just the rattling of the wheelchair and the rustle and squelch of plant life under the skinny tires. The occasional Power Bar wrapper and drink cup littered the path. Ben could see why Charlie complained. He preferred trails less traveled himself. Ones navigable by wheelchair hardly deserved the name.

Reading his mind, Gladys said, "Can you imagine Daphne Lindstrom used to come up to the Grove to get away from everyone?" She sounded a little out of breath. "It's not very far from town. We're practically there. She seems to be the only one besides the timber scouts who wandered around just for the hell of it. Of course, it used to take longer and feel more remote before everything got chopped down. If you look at the old pictures you can see the forest used to just swallow you up."

Ben nodded slowly. He knew. He had spent much time in the remaining pockets of North Coast old-growth forest, exploring, hiking, researching. While the trees here had come back in the last hundred years—nature was inexorable—the unmistakeable *crowdedness* of old growth was missing, where moss, flowers, trees, prickly salmonberry canes, and fungus fought for every square inch of real estate, the lush forest floor echoing in miniature the ecosystem of vast and towering redwoods above.

The trail narrowed.

"How much farther is Grand Daddy?"

"Maybe another couple hundred yards."

"Hold up. It's too hard to push me here. I'll get out."

"Do you need to use me as a crutch?"

"No, no. You go on ahead, and I'll come at my own pace."

The flora muted Gladys' footfalls after a few steps. Ben saw the white of her blouse as she vanished around a turn.

It took him several minutes, but he made his painstaking way after her. The absolute silence steadied him, as did the trunks of nearby trees. Nor did he need to ask when he had arrived—all at once he was in the heart of the Grove. On every side, draped in moss and lichens, the stumps of Daphne's once-mighty redwoods surrounded him.

The shrieking book fan was right—you could feel the "ghostly emanations" in this place. But the spirits haunting it were the trees themselves. After thousands of years standing sentinel, they had not abandoned their posts. His eye progressed from one stump to the next, the names Justine gave them in the book springing to mind: Demigod. Good Witch. Leviathan. Empress. Like signposts they led his gaze to the base of one mammoth, ancient, living tree that could only be the grandfather of all.

Grand Daddy. If it was imposing from a couple miles away, it was absolutely awe-inspiring up close. Twenty feet in diameter, he estimated. A good hundred-twenty, hundred-fifty feet on the leaning side to the lowest branch. Because of its tilt and redwoods' shallow root system, Ben could see where the angle put pressure—the carpet of roots struggled to cling to earth—but it looked stable enough. Redwoods had been known to bolster themselves against leans by growing more rapidly on their downhill sides. The Dyerville Giant might have leaned for a thousand years before it finally gave way. And the direction of Grand Daddy's lean was such that it would at least not fall back across the Grove clearing or trail. His eyes traveled the length of the trunk until branches hid it from view. Between the tilt, the sloping ground, and the second-growth trees obscuring Grand Daddy's top, there would be no telling the precise height without climbing to the top and dropping a tape. And who knew what mysteries it wore in its crown—a forest of its own, he imagined, sprung from soil that formed and accumulated over thousands of years. A secret world, hidden from terrestrial view.

It might have been five minutes, or even ten, before he remembered someone was with him. Gladys made no sound this whole time, and had Ben's neck not protested from being cranked back so long, he could have stared into the canopy for another hour, his hands itching for a rope and some Jumar ascenders.

But his neck did ache, and he came reluctantly back to earth, sighing. Even if he had his equipment, he was in no shape to be hundreds of feet off the ground, swinging and balancing. He began to apologize for his mental absence, but his guide's appearance startled him into silence.

She was pacing again. But not the thinking-while-walking sort she had done by the mill. This time, head thrown back, she strode dead-center down the former avenue, arms outstretched behind her, palms down, fingers spread. She was...trembling. No—*vibrating*, almost.

Ben blinked. *I'm losing it.* He massaged his temples and looked again. Gladys turned on her heel and paced back. Her eyes shone in the gloom, focused not on him but on Grand Daddy. Her back to Ben, she placed her palms against its trunk. The outline of her body had lost its discreteness. She was rippling, shimmering.

Stumbling, he sank against the nearest tree, not even checking first to see what should be avoided or observed or protected. The dull ache ever present at the back of his head awoke to renewed throbbing.

"Gladys? I think I've overdone it. Something's wrong with my vision."

Her voice floated back to him, oddly high-pitched. *"Who are you?"*

"What?"

"You heard me. You've come."

"What are you talking about? You brought me here."

"And you see me."

Oh, for God's sake, thought Ben. Talk about going off the Overhang. Bea was so right: he wasn't mentally up for jaunts in the forest with the town lunatic, no matter how good-looking she was. He ran his hands over his eyes. No use—she was still...shimmering, or something. He would have to ask Clyde the Veterinarian—did concussed *dogs* get warped vision?

"Gladys."

"Because I called you."

"Gladys!"

He pushed himself upright again, the sudden movement causing the forest to spin. Shutting his eyes against it, he staggered toward her like a drunken man. Gladys—or whoever she thought she was—screamed and retreated. *"Don't touch me! Help me! For the love of mercy, someone help me!"*

"Whoa—!" Ben halted in his steps. He held up his hands in surrender. "Hey. Okay. I'm not touching you. Sorry about that. I'm dizzy when I walk fast. Gladys…I'm gonna head back to town now." How he was going to manage a quarter-mile hike in his condition remained to be seen, but he was damned if he was going to linger in the woods with this woman and get accused of God-knew-what.

"Don't go."

He did not want to look at her. Everything else around him looked normal enough. But she took a step closer to him, and this time Ben was the one to back up.

"What's your name? I called you."

"Okay. It's Ben. Ben Platt. What's your name today?"

Gladys cocked her head to one side. *"You know who I am, don't you. I've been watching you. Because you can hear me."*

"I know who you are. You're Gladys Harrington." He kept his voice flat, reasonable.

"Yes, I know Gladys. She hears me, too. I tell her things."

"Uh-huh."

"Why won't you look at me?"

"Honestly, I don't feel great. You…hurt my eyes. I've got to go now, Gladys."

Her hand closed around his upper arm. *"Shane."*

Crikey. Heart hammering, he gently pulled free of her grip. "I'm going."

To his mingled surprise and relief, she did not try to follow. It took a full five minutes to reach the abandoned wheelchair, five minutes of physical and mental confusion. When he listened hard and heard nothing but forest sounds, he dropped into the shaky seat. A little recovery time. After all—what just happened there? The town historian and celebrity novelist went spooky and possessed on him? For real? Or was it an act—her way of showing him that she really was "spiritually-attuned"? She neglected to mention that, when she had these ghostly encounters, they all took place within the four walls of her own mind!

Surely she didn't do this often. People would know about it. Bea, at least, would have warned him. He frowned. He had chalked her reluctance up to concern for his physical well-being.

Ben was just wondering if he could make it back to the Dryad, using the chair alternately as walker and rest area, when the sounds of laughter and whistling carried up to him, breaking the spell. In another moment he glimpsed heads bobbing on the switchback below. A minute more and the hikers came into view, a pair of women in their fifties or sixties, the heavier-set one stabbing her way up the path with a walking stick while her companion trailed a few yards behind.

"Oh, hey there," said Walking Stick, the Marines' Hymn dying on her whistling lips. "You look awful. Need help?"

Her friend slapped her backpack playfully. "Don't be rude, Marilyn." She peeked around at Ben who was struggling to climb out of the chair. "You can walk!" she added in surprise.

"I'm okay," he said, as the chair threatened to topple over when he pushed up on the armrest. "Just a little dizzy."

Marilyn charged over and held down the other end until Ben regained his balance.

"Don't see any motor on this thing," she remarked. "You push yourself uphill with your toe, like a skateboard?"

"I—uh—had someone pushing me."

"Are they coming back?" asked the second woman. She had the luxuriant curls of a young girl, only they were white. "Otherwise we could wheel you back to town."

"After how you've been bugging me for months to see the Grove?" demanded Marilyn. "Ever since she read that blasted book," she explained to Ben. She turned back to her friend and gave an emphatic *thunk* with the walking stick. "First we'll have a look at the place, and then we can take him back. We're nearly there now. It won't take more than a few minutes."

"There's not much to see," Ben interjected hastily. He had no idea what was going on with Gladys Harrington but figured it didn't require more witnesses.

"Oh—are you in a hurry?" Curls asked, trying to mask her disappointment. "Of course we can help you now. Don't mind Marilyn."

Marilyn dug her stick in. "Knock it off, Judy. If there isn't much to see there, it will take us even less time." She scowled at Ben, clearly thinking him a selfish beast. "You can wait five minutes, right? Since Judy's come all this way."

He swallowed a sigh and sank back into the chair. Gladys would have to fend for herself. "I can wait."

⌇

There were no screams, at least. He assumed that if Gladys was still in Daphne mode and mistook Marilyn for Shane Derwent, Judy would come running, but the minutes ticked by uneventfully.

Then—faint at first, but growing stronger—the Marines' Hymn. Marilyn whistling. Ben tried to see up the path. Had she clubbed Gladys with her walking stick? But no, here came the two hikers, and with them a third: the author herself.

"…Never expected what happened with Brian Davenant," Judy was saying breathlessly. "I mean Shep, yes, and the son—that all made sense—but Brian just broke my heart!"

"What happy ending could there be between a ghost and a young man?" came Gladys' imperturbable response. She sounded her old self again. Or, her *new* self, Ben amended. Her 30ish self, instead of her 130ish.

She looked normal again as well. No more vibrating edges. To his surprise, she came right up to him and laid a firm hand on his shoulder. It was hot. "Feeling better now, Ben? It's getting darker, but if you're up to it you can lean on me the rest of the way."

"Rest of the way where?" he sputtered.

Gladys made a face. "Rest of the way to the Grove, of course. What else have we been talking about this whole afternoon?"

"It's amazing!" gushed Judy. "Just like she describes it in *Bury Me Not*. I kept thinking I'd see Justine Sauvee around every tree, and then out pops Ms. Harrington!"

"I've already been up to the Grove," said Ben, ignoring Judy. He held Gladys' gaze. "With you, remember? I…didn't feel right, so I tried to come back on my own and only made it this far."

"Don't be ridiculous. I've been sitting on Demigod's stump for the last half hour because you insisted you didn't need help."

"What are you talking about?"

"What are *you* talking about?"

"Uh—hey—time out," said Marilyn, making a T with her hands. "We'll let the two of you work this out. Judy and I will be on our way."

Judy looked disappointed. "I thought we were going to help push him back to town."

"He's got *her* to push him back to town," said Marilyn.

"Where are you headed?" asked Ben, not keen to spend more time with Gladys.

"The Dryad," said Judy. "The real Justine's old house."

"What do you know? I'm there, too. If you wouldn't mind lending me a hand, I've taken up enough of Ms. Harrington's time."

This seemed to recall Judy to herself. She laid an apologetic hand on Gladys' arm. "Of course! I didn't think of that. You probably have to prepare for your talk at the Blind Bard tomorrow, and there I was yammering on and on."

"We'll take him," said Marilyn.

"That won't be necessary," said Gladys. She grasped the wheelchair handles, and before Ben could react he was in motion, headed down the fork in the path that didn't lead back to town. "Nice meeting you both," she called over her shoulder. "Looking forward to more talk at the Blind Bard!"

"Gladys—seriously. I think I better get back to the Dryad and lie down a while." He kept his voice down although they were already out of earshot.

"I'll take you in a minute, but first we need to talk."

"Then let's talk here—you aren't taking me to the Overhang, are you?"

"And what if I was? It's part of the ghost walk." With a sniff, she jolted the chair over a snaking tree root and parked it alongside some withered salmonberry canes. Shriveled berries clung to the leafless twigs.

Ben winced. Waited for the predictable wave of dizziness to subside. When he opened his eyes again, he found Gladys standing right in front of him, arms crossed and eyes blazing. "I know you're eager to get away from me," she said, "but first we have to talk. I have to—you—look—you can't tell anyone."

This was too bizarre. "I'm not going to," he replied truthfully. Unless Gladys did this frequently, no one would believe him anyway.

"I had an—episode—didn't I?"

"Ye-e-es."

Her arms tightened and she kicked at some of the salmonberry runners. "Was it Daphne?"

He stared. "Is there—what?—is there like an array of choices?"

"Tell me."

"Uh—yeah. I guess you thought you were—I guess it was Daphne."

Gladys straightened. A pulse beat in her neck. "You think I'm faking it, don't you, Ben?"

"I'm gonna be completely honest with you and say I don't know what to think. Look—Gladys—are you trying to say this happens to you, and you don't remember afterward?"

"Sometimes." Her voice was small. "I haven't...that is...no one's seen me have an episode since I was a kid."

Call me Mr. Lucky, thought Ben. Despite the profound weirdness of the last hour, a stray insight streaked through him: she looked good embarrassed. It brought color to her face and a softness that was ordinarily lacking. It cost her to confront him, and as he stared at her, for once she was the first to falter.

Masking her discomfort, she pried shriveled salmonberries from the vine, chucking them down the path. She had a good arm, and he wondered if any of the berries were nailing Marilyn or Judy.

"So tell me, Ben—what did I do? Or say, I guess."

It was his turn to shift restlessly and look away. "Oh, well...something about how you wanted to talk to me because I could...hear and see you. And that you had—uh—called me. Then you said I was Shane."

A humorless laugh. "You must think I'm nuts. Because you're not even from around here. Why on earth would you have heard or seen Daphne? You only just heard *of* her."

The polite denial bubbling to his lips died there.

"What? Why do you look like that, Ben?"

There was no use, he supposed, in hiding anything. In such a small town, she was sure to hear it from Bea or Charlie. He licked his lips. "Because—well—if you're nuts, then I'm not much better."

Gladys held her breath and sunk into a crouch beside the wheelchair, her eyes searching his face. "Tell me."

Ben made a face. "It was a freaky thing. I thought my eyes were playing tricks on me because you didn't look...normal...You looked shaky or something—"

"Which could just be a result of your concussion," she interrupted.

"Which could just be a result of my concussion," Ben repeated, "except when you said—as Daphne—that I had seen you and heard you, that's what really did me in."

"It did?" Gladys leaned closer and her voice was barely above a murmur. "Because you have?"

"I don't know." Briefly he told her about seeing the woman in the woods while he was looking at the historical society book.

"That's only seeing," Gladys pointed out, when he finished. "That's not hearing."

He hesitated. This was probably stupid—he didn't trust Gladys any further than he could throw her—but he'd already blown it by saying he had heard Daphne. "The thing is," said Ben, "I may have heard her. I got this concussion when I fell out of a tree—I'm sure Bea told you—but I might not have fallen in the first place if I hadn't heard this...voice...calling to me. Asking for help."

"Ahhhh." Her eyes shone up at him in the gathering dusk. "That's our girl."

Ben's tired brain struggled with this. "I have no idea what's going on."

"I mean she chooses people she finds...sympathetic."

"I'm not," said Ben flatly. "Sympathetic. I've got enough going on. The last thing I need besides a head injury is to get latched onto by some ghost or whatever, and be expected to help her. How can I fix her life—*after*life, I should say—if I don't even have a good handle on my own?"

"It must be your love of the trees," Gladys suggested. "You share her consuming passion. That makes you sympathetic to her."

"Gladys, please. This has been a long afternoon. I'm not in a condition to win any arguments. Can we take up this topic at some later point?"

She broke into a smile. "Yes. Yes, absolutely. I'm sorry to badger you when you're not feeling well. It's just that I've never had anyone I felt I could share these things with. It's almost a relief to get caught in my secret! I know I've only just met you—I don't know what it is about you, Ben. But I feel it too, whatever Daphne feels. You can be trusted." Her hand snaked forward and grasped his. "We can keep each other's secrets, I think."

He remembered the warmth of that hand.

What happened next was a blur. Three things that occurred in such rapid succession that they felt nearly simultaneous. Any cause-and-effect he wanted to read into it had to be his own mind trying to make sense of it. At least, that's what he told himself as he lay in the Green Room that night trying to fall asleep.

The first was that Gladys' face drew so near his that all he could see were her soft lips and the appeal in her eyes. Whether he raised her up or whether she initiated he didn't know, but the next moment she was perched on his lap while the chair protested with great squeaks and groans. Neither of them paid the least attention. His hands found her waist and pulled her against him, and she bent her head to press her mouth to his.

The branch came out of nowhere.

With a whistling rush that Ben could only sort from memory, it grazed his tender left shoulder, a piece of it gouging a furrow from thumb to wristbone, before it landed with a splintering crash beside the chair. Gladys cried out in surprise, and they ducked their heads together to escape the rebounding needles and twigs.

Instantly the blood welled up from his gash, dripping onto Gladys' crisp white blouse and sending her scrambling to her feet. "Damn damn damn! Blood is so hard to get out. What the bloody hell *was* that?"

"A branch. A widowmaker." 200 lbs, if it was an ounce. He rose shakily to his feet to drag the chair away. "Come out from under the tree, Gladys."

His hand was stinging. "Wait till Bea sees me this time, I'm bleeding like a pig." It could have been the blood loss or the sudden movement, but Ben swayed on his feet. Gladys rushed over to prop herself under his clean side.

The third thing happened when she was assisting him back into the chair. Just past the thick curtain of her hair, Ben saw movement. White. It might have appeared or it might have been there all along—he didn't know or notice until it moved.

But he recognized it, even as it receded and shocked as he was.

The pleated train of a long white gown.

CHAPTER 9

The Journal

"Charlie, can I talk to you?"

It was nearly dark now. Ben found the innkeeper in the mud room, where he was dunking lamp globes in hot, soapy water. "I could dry."

Charlie tossed him a rag and nodded at the bench across from him. "Whatever you do, don't drop them."

"I know, I know," said Ben. "They're original to the house."

They worked in silence some minutes. Ben had to figure out how to dry the glass without his fingerprints smudging them up again, but once the task didn't require his full concentration, he said, "There's something I didn't tell you or Bea earlier."

With his fingernail, Charlie picked at a dried insect stuck to one of the globes. "What's that?"

Ben had mulled this over throughout the silent trip back to the Dryad. Down the bumpy trail, along the street where the children had been playing, around back of Etta's (no hideous mural on that wall at least), and then up the curving road to the bed-and-breakfast. By applying firm pressure to the back of his hand and elevating it, he succeeded in stopping the gash from bleeding, but he would need to do some cleaning up or Bea would think he murdered someone in the woods. Gladys brought the wheelchair to a gentle halt by the front porch and set the brake. When she came round to face him, he realized she was angry. Not at him, he didn't think, but before he could ask, she gave his good shoulder a squeeze and said, "I've got to go. If I don't soak this blouse in cold water, I'm vampire bait for sure. See you tomorrow, maybe? I'll leave the chair here in case Bea and Charlie need to get you around." Ducking down, she kissed him on the check. A peck, merely. She threw a last glance at the encroaching woods, turned on her heel and left.

If she wasn't angry at him, then what was her mood about? He had not mentioned his second sighting of the woman in the long white gown, but he had a niggling feeling he didn't have to. A theory was starting to form in Ben's head. One he fought against. Like any researcher, however, once the idea took shape, it ate at him. He wanted to test its plausibility. Its veracity, whether he liked it or not. Whether it made any sense or not.

Charlie rubbed the insect bits off on his overalls and set the dripping globe on the bench, reaching for another.

Getting his thoughts in order, Ben began his confession with the voice in the woods—the one that scared him out of the Douglas fir. Then he related his dream about the hand on the window. Then the vision at the edge of the woods, though Charlie already knew about that. Ben omitted Gladys' incident in the Grove, as well as their kiss—he was going to have to start keeping notes, to remember what he told to whom—but wound up with the widowmaker branch and the second glimpse of the white gown.

While he spoke, Charlie continued to dip and rotate and scrub, but more and more slowly. By the time Ben finished, the innkeeper was sitting back against the wall, eyes fixed on the ceiling and wet lamp globe forgotten on his leg. Moisture from it left a dark circle.

"So," Ben said, "I guess what I wanted to ask, Charlie, was: (1) do you think I'm crazy? And, (2) if no, then why not? I'm asking you because, when we talked this morning, it seemed like you had some idea of what was going on with me."

For a long spell Charlie said nothing. If not for his massive chest rising and falling slowly, Ben might have thought he'd been turned to stone. Maybe the topic of Daphne Lindstrom always did this to him. Through the Dryad's walls they heard the whirring of the vacuum cleaner—Bea taking care of any dirt her hiking guests tracked in before they headed back to town for dinner.

Charlie's gaze flickered downward. He seemed to notice the wet spot on his overalls for the first time and set the globe on the bench.

"Bea won't like that I'm talking about this," he said.

Ben felt guilty. "I know. I'm sorry. I gathered it was a touchy subject at lunch."

"She's a good woman. A practical woman. She likes talking Daphne Lindstrom as much as the next townsperson, except for how it connects to my family."

Which is—? Ben prompted inwardly. Aloud he said, "I wouldn't bug you about this, Charlie, but I don't know what my problem is—if I really just banged my head too hard and need Dr. Stevens to come out again, or if the whole town is playing some elaborate trick for publicity or whatever, or if I really am seeing or hearing something or some*one* that other people have seen and heard."

The vacuum paused. They listened as Bea slid some furniture against the wall to get underneath it. The low roar started up again. Charlie took a deep, wheezy breath, planting both booted feet squarely on the floor. "Your hand. It's bleeding again. Better press on it with the rag."

Ben obeyed.

"Guess you have a right to know now." Charlie's voice was low. Ben leaned forward to catch his words. "Guess seeing her twice gives you a right."

A "right"? His unwelcome visions gave him entrée into an elite society, then?

"But what I tell you, Ben, goes nowhere. I mean you can't tell anyone. Can't write a book about it or go on the radio or what-have-you. I've only ever told Bea. And she's really protective—made me promise not to talk about it with other people, and I've kept that promise."

"Charlie, I don't know. If you promised her…" Ben said reluctantly. He wondered at himself. Only a few hours ago Gladys' confidences struck him as unduly intimate, and now here he was trying to wring some from Charlie. "I mean, you barely know me. Not that I'm not dying to know, of course."

"Bea's got a good instinct about people," said Charlie, not heeding him. "I think she'd be okay with this. I'm only telling you right now because of what you been going through. Worse comes to worst we could say you made it all up because you had brain damage."

"Thank you," said Ben with a wry grin. "If I broke your confidence, I hope you would."

~~~~~

Charlie's Story

I was thirteen before I knew what happened to my father.

I knew how he died—the facts of it—from my own memories, but I didn't know what he went through when he was a kid. Not till his sister—my Aunt Rachel—finally told me. She said he was "eaten alive by curiosity." Aunt Rachel always avoided talking about him, but I think she had to speak up finally because I'd been acting strangely for weeks. Disappearing, going for walks in the woods, talking to myself. Aunt Rachel said she didn't put two-and-two together until I started acting funny, and that jogged the memory, like.

My father was five years older than her. Just old enough that she was a pest to him and not a playmate, so of course she used to tag along when she could, and when she couldn't, she would sneak after him. So when he started ducking around the woods like I did—at about the same age—she was right behind him, secretly. She said he went through a whole spell. He would go to the Grove, sometimes right off and sometimes after long wanderings, like he was trying to stay away from it but finally couldn't. She knew it was always on his mind because he'd always reach a point where he'd get real impatient with himself and curse or kick something or throw something, and then next thing you knew, off he headed for the Grove.

Once he got there he acted even stranger. He would sit for an hour, muttering to himself. Or pace up and down arguing. One time he even got down on his knees and hammered on the ground. And then the time that scared her most of all, she saw him talk to himself for a long time, and then he just started crying. Crying and crying. Her big brother!

That was too much for my eight-year-old aunt and she went and told their mother everything. It was a crazy story and Rachel was known for tattling and exaggerating, but my grandmother had already been noticing signs and clues on her own, so this time she took Rachel seriously. When my father came back in that afternoon, my grandmother asked him what was going on. She pointed out all the things he'd been doing, and even though she didn't say Rachel told her, he knew. He flew into a rage and started yelling about how he was gonna run away from home and how he couldn't stand the spying and all.

Now, my grandparents were divorced. Which never happened in their day and age. Grandma was the only divorced woman in Red Gap. Maybe in the whole county. And Grandpa lived far away in Los Angeles for his health. But he was a rich man, and he sent money all the time, regular. Well, when my father got out of control, Grandma wrote Grandpa Derwent, and next thing you know, my father got shipped back east to a boarding school.

That was all Red Gap saw of him for the next fifteen years. Right after high school he enlisted, and when the War ended he went to college on the G. I. Bill. By then my grandfather was dead and Grandma was going downhill, so Aunt Rachel wrote my father and asked him to come back and help settle everything. He didn't want to come back, but she begged him to help her and then he could leave again. So back he comes. And when she picks him up at the train station in Redding, he's got a wife—my mother—and a baby—me.

Aunt Rachel said everything was fine for a while. She and my mother nursed Grandma until she died a couple years later. My father got all the wills and estates settled and commuted to Eureka to work in an insurance place. He didn't go into the woods if he could help it, and he was always telling my aunt how much better the world was outside of Red Gap and trying to convince her to sell the house and leave. But she didn't want to go and leave everything. My father had been away a long time but that didn't stop everyone in town from looking at him a certain way. But he kept to himself and wouldn't be sucked into talking about the past or about his parents or grandparents or the old days. It wasn't till one summer. There had been a drought the couple years leading up to it and some kids were goofing around in the woods and started a fire. With the winds and all, there was a chance it would reach the town, so it was all hands on deck. Even my father had to wet a handkerchief and tie it over his face and head out to help. As far as Aunt Rachel knew, it was his first time going back deep into the woods since he was thirteen.

The men were gone forty-eight straight hours. They made some fire breaks. A few of them got trapped and swept over and didn't make it back. My father came straggling home another half-day after that, with my mother and aunt already going crazy with fear and Aunt Rachel starting to mumble about making arrangements. It's my earliest memory: Mom yelling at Aunt Rachel, "There aren't going to be any arrangements because he's coming home!" And then, like she willed it, he was stumbling up the porch steps. Black head to foot with smoke and soot. One of his eyebrows singed off. He scared me to death. But it wasn't all the dirt and ash that made him so frightening—it was his eyes. Like they had seen more than people are supposed to see.

After the fire he was distracted. I don't have any memories of him talking. Just Aunt Rachel and my mother, Aunt Rachel and my mother, while he sat there. He started taking long walks in the woods. Being gone and quiet and distracted.

Then one day when I was in the front yard making mud pies with Rube, this car pulls up and some men get out and say hello, boys, to us and go knock on the door. My mom opens, and they take off their hats and say something to her, and she screams and falls right down. They pick her up and Aunt Rachel has them lay her on the couch. I come over all in a panic because my mother was always so strong and Aunt Rachel shoos me away. She won't let me see my mother for hours, and when she does, my mother is all tucked up in bed even though it wasn't time to go to sleep. She takes my hand and hers feels hot and dry. She tells me that my father is dead. They found him at the base of Grand Daddy—all his bones broken and just some ropes in his hand.

At this point in the story Charlie drew his sleeve across his eyes again and fell silent. He and Ben were now sitting in total darkness. This was how Bea found them a minute later when she popped the door open and flicked on the light. Giving a startled yelp, she lost her grip on the vacuum attachment, and it clattered on the tile floor.

"For heaven's sake! I didn't know you two were out here, lurking in the dark! Are you *still* working on those, Charlie?"

"All done now," he said, avoiding her gaze. He began stacking the cleaned and dried lamp globes in a nearby picnic basket.

"I can't imagine you did a very thorough job if you couldn't even see what you were doing," his wife said dryly.

"I'm a man of many surprises."

"*That* I do know." She grinned at Ben. "How was your ghost walk? I see you survived—for the most part." Catching sight of his battered hand, she gave him a questioning look.

"Tree branch," said Ben.

"See any ghosts?" she teased, scrunching against the wall to let her husband pass.

Ben choked slightly. He played it off as a chuckle. "Oh, I'd say they were outnumbered by the *Bury Me Not* fans out prowling the trails. The walk should be a big hit, though," he added. "The woods are definitely…spooky."

"And what did you think of our most famous citizen?" Her tone was light, but he saw genuine curiosity in her expression.

The memory of his hands and mouth on Gladys flooded back. He hoped his face wasn't giving anything away. "She's—one interesting lady."

"Mmm…pretty, too, don't you think?"

He rose slowly to his feet. "Yeah. You could say that. And about eighty years younger than I thought she would be." He waved his hand in the direction of the mud room door. "I'm gonna go help Charlie put those back up. Unless you have another job for me."

Bea shook her head and stepped on the vacuum button to retract the cord. "Nope. But you two don't take too long. After I whip up some cornbread it'll be time for dinner."

Charlie saved the outdoor lamp globes for last. It was understood between them that Ben's job was to hand them to Charlie, but that he himself was not to do any ladder-climbing or balancing-while-holding-fragile-antiques. It amazed him how good Charlie's balance was for such a big man. Were he a hundred pounds lighter, Ben would be tempted to invite him free-climbing. That is, if his own head permitted it, he reminded himself.

"Your father," Ben murmured. "He must have fallen while trying to climb Grand Daddy."

"That's what they think."

"But why? What did he want to do that for?"

The ladder creaked as Charlie descended. He flipped up the

spreader locks and collapsed it. "Let's go put this back in the shed," he said. "And I'll go on with my story."

Charlie's Story

Like I said, all I knew as a kid was that my dad died falling out of a tree.

My mother hated Red Gap after that. She took us back to Redding, but her health never recovered, and by the time I was eight, she was dying. Her own family'd gone in the flu epidemic of 1918, so that meant the only relative I had left in the world was Aunt Rachel. Back I came.

The Gap is the best place in the world to be a boy. With the River and all the downed trees and hollowed-out trees you can do all the exploring you want. Plenty of adventure and lack of supervision. Aunt Rachel left me to myself, pretty much, so long as I did the chores she gave me and showed up by dinner time every day. When I got tired of the trees, there were the animals. I had pet raccoons, nursed an owl with a busted leg, watched beavers building a dam. When the weather was bad, me and my friends broke into the old mill and had secret club meetings. Everything was great. And if people thought things about my family or what happened to my dad or granddad, no one told me. No one talked about the Lindstroms back then, either. It was all forgotten. All quiet, I thought.

It wasn't until I was thirteen that everything came apart. That was the year they built the Come On Inn. Ever since the old mill office burned down, the lot was just a heap of dirt and trash and rubble, but the Archers—Joyce's parents—got all that hauled away. Then, when they got the backhoe in there to dig out for the new foundation, it hit paydirt. All these metal boxes and a safe. The Archers were all for opening everything up right there on the spot, but—their bad luck—everything is everyone's business in a small town. Word flies up the street to Etta's and, next thing you know, a few citizens think this could be the start of something big and decide to form a historical society, and first thing they do is tell the Archers to turn that stuff over. This gets to be a big argument, and meanwhile the Archers want to keep going with the motel construction because darned if they aren't renting that backhoe by the day from over in Eureka, so everyone agrees to store the boxes at the mill until the smoke clears. They move the stuff up there and put these big padlocks on the front and back doors.

Well, me and my friends weren't using the front or back door to get in anyhow. We shinnied up where the water wheel was housed, though by now most of the teeth were rotted or broken. The very day they put the boxes in, our club met and we pried some of them open.

Most of it was dull stuff. Lumber company books, payroll records, company correspondence. But one box had another one nested inside it. A leather one, with the edges all crumbly. We all looked at each other funny. It didn't feel like we'd get in trouble for opening the boring boxes, but this one—this one felt private.

And it was.

There were photographs of a young woman in old-fashioned clothes and one of a couple on their wedding day. There were letters, the ink all faded on yellow paper. There were some newspaper clippings. And a leather journal with a ribbon marker.

The other boys weren't very interested. After making some fun of the pictures, they replaced the stuff and went back to drafting our club by-laws. I wouldn't have cared much either. History was my least favorite subject. But just before I put the journal back in the leather box, I kind of riffled the pages. They were just the right weight and thickness I was thinking, that if I drew something on every page, I could make one of those animations. Mickey Mouse jumping over a ball, or the sun rising over mountains. I flipped once, twice, and when I did, a word stood out from all the old-fashioned writing.

Derwent.

That knocked me flat. What was my name doing in there? Did this belong to some ancestor of mine or to someone who knew my family?

All at once it was like something was loosed inside me. All the things no one talked about. I remembered the couple times I tried to talk to Aunt Rachel about Father and she changed the subject. Or the times I asked why my grandparents divorced, and she told me to hush up. I remembered busting in the back door at Rube's house to see if he wanted to catch frogs and making a roomful of grown-ups go dead quiet like they'd seen a ghost. Mrs. Benson said, "Speak of the devil—your ears ringing, boy?"

With so many memories flooding back, I didn't think twice. I took that journal and stuffed it up my shirt.

There was no safe place in the house to keep that thing. Even though my aunt had so many secrets, she didn't believe in *me* having any. She was always digging through my room for contraband or listening in on my conversations with friends. So I decided to hide the journal the only place I knew she wouldn't look: the woods. In the Grove, to be exact.

You don't grow up knowing your dad fell out of a tree without going back there and exploring around. Rachel knew I spent time there, but she didn't say anything. I could just tell it upset her because her lips would get tight. I think she thought if she never talked about it, it would just stay asleep.

So as soon as I could, I took that journal and hiked up to the Grove (there wasn't any trail back then). I wandered around and around and looked under things and over things until I found a couple possible hiding places. They weren't very dry, but curiosity was making me impatient. So I took a seat on the stump of Prince, where the moss covers a dip in it and makes it like an armchair, and started reading.

It was Pall Lindstrom's journal, sure enough. He had a big book plate in the thing with his name all fancy. Maybe someone gave it to him as a gift because he wasn't much of a journal-keeper. He'd go for long spells between entries. Sometimes he would just write about the weather or how the mill was doing. A line here, two lines there. The handwriting wasn't too hard to read—he made his P's funny—but it was small writing and hard to make out when you're in the woods with no flashlight. I flipped to the middle, trying to guess where I'd seen my name.

> *That Derwent showed up at the reception drunk as a fiddler, shame to him and his wife who is expecting. D insisted on talking alone to him and got him to go home.*

That got my attention, all right. A Derwent—any Derwent—*drunk*? Aunt Rachel never kept a drop in the house. I'd heard other people complain about it and tell her Prohibition ended decades ago. I shouldn't have skipped around. What did I miss? I went back to the very beginning.

And that was how Daphne Lindstrom got under my skin. I hid the journal wrapped in newspaper and a burlap bag in one of the fir trees near the Grove. I figured anyone who came up there was there to see Grand Daddy, and not any of the piddly firs poking up here and there. Every chance I got, I snuck away to try to read more. I got smarter and brought a flashlight and my aunt's magnifying glass.

Daphne Lindstrom got under my skin because she got under Pall Lindstrom's skin. This not-very-wordy guy who wrote about the weather in more detail than about her. But the weather never affected him like she did.

> *Stir in town. Arthur Chase's daughter returned from sanatorium in the Valley.*

> *Miss D. C. most beautiful girl I have ever seen.*

> *Miss D.C. passes the office each morning and afternoon on her way to and from the schoolhouse. She is the eldest girl in the school as a result of her year-long absence, and, I believe, more of an assistant schoolmistress than pupil. She has always in her train younger boys and girls.*

Miss C stopped outside, talking to the boy who carries her lunch pail. I hastened into the street on pretense of hiring the young man as an errand boy. This Albert Turner is a favorite with her. She smiled upon me for my troubles.

Escorted Miss C home from church. I cannot be certain of her affections. She is changeable.

Learned that bucker Shane Derwent was formerly a suitor of Miss C.

Derwent is a rough, uncouth young man, surly with me to the point of insubordination. I do not permit myself to imagine the two things are related.

Sought Miss C and found her by the tree she calls Grand Daddy. She was weeping. Furious at me. Told me never to follow her again.

I cannot rest. Miss C haughty and indifferent.

Would not speak to me.

Accepted a glass of mulled wine from my hand at the Christmas Fair.

Derwent injured by felled tree rolling suddenly downhill. I ascribe it to his carelessness and frequent inebriation.

Have not seen Miss C for several days and hear reports of her illness.

Albert declares Miss C on her deathbed. Cannot sleep.

Miss C has returned to school! The illness only added to her pale, ethereal charms. She accepted my congratulations on her recovery with indifference. When I dared express my hope that she would live to grace our lives many, many more years, she replied, "Mr. Lindstrom, your constancy would fatigue the sturdiest constitution."

Derwent has returned to work. He moves more slowly now. I would be tempted to fire him, were it not for his new sobriety and the news that his already much-put-upon wife is in the family way.

The most joyful day of my life. Miss C consents to marry me.

~~~~~~~

Charlie fell silent. He scratched his head with both hands, setting his wild white hair even more on end.

With difficulty Ben resisted the urge to shake the older man by the shoulder. Had he sensed that Charlie paused for dramatic effect, impatience would have won out, but Charlie was biting his lip, his brow furrowed.

The situation resolved itself when Ben sagged against the worktable, knocking a pair of wood clamps noisily to the floor.

Charlie's gaze returned to him from far places. "Watch out there." Taking hold of Ben's elbow, he steered him out of the shed and locked the door behind them.

"What happened next, Charlie? Was that the end of the diary?"

"Nope. But I didn't get any further in my reading that day because that was when I met my unexpected visitor."

"Your aunt?"

"Heh. No, but she would have scared me too. It wasn't Aunt Rachel." Charlie put out a hand to stop him. They stood just outside the pool of light from the back door. Ben saw the swift shadow of Bea flit across the curtains: stove to table, table to refrigerator.

"It wasn't Aunt Rachel," said Charlie again. "That was the first time I saw Daphne Lindstrom."

CHAPTER 10

Blindness and Silence

Rain was falling.

Ben lay in bed, arms crossed behind his head, listening to the water come down. There was no storm, no wind. Just the rain, steady and drumming.

Nor was there any hope of sleep. For one thing, he had slept too much the past few days, but more importantly, his mind was too full. He marveled briefly that the concerns which had obsessed him not twenty-four hours ago—his faithless girlfriend, his destroyed career, his uncertain future—seemed now distant. He could even say *irrelevant*, compared to what occupied him now.

Charlie had seen her.

The story waited through dinner. If Bea suspected anything off about Ben, she attributed it to his concussion. For his part, Charlie flipped the switch back to "normal," and he and his wife discussed bookings, wiring in need of repair, squirrels raiding the bird feeders. Ben would have exploded with impatience had he not also discovered himself to be ravenous and Bea a splendid cook. With each successive serving he grew more apologetic and she more pleased. "No, no, don't be sorry! I couldn't be more flattered that you like the chili, and your appetite is a good sign. Wait till you have the cherry danishes I'm making for tomorrow."

Then after dinner the guests trickled back in, shaking raindrops from their fleeces and windbreakers and heading for the Dryad's library to sip port before the fire. Ben greeted Marilyn and Judy before pleading headache and shuffling upstairs to the Green Room.

Sometime later there came a knock. Shoving *Bury Me Not* under his pillow, he opened to admit Charlie. "Not gone to bed, huh?" the big man asked.

"Not while there was a chance you'd come talk to me some more," said Ben. He gestured to one of the armchairs, but instead of sitting, Charlie made a loop of the room, brushing his fingers along the wainscoting and peering blindly from the window.

Ben wondered if he regretted saying so much already and cast about for a way to renew his trust. He joined him by the window.

"Her hand—the hand I saw—slid along right about here," Ben offered. "It was pale. With long fingers. She was wearing a gold ring." He shivered. "I thought I was asleep."

Charlie said nothing. Ben tapped his sleeve. "And I forgot to mention that this afternoon, when I got up from reading on the bed, there was this weird … pulsing in the wall. I couldn't figure out what it was."

"Mrmm," Charlie grunted. He rested his own hand against the wall briefly. "Yeah. I've felt that too, from time to time. People like Gladys would tell you it's Daphne's heartbeat. Treehuggers would say it's the dead redwood's heartbeat. This house, you know, it's built entirely with the wood of one tree. The one Daphne Lindstrom called Good Witch."

"But how—wasn't the Grove logged before the Lindstroms were married?"

"Uh-huh. They started the year that Daphne was at the sanatorium, matter of fact. But you've seen the size of those trees. They didn't do them all at once. When she agreed to marry Pall Lindstrom she asked for two wedding presents: that they never touch Grand Daddy and that he build her a house with whatever Grove redwood the lumber company hadn't shipped yet. That was Good Witch." With a sigh, he lowered himself into an armchair.

"Where did Good Witch stand?"

"Closest to Grand Daddy. He didn't start leaning till after she was felled."

"I'll bet their crowns were so interwoven that she probably half-pulled him down," said Ben. There was another pause. He took a seat in the armchair opposite Charlie. "So…did you learn all this from later entries in the journal?"

Charlie nodded. "And the lumber company records. Seems everyone knew Daphne's names for the trees. It was an easier way to keep track than using coordinates or some such."

"Do you still have the journal?"

Slowly, Charlie shook his head.

"What happened to it? The historical society?"

Another negative. "They don't know of it to this day. No. It was Aunt Rachel. When I—the time I…brought it back to the house I got grounded. Which meant I had to try to hide it somewhere right under her nose. It was only a matter of time before she discovered it. And when she did, she burned it."

Ben exhaled in dismay.

Charlie looked up at him, half-smiling. "Yeah, too bad. For Pall Lindstrom's legacy, I mean. It was okay for me. By the time she found it, I'd read it through a bunch of times and knew every line that related to my family or Daphne."

"Still…" said Ben regretfully. He would have liked to page through it himself. "But why do you say it was too bad for Pall Lindstrom's legacy?"

Charlie snorted. "Because of *Bury Me Not*, of course! If Gladys Harrington knew about the diary, she probably couldn't have pinned her character's disappearance on the husband. Pall Lindstrom knew nothing—he was beside himself. There was never any hint of guilt or knowledge. He fell apart. The diary just peters out like he couldn't bear to think about his life anymore. And that wasn't the only part that wouldn't have worked for the book. Gladys makes out like Daphne was crazy jealous of all the women looking at Pall. That it was her jealousy that pushed him over the edge. Shane Derwent was just there to be her whipping boy. The mill manager husband in *Bury Me Not* strangles the Daphne character because he's tired of her moods and wants to run off with his half-breed lover. Crazy. There never was anyone but Daphne for Pall Lindstrom, and at the same time he never felt even one day in his life like his wife really loved him."

Ben absorbed this. "You know, Charlie—this afternoon when Joyce was giving me the tour of the Come On Inn, she said she didn't think Pall Lindstrom killed his wife either. She was going to give me her own theory, but then Gladys showed up."

"Joyce'd probably like the murderer to be someone in *her* family," said Charlie derisively.

"Well, did Lindstrom have an idea himself, then?"

"Mmmph. Not in so many words. He was a serious guy. Man of his word. He wouldn't go throwing accusations around, even in his own journal."

"But you think he had…hypotheses?"

"Oh…" Charlie tapped his fingers on the armrest. "I guess I'd have to say that, if you read between the lines…I guess I'd have to say he always thought there were…feelings between his wife and Shane Derwent."

"You mean that maybe she ran off with him?"

"No, no. Shane Derwent lived out the rest of his life in Red Gap. That's why we Derwents are still here, a hundred years later. No, I mean Pall Lindstrom probably thought it was Shane who got jealous and killed her, if really she died that way."

"Then why wouldn't Lindstrom tell someone about his suspicions?"

Charlie shrugged. Shook his head again. "He had no evidence of anything. It would have been just his fears talking. She was *never found*. Derwent didn't act like a guilty man. He kept living and working in Red Gap. He went on worse and worse benders, but if you went around accusing every drunk logger of murder, there wouldn't be anyone left to cut the timber."

There was a rattle at the window and both men jumped.

"There's the wind picking up," said Charlie. "We'll have rain tonight."

Ben rubbed the back of his neck where the hairs were prickling. The foul-play theories were all well enough, but he set them aside for a more urgent question. "Charlie—what did you mean when you said Daphne Lindstrom visited you in the woods?"

"Just that." Gripping the scrolled armrests of his chair, Charlie stared at the wallpaper ivy over Ben's head. "I was in the Grove. Sitting on Prince's stump, like I always did, the journal open in my lap. And there was this rustling. A swishing sound. You know woods— they're full of noises. I paid no attention. I was reading about when Daphne went really downhill a few months before her disappearance. Lindstrom shipped in a doctor all the way from San Francisco to see her. The rustling got louder, but I didn't look up. Not until I heard the voice."

"Voice," said Ben. He seemed to have some obstruction in his throat.

"She said, *'Help me.'*"

Ben jerked upright in his chair, tipping the two front legs off the floor and landing again with a thump.

"I looked up then," said Charlie, the words coming faster now. "There was a woman standing there, not twenty feet away—that would've been enough to scare the bejesus out of me because I never ran into anything but deer or raccoons out there. But it was worse. It was the woman from the old pictures. I'd only seen them that one time, but I recognized her. She had on the white dress from the wedding shot and her thick, curly hair was half-undone. She held up her hands to me." He demonstrated.

Ben's own hands broke out in a sweat. "And then what?" he pressed. "What happened next?"

"What do you think happened? I was thirteen years old and by myself in the woods. I completely lost it. Screamed like a girl. Went tearing home without having the guts to look over my shoulder. It was only when I launched myself up the porch steps that I realized I'd at least managed to grab the journal. I heard my aunt inside, marching to the door to see what the ruckus was about, and that made me all clumsy and hamhanded. I dropped the damned thing and it fell open and I didn't have time to do more than kick it under the porch swing before she had the door open to ask me what in Sam Hill I thought I was doing. I couldn't string even two words together to answer. Rachel was a foot shorter than me by then but she still grabbed my collar: 'You been fooling around in those woods again?' When I said, Yes, Ma'am, that was all she needed to hear. I was grounded for three months. I was not to set foot in the woods—not to go near one single tree—if I knew what was good for me. She needn't have bothered. At that point I was so worked up that the woods were the last place I wanted to go. Not with what I'd seen.

"I did want the journal back, though. I waited until she was snoring away that night and then snuck back out to the porch to get it. It still lay open, and somehow this little sprig of fresh redwood had blown up the steps across the pages. There was Pall Lindstrom's last entry. June 27, 1895: '*She is truly gone. Past all hope, all cure, all help. The riverbed has dried up but yielded no secrets. I see the pity in the eyes of my fellow townsmen. All but those of Derwent. In his, naught but hostility. Perhaps he blames me.*

"'*There are whispers I catch as well: that when Derwent is in his whiskey he talks of seeing her, hearing her. But this must be the product of liquor and fantasy. For me there are no echoes of D. Only blindness and silence.*'"

Speaking of blindness and silence—the wind had stopped. A glance at the window showed Ben only his own face, but he rose to shut the curtains. He had no desire to see another ghostly hand. If Shane Derwent's visions sprang from liquor and fantasy, and his own from concussion, what could explain Charlie's?

"Pall Lindstrom never saw the ghost then," said Ben. "Or whatever she is. The vision."

"If he did, it wasn't before July, 1895. Now no one will ever know."

"But you—did you ever see her again, Charlie?"

The man gave a loud sniff. His eyes were suspiciously moist again and Ben felt like a brute for hounding him.

"You've got to understand," said Charlie. "My family had a history."

"Yes," said Ben. He didn't know what his companion was getting at.

"I had reasons for never wanting to see her again."

Who needed reasons? Ben thought. Most ordinary people didn't go around wanting to see ghosts.

Charlie must have read his expression because he crossed his arms over his chest. "Look here, Ben—my dad must have seen Daphne. Not just seen her—heard her! Think what Rachel saw in the woods—my father talking to himself and even crying. And then never wanting to go back to the woods once he returned to Red Gap. Not till he was forced to by the fire, and then it all started up again. What was he trying to do when he fell out of Grand Daddy? What was he thinking, trying to climb a 350-foot redwood? The man was crazy, and it was Daphne Lindstrom's ghost that did it." Charlie was pounding the armrest by this point, and a vein throbbed in his forehead.

"I get it, I get it," soothed Ben. "Of course you didn't want to see the vision again."

"And then there was my grandfather," Charlie went on, hardly hearing him. "The one my grandmother divorced. The man was a raging alcoholic. Moody and violent, Aunt Rachel said. She wouldn't talk about him except to say that leaving Red Gap was the healthiest thing he ever did. It was Daphne again—it had to be. I know it was." His voice rose alarmingly by the end of this speech.

"Shhhh…" urged Ben. "Bea will hear you. Or the guests—"

"—So I had a few options," said Charlie, dropping to a stage whisper. He spread out his hand to count them off. "I could try to get my aunt to move us out of Red Gap—which I already knew from my father's efforts was a no-go. Or I could try to stay out of the woods the rest of my life, terrified of them. Or maybe I could drink myself into oblivion like Shane Derwent and my grandfather. Or," –he grabbed his ring finger with his other hand and shook it— "I could decide that all that craziness was going to end with me. It was finished. Done. It didn't matter if this Derwent ever saw her or heard her again." (Jabbing his chest with his thumb.) "Hell, it didn't matter if I found her having a tea party in the Grove with Elvis and Jimmy Hoffa! I decided Daphne Lindstrom was not going to exist for me. The woman was dead to the whole rest of the world—had been for almost seventy years—and she was gonna be dead to me too."

The lights flickered. Down the hall a door closed. There were footsteps outside the Green Room, and they heard Marilyn: "No, you go ahead, Judy."

Ben slumped back into the armchair and waited for the noises to subside.

"Well, your plan worked," he said finally. "I mean, here you are. Not crazy, not drunk, not afraid to go into the woods."

Charlie gave a noncommittal grunt.

"You got everything under control," Ben went on. "So much so that you didn't have to try to escape like your grandfather and father did. You live where you wanna live, you're married, you do what you wanna do. Life is fine." He sighed, shaking his head. "And then along comes Gladys with her lousy book and, next thing you know, a million tourists and ghost-hunters descend on you. Like that isn't bad enough, then a day comes when some guy with a messed-up head even shows up, saying he's seen someone. Everyone bugging you and resurrecting ancient history and wanting to talk about Daphne Daphne Daphne. That dead woman that you haven't seen in—what—forty years?"

"I didn't say that," objected Charlie.

Ben rubbed his temples. The sharp outlines of the room were starting to blur again. It really had been quite a day.

"I didn't say that," repeated Charlie. "I said she was dead to me. That she wasn't going to have any power or say in my life."

"Oh. I misunderstood. All right. Then you mean you *have* seen her again. Since that day with the journal."

The answer was slow in coming. "I...have. I never acknowledged her, but I have."

Ben whistled. "Once? Twice? Did she ever say anything again?"

"She hasn't spoken to me in years."

"But you've seen her."

The blue eyes met his squarely. They were dry now, dull.

"What I'm trying to say, Ben—if you'll let me get the words out—is that I saw Daphne Lindstrom again, all right. That day when she scared me sick was just the first time. Since then, well, I've seen her nearly every day of my life."

~~~~~

Ben threw off the covers.

The porch lights stayed on all night at the Dryad, making the curtains glow faintly. Shadows of raindrops tracked down their lengths.

He pressed a button on the side of his wristwatch and the face illuminated: 1:39 a.m. Thank God. He could take more medicine. Shortly after he had bid Charlie goodnight, Bea had tapped at his door. "I just wanted to give you this, Ben. It's the key to the medicine cabinet in the bathroom down the hall. There's more aspirin in there if you need it tonight."

He did. And some kind of sleep aid, if they had any. He wondered if those two kinds of drugs should be mixed, but decided that—apart from any fatal combinations—they could hardly make matters worse.

The deserted hallway stretched endlessly in the gloom. A couple bluish nightlights marked his progress as he groped his way along. By the time he reached his goal he had to sit on the edge of the tub for a minute to regroup. Turning on the light sounded unappealing, but no way would he be able to unlock any cabinets and drug himself up in the dark—with his luck he'd probably eat the Drain-O. He covered his eyes with his hands and tugged on the pull cord.

Light from the overhead fixture flooded the bathroom.

After a moment, Ben cracked his eyes open, catching his haggard, sleep-deprived reflection. And something else.

Bea had changed her mind.

Maybe it occurred to her that the sampler Ben discovered that morning belonged in the room where he found it. Where Daphne Lindstrom herself had placed it. For Bea had hung it up again, directly beside the mirrored vanity. When he read the verse this time, the voice in his head no longer sounded like his own.

> My life is like a frozen thing,
> No bud nor greenness can I see:
> Yet rise it shall—the sap of spring;
> O Jesus, rise in me.

CHAPTER 11

Encounter

Ben sat up. The rain had stopped and bright moonlight spilled over him. The rope attaching his climbing harness to the tree wound around his ankle. If he had tumbled from his hammock in his sleep, he would have been strung up like the smoked ducks in Chinatown restaurant windows.

"Is that you moving around, Ben?" came a laughing voice, pitched low not to wake the others.

He grinned upward to the branch where Courtney's Treeboat hitched in. "You up too, babe?"

"I can't sleep," she whispered. "The moonlight is blinding after that rain. Besides—this is freaky. The way the tree rocks scares the crap out of me. Whoever sleeps 320 feet off the ground?"

"Must be that extra seven or so feet you have on me. I slept just fine at 313. Should I come up and check it out?"

"Are you crazy?" she squeaked. "Climbing at night? Stay where you are."

"No way," said Ben. "You're the one who said it was so bright out." He unclipped the rope and shook it off his ankle. Stepping out on the branch, he free-climbed up to her. Her hammock swung as he crammed into it.

Courtney smothered a shriek and buried her face in his down vest. "Idiot."

"Let's climb all the way up," he urged. "Don't you want to see how the top of the world looks by moonlight?"

"I'm *not* unhitching, Ben," she answered. "God knows which branches are rotted or about to fall off."

"I'll go first and check them out."

"What, by falling hundreds of feet and cratering out when you discover that, oh, *that* was the rotten one?"

He made chicken-clucking sounds in her ear, and she socked him in the gut. "Go yourself, Spiderman."

Kissing her hard on the mouth, he obeyed.

Up, up, up.

He felt his way, tugging hard on each branch before entrusting it with his full weight. But the tree was sound, bearing him with no false steps. Just before hoisting himself onto the highest solid branch he called over his shoulder, "It's a cakewalk, Court. Get up here."

There was no answer.

The view from the top surprised him. After all, this tree, which the team christened Hightower, stood shoulder-to-shoulder with a dozen other coast redwoods, ancient in age, their crowns interlaced for centuries as they muscled their way from the narrow alluvial flat into open sky. From the pinnacle, Ben should have looked out on the tops of all Hightower's fellows, but instead Hightower stood alone, the rest of the forest petering out more than a hundred feet below. Unimpeded, the breeze riffled his hair and tapped the tight, juniper-like needles of the upper canopy.

As he puzzled over Hightower's mysterious isolation, he became aware that, though the branch beneath him was solid as iron, it was also several degrees off horizontal. Not just the branch—everything. He was leaning forward slightly, into the trunk, his weight on his toes and the balls of his feet. Had it been this way a second ago? The moment he made this realization, the angle of tilt seemed to increase. Ben scooched closer to the trunk, fighting a bubble of panic in his stomach. He was being paranoid. This was Hightower. Not the Dyerville Giant. So why the hell was it leaning?

"Take my hand."

The voice came from above him. Calling out in shock, Ben looked up to see just that: a long white hand, silver-smooth in the moonlight, extended toward him. He closed his eyes. Swallowed. Opened them again. The hand rotated slowly until it was palm up, a wide gold ring gleaming from the fourth finger. Those fingers curled, beckoning. Against his will, his gaze followed the hand to an arm, tightly sleeved. Hand bone connected to the arm bone. Arm bone connected to the shoulder bone. Shoulder bone connected to the neck bone. Every inch sheathed in material as white as the hand. Covered buttons, lace. Neck bone connected to the—

"Benjamin!"

The hand caught his wrist. He shuddered against the cold that swept the length of his arm.

"Let go of me," he shouted—only to find the words sucked from him. The hesitant breeze was gone, lost in the sudden gale that blew up, pressing, leaning against every inch of Hightower. The tree gave a low, rumbling groan. Branches whipped him across the face, causing his eyes to sting and water. Through the blur he saw the woman—her long white dress, the wave of her shining hair around her icy face. The wind that assaulted him had no effect on her. She stood, white and still on the branch directly opposite him, her other arm wrapped about Hightower's trunk. Despite his efforts to jerk away, her hold on him tightened.

"This wind—" gasped Ben. "I think Hightower's going down." He pictured the shallow root structure, a pancake of crisscrossing filaments. Sufficient when one redwood grew surrounded, sheltered, by its fellows. Without them, the roots' grip on the earth would be no more effective than broom strands skittering over ice. "We've got to—try to—descend before it goes."

She smiled then, almost tenderly. And though she did little more than whisper, her voice carried easily to him. "At last. Ben—I thank you."

Again Ben awoke. Again he sat up. This time there was no mistaking reality, however, because the sudden motion brought on a wave of nausea. His heart was trying to escape his rib cage, so hard was it pounding, and he felt the trickle of sweat between his shoulder blades.

Good God.

The sound of rain at the window soothed him. There was no clear night. No moonlight. No violent wind. He was not 350 feet up and about to die. He was alone.

Or nearly.

When he swung his legs slowly to the floor, there it was. The pulsing he had sensed once before. The heartbeat of Good Witch. His breath escaping in a hiss, Ben placed a hand against the wall. Almost immediately heat flowed through it, searing along his fresh scar.

She was there. Certainty filled him, though he could not have explained to another how he knew.

Rising with effort, he swayed to the window, blowing on his hand to cool it. Ben brushed aside the drapes and peered through the rain-glazed glass. Below him on the brick walkway that led to the back porch, her face turned upward, stood the woman. Unlike the one in his dream, this one bore no immunity to the weather. She was drenched, from her waist-length rippling hair to her sodden gown. Her pale skin glowed, radiating from some inner source. She lifted one hand, the shape and gesture already familiar to him.

He stumbled back against the bedpost, his whole body shaking.

What did she want from him?

Why trouble him? Why appear and re-appear to him? Why call to him? Why throw *branches*? He was no Derwent, that she should pursue him to drive him mad. He was nobody to her, and she should be nobody to him. Ben's joking manner, always at hand to fend off life's awkward or painful moments, failed him now, and he only knew, in the pit of his stomach, that he was afraid.

He could go back to bed. Pull the covers over his head. Wait for daybreak and the other bed-and-breakfast guests to drive her away. And then what? Spend the rest of his time here looking over his shoulder, refusing to go outside or look out any windows. Then, when he was well enough, get far, far away and forget that Red Gap and its inhabitants, dead or alive, ever existed.

It was do-able. Cowardly and unsatisfying, but do-able.

Waking Bea and Charlie felt equally untenable. Even if he figured out which room was theirs without rousing everyone in the place, he didn't imagine they would thank him, having made their feelings on the family ghost like crystal.

You can do this, Ben told himself. You can *do* this. You climb 300-foot trees, for God's sake! This is nothing. Man up. Maybe it's like with Gladys—the ghost lady wants my help, and once I do whatever it is, she'll leave me alone.

He realized he hadn't asked Gladys if the ghosts did indeed leave her alone after the fact. Daphne didn't. Clearly. Though maybe that was because Gladys had been unable to help her..?

Gathering his shredded nerves, he returned to the window.

It was a double-hung sash of four panes. From the effort required to slip the latch, Ben suspected it was rarely opened, and he muttered an apology to Bea under his breath. He sensed the woman below, watching, impassive, as he struggled to raise the balky thing. The sash jammed a couple inches up. Ben cursed and hauled on it before it gave way with a screech, flinging upward and causing the panes to rattle. Loud enough to wake the dead, he thought wryly—if she weren't already awake.

Given his dizziness and the steady downpour, he wasn't eager to thrust his head out the opening. Still, it did seem churlish of him to stay tidy and sheltered while she soaked to the skin, even if she had been dead for over a century. Then again, Daphne Lindstrom went where she pleased. If she wanted to come in out of the rain, she would, presumably.

They stared at each other. Her gaze unsettled him. Whatever she was, she had no need of blinking, apparently.

She appeared solid enough, the way the raindrops coursed down her marble cheeks. Maybe she couldn't walk through walls. Not that staying inside was doing him much good, Ben thought. With the way he was sweating, it was a toss-up who would be drier in five minutes.

"You were the one who wanted to talk to *me*," he muttered, wiping his hands down his flannel pants.

"*Yes*." She spoke as quietly as he did.

Damn. Ghosts had good hearing.

He tried again. "Uh...who are you?"

"*One who has waited long.*" Her lips barely moved. As in his dream, she had no need to raise her voice to be heard. It came to his ear from no particular direction, coaxing, musical—thoughts made audible. He was relieved to find the sound wasn't high-pitched, as when she spoke through Gladys. *If* she spoke through Gladys.

So many questions.

"*I had a name, once,*" she murmured. "*It has slipped away. I remain.*"

Indeed.

His fear receding the slightest bit, Ben leaned out. Cold drops spattered him as he clutched the sill to keep his balance. "You've—uh—asked for my help. I don't know what I could do for you. What did you mean?"

"*You wander my woods.*"

"Well—sort of. A lot of people do."

"*You belong.*"

The choice of words surprised him. It was always how he had put it to himself. He *belonged* in the woods. Then Gladys was right? Daphne felt sympathy with him? Of course, she also called them "her" woods. Possibly she resented his intrusion.

"I was passing through," he said. "Until my accident."

"*You... climb.*"

"Yes," Ben said, uncertain whether this helped his cause. "I do climb."

There was a silence. He felt the tingle of cold where rain penetrated to his scalp.

The corners of her mouth curled almost imperceptibly. "*You climb. One might venture to say with more* daring *than skill.*"

"What?" he yelped. "No. No—that's not right. There's nothing wrong with my skills if no one is trying to—to mess up my concentration." No one dead and spooky, he added to himself.

"*Should not single-mindedness be numbered among the necessary skills?*"

Who did she think she was? Fleetingly, Ben considered telling her what she could do with her climbing critique and then slamming the window shut. This must be why, after a hundred years, she still couldn't get anyone to help her.

To his amazement, her pale lips parted and a smile dawned on her face, gradual and half-puzzled. She touched her hand to her mouth as if to assure herself it was happening. It was, and she raised her eyes to his again, now beaming.

Ben gawked.

He had not been prepared—the transformation was so complete.

She might be undead and a century older than he was. She might roam the woods, scaring people out of trees and hurling branches at the unwitting. She might be half-drowned and wearing clothes more appropriate to his great-great-grandmother. She might even have an uncomfortably sharp tongue. But all those thoughts fell away, leaving only Pall Lindstrom's sunstruck, dazzled words: *Miss D. C. most beautiful girl I have ever seen.*

When she spoke again, it took him a second to identify the note in her voice. "*You were so very high. Did you not think to hold fast?*"

There was no other way to describe it, however.

She was teasing.

How long it took him to get downstairs he didn't know. Besides his condition, he dreaded waking anyone. They would surely think he'd lost it, staggering around in the dead of night at a semi-invalid's top speed in order to meet the town ghost outside. Even Charlie would shake his head and repeat his parting words: "I told you all this as a warning, Ben. Like I said, she can't be helped. If she's appearing to you that's not a good thing. Ignore her. Your head'll get better, and you'll be on your way soon enough. Pretend you never heard of the woman."

There was one bad moment at the bottom of the stairs, when the newel post he grabbed turned out to be a nymph statuette. It would have tumbled noisily to the wood floor, had he not instinctively broken its fall by sticking out his leg. Broken its fall by breaking my shin, thought Ben, hopping on one foot and mouthing swear words in the darkness. Slapping it back on the pedestal and hoping it was facing the right direction, he groped his way across the parlor, down the hallway, past the dining room to the back door.

Through the leaded diamond-shaped panes he saw—half-relieved and half-alarmed—that she was still there. Ben tried to imagine inviting her in to drip all over Bea's carpets and found he lacked the courage. Not to mention how bizarre it would be if Bea or one of the guests rose in the night to investigate suspicious noises.

His eye fell on the umbrella stand by the door. Selecting the largest one, he ventured out into the wet.

She stood motionless, studying his approach, not moving even when he raised the umbrella to shelter her beneath it. The smile which so altered his opinion of her looks had vanished, though Ben thought he still detected traces of it in her eyes.

She was overwhelming. Lit from within. Her eyes, which should have been muddy in the dim porchlight, glowed. They were green at their centers, shifting to hazel and then brown at the edges. Her features seemed carved—inhumanly distinct—just as her skin was strangely uniform and flawless, its pallor reminding him of moonstone. While she came only to his chin, he remembered the directness of her gaze, the challenge in it, from the photograph. No shrinking violet, Daphne Lindstrom.

They stood a long minute. No sooner had Ben taken in her appearance than he was distracted by a discovery: his head—his shoulder—his hand—for the first time in several days they no longer forced themselves on his awareness. They were … *well*. He raised his hand slowly and turned it to look for the gash, not the least bit surprised when he saw only smooth, unbroken skin. And his head—tentatively he reached for the sore spot, only to find it felt like any other part of his head. No knot, no tenderness. The dizziness was gone.

"What the hell?" Ben wondered. He nearly forgot her in his bewilderment. He snapped his head back and forth, lolled it around in a circle. Nothing. "Hey!"

"*You marvel,*" she said, the sound of her voice recalling him abruptly to their situation.

"Yeah." He ceased experimenting but was unable to prevent a grin. "I feel all right again. I haven't felt good since—"

A hint of her luminous smile returned. He supposed ghosts did not apologize.

"All right, then," said Ben. "I haven't felt good since I took my fall and banged up my head and shoulder. Why do they feel okay now?"

"*There is no physical ill here.*"

"Here?" Ben echoed. "Where? In the yard?" A thought occurred to him, and the umbrella slid several inches lower. "Wait—am I dead? I died in my sleep. Or I fell down the stairs a minute ago."

The smile did return now. She even convulsed in a silent laugh. *"You live yet, Benjamin Platt."*

"Then what did you mean 'here'?" he asked when he found his voice again.

"Here. Where I am. I know not where it is, precisely. Neither heaven nor hell. I exist, merely." She gave a measured sigh—or it could have been the wind around them.

"But then, if I'm still alive, why am I not unwell anymore?"

The shades shifted in her eyes, the green radiating from the centers. *"I am encompassed. Beyond certain boundaries I may not stray. But when I… draw near… to the living, they may pass some ways into my world."* Her gaze dropped, and as she stood with her arms hanging immobile by her sides, Ben felt a weight in the air between them.

"Others, then, have 'passed' into your world."

The palpable despondence thickened. *"For a time. But they have gone."*

He had never reflected on what all those dead Derwents looked like from her perspective. "Do you know who they were or where they went?"

Slowly she shook her head. One tick back and one tick forth. *"Who they were I can no longer say. I have called to many but gone unseen, unheard. Even those who heard me have gone. Some to flight, some to madness, some to death."*

It was a bad track record. As if Ben needed reminding. The fear which had nearly faded came roaring back in his gut. When he tried to speak again, his throat felt like someone had rammed it full of cotton balls. "It is a little—uh—unnerving to talk to someone who isn't all the way—you know—dead or alive. I don't know myself why I can hear you. See you." He gave the umbrella handle a nervous spin, sending a carousel of drops flying. "If you don't mind me asking—why have you spent all this time trying to reach people, when it hasn't been working out? Why don't you just…move on?"

Her gaze swept back to him. "*I am bound. Tied to this existence. Do you not trust that I would move on, were I able?*"

"How are you 'tied'?"

"*I made a pact, when I was living. To be certain, I meant no more than a schoolgirl's vows, uttered in passion and heat when the blood is young. The ritual with which I solemnized my vow sprung from my own imagination. But I was taken at my word. To my eternal sorrow.*"

Ben heard her breath quicken. But the wild thumping that filled his ears had to be his own heart. "What was your vow?"

"*There were certain trees in the forest very dear to me.*"

"The Grove," he said.

She pondered this. Nodded. "*The Grove. So the townspeople called it. These trees, redwoods—they were my paradise. My heart beat with theirs. But all around them their fellows were falling, fed to the saws and the appetites of men. When my trees were threatened, I was threatened. I vowed they should never fall while I lived. That I would protect them as my own blood and bone.*" Her voice had fallen to no more than a whisper, but it carried to him no less. "*I cut my skin. Pressed it against the living wood to prove my good earnest. I took the soil that nourished them and ate of it.*"

With difficulty Ben tried to hide his dismay. Not that it mattered. Her green eyes stared through him, beyond him. "*I failed them. A girl of fifteen. I could not prevent the destruction that came to them. My family sent me away to an asylum where I had battles of my own. Between my trees and me, I felt the bonds weaken and grow thin. I thought them broken. But they were not. Like the forest in drought, they only lay sluggish and dormant. After my return, the one remaining tree called to me and reminded me of my promises.*"

"Called to you?"

"*My heart broke to witness the devastation—as if pieces of my own body had been put to the saw. But I heard the call—the bond was* undiminished. Had grown stronger even, to what remained. It must be protected at all costs."

"Protected," repeated Ben. "Is that why you married Pall Lindstrom?"

"Pall...Pall... Lindstrom." She tried this out. "Yes. I married Pall Lindstrom. He had the power—the authority—to help me fulfill my vow. Only the one tree. Pall Lindstrom did not have my heart, however. It belonged to another. But I did what I needs must. I kept my promise."

"And then what happened to you? You disappeared."

"My life was unbearable. I begged for release. But redwoods—they might endure thousands of years. I had Pall Lindstrom's word that he would never allow harm to come to the remaining tree. I could... abandon my guardianship. Or so I hoped. But you see it continues."

Which didn't answer his question.

Despite his burning curiosity, hounding her about the circumstances of her death felt tacky. He let it go for now.

"It's been over a hundred years," he said. "You succeeded. No one will touch the tree now because you—it—has become famous."

Another mournful nod.

"Can you just—er—tell the tree you think your job is done? Maybe it will release you, or whatever."

"That cannot be."

Oh.

"So, is that why you try to... contact... people? You want companionship?"

Her eyes lost their faraway look. Met his head-on. "How forgetful of you, Benjamin. Do you not recall I begged for your 'help'?"

"No, no. I remembered. For some people, 'help' could mean companionship," he added, somewhat defensively.

She raised one eyebrow in the mildest skepticism.

"So—" resumed Ben, "all the people you talk to—you ask for their help?"

"*I do. I have.*"

"But how on earth could I—could they—could *any* of us help you? Look. I'm a scientist. A botanist. I don't do otherworld things. Metaphysics."

Another smile crept across her pale countenance, part-hopeful, part-cajoling, completely dazzling.

Oh, God, thought Ben. Here comes the crazy-making part.

He took a deep breath. Asked again. "What could someone like me do for you?"

Her fingertips brushed, light and cold, across his knuckles. Looking down, he saw those knuckles were white from their death-clutch on the umbrella handle. He tried but could not relax them, especially when her touch came to rest on the back of his hand. He waited for the cold to rush through him, as in his dream, and though it did not come, he still shivered.

"*Benjamin,*" said Daphne Lindstrom. She drew a hair closer. The silvery mist of her breath curled up to caress his jaw. "*I asked one thing of them. I ask but one thing of you.*

"*You must bring down the tree.*"

CHAPTER 12

Fever

"Aww, hell," rumbled Charlie. "What now?"

There was some heap of something on the grass out back, barely visible in the pre-dawn.

"What is it?" asked Bea, sliding the cherry danishes off the sheet pans onto cooling racks. "More litter? Beer cans?"

Her husband grunted again. He set his mug on the counter and reached for his hat with the flaps.

"Well, whatever it is, don't take too long about it. You were going to slice fruit for me."

First off, the back door was unlocked, and he was certain he locked it. Next thing, blamed if his favorite umbrella, the giant one he found at a golf store in Redding, wasn't blown clear across the yard against the trees.

From the perspective of the back step, the heap of something took on definition. A body. Charlie straightened up. With a glance at Bea, he grabbed another of the umbrellas from the stand before pulling the door shut behind him.

It was the young man. Face-down in the wet grass, his t-shirt and flannel pants soaked and molded to him.

Charlie gave him a poke with the umbrella tip.

Nothing.

Another poke. This one on the behind.

Nothing.

He flipped the umbrella in his hand so that he held the spiny ferrule. Cautiously he extended the curved wooden handle close to the back of the young man's head. "About...*there*." He jabbed once.

"Ya-a-a-a-aghh!" hollered Ben, rolling to his side and waving his arm blindly to fend off his assailant. Squinting, he recognized Charlie and broke off with a groan.

The back door banged open. "Charlie—Ben—what on earth?" cried Bea. "Ben, what are you doing out here? And Charlie, what were you thinking, pressing on his head like that?"

"Thought he was drunk or dead," mumbled Charlie.

"If I was, that would've brought me back," said Ben. He made a feeble attempt to sit up before every muscle and bone in his body objected and he sank down again.

Heedless of her slacks, Bea knelt in the grass and put a hand to his forehead. "You're burning up! No wonder, in these wet clothes. And look at the welts on your face from the grass—you must have been lying there for hours."

"Can't lie there now, at any rate," Charlie said. "Guests'll be down soon."

Ben didn't think he was capable of self-propulsion. "Euuuhh—maybe you could just cover me with some leaves—a lawn ornament or something."

"Don't be ridiculous," chided Bea. "Charlie will help you inside."

Charlie was going to get his favorite umbrella. "We don't encourage drunkenness," he threw over his shoulder.

"I wasn't drunk!" protested Ben. He heaved himself up on his elbow, gagging when the Dryad and Bea revolved around him like a model of the solar system. "Though I do feel hung over. Or worse."

Charlie's work boots entered his field of vision again and ever-so-slowly Ben tilted his head back to look at him. "Could have been the drugs."

"Drugs?" asked Bea. Charlie's eyes touched on Ben's and looked away. He made a business of shaking pine needles off the golf umbrella. "Charlie," his wife remonstrated, "for heaven's sake, worry about that silly thing later and help Ben up!"

"Took some more aspirin and a sleep aid," muttered Ben. He bit back another groan as Charlie grabbed him under the arms and hauled him up.

"But how did you get out here?" Bea persisted, trying to prop him up on the other side as they shuffled back toward the house. "Did you sleepwalk?"

Ben felt Charlie's arm stiffen around him. And despite his own muddled head and developing fever, Ben understood what it meant. Charlie *knew*. He knew what had drawn Ben out in pouring rain, cold and darkness. He knew and did not want his wife to know.

At the same time, Ben couldn't think fast or straight enough to come up with a lie. "I thought—I thought maybe I heard something outside."

"Heard something..?" echoed Bea. Her worried gaze sought Charlie's as they lowered Ben onto a chair, but Charlie was plucking at his own shirt where Ben's had dampened it. "What did you hear?"

"Drunks?" suggested Charlie. "Sometimes after Etta's closes they come up this way. Or deer. Coulda been a deer."

Ben pulled a face at Charlie that meant, *A deer, for God's sake? Like I'd ever follow one of those again.* He was starting to shiver. "M-m-might have been dr-drunks."

"Oh, Ben, look at you," fussed Bea, distracted. "We can figure out what it was later. In the meantime we better get you out of those wet clothes and back into bed. I knew you shouldn't have gone walking with Gladys yesterday. Your first day up since the accident. You pushed yourself too far. Take him upstairs, Charlie. I've got to finish breakfast.

But later I'll call Dr. Stevens and have him come out and check on Ben again."

"It's just a-a f-fever," said Ben. "A cold. Don't bother."

"You don't think it's your concussion, then?" Bea persisted.

"J-just a cold."

"Well…someone needs to make sure. I'll call Clyde."

"Clyde the v-veterinarian?" Ben dragged his mouth into a grin. "Dogs don't get fevers, do they?"

"They get fixed, is what they get," said Charlie, hoisting Ben to his feet again.

"Then I really don't want Clyde to come over."

"Very funny, you two." There was a hiss as the first drop of coffee splashed into the carafe on the sideboard. Bea clapped her hands. "Seven o'clock! Go on up. And don't worry, Ben. We won't let Clyde fix anything but your head."

"It was her, Charlie."

Charlie said nothing, only peeling Ben's t-shirt over his head. He wadded it in a soggy ball and threw it on the braided rug. "Lay back so's I can rip your pants off."

Ben passed over the joke that came to mind and obeyed. "You heard me—it was *her*. Why else would I go out in the dead of night when I felt like crap?"

"Mmmph." Charlie spotted the open window. He wiped the sill with Ben's flannel pants and tugged the sash down. The latch locked with a shriek. Then Charlie dug in the chest of drawers, tossing out another t-shirt and some gray sweat pants. "Need new underwear?"

"I know you've been acting like you don't see her or hear her," said Ben, "but did she ever say to you exactly what kind of help she wanted?"

"Don't go down this road. I'm not gonna go down this road."

"Charlie—believe me—I wouldn't ask unless it was really

important."

"Not gonna go down this road. You sleep it off."

Aaagh. Ben's head was killing him and Charlie was frustrating as hell. Given his bumps and bruises, not to mention the last few hours he spent collapsed on the ground, no position on the bed felt comfortable. But anything was better than sitting up.

"I felt okay around her," Ben mumbled against the pillow. "Not sick or sore, I mean. I don't want to help her, but I felt better."

Charlie yanked up the covers. Dropped an extra afghan on top.

"And you didn't mention—"

"Gotta slice bananas," said Charlie.

"—What she looks like when she smiles."

But the door had already closed behind him.

Charlie took the knife from Bea. She'd done the bananas, so he tackled the apples.

"That strata isn't setting up very fast," she said, shutting the oven door. "I knew I shouldn't have tried a new recipe."

"Too much milk," said Charlie.

"It was only a half cup more than the other recipe." She crossed her arms over her stomach, tapping her elbow with the oven mitt. "Well?"

"Well, what?"

"He's not getting better, is he? I thought he was, but he isn't. What on earth was he doing outside?"

"What do you want to do?"

"Do you think you should drive him into Eureka today? He could see Dr. Stevens. Or else you could take him all the way back to the University and he could go to the campus clinic."

Charlie balanced the Fuji on the wooden board and sliced through the core. "He needs to sleep today," he said.

"First thing tomorrow, then? Or day after tomorrow."

"I don't think he'd go," said Charlie. He poked a seed out with the tip of the knife. "And I thought you wanted him to stay."

"I do want him to stay! You know I like him and have plans for him, but not if it isn't the best thing for Ben." She plumped up the daisies in their vase, pulling off a droopy petal or two. "It isn't natural, is it, that no one seems to miss him? If he's all done with that canopy project he talked about, shouldn't he go write it up or something? I have a feeling that everything isn't right. Maybe he's avoiding something. So maybe the best thing to do would be to send him on his way."

"I don't think he'd go," Charlie repeated. He started on a new apple. "Or, he wouldn't want to. He…likes it here. And I think he—uh—he likes Gladys, you know."

"She appears to like him, at any rate," said Bea. She smoothed her apron. "You tell me, then. If you don't think he's dying and you don't think he wants to leave, what *do* you think is going on with that young man? Why was he in the yard, of all places?"

Charlie shrugged. "He's got a concussion, he did too much too soon, and then he took drugs you shouldn't take together."

She came up behind him to lean her forehead on his shoulder. "And that's all?"

"Any one of those by itself is enough to make a person not all the way right. The three together—that's when the UFOs kidnap you."

"Yesterday, when he said he saw that woman in the woods—"

"Don't worry about it, Bea."

"Mmm. Do you think—do you think he thought he saw her again last night?"

Charlie dumped the apples into the fruit salad. "He said he heard something, not saw something."

"You know what I mean. Do you think he really did?"

"I think," said Charlie, running the scrubber over the cutting board and rinsing it off, "that people come to Red Gap full of ideas. If they see something or hear something, it's because they want to."

"That's not fair, Charlie. You know very well that that doesn't apply to Ben."

"Who says? He spent the afternoon with Gladys Harrington. She's enough to fill anybody's head with nonsense."

"But he saw the woman in the white gown before he ever met Gladys."

Charlie whipped the dish rag off its hook. "What do you want, Bea? You're the one who said he was all addled because he didn't know if what he was seeing was in the book or out the window."

"I know, I know." Her brow creased. "But—for whatever reasons—he might be—*susceptible*—"

Their eyes met. He knew she was thinking of Shane Derwent. And Lucas Derwent. Charlie's father—Charlie himself.

"Do you think he could…harm himself?" Bea asked.

A squeak and rumbling overhead alerted them: the first guests were up and using the bathrooms.

"We won't let him," said Charlie.

She chewed her lip. "Maybe you should…warn him."

He nodded once.

A flush rose to her cheeks. To hide it, Bea turned and opened the oven door again. She jiggled the pan. "Looks about right, now. I'll shut the oven off but leave it in there to keep warm."

"You told me you didn't want me talking about…my family and Daphne."

"I don't! I still don't. You made different choices than your family, and they've worked out. But he's such a nice young man. If he's…vulnerable…or something, and if you think he wants to stay here longer, maybe you could just share a little of your experience. Like you said, everyone else has their ideas, and they'll all be encouraging his—his unhealthy tendencies. You could…set him straight, like. I don't want *you* opening a can of worms, of course…"

"I'll be all right." Charlie cleared his throat.

Bea's arms came around him. She rested her head against his chest. "I love you, darling. You're a good man. Warn Ben, please. But then I want you to promise me that you won't let yourself get sucked into it."

"I haven't, all this time."

"But promise me now. Promise me you won't talk about it more than you have to. Won't *think* about it."

He squeezed her. Rested his chin on the top of her head. "I promise."

"Knock knock. It's Sunday. Got any more of those cherry danishes?" A lean, mustached man in faded jeans and a long-sleeved camouflage shirt peered into the kitchen where the Derwents were cleaning up.

"Looks like you just came from church, Clyde," said Charlie dryly, indicating the sticks-and-limbs print on the man's shirt.

"Best church of all—church of God's Great Creation," retorted the veterinarian. "Took my boy out this morning for a little crossbow practice."

"Isn't the season over?" asked Bea. There were two danishes left, but she smacked Clyde's hand when he tried to slide both of them onto a plate. "I'm saving one for Ben."

"I dunno if one piddly danish is enough pay for a house call," complained Clyde. "And this is my second time."

"Have some coffee to go with it," said Charlie.

"Don't mind if I do."

"Well?" prodded Bea. "What did you think? How's the patient?"

"Like you said, he's got a fever," Clyde answered around a mouthful of pastry. "Probably a virus, but we can't rule out tapeworm."

"Clyde Sills!"

"That's Dr. Sills to you, Beatrice. Hey hey—just kidding," he added, when Bea made to confiscate his treat. "What do you want me to say? The boy has a cold."

"I know he has a cold. I told you to check on his head. His mental state."

"Do I look like a psychiatrist to you?" This time Bea did take his plate. Clyde held up his hands in peace. "Okay! Here is my unexpert opinion: he's a little agitated."

Bea and Charlie exchanged glances.

"About what?" said Charlie.

"Hard to say. He wasn't saying much of anything. I was feeling around on his head and shoulder—did this hurt—how about here—how about here—what about on a scale of 1 to 10, with 10 being agony and so on—he's at about a 3 or 4, depending on what I touched. But it's the the side effects: dizziness, seeing things."

"Seeing things?"

"That's what I wanted to know, too," said Clyde, "but then it's like his eyes come into focus and he's looking at my shirt. 'Are you a hunter?' he says. And I says, 'Yeah.' And he says, 'Aren't you supposed to be a veterinarian?' And I says, 'Not just supposed to be—I *am* a veterinarian.' And he says, 'So some of the animals you heal and some of them you blow their brains out?' And I says, 'Well, there's animals and then there's *animals*. Not that I blow anyone's brains out.' And I tell him about my top-of-the-line Excalibur crossbow with the fiber-optic sight and the sling studs that de—"

"Yes, we know about your crossbow," Bea interrupted, to head Clyde off at the pass.

He looked slightly hurt but drew himself up and continued. "So I *tell him about the crossbow*, and the guy gets this funny look on his face. You think he's one of those PETA nuts who pickets things and throws paint on people?"

"I don't think so…" said Bea uncertainly. "I mean, Ben does like trees and nature."

"He did go after that injured deer," Charlie pointed out. "It's how he got in trouble in the first place."

"He eats meat, though." Bea smiled in relief. This settled it in her mind. "He's no fanatic."

"Well, like I say, he looks all funny about it, so I says, 'What is it?' And he says, 'What? Nothing.' And I says, 'You got this funny look on your face when I talked about my crossbow. You not a big fan of traditional weaponry?' And he says, 'I dunno about traditional weaponry, but I have no problem with a crossbow. Shot one a few times myself. Just a standard model, though. I bet your Excalibur would go higher.' And I says, 'What do you mean *higher*? We're shooting black-tail deer, not hot air balloons.' And he says really quick like, 'That's what I meant. I meant *farther*, not higher.' Then he says he doesn't feel so hot, and thank you so much Dr. Clyde, but would I mind if he went to sleep now?"

Charlie let out a great harrumph. "So are you telling me, Clyde Sills, that Ben tells you he's seeing things, and instead of finding out what, you have some big conversation about your blamed crossbow?"

"Hey, Derwent. You want a professional opinion, go hire the right professional. But I think even the psychiatrist would say you got to let the patient direct the conversation. It's revealing."

"What did your conversation reveal, then?" puzzled Bea.

"That he knows how to use a crossbow," said Clyde. He stood up and put his plate and mug in the sink. "And I would say that's a useful fact. (Thanks for the goods, Bea.) See, you don't want a guy who's concussed and dizzy and possibly seeing things anywhere near a crossbow. Who knows what he'd hit. He better stay in bed."

Charlie chuckled. "Thanks for the diagnosis, Einstein."

"$E=mc^2$. Where you headed, Derwent? If you can sport me a ride over the Ridge, Halladay said his rooster's looking peaked."

Despite telling the unusual hunter-veterinarian that he wanted to sleep, Clyde had no sooner gone downstairs than Ben crept, shivering, to the chest of drawers, to dig out his iPod. No hope of sleep if there was any chance he'd hear voices. Or one particular voice, he should say.

He suspected Daphne's was not the sort to be drowned out, but it was worth a try. Popping the earbuds in, he settled back with a muffled moan, pulling the covers to his neck. God, he must have imagined it—feeling *well* last night. The fever did funny things to his ears. The music would be faint one minute, drowned out by ringing, then loud, then faint again.

You must bring down the tree.

I'm losing my mind, thought Ben. No—I've already lost it.

The tree.

"You can't be serious," he had said. He pulled his hand away from her touch.

"*Never more so.*"

"I won't do it."

She said nothing.

"You have the wrong guy. I'm a student of trees. I try to help them live, for Chrissake. I don't take a chainsaw to them."

"*I leave you to consider.*"

He watched her retreat, measured, unhurried. With each step she took, he felt his injuries and symptoms make themselves known again. The volume on them being turned up steadily. His legs wobbled. His head felt like she had taken a mallet to it. Even the faint glow she trailed struck his eyes like daggers, forcing them shut.

He buckled. Hit the grass like a puppeteer had clipped his strings. And there he lay till Charlie found him.

You must bring down the tree.

Like hell he would.

He was not going to think about her.

He was not going to think about her.

He was going to sleep, and when he awoke, this would just be another colorful dream, brought on by a blow to the head and mixing drugs.

He was not going to think about her.

A crossbow.

He remembered Ed Wilson handing him the Barnett Trident II. "You take the shot, Ben. You have the best luck."

"How are the rest of us supposed to get any better if Ben always gets to take the shot?" demanded Courtney. Ed Wilson chucked her on the cheek (was that part of the memory, or did his imagination supply it, after the fact?). "You're not doing it, Courtney, because no one here wants to get killed."

Ben pointed at a branch. "125 feet. Too high, you think?"

"Not for you, Buddy."

He took the shot.

Mount a reel on Clyde's Excalibur and he could launch a line 150 feet up Grand Daddy. Maybe higher.

Free-climb after that.

Not that he was thinking about it.

CHAPTER 13

Soup to Nuts

"Well, aren't you a fragile little thing?"

In the doorway stood Gladys Harrington, a miffed Bea bobbing over her shoulder.

"Bea wouldn't even let me see you yesterday."

She was seeing him now. Ben had thrown off the covers to cool down, and Gladys' eye ran over his bare shoulders and chest.

"He was scarcely coherent yesterday," said Bea. She pushed past Gladys into the room, twitching the bed sheet casually to cover him up. "How are you feeling today, Ben? Can I get you something?"

"Better. Definitely better." Actually he still felt like crap, but he wasn't going to admit to it after Gladys called him fragile. It wasn't a total lie, though. The worst of the fever was past and there was no dull ache in his shoulder. Even the seasick feeling that accompanied his concussion was muted today, if only because his entire head felt like a taxidermist had shot it full of polyurethane.

Bea pulled two extra pillows from the wardrobe. "Think you can sit up a little?" She waved away Gladys' half-hearted motion to help and slid them gently behind him. "How about your shirt?"

A fit of coughs took him. He tugged the t-shirt over his head but had to stop before he put his arms through, gripping his forehead in hand because the hacking felt like it would jar his skull apart. "Excuse me."

"Some soup would be good for that," said Bea. "I made it last night, if you think you could manage."

He smiled. "That'd be awesome, Bea. Sorry to give you and Charlie so much trouble."

"Don't mention it." She glanced at Gladys, but the woman made no move to follow her out. "I'll just leave you two to talk, then."

Gladys waited a beat, listening for Bea's step on the stairs. Then she clapped her hands together and followed the perimeter of the room, running her fingers over the table, mirror, bedrail, window panes, wainscoting.

"Why do you look so thrilled?" asked Ben.

"Because I've never been in here without Bea or Charlie hovering over me, waiting for me to get out. This room is amazing. Which do you think is the real Daphne?"

"What do you mean?" He fiddled with the sheet, watching her from the corner of his eye. He had met the real Daphne. Had Gladys?

"Daphne the decorator. Don't you think it's strange that the rest of the house is Victorian overload—William Morris on steroids—and things are so simple in here? This wallpaper…" she traced the ivy pattern with her finger "…there's space around the vines. Every square inch isn't crammed with flowers and squiggles and scrolls and things." Smiling, she came to sit on the bed beside him. Ben sat up a little straighter. "You're gumming up the works, you know. This room is a hot ticket, but no one can see it since you became the Dryad's Resident Invalid. I even offered to move you to my place, but Bea was adamant."

"You did?"

She was wearing some kind of slinky red knit top that emphasized her cleavage and narrow waist. "I did. She wouldn't hear of it. So my poor weekend audience at the Blind Bard had to satisfy themselves with pictures of Daphne's room that I passed around."

"Maybe it's not so bad," he said. He tried to keep his gaze above-the-neck. She had wound her shining dark hair in an intricate coil and speared it with a tortoiseshell comb. "It leaves them wanting more."

"So it does."

She slid off her shoes and swung her legs up, cuddling into his side. "See? I wore a more practical top today, for kissing a dangerous man like you. Stretchy, so I can get my arms around you"—she demonstrated—"and red, so you can bleed all over me."

Despite his lassitude and stuffy head, Ben was sharply aware of her breast against his arm. The sensation was far from unpleasant. His nervous cough brought on genuine ones. "I can't kiss you," he said when they subsided. "With my congestion I'd suffocate. Plus I'm probably contagious."

"I know," she purred. She pressed against him once more. "Poor sufferer."

A floorboard creaked in the hallway. Gladys shot up, straightening her top, but whoever it was went on by. Winking at him, she resumed her seat, this time leaning against the bedrail at his feet. "Seriously—if you're so sick, maybe I should check you into the Urgent Care in Eureka."

"I'm getting better. Just slowly. This deal wasn't related to the concussion."

"But how long are you planning on clogging up the works here? The Derwents have a business to run. Staying at my place would have obvious benefits, but, no, we all want to fight over you. It's not often anyone as interesting as you comes to Red Gap."

"What are you talking about? New people come through here all the time, thanks to you."

Gladys shrugged. "Mostly women. Book tourism doesn't seem to be a male pastime. That's what makes you so special, Ben. You never heard of *Bury Me Not,* and you're most definitely male." Casually she tucked her legs under her, brushing against his beneath the sheet. "Tell me—what *were* you doing so close to Red Gap?"

"Didn't Bea say?" This again. He looked out the window. "I was finishing up a project with my advisor and some other grad students. I thought I'd take a shortcut but ended up hitting a deer—"

"I know that part," she interrupted, smiling again to soften her abruptness. "I meant, why were you there alone? I thought tree-huggers would at least carpool. And how come no one seems to care that you've been laid up here for nearly a week now?"

Ben felt heat rising in his face that had nothing to do with his dwindling fever. "I…uh…had a bit of a falling-out with my advisor. No one was with me because I cut out early. I doubt anyone at the U even realizes I'm gone because the rest of them won't be headed back for another couple weeks."

She looked as if she'd like to ask more about this but then let it drop. "I see. But there's no one to be surprised and delighted when you show up earlier than expected? Your parents?"

"I don't live in their basement, if that's what you're getting at. My parents retired to Arizona. We're already on the semiannual visits rotation."

"I forgot how lucrative being a graduate student was," said Gladys dryly. "Of course you have your own place. How about a girlfriend, then? A tender, nature-loving soul mate who crosses the days off the calendar until you return?"

Ben had no desire to talk about Courtney. "No. No one."

"Mmm…lucky me." Gladys ran a hand over the sheet and up his leg, only to have Ben cry out and nearly kick her when she pressed on his bruised shin. "What the hell?"

"Sorry. I—" He *what*? He wasn't about to explain that he'd dropped a nymph statuette on his leg when he was sneaking out to see Daphne Lindstrom. "I hurt my leg, too."

She rolled her eyes. "For God's sake. You are in sad shape."

"This isn't the norm for me," said Ben, irked. "I've had a bad run."

"Mmm ... I know what those are like."

Ben didn't know if this was a hint that he should follow up on or just a sympathetic comment. Not that he wanted Gladys disgorging more deep dark secrets. Especially when the questions crowding his mind had more to do with Daphne.

"How'd it go at the Blind Bard?" he asked finally.

"The usual. Tip-top. A-1."

"What do you do there?"

"Give a little background on Red Gap and its colorful history. Take questions. Read a chapter. Sign books."

"Would you have taken people up here to the Green Room, if I weren't laid up?"

"Nah. Otherwise how will we sell our ghost walk? But most people would have tried to take a look at some point. It's fine. Ray brought a selection from our Historical Society 'archives,' and folks just eat that up."

Ben thought back to Charlie's findings at the mill. "Ledgers from the lumber company and such?"

"It depends from week to week. This week it was pictures—the usual suspects. Some logging memorabilia." Gladys rose from the bed, tucking a stray lock back into her coil of hair. "He never consults me, of course." She began folding the dangling afghan Ben had kicked off. "This time Ray even had a letter."

"From who to who? A love letter?"

She gave a mirthless laugh. When she tried to drape the afghan over the blanket rack, a quilt slid off, and she bent to retrieve it. "Of sorts. It was to Mr. and Mrs. Arthur Chase—Daphne's parents—from a doctor at the Napa State Asylum for the Insane."

"Asylum for the Insane? You mean where—"

"Yes," said Gladys shortly. "The madhouse where the Chases had their daughter committed."

"Wow. What did the letter say? 'Your daughter's still loony tunes?'"

"If she wasn't when she went in, a year at Napa would've done the trick," flashed Gladys.

Ben held up his hands. "Sorry. Just being facetious. I'm sure it wasn't any picnic. At least she was only there the one year, right? I've actually spent some time in Napa because my mom's parents live there. The asylum must be gone because I never remember seeing one."

"It's outside of town. The building Daphne knew is gone now, but the asylum lives on," Gladys snapped. She crossed her arms over her chest. "It's known as the Napa State Hospital nowadays. Home for you-name-it: mood disorders, anxiety disorders, personality disorders, schizophrenics. A place to store people you don't know what to do with." She glared at him as if he were personally responsible for this inadequacy.

"Oh," said Ben. What was the woman's problem? It wasn't like he had ever committed anyone, much less Daphne.

To his relief, the sound of Bea's muffled voice carried to them, followed by the rattling of dishes as she ascended the stairs. Gladys uncrossed her arms and smoothed the anger from her face before springing up to get the door.

Bea buzzed in, tray in hand, bowl of soup steaming. "Chicken noodle," she announced. "Best kind for a cold."

Ben dragged himself more upright because Bea looked like she might do it if he didn't. "This smells great. Thanks. You spoil me."

Bea's gaze flicked over to Gladys who was smiling benignly. "No trouble at all. Could I get you something, Gladys, since it looks like you'll be staying awhile?"

"Don't bother. I'm great." Gladys ignored the hint.

"All right, then." With one last glance at Gladys' discarded shoes, Bea left. Gladys extended one stockinged foot and prodded the door shut behind her.

"I'm telling you, Ben—come recuperate at my place. How much

mothering can you take?"

He was relieved her mood had passed. "No way," he joked. "Bet you can't cook like Bea."

She watched him beneath her lashes. "I have other skills. Plenty of them."

"I'll bet." He focused on the soup. Flirting was not his forté. Courtney used to say he was as unsubtle as a tree stump. How had he managed to kiss this woman a couple days ago? Maybe Gladys had come at him first. He couldn't remember.

"You wanted to know what the letter was about?"

Letter?

They had bonded over their weird encounters with Daphne. That was it. And somehow she ended up on his lap. This was not advisable. Getting involved with her. Her interest was flattering, and she sure did look good, but the woman might as well have *High-Maintenance* tattooed on her forehead. Not to mention her admitted "episodes"—! Didn't he have enough mental problems without taking on hers?

"The *letter*," Gladys said impatiently. "From Napa. From the insane asylum to the Chases."

"Yeah." Ben snapped back to the present. "What did it say?"

"That they did not recommend the patient be released yet. She showed little sign of her 'melancholia' when outdoors or at farming tasks—"

"Farming tasks?" he interrupted. He had been picturing a ragged, teenage Daphne chained to a wall while benighted doctors bled her or doused her with buckets of cold water.

"—But that when around other 'inmates,' she withdrew, becoming sullen and mute."

"That doesn't sound so bad," Ben said cautiously. "If some of the other patients really were insane, I could understand her withdrawing."

"All the state hospitals were wildly overcrowded," said Gladys. "This was before drugs or patient rights or anyone knowing what else to do with the mentally ill. Which means Daphne spent most of her time around other people. Which means she spent most of her time sullen and mute."

"Well, how'd she get out, then?" he said, fed up with her know-it-all attitude.

"I've asked her."

Right, he thought. Here we go.

"There were only two ways out of the Asylum," Gladys continued. "Death or discharge." Rising from the armchair, she wandered to the window. Bea had looped back the drapes earlier, but the day was so foggy and wet that Ben doubted much could be seen. "We know she didn't die, so she had to convince Dr. Reed—who wrote that letter— that she was fit to return to normal life."

Ben studied the curve of her back. He really shouldn't encourage her. But he couldn't help it.

"How exactly do you ask Daphne things? Do you see her—or is it during an—uh—episode?"

Without turning to look at him, Gladys tapped the window panes with her fingertips. "This sounds dumb. Or crazy. But I feel her. I know enough about her that I can pick out her voice."

Given his most recent experiences, Ben was in no position to judge anyone dumb or crazy, but he squirmed nonetheless to put himself in the same bucket as Gladys. "Take a couple days ago, for example," he said. "When you spoke to me in the Grove. Or Daphne spoke to me through you. Can you remember any of it afterward?"

She shook her head. "I can't when it's like that. I'm talking about times when I'm very focused on her. Looking at her pictures, reading about her, *writing* about her, being places that were significant in her life."

"So when you say you 'asked' her how she got out of Napa—"

"I've spent a lot of time sorting and archiving and studying all the historical materials we've collected," Gladys said hastily. "Including this letter. I've thought about this letter a lot. There isn't much that survived in Red Gap from this period in Daphne's life. I focused on the letter. And then I knew."

He waited. "Well? Then what? What did she tell you?"

At last she looked at him. Gave him an arch smile. "Why, Ben—it's no secret what she told me. Thousands and thousands of people already know, in seven different languages."

"Are you saying that *Bury Me Not* is all based on things you learned from Daphne?"

"Let's say it borrows heavily. What do they say in the movies? 'Inspired by real events'? 'Based on a true story'?" Seeing that he had finished his soup, she whisked the tray away and resumed her seat on the bed, as close as she was the first time.

"You're saying she told you that Pall Lindstrom killed her?"

Gladys pouted. "We already talked about this. Or did the fever burn that out of your head?" She snuggled into his side again, draping his arm around her shoulders. "I told you that I'm not 100% dead certain on it. Daphne has been rather close-lipped. I had to use my imagination, based on the evidence at hand."

Her breast was pressing against his rib cage now, but Ben was determined to get his answers. "You could have gotten it wrong, though."

"I suppose Charlie's been telling you that. He's always been a grump about the book, but what would you expect from a Derwent?"

"But why do you think you still experience her? You don't mention recent 'episodes' with those other ghosts in your life. They must have left you alone after you did what they wanted."

"They did." None too gently, Gladys sat up, narrowly avoiding knocking his chin with her head. "I guess I wasn't able to satisfy dear Mrs. Lindstrom."

"You think because you got some of her story wrong, or because she wants something else out of you?"

"I don't know."

"Can't you ask her?"

"It's not a telephone line, Ben!"

"Something's wrong. Otherwise she wouldn't still appear to people like me and ask for help."

"If you're so smart, and you're the one who *does* see her, why don't you ask her yourself?"

It was on the tip of his tongue to say, *I have*, but he held back. Why, he couldn't say. An urge to protect Daphne, perhaps. Or himself. They would run him out of town, invalid or no, if he told them Daphne asked him to fell Grand Daddy. That made no sense whatsoever. It had to be a misunderstanding—fever taking him and twisting her words. No, no—it was worse than that. There was no ghost, and he had imagined everything from first to last. Concussion, insomnia, drugs, fever.

"I'm in no condition to talk to anyone," said Ben.

Gladys sighed. She ruffled his hair gently. "You already have some gray. How old are you, Ben?"

"Twenty-eight." He wondered how old she was.

She lay down, pulling on his arm. "Aren't you tired of sitting up now, Sickie? We've talked enough. Why don't you relax?"

Hooking up with her was not a good idea. He could think of fifty reasons, in fact, for why it was a *bad* idea. Not least of which was that another face now hovered at the edges of his consciousness.

Gladys took his hand and placed it on her backside.

Maybe not fifty reasons, Ben said to himself. More like ten.

"I feel like hell," he muttered.

"Then feel me instead."

The timid knock turned authoritative when it was ignored.

Ben and Gladys disentangled their lips and limbs so hurriedly that Gladys rolled onto the floor as the door was opening. "Oh, hey, Bea," said Ben. "The soup hit the spot."

"Glad to hear it," said Bea. She kept her eyes resolutely off them as

Ben tugged the sheet back up and Gladys straightened her knit top. "Sorry to interrupt. I couldn't wait any longer to run the dishwasher."

"Of course," said Gladys. "I was just going to bring the tray down."

Bea picked it up from the floor. "Don't trouble yourself." She paused in the doorway. "And, Ben, you might want to take it easy so you don't have a relapse." Bea sounded like she was smothering a laugh. "All that talking can be so exhausting."

They listened to her retreating footsteps.

Gladys slipped her shoes back on. "That's it," she whispered. "I feel like the dorm mother just caught me. Move over to my place. Think about it."

"Come see me tomorrow?" he grinned.

"Only if you're well enough for me to get you out of here—wheel your sorry ass around town again. I can't have Bea feeling so superior to me." She leaned over to give him a lingering kiss and one more look down her neckline.

"Hey," Ben said, when she reached the door. "You never did tell me how Daphne said she got out of Napa."

Gladys shook her head mockingly. "I have too, young man. Think of the last ten minutes as your hint. Dr. Reed was only in his twenties when Daphne came through his asylum. A young doctor, a beautiful, troubled girl—she hardly needed to tell me. Because what does any person want more than love?"

But Gladys was wrong, Ben thought, as he lay back and stared at the ceiling. Because if it was true, that Daphne had pretended or offered love to Dr. Reed, she had done it in exchange for the one thing she wanted more.

Even more than love, Daphne had wanted her freedom.

CHAPTER 14

The Overhang

She would not come.

He expected her. That night, after the Derwents and the Tuesday night guests had gone to bed. A hush fell over the house. Ben sat in the armchair, fully dressed, ready to venture into the soggy wet, if she should appear.

He laid a hand against the wallboards. No pulse. Nothing.

Why, then, did he feel she was somewhere just out of sight? As if she were waiting on him. She should come.

He wanted to see her this time. Now, when he felt relatively well. If only to confirm that he hadn't dreamed it all. He wanted to ask her, *Did I understand you right? More than anything, you want your freedom?* And he needed to tell her that he could not, could not, give it to her.

No raindrops coursed down the window panes tonight, but the fog continued impenetrable. In her white dress it would be nearly impossible to see her, even if she stood just below him, as she had before.

Ben threw the protesting latch and forced the sash up, thrusting his head out. The cold air counteracted the wave of vertigo this motion brought on. He thought he saw movement—in his mind there was a swishing sound, a footstep. But then there was nothing but the fog and its damp fingers on his cheek.

She did not come.

~⁓~

"Gladys mentioned taking me for another stroll today," said Ben. He was stacking all the dirty dishes he could reach, balancing the silverware on top, for Charlie to take to the kitchen.

Breakfasts at the Dryad were served buffet-style. Apart from the dining table for six, several smaller round tables seating twos and fours crowded the room. Ben had come down to find those filled, leaving him to join a mom and her two homeschooled teenage daughters at the large table. The older girl had been shy or cool or something, not looking at or talking to him, but the younger one plied him with questions about the Green Room. Did he feel anything? See anything? Hear anything? "Nothing last night," he replied in all honesty, between bites. "You could take a quick look in there this morning, if you like, if it's okay with the Derwents." The older girl stopped pushing her eggs around her plate to share an excited look with her sister. Their mom sighed with relief. "You've made my day. They were begging me to spend an extra night because they didn't want to go home without seeing it. We've visited everything else twice over."

Charlie gave him a washcloth to wipe down the table. "Not that big a town," he said. "Lousy day for a walk, too. Foggy."

"Hey, Innkeeper—don't let Bea hear you talking like that," Ben teased. He passed Charlie the half-empty cream jug and the jam server. "No, I was thinking I'd like to go by the mill again, take a look at the railroad tracks. Maybe follow them a ways and see where they ran the lumber and shipped it out."

"That'll be a bumpy ride," said Charlie. "Don't know if a wheelchair could make it. But the Overhang isn't much past it. It looks down on the deepest part of the river, when it's running."

The Overhang was where Daphne's things had been found, Ben

149

recalled Bea saying. And where Gladys had set the supposed murder. He strove for an offhand tone. "I'd like to see that, too. And then maybe finish up with a look at the historical society stuff."

"What for?"

Ben scraped crumbs off the table surface into his hand. "Just to get more of a bearing on things. You can't blame me for being curious."

"Are you sure it isn't Gladys you're curious about?" Charlie gave one of his wheezy laughs, and Ben knew Bea must have mentioned yesterday's messing around.

He focused on scrubbing off the jam the younger daughter had dripped from the server to her plate. "I don't know what your issue is. At least Gladys is alive, and everyone agrees she exists."

Charlie made an indeterminate sound and chose that moment to disappear with the dishes. When he returned a few minutes later, Ben was wiping down a smaller table. "Finish wiping or run the carpet sweeper?" said Charlie.

"I'll wipe," said Ben. "That way I can sit." He watched his host, trying to measure that morning's degree of openness. Not very, he would guess, to judge by how Charlie determinedly kept his back to him. "Hey, Charlie. Speaking of the girl not everybody sees—"

"This guy got some ketchup on the chair." Charlie pointed. "Bea won't be happy about that."

"Speaking of the girl not everybody sees," Ben persevered, "has she shown up for you, in the past couple days?"

Charlie's carpet-sweeping accelerated. He glanced kitchenward, as if he expected the door to swing open. When it didn't, he drew closer to Ben. "Promised Bea I wouldn't talk about it any more than I had to, to warn you."

"Which you did," said Ben. "Warn me."

"Which I did," Charlie agreed. "Wouldn't want to encourage you— bad luck for everyone else who got wrapped up in it."

"I understand," Ben said. "And I don't want to drag you down or make you do something Bea doesn't want you to."

"That's right," said Charlie.

They worked in silence another minute, the rolling of the sweeper and squeaking of the washcloth the only sounds.

"You seen her?" asked Charlie.

"Not since you found me outside. I kind of expected to last night, but no." Ben couldn't shake the feeling that he *should* have seen her, if she wanted to be found. That she was watching, just out of sight. "It's weird," he added lamely.

"Know what's weirder?" said Charlie. He held out his hand.

Ben tossed him the washcloth. "What?"

"This has been the first week of my life since I was thirteen—not counting the times I've been away—that she hasn't shown up even once."

Ben's eyes widened. "You haven't seen her for a whole week?"

"Not for seven days. It's funny. Ben—I haven't seen her since you showed up."

Gladys breezed up around ten o'clock, armed against the fog in a fleece, rain jacket and wool cap. Ben had been waiting in the parlor, flipping once more through the town history. If concentrating on Daphne's artifacts brought her to life for Gladys, it might work for him.

Come on then, he muttered to himself.

Half an hour passed. Nothing.

"Where to today?" asked Gladys when he opened the door. "I wheel at your command."

Ben outlined his itinerary. "I think I could walk some of it, feeble though I am," he said.

"No way," said Gladys, taking hold of both his hands and dragging him toward the rickety wheelchair. "I'm not explaining to Bea when you go dizzy on me and pitch off the railroad trestle. She already disapproves. Sit tight a minute while I run in and tell her I'm taking you to Etta's for lunch."

From the vantage of the Dryad, the rest of Red Gap might not have existed, the fog enveloped it so completely.

Daphne could walk alongside us the whole way and I wouldn't see her, Ben thought. The idea bothered him. But I would *feel* her, he added. I don't know why, but I would. Was it because they had spoken? Because she had touched him? And why had she abandoned Charlie, after appearing to him for decades? Did it have something to do with his own arrival?

"Boo!" Gladys materialized beside him again, landing a kiss on his cheek and giving his ear a playful nibble. "All set. You're mine, for hours and hours."

He shifted in his seat. Surely this had nothing to do with it. Daphne wouldn't be avoiding him because of Gladys. After all, she *possessed* Gladys from time to time, as the mood took her. It was one of the reasons he looked forward to a few hours with her today: he wondered if she would have another Daphne episode. Now that he knew what to expect, he wanted to test it. Was it for real? If it was, why would Daphne need to inhabit another body, when she already had one perceptible to at least a few other people? And if it wasn't for real—well, he had no idea what that meant.

Nor did he know how the falling tree branch fit in. Aggression or mere coincidence? Coincidence, fine. But if Daphne objected to him getting involved with Gladys...

I'm not getting involved, Ben explained to himself. It's nothing. She looks good and she wants to mess around and I'm on the rebound and I'm okay with that. All casual. It might go somewhere or nowhere. He just planned to enjoy whatever came his way.

They descended into town in silence, Gladys' hands on the chair rather tense until the sidewalk began. ("Thank God—you should see how Ray takes corners in his pickup. The guy's half blind.") Few people were out and about. What ones there were loomed suddenly out of the mist, startling Ben, before receding again, a mitten raised in greeting or a remark muttered about the weather.

Just past the Come On Inn on the downhill side, the mill looked even more dilapidated in the gloom. When Ben wiped a grimy window and pressed his face to it, he saw that several panes on the adjacent north wall were missing and part of the ceiling caved in. Apart from a few rusty chains and a saw blade or two scattered across it, the floor was barren, dusty. The south and west side walls hardly deserved the name, being slapdash affairs of random leftover lumber, nailed together to close off the space after the mill shut down. When they circled the building, he saw remains of rail tracks leading to and away. Four sets. Enough for a log train bound for the coast and smaller engines running to and from the timber fields.

"A pretty big operation," said Ben.

"Not too shabby, considering the lumber company started as a two-man, two-axe outfit after the Gold Rush. It didn't take the owners long to figure out there was more money in timber than in standing in rivers all day, fighting over a few nuggets and flakes." Gladys made a sweeping gesture. "Here the gold just stood there—it had for centuries—waiting for you to come hack it down and chop it up."

"Still," Ben said, "it's pretty amazing how they managed to tackle Daphne's trees."

"I think that's why they didn't touch the Grove for almost fifty years. Only when they'd logged all the bigger firs and smaller redwoods did they start looking at it covetously."

Ben pondered this. "It was probably more than just what-else-is-there. I mean, you have to have pretty developed access and expensive manpower and equipment to deal with trees that size." Which was one more reason Daphne didn't know what she was asking for. Even with a modern chainsaw it would be like trying to go after the Washington Monument with an electric carving knife.

She had waited decades too long to abandon her post as tree guardian. She should have made her demands back when Red Gap Lumber Company was still in operation. Of course, considering all those tortured Derwents drinking themselves senseless, running away, going nuts—maybe she had.

Charlie was right. There was no question of wheeling Ben along the overgrown tracks.

"How far to the trestle?" he asked.

Gladys was retrieving her knit gloves from an inside pocket. "If you follow the tracks, it's maybe a quarter mile. The teenagers do it. I think there's some covert bungee-jumping off it, even though it wouldn't take more than a tremor to level the whole thing."

"Charlie says the Overhang isn't much past it."

She looked at him sharply. "It isn't."

"Well, is there another way to get there?"

Shrugging, she replied, "There are a million ways to anywhere. If you've had your fill of the mill and railroad tracks, I'll take you."

Unlike the route to the Grove, the way to the Overhang showed evidence of heavy traffic over time. The trees encroached on either side, but Ben detected traces of skids, wagon ruts, half-buried logging debris. The old road paralleled the tracks but followed a steady incline, the fog thinning as they climbed.

"I should walk."

Her mittened hand dismissed this, although she sounded breathless when she spoke. "It isn't much farther. Tell me—what do you know about the Overhang?"

"Bea says it's where Daphne's things were found, after she disappeared." He blew on his own hands and tucked them under his thighs. Better not to mention Charlie spoiling another element of Gladys' precious plot. "She leave anything out?"

"Nothing she would call important, since the Derwents only grant the bare facts," said Gladys. "Daphne disappeared. A few days later someone found her hat and basket there."

He let his head hang back, trying to see her expression. Overhead the treetops pirouetted and he shut his eyes. Gladys made a sound in her throat. Her lips brushed his forehead. "Just over this last rise."

When the wheelchair came to a halt, he looked around. They seemed to be at just another bend in the road, but Gladys pointed past him into a tangle of trees and ferns. "Follow the cigarettes and beer cans. The trestle isn't the only teen hang-out."

Looking down, Ben detected a path through the foliage, dotted, as advertised, with the occasional piece of litter. It wound past a clump of Doug firs and a spindly, outlying redwood or two, ending abruptly in an open space no larger than a living room. The clearing was bounded on three sides by trees and on the fourth by a drop into space. Slowly, Ben ventured closer to the edge, keeping one hand on the lone fir guarding the cliff.

The Overhang, indeed.

Although their climb had been steady, it had not been steep, so the depth of the ravine surprised him. The ground must have cut away sharply under the railroad tracks, and he thought he spied, some distance away, the criss-cross ties of the trestle.

What was it? 100 feet down? More?

Gladys joined him, her arm sliding around his waist to steady him. Together, they peered down. The Yoak River was scarcely more than a large creek at this point in the year. Ben could make out the boulders which punctuated it. *The riverbed has dried up but yielded no secrets.*

Daphne must have disappeared when the river was high; otherwise it would have been obvious that she had not thrown herself from the Overhang. She would have fallen on the rocks or even to the side of the water.

"What happens here—in the book?" Ben said suddenly.

"You mean, what did Daphne say happened?" She read him too easily, how he had wanted to avoid putting it that way. Releasing him, she backed away a step, leaning against the fir. "Well, as I said, I'm not 100% positive. What I do know is that she would come here often. Maybe climb one of these trees."

"Climb?" interrupted Ben. "In a dress?"

"Maybe, maybe not. Turn-of-the-century fashions were loosening up. There's a reference in one letter from Mrs. Arthur Chase to her sister, complaining that she caught ten-year-old-Daphne in the trees again, clowning around in boy clothes—"

"You don't think she was running around the forest in boy clothes after she was married, surely." His brow furrowed as he inspected the surrounding trees. Yes, several offered obvious climbing routes, but for *Daphne*? Vividly he recalled her standing beside him under the umbrella. She was 5'5," tops—and with that gown constantly dragging behind her—! Of course, that might have been her wedding dress.

Gladys made a huffing sound. "Oh, probably not, but we don't know. In any case, I think men underestimate what a woman can do in a dress, particularly if she's worn one all her life. So whether she climbed the trees or just hid behind them up here, it gave her a view of the loggers as they went to and from their work. Shane Derwent passed this way a few times a day. After he was married and she was married, the Overhang became the only place they could 'run into each other' without raising eyebrows."

"I thought everyone knew she liked to wander around in the woods," Ben interposed again.

"Wander the Grove, yes. But this is different. The Overhang is right off the loggers' beaten path. A woman would need an excuse to be here. I think that's why she was never without her gathering basket. Though what she could get here I don't know."

He tore his gaze from the trees to inspect the vegetation at their base. "Summer would be no problem," he said. "She could collect any number of things: strawberries, huckleberries, flowers. In the fall or winter—" he brushed some vines of holly-shaped, glossy leaves with the toe of his boot "—this stuff would work. Oregon grape. Indigenous people used the bark for all kinds of things."

"Well! I wish I'd had you around to consult when I was writing *Bury Me Not*," Gladys said wryly. "I just said she had some generic bark in her basket."

"Okay, then," pursued Ben, "Daphne comes with her basket and either climbs a tree or hides out like she always does, hoping to meet up with Shane. Then what?"

"Then…" Gladys drew close to him, her eyes gleaming in the murky light. "…He came. For whatever minutes they could steal that day, the lovers were reunited." Lightly, she pressed her mouth to his and he felt a low laugh vibrate in her throat.

Enjoy whatever comes my way, Ben reminded himself. Though, if they were going to hook up, he would way rather do it indoors than out here in the cold, where they could barely feel each other through the cumbersome, noisy layers of down, fleece and Gore-Tex. Not to mention, kissing Gladys Harrington in the woods had its risks. He cracked an eyelid to make sure they were in the middle of the clearing. Yes. If the 200-pound widowmaker a couple days ago *was* aggression and not coincidence, Daphne was out of luck here. She would have to barrel them off the Overhang if she objected.

The thought no sooner came to him than he felt it. Again. Her presence.

Ben's head whipped up, and he ignored Gladys' grumblings to scan the woods.

Nothing. No white dress, no curling hair, no hand.

This bug you? he asked. Show yourself.

He lowered his head again, kissed Gladys for all he was worth, until the sensation of being watched made it impossible to continue. Again he pulled back; again he did a sweep of their surroundings. Nothing.

"What is it, Ben? Is someone there?" She clutched him and glanced nervously about.

Frustration filled him. He wanted to yell, You have something to say to me? Say it! To his companion he said only, "No. No one."

Gladys shivered, drawing his attention back to her. But she was just Gladys. No one else in there at the moment. His disappointment must have shown because she made a face. "What? You were hoping we'd get impaled by another killer branch?" She drew his head down again. "We'll have to make our own excitement."

Ben resisted this time. "It's nice, but I can barely hear myself think over all the Gore-Tex friction." He smiled and rubbed at her mouth to wipe away the pout. "Finish your story, and let's get out of here."

"All right, then," Gladys relented. She resumed her hushed, dramatic voice. "The lovers met that afternoon. But unbeknownst to them, there was a witness. Pall Lindstrom saw Shane Derwent coming away from the Overhang. Fury filled him. The rage that sweeps like a forest fire. He waited to see if his wife would emerge. But when she didn't, and the sounds of other people died away, he came up here to confront her."

Possession of another kind took hold of Gladys. She drew back, seeing the scene play in her mind. "I think he demanded an explanation. Daphne faltered. She showed him the basket. Said something about collecting bark. Why then, Pall wanted to know, did he see Shane Derwent leaving her a few minutes ago? Daphne backed away from him. She stammered something about brewing a tonic for Margaret Derwent, who was feeling unwell with pregnancy. The excuse did not satisfy. Pall came after her."

Gladys took both of Ben's hands in her own and placed them around her neck. He felt her pulse racing below his thumbs and the hum of her vocal chords when she spoke.

"He took her white, swanlike neck between his two hands. Those same hands which had held hers on their wedding day, when he

promised to love and keep her till death did them part. Her eyes plead-
ed with him. Her mouth worked, but no sound emerged. It would be
so easy, Lindstrom thought. There was no one near. The silence was
complete. This was his moment. It was then, I think—in the throes of
this jealous, unreasoning fit—that he strangled her."

CHAPTER 15

Traces

There wasn't much of a crowd at Etta's.

Tourists paid obligatory visits for its historical value before fleeing to the cozier restaurants and cafés. Ben himself cast hopeful glances toward the Lazy Lumberjack and the Five-Spot before Gladys parked the wheelchair on Etta's porch.

Inside was wood, wood and more wood. Floors, wallboards, bar counter, furniture. Sawdust shavings on the floor. Photographs of loggers turning trees into lumber. Ben recognized some of the shots from the historical society book. The bar lights were suitably dim, although he suspected the effect derived from a patina of grime on the fixtures, rather than a deliberate attempt at ambience. The booth Gladys led him to, after greeting some of the customers at the bar, boasted the same tacky layer of God-knew-what. "Non-stick coating," she said, when Ben inspected the residue on his hand.

A weary blonde floated over to stare dully at Ben, her hands on her hips and her back sagging into a question mark. "What'll it be?"

This was the waitress, then. He glanced around for menus and came up empty.

"Chili for me, Emma," said Gladys. "And an iced tea. You covering for Alice today?"

Emma nodded. "There was a guy in here 'bout twenty minutes ago, asking for you," she added listlessly.

"Book fan?" asked Gladys.

Emma shrugged. "Didn't ask. Told him to check over at the Blind Bard." She turned to Ben. "Burger, tuna sandwich, chili, soup-of-the-day-which-is-tomato. You the guy staying at the Derwents?"

He nodded. He was also the guy wishing he could go back to the Derwents' for lunch. "Uh... I'll have the tomato soup." If it was *du jour* at least it would be fresh, he hoped.

It wasn't. As a never-married graduate student, Ben was something of a canned soup connoisseur. He recognized the Campbell's Old-Fashioned Tomato Rice, even under a dollop of sour cream.

"You know how in old churches the rich families had their certain pews?" Gladys asked between bites. She was dipping the wedge of French bread in her bowl and didn't seem to mind that her chili looked every bit as canned. "The same is true for alcoholics in small-town bars. That stool at the end there—that was the Derwent spot. Shane, Lucas, Byron."

"Byron."

"Charlie's father."

He remembered. "Fell out of Grand Daddy to his death. And Lucas—he and his wife divorced. The grandmother stayed here, while he went to L.A. somewhere."

Gladys' eyes widened in appreciation. "Check you out! One week and you're already an expert."

I should shut my mouth, thought Ben. I'll get Charlie into trouble on every side. He took a sip of his ice water, ignoring the cloudy film on the glass. "Your turn to talk. I want to know about you. I know you came to Red Gap to make a clean start, but why here? How did you even hear of this town?"

Before she could answer, oblique daylight flooded Etta's as the door opened. It was so dim in the bar that Ben could only make out a shadowy figure, backlit, but the same gray beams that obscured the newcomer threw a spotlight on Gladys and him. The stranger liked what he saw. He let the door fall to behind him and made his way toward them in the gloom. The town had seen too many new faces recently to bother with this one. Only Emma took note of him from behind the bar. She jerked her chin at Gladys. *That was him I told you about.*

He was a man in his 40s, of middling build and a slight paunch, with rebelliously thick black hair that made Ben wonder if it was real. He retrieved a business card from the inside pocket of his suede sport coat and extended it to Gladys. Ben noticed his hand, too, was particularly hairy, as if he wore wiry black fingerless mittens.

"Pardon me for interrupting your lunch," he said. It sounded like gravel collected in his throat. "You didn't return my calls, so I took the risk of driving up."

Gladys' jaw was set. She glanced once at the proffered card and tucked it in her pile of discarded outerwear before Ben could see it. "I'm sorry you took the trouble. I've been very busy. I would have called you back at a time more convenient to me."

The man's somewhat bulging eyes swiveled over to Ben and back. "Yeah," he said. "Again, I apologize. I did hope there would be at least one 'more convenient time' for you in the past six months."

"Alas." She smiled blandly. Turned back to Ben. "You were saying—? Something about Oregon grape's homeopathic qualities."

"Uh," he jumped in, "yeah. As a laxative. The root."

"Carson Keller," said the man, thrusting the hairy hand at Ben, who could not avoid shaking it. "Filmmaker."

"Wow," said Ben. "Ben Platt. Tourist. You want to make a movie version of *Bury Me Not*?"

"Not at all," Gladys said tersely. "He's not that kind of filmmaker. He wants to make a biography—of me. Mr. Keller, while I am extremely flattered by the attention, if I had found the convenient time to call you, the first thing I would have said is that I am a very private person."

Ben coughed. Reached for his water glass.

"Exactly," said Keller. "A very private person. All the more reason why you might want a say in any media representations of you. However private you might be, your book's success has made you into a public figure. I realize you find the interest in your personal life repugnant, but I assure you I would be willing to grant you some creative say if you would favor me with a few hours of interview time."

"I'll consider it." Her tone was not especially convincing.

Keller grabbed a lock of his thick hair and tugged it thoughtfully. "When it took so long to hear from you, I did start doing some research. Spoke to some folks in Mountain View. Old neighbors, that sort of thing."

Gladys' eyes flashed. "I said I'll consider it."

He bowed. "Thank you, Ms. Harrington. My card has my cell phone number, but I'm afraid coverage is spotty here. You can reach me at the Come On Inn in the next few days."

She nodded. He took his leave, bathing Ben and Gladys once more in pallid light as the door to Etta's opened and shut.

Gladys returned to eating her chili as if nothing had happened.

Ben sat back, no longer hungry. "Well? What was that about, Ms. Private Person?"

"It's self-explanatory, I'd say."

"What's the big deal about talking to him? Apart from the fact that he has super scary body hair. He might go off and make a really creepy biography of you if you don't intervene."

"I don't want him to make *any* biography of me."

"Clearly. But not wanting him to doesn't mean he won't."

"I know that," Gladys snapped.

"Then why not talk to him?"

She smacked her spoon down on the gummy table. "If I gave in to every lousy person that wanted something out of me there'd be no end to it! I don't want him to make a movie about me. I don't want him digging around in my life. Look at him—he's no Ken Burns. There's no big Macarthur Foundation grant behind him. I'm hoping, with enough discouragement and with waning public interest, he'll just give up and make his dumb video about someone else."

"Is this what you say to the guy who wants to make a *Bury Me Not* movie?"

She blinked. "You mean the 'guys,' plural. They're in talks with my agent."

"So, you're not opposed."

"That's a movie about the book—not *me*!"

"Well, I don't know how you expect public interest to wane if you're willing to allow a film adaptation."

"Oh, don't be logical with me. I can't stand it!" Gladys started digging through the outerwear pile for her wallet. He made a perfunctory gesture of pulling out his own empty billfold, only to have her say, "Don't bother. I told you this one was on me."

While the haggard Emma made change, Ben inspected the Derwent end of the bar. The stool was worn unevenly; it fit his backside if he sat forward with a foot on the rail. Here it was that Shane Derwent drank away his grief and Lucas his obsession. He wondered if Daphne had chosen to approach Charlie's father and Charlie himself at so much younger ages to forestall any escape into liquor. A trade-off, for sure. They might stay sober, but you could hardly expect adolescent boys to fell a redwood centuries old.

"Did you see these?" Gladys broke into his thoughts. She pushed his elbows aside and pointed to letters carved into the edge of the bar counter. A series of Ds, regular as fenceposts. And at the very end, a handful of rough, parallel, squiggly gouges beside an eye.

"Is that supposed to be a face?"

"Her face, yes. You have to back up a little to see it."

"Or be half-plastered."

"You've seen her—at least from a distance—do you see a resemblance?"

Ben stared at the crude carving to avoid Gladys' questioning look. The woodsy intimacy which prompted his confession the other day had vanished, and he balked at announcing he had since encountered Daphne at much closer range. Call it instinct: you did not tell one woman that you were thinking about another. Especially when the first woman was volatile and the second deceased. "The hair, maybe. Are we all set? I'm looking forward to seeing the historical society stuff."

There were two churches in Red Gap, neither of which met in a church building. The Catholic congregation shared digs with the community center, and the non-denominational flock gathered in the K-12 school gym. Which meant the former St. Olaf's Lutheran Church could be rented out to the Red Gap Historical Society at rock-bottom prices.

The card taped to the safety glass alongside the vestibule door read: "Historical Society Museum. Open Tues-Sat 2:00-4:00 p.m."

Gladys knocked, but when no one came she stalked off to search under various potted plants for the key.

It smelled musty inside, a rich mix of moldering red carpet, furniture polish, candle wax, and clothes too long in the wardrobe. Although several stained glass windows remained, all other traces of the little church had been removed. Instead of an altar, the chancel featured a large glass case in which several books lay open beside old newspapers and correspondence. Beyond it, the former apse housed a replica schoolroom, complete with blackboard and antique desks. Running the length of the sanctuary were everything from mannequins in period clothing to enormous regional maps and photographs to sample products made from fir and redwood. The pews had yielded place to an exhibit of logging equipment from different ages, and the enormous cross-section of an oversized coast redwood filled the entire rear wall like the cork to a bottle. Ben smiled to recognize that the presence of this monster evoked church-appropriate reverence in him. He couldn't help but feel he should mute his footsteps and keep his voice low.

Skirting the Dolbeer donkey engine with its trademark vertical capstan, Ben approached the slab. "How long did you stand?" he murmured. "Two thousand years? More?"

"It's from Demigod," volunteered Gladys at normal volume. She was straightening a stack of informational cards by the entrance. "Ray insisted on marking all those tree rings at important dates, even though I told him the thumbtacks were kind of a redwood cliché. How many births of Christ can you stand from Santa Cruz to Arcata?"

"The Lincoln assassination is an original touch anyway," said Ben, fingering one of the markers. The same could be said for "Baseball's National League founded (1876)," which was the last ring highlighted before "1889: Tree felled."

Demigod. He pictured the Grove, the stumps. This one had stood next to Empress along the outer ring. Affecting nonchalance, he pressed his whole hand against the slab. But there was nothing. Not even his own pulse.

It was getting harder to hide his reaction from himself. He wanted to see Daphne again. It had gone beyond dread curiosity to eagerness, and the longer she hid herself the more anxious he became.

"Do you think you'll be okay by yourself for a bit?" asked Gladys. "I have some phone calls to make. I'll lock the door so no one else bugs you."

"That'd be fine," answered Ben, trying not to sound too enthusiastic.

"If I'm not back before you finish up, just have a seat. Or you can let yourself out through the sacristy and wait for me back at Etta's."

"Got it."

The key had barely turned in the lock before Ben began pacing the room impatiently. Where to begin? He blew past the early log-ging equipment—axes, wedges, mallets, whipsaws—and took the two steps to the chancel. The open books in the display case were Red Gap Lumber Company ledgers, most likely the same ones Charlie and his friends had discovered all those years ago. The first volume was a minutes book from shareholder meetings, and the second contained a time roll for 1893. Among the several hundred names he found Shane Derwent at a monthly wage of $55 and one Albert Turner at $8.

The newspaper beside the ledgers was laminated to prevent further yellowing. In block letters the headline of the *Humboldt Standard* pro-claimed, "Red Gap Woman Continues Missing, Believed Dead." The article told him nothing he didn't already know, though the reporter described Mr. Pall Lindstrom as "stricken a mortal blow of grief" and Mr. and Mrs. Arthur Chase as "wan yet stalwart." Both parties refused to comment on the situation.

Ben proceeded to the letters. No correspondents he recognized. He was tempted to move on until a portion of the hurried, spidery script leapt at him: "Have pity on me and write again very soon. I long to learn the aftermath of Daphne Chase's return. I heartily concur—a twelvemonth's treatment in the insane asylum was all too brief in this instance. Such unwomanly, violent behavior as she demonstrated last year! It beggars belief. I could scarce keep my countenance when I read your description. You, I trust, have offered your advice to [illegible] ..."

His breath escaped in a hiss. Stupid old busybody. But in such a provincial place, Daphne's adventures must have supplied the town gossip mill 24/7.

Nell Holloway's acquaintance with her neighbors' misfortunes was sec-ond only to Almighty God's.

He straightened with a jerk that caused him to stagger, as his brain caught up with his body. The hairs on the back of his neck prickled. Where had that thought come from? Ben steadied himself against the glass case. There was no point in looking around. He knew he was alone. He *felt* he was alone. What then—?

"Nell Holloway"? His eyes returned to the letter's salutation. *My dear Ellen*. Ellen. Nell. He might have, Ben counseled himself, supplied the nickname in his mind after reading the salutation—though he'd never known a Nell in his life—but where did the Holloway come from?

He felt the eagerness to encounter Daphne again draining away, replaced by apprehension. In his desire to see her, was his mind conjuring her from thin air? Allow me to clarify, he thought: wanting to see her does not mean I want her inside my head. Like his head wasn't messed up enough as it was? "God," muttered Ben, "I'm the first guy on earth to develop schizophrenia from a concussion." Maybe he really ought to take Gladys up on that offer to drive him to the Urgent Care in Eureka.

He had to get a grip. Turning his back on the disturbing letter, he shuffled the length of the sanctuary, avoiding anything that might be Daphne's or touch on her. But what did not? He ended up studying the axes, distracting himself with their macho names. Red Warrior. Choppers Pride. King of the Forest. "In the early days of logging," read the plaque, "it might require a crew of two choppers up to one week to bring down a larger redwood." Exactly. How long would it take a crew of *one* chopper, if he were so inclined? And how on earth would he manage this fortnight of vandalism on one of Red Gap's main tourist attractions without attracting anyone's notice?

Not that he was going to. This just cemented it. Not that it needed cementing. Ben dragged his hand through his hair. Lord.

"We need to talk," he said to the room at large. "I told you I couldn't do this. I won't do this. But I need to talk to you. If you're there. If you exist."

No response came. He had no companions in the museum save the mannequins. Sighing, he scrutinized the one labeled *Ladies' Walking Suit, 1890s*. Gladys was right—you could climb a tree in this. The skirt was shorter than he imagined, some ways above the ankle, and free-swinging. He wondered who the outfit had belonged to, but there was no indication.

He returned to the gossipy letter. Re-read the passage. No thoughts streaked through his head but his own.

He crammed into one of the schoolroom desks. Ran his finger down grooves and initials scratched in the wood by countless pupils. Among them was a series of Ds, as at the bar, and he wondered if Shane had inscribed these ones as well. Rubbing them didn't work as a magic summons. Most likely Shane Derwent had made the same discovery. The photograph from the town history book hung on the apse wall, with the students lined up, Shane holding Daphne's braid. A note was posted to it: "Share your memories with us! If you can identify any children in this picture, please alert the curator."

Discouraged, Ben made one more desultory circuit of the museum. He wondered where they stored all the items not on display. Ray's secret archives, as it were. The curator's desk, tucked in a corner behind a coat stand, was locked. Another dead end.

Fine.

"You wanna stay hidden, stay hidden," Ben announced aloud. "But you just try to free yourself on your own. You just... keep trying your lame methods for another hundred years and see how that works out for you." Rising from behind the desk, a wave of dizziness caught him and he stumbled against the file cabinet. The stack of mail balanced on top slid off, sending envelopes and a package or two sailing, to fan across the worn carpet like a banner unfurling.

He cursed and got down to retrieve everything, slapping it back on top of the cabinet any which way. One bubble envelope had burst open, spilling its contents of a dark blue, clothbound volume stamped in gold. The cover letter, which had been taped around it for added protection, slipped off. "... happy to report the binding was repairable. It would be cost-prohibitive to restore the damaged page, but I have

located another copy of the book and enclose a photocopy of the unreadable poem on acid-free paper in the appropriate spot."

Grimacing, Ben retrieved the book with light fingers, hoping impact with the floor hadn't undone its repairs. *Goblin Market and Other
Poems*, read the spine. *Christina Rossetti*. He ticked through the pages,
frowning at the beautiful-yet-disturbing pair of engravings—a strong-
jawed woman with flowing hair, surrounded by sinister creatures bearing food. He had never been much for poetry, though, and was about
to shut the book when his thumb caught on a page, pulling it out.
"Damn it," said Ben. Fortunately, it was only the photocopy the book
restorer mentioned, and he carefully replaced it.

"'A Better Resurrection,'" it read.

> I HAVE no wit, no words, no tears;
> My heart within me like a stone
> Is numb'd too much for hopes or fears;
> Look right, look left, I dwell alone;
> I lift mine eyes, but dimm'd with grief
> No everlasting hills I see;
> My life is in the falling leaf:
> O Jesus, quicken me.

His breathing accelerated. He recognized this verse. Not the words
exactly, but the tone, the rhythm, the theme.

His eye rushed to the second stanza, and when he read it, a second
voice joined his.

Coaxing, musical—thoughts made audible.

> My life is like a faded leaf,
> My harvest dwindled to a husk:
> Truly my life is void and brief
> And tedious in the barren dusk;

My life is like a frozen thing,
No bud nor greenness can I see:
Yet rise it shall—the sap of Spring;
O Jesus, rise in me.

Yes, the same voice whispered. *This is mine.*

"Daphne?" Ben shot to his feet. Paid for it, as the world rolled beneath him again. He stuffed the book under his jacket. Prodded the bubble envelope behind the file cabinet with his toe, all the while looking and looking. She was here. Where?

Across the length of the sanctuary, a flash of movement caught his attention, someone passing by the window closest to the vestibule.

As quickly as he could, Ben made his way to the door. He struggled briefly with the deadbolt and flung it open. "Where have you been?"

"You were expecting me?" the observer replied.

No moonlight-pale Daphne Lindstrom faced him, however. Nor was the voice that addressed Ben the one which still echoed in his head and whose owner he felt even now slipping away from him. This visitor was someone rather less welcome.

Ben gaped, sick and breathless, at the wild-haired Carson Keller.

CHAPTER 16

The Summons

"Are you—following me?" Ben managed. He felt the poetry book sliding down his torso and crossed his arms over his stomach, grateful for the lumps and layers of his jackets. His mind was racing. The vestibule side of the nave had only two stained-glass windows intact; the others had been replaced by windows of decorative beveled panes, some transparent, others opaque. Most likely Keller could not have observed him unless he pressed his face directly to a transparent pane, but that was cold comfort for Ben.

Carson Keller shook his head, a grin twitching the corners of his mouth. "No offense, Ben—can I call you Ben?—but I've got bigger fish to fry." He bounced on his toes to dart a look over Ben's shoulder.

"She's not in here," said Ben. "And the museum's closed. Were you following Ms. Harrington, then?"

Keller's grin faded. "This happens to be a primary place of interest in a small town. While I'm in Red Gap, our paths are sure to cross several times a day, and I can't have you making accusations. C'mon, relax." He gave Ben a placating punch in the bicep. Ben felt the Rossetti volume squirt out, and only by lunging clumsily was he able to arrest its fall.

"Errrgh." He sank down onto the step.

"You all right?"

Ben massaged the base of his skull. "Just a low-grade headache," he lied. "Sudden movements don't agree with me."

Keller joined him. "Sorry to hear it. You caught the book, though." He rotated Ben's hand to inspect the title. "'*Goblin Market and Other Poems.*' Never heard of that one. Not that that's saying much. You like to carry your favorites around with you?"

"I'm—uh—just borrowing it from the museum here. I wanted to show it to someone."

"Ms. Harrington, maybe?"

"No."

"You know her pretty well? A fan of her books?"

"I've actually only read a few chapters of *Bury Me Not*. And that was since I came here. I never heard of her otherwise."

"But you two seem to have hit it off," persisted Keller. "Having lunch and all. Let me buy you a cup of coffee. I'll even take you to a nice spot—not like that dive you were in."

"No thanks."

"Just a friendly conversation."

"I'd rather not."

Keller shrugged. "Maybe some other time." He stretched out his legs, crossing his ankles. "Funny town, isn't it? Full of interesting characters. Like that Joyce who runs my motel. She watches me like she expects me to steal something. And when I mention Ms. Harrington she gets all uptight. You can tell there's no love lost, but neither is she going to open up. I'm an outsider. That's how it goes."

Ben said nothing. He had forgotten till now how Joyce had been on the point of telling him her own Daphne theory. "Maybe it's because they know you want something out of them. If you minded your own business, they might open up on their own."

"You found that to be the case, then?" Keller studied Ben's face with renewed interest.

It was Ben's turn to shrug. "I don't know. That just works for people in general, I think." He glanced at his watch. How many phone calls was Gladys going to make? He could attempt the uphill climb to the Dryad under his own steam, but he didn't especially want Keller following him.

"The wheelchair must be for you," Keller said, jerking his chin at it. "For that head of yours that doesn't like sudden movements. This is a strange place to play tourist. I mean, you have trouble getting around on your own, the weather is crap, you never even heard of the books. What brought you here?"

Ben swallowed. "It was the trees. I—uh—I'm a big fan."

"So you came to check out Grand Daddy."

"That's right."

"Plenty of other parks with more trees."

"Smaller trees. Or harder to get to. Grand Daddy's pretty amazing."

"Yeah." Keller mulled this over. Scratched the thick black fuzz on the back of one hand with the other. "You one of those Earth First! freaks, Ben? Like the nut who camped out in that redwood for a couple years?"

"You mean Julia Hill?" Ben laughed. "I've met her. She's not a freak. Just single-minded. Earnest. She means well." *Should not single-mindedness be numbered among the necessary skills?*

Keller made a dismissive gesture. "Well, that could go for all freaks, couldn't it. Everyone means well."

"Including you, I suppose."

"Including me. Remember that. And no offense about not wanting to do your biography, Ben Platt. I'm sure it's fascinating—mysterious invalid environmentalist on vacation. I'm just not sure it would sell." He uncrossed his ankles suddenly, landed his feet flat on the step. "Oop—time to tuck away your favorite poetry book again."

"Huh?" Ben followed his gaze to the corner, where Keller's superior powers of observation had spotted Gladys crossing the street toward them. Without thinking what his companion would make of it, Ben obeyed, stuffing Rosetti back under his layers.

"I'll be going," Ben said. Grabbing the railing, he prepared to haul up on it, but Keller caught him under the other arm and spared him the trouble.

"Hello again, Ms. Harrington," he called. "Just having a nice chat with your friend. Hope you have a good afternoon."

Gladys' eyes were stormy. She hardly acknowledged Keller as he strode away. "Get in," she ordered, yanking up the wheelchair brake.

"Whoa, there," said Ben. He checked to see if the filmmaker was out of earshot. "Don't get all up in arms. Keller cornered me here. I didn't seek *him* out."

"Whatever." She pointed at the seat.

"No, come on, Gladys. I didn't tell him a thing about you or grant him any interviews, so don't get all bent out of shape."

"I'm not *bent out of shape*," she hissed. Taking the chair by the handles, she whipped around behind him and knocked the back of his knees with it so that he sprawled into the seat.

"For God's sake, Gladys!" he complained as she charged up the sidewalk with him. "What the hell is your problem?"

"My 'problem,'" she huffed in his ear, "is that I've shared some pretty confidential things with you, and it may have been unwise, since I hardly know you, but it's done. And then what do I find except you *talking* to the creepy guy I just got done telling you I wanted nothing to do with! Other than that, I'm perfectly fine."

Ben shielded his eyes with his hands so that he could twist in the chair to face her. "Do we really need to go this fast? Okay, look—for one thing, as I already said, he cornered me. And for another, if I'm totally rude and blow the guy off, then he's going to jump to conclusions and think I'm being really protective of you, which to his mind might imply there's more between us than there is. If he starts thinking that, then he's doubly interested and doubly a pain in the ass. Am I right? Whereas, if he thinks there's nothing going on—"

"And there *isn't* anything going on—" she said through clenched teeth.

"And there isn't anything going on," Ben repeated.

That answered one question, at least. Despite himself, he felt a twinge of disappointment. Did that mean she wasn't up for a fling, after all? He swiveled forward again, massaging his temples. It's cleaner this way, he reminded himself.

Gladys maintained a stiff silence the rest of the way up the hill, not even responding to Ben's gasp when a pickup truck burst fully-formed out of the fog and forced them to the edge of the road. "You weren't kidding about Ray's driving."

She wasn't kidding about anything, as a matter of fact, since she wasn't talking. He wondered how much angrier she would have gotten if he'd actually dished the dirt with Keller. Ben was too tired to care, at this point. It could all be patched up later. In the meantime, all would be right with the world if he could just find his way to some aspirin and a nap.

~⁓~

"Daphne. *Mrs. Lindstrom.*"

Hours later he sat with *Goblin Market* open on his lap, the window raised high. It had rained in the late afternoon but by evening nothing remained except the lowering clouds, the ubiquitous fog. Exposing the book to the damp would probably finish it off, but he had to try. She had answered him in the museum—would she do it again? Could the book act as a summons?

"Daphne," he murmured again. It was a strange volume. In nearly pristine condition, apart from the one poem, so faded as to be nearly obliterated. No inscription, no marginalia. He inspected the peculiar engravings again and flicked through the other poems before returning to "A Better Resurrection." Self-consciously, he began to recite it under his breath, straining to hear the other voice join his.

The words hung in the silence.

With effort, Ben relaxed his muscles, every inch of him aware and waiting. *Listening*, if that word could be used to describe one's whole consciousness. She was—

Tap.

At the sound, his head snapped up. He braced himself for the resultant dizziness, almost welcoming it.

There was no hand at the window, sliding against the panes. It had been a piece of flotsam, tossed by the wind. And yet—he knew.

At long last, she was here. Nearby.

Ben replaced the book in its bubble envelope as gently as haste allowed and ducked beneath the raised sash.

Yes.

At the edge of the woods, Daphne Lindstrom emerged, her head turned upward as if weighted back by her luxuriant hair, dry again and pinned up and back. From this distance he could not read her expression.

"Wait," he whispered, knowing she could hear him. "Please—wait there."

Familiarity made his escape outside easier this time, and he ignored his head's protests and the weak coughs that racked him, knowing they would disappear as soon as he drew near her.

She stood where she had met him the other night, at the center of eddying fog from which crept wisps and tendrils to encircle him. And as before, he felt perfect wellness steal over him, his ailments vanishing as if they had never been. He raised a hand, to which she did not respond, but her hazel gaze fixed on him and her lips parted.

He took her in with his eyes. She had certainly emerged none the worse for wear after being half-drowned the other night. Not only was her hair as neatly coiffed as it could be, but her gown was immaculate from lace collar to pleated train. From beneath the scalloped hem he saw the tip of a white kid slipper. No lying face-down in the grass and mud for Daphne Lindstrom. He wondered if ghosts had some kind of home base where they could get cleaned up. Sort themselves.

"You've made yourself scarce," Ben said, when she made no move to break the silence. "Why did you come this time?"

"*You sought me.*" Excitement washed over him at the sound of her voice, accompanied by a chill. It was exactly the warm alto he had heard in his head, plucked from the air.

"Yes. I 'sought' you. But I have for a couple days now. And you didn't come then."

Her smile broke over her. There was nothing tenuous about it now. He felt his breath come short. "Daphne—if I could call you that—something strange has happened. When you didn't come the last couple days, I started to wonder if our meeting was brain damage or me losing my mind."

The smile became wry. "*My continued existence is all too certain.*"

"I couldn't see you," he continued, "but I could *feel* your presence somehow. I kept waiting for you to appear because I thought you were there sometimes, just out of sight. Avoiding me, maybe. Were you? Or was that all just me?"

She lowered her gaze, leaving him suddenly cool. "*There were obstacles.*"

"What do you mean, obstacles? To you coming, or obstacles that prevented me seeing you?" His hands came up and dropped to his sides again. "Because, not only could I sense your presence at times, or whatever was happening, but sometimes I even thought I could hear you. Not audibly. But in my head."

Her eyes, with their unearthly light, met his once more. He watched the green of her irises radiate into the hazel and brown. "*I am here now.*

What did you wish so urgently to tell me?"

Which meant, he supposed, that she was not going to answer his question. He shook his head. As if a ghost needed to cultivate a sense of mystery! Women were women, apparently. Even undead he couldn't communicate with them.

He had better just explain himself before the so-called "obstacles" forestalled further conversation.

"Okay. Daphne, what I've been wanting to say is that...what you asked...I don't...I'm not certain that it's possible." He found, when he was finally face to face with her, that his earlier defiance had evaporated. Regret tinged his words.

She knew immediately what he referred to, and her countenance dimmed. *"Not possible?"*

The regret grew. "I'm very, very sorry. I would like to help you." He found this was true. "But there are..." his grin was rueful "...obstacles."

She caught his irony. *"On your part as well?"*

"Yeah. Though I doubt they're the same ones. Please—I need to explain this to you. Is this where you want to talk?" He glanced involuntarily at the house where all lay still and dark, save for the light in his room.

"I am bounded."

He sighed. "No house, I take it."

"Come." Her ivory hand descended lightly on his forearm, sending a thrill to his very fingertips. Without thought, he reached to cover that hand with his own, another shock coursing through him. What was she?

Effortlessly, she withdrew, her skin sliding beneath his palm: cool, dry, soft. The hint of a smile curving her cheek, she preceded him into the woods.

Just under cover of the first grouping of firs the Derwents had placed a wrought-iron bench facing the house. It was here Daphne led him. Turning, she swept the short train of her gown to the side and seated herself.

"*Speak.*"

Ben stood awkwardly before her, uncertain whether she meant him to share the bench. "I don't know where to begin."

That flash of humor. "*I have no shortage of time.*"

"I guess you don't. Okay, then. Hear me out." He drew a step closer. "How certain are you that your existence is tied to the remaining tree? You seem as…real…as existent as ever, considering that most of the Grove was logged long ago."

"*I doubt not that if all the trees yet stood, I should be stronger still. As it is, but few can see me, as you know.*"

"Well, that's conjecture, really. Maybe you're still around for some other reason. I know some people would say that other…ghosts… exist, even though they're not tied to trees or anything."

"*I know nothing of others,*" she said simply.

"But you see what I'm getting at, don't you? You might just—" he struggled for the right words, only Gladys' coming to mind, "—have unfinished business. And once that unfinished business gets taken care of, you'll be free. There's no need to do untold environmental damage to the tree you've always loved."

"*The only business remaining is Grand Daddy.*" She was firm. "*The remaining tree is the source. You understand, do you not? The other trees are gone, dead. But I live on because the remaining tree lives on. The fallen ones weakened me but could not take me because they were not the source.*"

Ben ran both hands through his short hair and dropped onto the bench beside her. She made no movement in response. "But, Daphne, why would one tree be more important than the others? You think it's just by chance that the one surviving tree is this 'source'? That you wouldn't be around if only Empress was left? Or Good Witch or Prince?"

"*Grand Daddy is the source. The source of their life and of mine. I am certain. Did you not call yourself a 'student of trees,' Benjamin?*"

He stared at her as his mind worked, watching the rings and

gradations of color shift in her eyes, rippling outward. Rings. Lines. *Outward.* He inhaled sharply. "The fairy rings."

"Yes." Her smile lit the semi-darkness. "*The Grove was not born of seed cones.*"

Despite the weirdness of the situation, Ben couldn't help but grin at her in admiration. "Bea is right—you would have made quite the botanist. In fact, I don't know how you know."

"*A hundred years is a very long time to observe and learn.*"

"But you're right," he marveled. "The other trees in the Grove were sprouts, not seedlings. Sprouts from Grand Daddy's roots. That's why they radiated in a circle of lines from it. Grand Daddy is so old it probably doesn't produce many seed cones anymore, and what ones it does make, I bet, have pretty low viability. So sprouts. A fairy ring of genetic clones."

"Klon. *Clones,*" Daphne murmured. "*A fitting name for them. These 'twigs,' however, were veritable colossi. Yet it was Grand Daddy who gave them life. So you see, it is indeed the remaining tree which must fall.*"

Ben felt his heart sinking somewhere in the vicinity of his stomach. So much for convincing her that Grand Daddy had no connection to her continued existence; instead he found himself persuaded. Which only made things worse.

"Daphne," he began again, "you might be right, but it doesn't change anything. Like I said, I can't help you—"

"*Because of the 'obstacles'?*"

"Because of the obstacles. Firstly, damaging something as ancient and enormous and beautiful as that tree goes against everything I believe in—"

"*As ghosts do not?*" The smile lurking in the corners of her mouth didn't reach her eyes.

"—And secondly, even if I lost my mind and decided to go along with your plan, there's no way it could be done! I can't grab an axe and hack at it for weeks with no one noticing. I can't even steal a chainsaw and hope no one sees or hears me. Even with modern equipment it would still take hours, and I don't know what I'm doing. I'm not a logger. I'd be way more likely to kill myself with a chainsaw than Grand Daddy. Then I would be dead, the tree would go on, and you would be back at Square One."

While he spoke, a faint flush spread up Daphne's neck and face. A gauze of pink across her moonstone skin. Ben couldn't tell if it was grief or embarrassment or frustration.

"And supposing I lost my mind and attempted it—somehow felled the tree. That wouldn't mean the stump couldn't still send out root sprouts. They wouldn't be as...strong...maybe, but—" he blundered along—"but—coast redwoods grow like crabgrass, in their own way."

"I'm sorry," he said again, uselessly.

He saw her throat work before she mastered herself. The lace of her high collar ended right at the hollow of it.

"You are a friend, Benjamin Platt."

Ben snorted at this, looking off into the trees in disgust.

"A friend of nature, indeed. But also a friend to me." So lightly it could have been a curl of fog, he felt fingertips touch his hair. He held his breath. *"Forgive me for troubling you so. I grow too forward, too impatient. You are correct in supposing the tree cannot be taken down by such means. As you say, leaving a mere stump would not guarantee that the roots would not sprout anew, recalling me from the brief liberty of my rest."*

As he turned to read her expression, her hand drew back. With lowered eyes, she clasped it with the other in her lap. "You mean it?" he asked. She gave up? It couldn't be that easy, surely. "You mean you're willing to abandon your plan—I don't have to chop the tree down."

"No, Benjamin." She held herself unmoving. The pink of her cheek deepened. *"I fear the only certain way to kill it, then, is to uproot it altogether."*

"Do *what*?" He found himself on his feet again, pacing back and forth before her. "That's—that's—you've got to be—" No coherent thoughts came to his assistance. He sputtered himself into dumb-founded silence.

Daphne waited. *"The task would not fall to you alone. I could help you."*

An incredulous laugh burst from him. "You'll help me topple a two-thousand-year-old tree that weighs more than a 747. Well, that's a relief."

"Need you mock me?"

"Need *you* be completely out of your mind?" The utter ridiculousness of her proposal made it easier to refuse her. "Daphne. This suggestion is no different from the first. Except that it's ten times more impossible."

"The tree leans."

"It does," he admitted. "And with the rest of the Grove logged, Grand Daddy has lost a huge part of its protection from the elements. The surrounding slopes offer some shelter, but it's just a matter of time till some monster windstorm takes it out. I'm amazed it's held up this long. You don't need me. Nature will finish the job."

"And yet the tree has leaned for a century, weathered countless storms, survived wind and fire and flood." Her voice trembled. *"What if it endure another hundred years? Two?"*

"It can't," he declared. "It won't. There was another redwood like it, not too far from here. Even bigger. The Dyerville Giant, they called it. A windstorm knocked out some of the nearby trees, leaving it exposed like Grand Daddy. The Giant was already a leaner, too, and sometime after that storm it fell." He bit his lip, pacing away from her. It occurred to him that the Giant crashed down within the very month of becoming vulnerable—no decades intervened.

As if she read the omission in the set of his shoulders, Daphne said only, *"You will not help me then. You bid me wait, trust in the workings of nature, however slow."*

He could feel her disappointment open a distance between them, as if she were receding, though she had not moved from the bench. He thought of her patient, daily attendance on Charlie, years and years of waiting to see if he would acknowledge her again—all that, only to vanish from his life over the past week. Would she abandon him as well? Ben had only seen her the few times, had only spoken with her twice, and yet he felt the potential loss more keenly than he liked.

She arose, smoothing her skirts.

"Wait—Daphne." Impulsively he reached for her, but she eluded his grasp with no appearance of haste. "Is there no other way I can help you?"

The faint shadow of her smile wavered briefly and was extinguished. "*What would you suggest, Benjamin?*"

"Well," he said, "there's ... there's companionship."

Her eyes darkened, the brown growing more pronounced. She said nothing.

"It must get lonely," he continued awkwardly, "wandering around trying to talk to people, mostly unsuccessfully. I mean, I do hear and see you after all." And touch you, he added to himself. "I could keep you company."

"*How kind. I thank you, Benjamin. But I am well-accustomed to solitude.*"

"No, hang on." He caught at her arm as she made to pass by, his hand closing on the puffed sleeve above her elbow. For an instant he felt the live tension of muscle and bone before quickly releasing her. "I don't say it to be kind. I would like to see you again."

Her color rose and ebbed, leaving her paler in its wake. "*There was a time...*" She broke off. Shook her head. "*It is impossible. You belong to your kind. You do no more than pass through my world. This very time with me will weaken you, Benjamin. I bid you farewell.*"

He stood for a long time after she had gone, staring blindly into the dark forest as his all-too-mortal self returned, with its familiar pains, the aftermath of injuries and sickness. Beyond these he felt a paralyzing fatigue. Was this the weakening she referred to?

But it was none of those things that held him there.

What rooted him to the spot, one hand clenched along the back of the bench for balance, was the pervasive fear that he had seen Daphne Lindstrom for the last time.

CHAPTER 17

A Chink in the Armor

"Bea, do you have internet access here?"

Ben poked his head around the office door. Standing just off the kitchen, the office was the one exception to his hostess' professional neatness, crammed as the small space was with two desks and computers, two printers, file cabinets, the stereo system which piped music throughout the downstairs, heaps of books, piles of papers, racks of CDs, photographs of the Derwents and their twin daughters at various ages and stages, and half-opened boxes from which tumbled customized blue stoneware "The Dryad" mugs, postcards and t-shirts. Mounted on the wall above Bea's desk was a complicated-looking telephone and above Charlie's, a flat-screen tv.

"Oh, heavens, Ben," she cried, spinning on her rolling chair. "I never like anyone to see this disaster of a room, especially the guests!"

He grinned. "After so many days, I'm practically family. The poor relation who does odd jobs to earn his board."

"Well, thank you for helping Charlie rip out the vegetable garden yesterday. It can't have been very fun, in all that mud and rain."

"Way funner than nursing me, I bet," he replied.

She waved this off. "Stop, Ben. A little nursing is good for the soul.

After Rachel and Megan went off to college I haven't had anyone to bother with, other than the occasional guest with stomach flu. And that's no fun at all because half the time they think I gave them food poisoning."

"Really, though, Bea—you've gone above and beyond. Gladys says I should get out of your hair. She's offered me a ride if I want to go to Eureka or back to the U. I'd rather not drive myself, but if someone else took me … It's not like I'm going to die or anything."

Bea looked at him thoughtfully. "Of course not. Certainly you'd survive if you went now. Is that what you want, Ben?"

He looked away. Want to leave? It was the last thing he wanted. At first his health had kept him in Red Gap. His health and—if he were being honest—the fact he had nothing to return to. But now—well, now wild horses couldn't drag him away. He didn't know how Charlie's grandfather or father managed it. If the Derwents ever kicked him out, he would throw himself on Gladys' hospitality, however perilous that might be.

Bea rapped her knuckles on the desk. "Exactly," she said, forestalling his excuses and explanations. "You're honestly welcome to recuperate here longer. In fact, I hope you will. I have plans for you, remember?" Scooting her chair as close to her desk as possible, she pointed at Charlie's computer. "Can you eke by me? Charlie's password is 1234 or something useless like that. I hope it won't bother you if I'm in here. I might have some phone calls."

His smile was grateful. "Actually, yeah. Would you please get out of your own office so I can send some email and play FreeCell?"

Bea made a face. "Don't even mention that game to me. I swear if it's not Texas Hold 'Em with Charlie, it's FreeCell."

Sure enough, Charlie had a few windows running. Ben minimized them and double-clicked on the browser.

"It's about time you contact someone from the outside world," said Bea. "I still can't imagine you didn't think anyone would notice you've been missing for nine days."

He was relieved when the phone rang, sparing him another rehearsal of why no one in the world cared where he was.

His inbox was stuffed with departmental mass mailings: barbecue invitations, upcoming conference registrations, calls for papers, nags about filing student grades and keeping the mailbox area clean. Ben deleted most of them. A quick scan showed no message of mass destruction from Ed Wilson yet, thank God, which meant the team was still in the canopy where they should be. Just in case, though, he edited his autoreply. Instead of "I will be out of the office in the redwood canopy until late October," he modified it to "I will be on personal leave until late October with limited phone and email access." Let them make of that what they would. He considered shooting an email to Lance's girlfriend Sherry about the totaled car but decided it would open a can of worms prematurely. Sherry wasn't missing the car, and Lance didn't need it where he was. Leave it at that.

Only when he logged out of his account did he realize there had been no message from Courtney. She apparently hadn't suffered any emotional sea change and slogged miles through redwood jungle to the nearest internet café, desperate to reach him. There had been no remorse, and he had neither searched for it nor noticed its absence. His relationship with Courtney might have come from another lifetime, it felt so remote. Ben pictured her gray-blue eyes and long ashblonde hair forever pulled back in a ponytail. Her tall, athletic build with surprisingly full breasts stuck on almost as an afterthought. It irritated Courtney that people thought she'd had a boob job. But even as he considered her, the features blurred. The eyes darkened to hazel and green; the hair curled and escaped its trappings; Courtney's frame shrank until she had to tilt her head back to look at him…

"She didn't come by yesterday," said Bea. She made a last notation in the reservation book and shut it with a clap. Ben hadn't even heard her get off the phone.

"Who?"

"What do you mean, 'who'? Gladys. Weren't you listening?"

"Uh…"

"I thought you two were really hitting it off."

His thoughts were too scattered to lie. "Oh. She's mad at me, I think." He'd forgotten all about Gladys' temper as well. She'd probably waited all day yesterday for an apology, though he still didn't know what he had done to apologize for. Exactly nothing.

No, his thoughts had been elsewhere yesterday. After sleeping off the "weakness" Daphne predicted, he had risen at noon and donned mud clothes to help Charlie rip out squash vines and rotted tomato plants, spent cucumbers and bolted greens.

His thoughts had been with Daphne Lindstrom. With the other woman he had not wronged. Then why did he feel as if he had? No, it wasn't that. She had not been angry in her dismissal, or reproachful. She had merely acknowledged his refusal and moved on. Whatever she would try next, if she had a plan in mind, it would not involve him.

He should have been relieved. Compared to all those Derwent men, he'd gotten off scot-free. Instead, his feelings were a morass of regret, depression, anticlimax.

"She can be sensitive," said Bea. "Colorful people usually are."

"Gladys."

She whipped off her glasses and stared at him. "Of course *Gladys*! Are you feeling okay, Ben?"

"Sorry. I'm tracking now. And I feel fine. Better than I have for days." He opened another browser window. "Maybe I'll give her a call later."

The phone rang again. When Bea answered, Ben rotated slowly on Charlie's chair, reaching over to twitch aside the curtain covering the narrow window. It was raining again—or raining *still*, he ought to say—but lightly. He realized with a start that the sliver of forest visible from this angle was the same entrance to the woods he and Daphne passed through not thirty-six hours ago. Foliage hid the wrought-iron bench from view, but he knew exactly where it sat.

"I'd say your best bet for availability before spring would be on Tuesdays and Wednesdays," Bea was telling the caller, before her voice cut off like someone switching radio stations. Instead of reservation details, other sounds filled Ben's ears: the gentle thrumming of rain on forest canopy, the sporadic drip of run-off, the soggy, muted susurration of footfalls in dampened mulch.

The view from the window yielded to woods all around him. He was in the Grove. Grand Daddy loomed beside him solid as Gibraltar, leaning away to the south. Lightly, he ran a pale hand down the tough, stringy bark to where the tangle of roots tugged upward from the earth. Only the massive height and girth of the tree they anchored could make such roots appear inadequate, most of them being bigger than a man's arm, others than a man's leg. He traced one of the larger ones through its twists and convolutions until it plunged into the ground. At the intersection of wood and soil, his hand rested thoughtfully, the wide gold band on his ring finger gleaming in the dim light.

"—Full-size beds," Bea said, "because they're original. But we do have some air mattresses because we know some folks need more sleeping space."

The forest scene was gone. Through a whirling head, Ben became aware of his hand on the mouse, the sag of seat cushions beneath him, the oven buzzer beeping in the kitchen. Bea heard it too and brought her call to a close as quickly as she could before slipping from the room.

An unsteady laugh escaped him. "Well, what do you know?" He rose from the chair, slapped his palm on the surface of the desk, revolved on the spot because the space was too small for pacing or jumping.

What, indeed. Because that was no daydream.

He had been inside her mind—her consciousness. Daphne's!

There was no other explanation for what just happened.

But *how* had it happened? And why?

"It's what Gladys said," he muttered. "When I'm someplace meaningful to her, when I'm focused on her..." It didn't explain why he thought about her all day yesterday to no purpose, or why he should connect with her here, in the Derwents' cluttered office. But there it was. He pushed aside a mug box with his foot in order to stand right up against the window. Stare out with all his might. *Daphne.*

The scene before him wavered. He heard the drip of rain but also the clatter of baking pans on the counter. The roots underfoot again; the edge of the file cabinet against his arm. A lock of curling hair thrown across his vision as his head turned; the throb of his own head protesting this effort at concentration.

No.

The thought, the one word, pressed briefly upon him and vanished.

"Daphne," Ben said through gritted teeth. "Let me in."

No.

And then the sense, hard to describe, yet certain despite its unfamiliarity—a door closing. A curtain drawn.

He was back in the office. Alone.

He tumbled into Charlie's chair. The computer screen had gone to its sleep mode, curving lines of color sweeping and looping across the black, pen strokes of an unseen artist.

Somehow—however it had worked—he had been inside her head and then...shut out.

She was inspecting the roots of Grand Daddy. The fragile network of fingers that grasped the spinning planet and drew moisture up hundreds of feet to the grow zone. Daphne had closed herself off, but Ben knew what she was seeking as clearly as if she had told him. Grand Daddy's vulnerability.

He jiggled the mouse. How was it exactly that the Dyerville Giant fell? And so quickly? Daphne was right—a century of exposure and wind had not been enough to finish Grand Daddy—why had it worked on the Giant with such brutal efficiency?

A quick search brought up thousands of links and photographs. Especially popular were shots of hikers clambering into the upended cavern of roots or measuring their height against the fallen trunk like so many proverbial ants on a log.

Skimming the search results, Ben found the key piece of information buried several pages down in a book quoted by one of the articles. According to the excerpt, in the initial windstorm, one of the falling trees had slammed into the earth some distance from the Dyerville Giant, but in doing so, it damaged the Giant's root structure. When another falling tree then tipped against the Giant itself, down they both came.

Ben's mind replayed the scene he had observed through Daphne's eyes. The massive roots radiating from Grand Daddy's trunk, spiraling, tangling around and over each other until hidden underground. But he knew that underground these same roots rapidly diminished in size, dwindling to mere strands, racing up to a hundred yards in every direction to absorb as much surface moisture as possible from the steady rain and thick fogs. What these delicate runners lacked in strength and depth they made up for in cooperation. The threads from each tree interlaced and wove over time with those of fellow trees. A hidden, terrestrial web that echoed the one far above. While Grand Daddy no longer had the protection of the canopy—it faced the elements alone—the complex tapestry of root filaments survived, the fabric under pressure as the tree leaned, but holding.

With a glance over his shoulder, Ben closed his numerous browser windows and maximized one of Charlie's poker sites. He leaned across the desk to pull the curtain shut.

"Bea," he called into the kitchen, "do you have Gladys' number?"

If she had not agreed to meet him at the trailhead, he doubted he would have recognized her. Gladys had scraped her dark, glossy hair back into a topknot and sported one of those odd headband-earmuff deals in some shade between gray and beige. Because of the everlasting mist and fog, layers of outerwear concealed her curvy figure, and the pallid light did little to flatter her skin or the circles under her eyes. She wore no make-up but a dash of lipstick, an incongruous note that contrarily made her look older. Ben wondered if she'd caught his cold but knew better than to ask, since he had once made that mistake with Courtney, only to have her snap, "Why does everyone say that, whenever I don't have make-up on?"

"Up for another stroll to the Grove?" he asked when she reached him, striving for a cheerful tone. "Bea insisted I bring the damned wheelchair in case the so-called hike wipes me out, but at least you won't have to push me up the trail."

"Whatever you say, Tourist," she shrugged. "We're all here for your amusement." Zipping her jacket to her chin, she marched past him.

"Hey." He caught at her elbow. "I don't want to put you out or anything. I thought you might like to come, hang out."

"I'm here, aren't I?" she countered. "Hanging out with you instead of working on my screenplay adaptation, like I promised my agent."

"Yeah. But we ended on kind of a not-so-good note the other day, and it looks like that's still the case. What's bothering you, Gladys?"

She jerked her elbow away. "Nothing."

Ben rolled his eyes. "Let me guess what the nothing is, then," he called after her retreating back, "You're still ticked about me talking to Keller."

"I said nothing's wrong!"

Whatever fleeting attraction he felt for the woman was fast withering away, but with a grimace he set off after her.

She set a cracking pace, her progress occasionally slowed by the intermittent fans who accosted her. When Ben entered the outskirts of the Grove some fifteen minutes later, he found her surrounded by a group of teenage girls and their mothers, fielding questions and pointing out the stumps which played a significant role in the book.

Ben took the opportunity to enter alone, his senses alert. Nothing unusual caught his eye or reached his ear, but he had an impression of something behind the closed door slipping away—a person disappearing up a winding staircase.

For the second time he approached Grand Daddy. He had been too focused on the canopy on the earlier occasion to notice the layout of the now-overgrown stumps, how they radiated irregularly from their parent tree, jewels springing from the root crown. Grand Daddy itself reared up nearly from the lowest part of the flat, the ground sloping slightly downward to it on all sides but one. Slowly Ben circled until, like the tongue of a board sliding into its fitted groove, what he saw matched what he had seen through Daphne's eyes some hours ago: the north side of the tree, where the vast roots had been partially wrenched from the rain-softened earth by the immense weight of the lean.

As she had earlier, he ran his hand downward, the length of a larger root. Crouching and fumbling in his chest pocket for the flashlight filched from Charlie's toolbox, he aimed the beam along the underside.

At its worst points there was enough space for a man to crawl underneath—a big man. Charlie, even. That the underbelly of the tree had been long exposed was clear from the well-established forest life the light revealed. Myriad fungi, some moss, beetles. Fairly extensive root rot. He had not been lying to Daphne when he told her Grand Daddy's fall was inevitable.

You see what I mean, Ben said inwardly. And it won't be another hundred years, either.

He had the image of her hesitating, absorbing this, before turning from him again. Ascending.

Sitting back on his heels, he clicked off the flashlight.

Any bald attempts to hurry the tree along were out of the question—axes, chainsaws, tractors—far more plausible would be sabotage to the redwood's invisible anchors. The mat of root filaments running underground a hundred yards in every direction. One could reproduce the fatal action of the Dyerville Giant's arboreal assailant, cutting through Grand Daddy's weakened hold on the earth. If it were done even just twenty-five yards off, he doubted any of the Grove visitors would notice. Ben remembered Charlie hiding the journal in one of the Grove's disregarded fir trees—nearly in plain view. It might be there still had Daphne not frightened him that first time.

Well, he thought. I was right about Grand Daddy falling sooner or later, and I was wrong that there was nothing I could do to help.

He raked a hand through the rich forest mulch, clenching it in his fist.

Why the hell am I considering this? I told her I wouldn't. So why the hell am I?

"Find anything interesting?" Gladys appeared over his shoulder. When Ben glanced around, he saw that the crowd had dispersed following the impromptu Q&A session. They were alone. Her surliness appeared to be in temporary remission.

"Grand Daddy's got some pretty bad root rot on the underside," he heard himself say. "Makes sense. A hundred years or so of exposure to moisture and bugs and invasive fungi."

"You think the tree's diseased?"

"I'm not saying that. I'm just saying its hold on the ground won't last forever." He kept his eyes on the roots, unwilling to let her read his expression.

"That would be a shame," Gladys said slowly. She hunched down beside him. "You're the redwood guy. Think anything could be done about it?"

"What do you mean?"

"I mean, is there such thing as redwood retro-fitting? Could it be propped up?"

He shook his head. "You don't prop up a thirty-story building. The only props were the other trees."

A gust of wind buffeted the branches far above them, loosing a shower of drops onto their heads. Gladys laughed. "You look like a Christmas tree. The water sits on the ends of your hair like ornaments." With her fingertips, she poked a couple of the water droplets, her soft touch reminding him of another hand brushing against his head.

A pang ripped through him.

He wanted to see her again.

He didn't care if Daphne wanted to see him or not. She couldn't give up on him so easily. Maybe they could work out some middle ground. What that could possibly be he had no idea, but there had to be something.

"Are you okay?" Gladys asked. "I know I've been kind of hot and cold lately."

"What?" He stood up, dumping the fistful of mulch. He wiped his hands on his jeans.

She rose as well, giving him a tentative smile which he didn't even see. He was thinking too hard. The ghostly Daphne wouldn't come. Not now, with Gladys around. Considering her recent silence and re-fusals, she probably wouldn't come even if he were alone. Could he summon her in Gladys? Could Gladys summon her?

What had Gladys been doing the other time, when she had her "ep-isode"? Just walking around, he thought. She put her hands on Grand Daddy, but she was already not herself when she did that. She must have been focused on Daphne beforehand, thinking about Daphne.

"I found something," he said abruptly. "Before Keller interrupted me at the museum."

Gladys stiffened. "I saw that guy yesterday, poking around the Bard.

And Alice said he came into Etta's before closing and bought everyone a round of drinks, the bastard."

Cursing himself for mentioning the filmmaker, Ben tried again. "It was a poetry book. With this one poem in it that I've also seen at the Dryad. A Christina Rossetti one. Have you heard of her?"

"No-o-o..."

"Me neither, but it was a poem about feeling dead and wanting to live again." He wished he could remember the words.

A Better Resurrection.

"Yes!" Ben exclaimed. "It was called 'A Better Resurrection.' His heart gave a lurch—he didn't know if he'd remembered or if Daphne had put the thought in his head. "'My life is like a faded leaf...uh... My life is like a frozen thing—'"

No bud nor greenness can I see—

"'No bud nor greenness can I see—'"

Yet rise it shall—the sap of Spring—

"'Yet rise it shall—the sap of Spring—'"

O Jesus, rise in me.

"'O Jesus, rise in me.'"

While the verses came slowly to him, Gladys sagged against Grand Daddy. She covered her face with her hands. Trembled.

When the final words floated away, Ben didn't dare breathe. Didn't dare stir. He prayed no one would come upon them—interrupt what he hoped was about to happen.

Come back, Daphne.

Gladys' head drooped. A shudder swept through her and her arms flew outward, as if she were about to propel herself into the forest by pushing off the vast trunk.

Moments passed. The Gore-Tex of her jacket scraped the bark as her body shook, her knot of hair snagging on it and tumbling from its coil. If she noticed, she gave no sign.

"'My life is like a faded leaf,'" he whispered.

"Aaaaaahhh." The exhalation broke from her, and the sound of it set her free. She danced away from the tree into the open, spinning round and round. Her hands patted her clothing experimentally as a smile broke over her face. Ben recognized the radiance, translated through Gladys' features, and an answering excitement swept him. She could not want to close him out entirely—not if she still chose to inhabit Gladys.

She had panicked the first time he tried to approach her, but surely she knew him better now? It hardly mattered—the effort to restrain himself was too great.

"...Daphne?" He took a half-step toward her.

She turned back to him then.

Shyly, she stretched out her arms.

"Benjamin. I knew you would come."

Chapter 18

Parts of the Whole

Her movement startled him. Not that an embrace was unwelcome, but given her former reserve it was unexpected. Ben had taken several steps toward her before he halted again.

"…Daphne, right?" he repeated.

Her arms dropped, the glow fading from her eyes. "*I am too forward.*"

It was jarring. To hear the same words she had spoken to him the other night, but now in the high-pitched voice issuing from Gladys. Like having a new actress take up a familiar role after the first one opted out of her contract.

"Why have you come back?" he asked. When you told me being together was impossible, pointless, he wanted to add.

"*This is my home.*" The trace of a smile. "*You have sought me. Why have you come, Benjamin?*"

"I wanted to see the Grove again, now that I'm feeling better—" It occurred to him that, while this was true, he could still feel his sundry ailments if he focused. No sensation of complete well-being overpowered him. Was that because of Gladys' body or because this was not Daphne? "And I wanted to talk to you again. See you again."

His supplementary awareness caught an impression of her listening, even holding her breath. Well, of course she was listening. They were having a conversation. He studied Gladys. She held so still she might not, in fact, be breathing.

"Tell me—" he fumbled, "why do you choose to use Gladys?"

Anger whipped along his new nerve endings. The bolt was so sudden and so suddenly gone that he might have imagined it, except his body still buzzed with the shock.

"I do not 'use' her. Her sympathies make me welcome. You cannot understand the hunger for the living—what you have without effort or cost."

"Sorry. It was a poor choice of words. I guess I don't understand." He tried again. "What can you do when you…share…with Gladys that you can't do on your own?"

"I have yet to discover fully. The sensation in itself intoxicates." She was rotating her arms, inspecting Gladys' clothing. Reaching up, she pulled off the fleecy earband to examine it, bemused.

It made no sense to Ben. How could she, on the one hand, beg him to end her endless life, and on the other "hunger for the living"? Ghost-Daphne had never mentioned being tempted by the living. And if Gladys didn't know Item #1 on Daphne's priority list, she couldn't possibly be speaking for her. Except—what to do with their strange new connection? The impressions that flitted through? What to do with the echoes of Daphne's words and sentiments?

Doubt prevented him being candid. "Tell me—what do you want most to do? How can I help you?"

"I want to live."

"But—"

"Not that half-life I experience." She cut him off, her fingers raised as if she thought to put them to his lips. *"No! That ghostly lingering, unseen and unheard by most. Such an existence stretches to eternity and fills me with despair. I would rather cease to be than continue so. But to live again—"* she pressed her fists to her chest *"—to live as she lives—that*

tempts me more than death."

Not a contradiction, then, but a new direction? He wondered—hoped—it might have something to do with him.

It could be that sharing one body had its drawbacks: neither one had clean dominance. There had to be blending. Compromise. Daphne in Gladys' body was no longer Gladys and not quite Daphne. She was some third entity.

All he knew was that, if there was any Daphne in there—any at all—he didn't want to drive her away.

"What is it, then, about Gladys' life that attracts you?"

The answer was immediate. *"Her freedom."*

"Freedom." A shiver coursed through him. "Yes."

"Her utter liberty from the constraints of husband and family and society. She may go where she pleases. She may pursue her interests. Her work gives her independence."

"Oh," he said. "That kind of freedom."

Her smile was rueful. *"Those freedoms were unobtainable when I lived. Yes, I covet those. She is free, moreover, from the burdens of the dead, where time lies in every direction, a desert stretching to eternity. I have walked and walked these hundred years, only to arrive where I have always been. Nowhere. And alone."*

"There have been people," Ben said, thinking of the Derwents and himself.

"They do but pass through."

The words jolted him out of the present. He was back at the wrought-iron bench, on the edge of the Dryad lawn. *You do no more than pass through my world.* The feel of her arm in his grasp before she withdrew. The utter bereavement when she was gone. Nowhere and alone.

His breathing quickened as he stared at Gladys. It *was* her. It had to be. To what extent remained to be seen. But if Daphne had changed her mind—if part of her wanted to live again—that was enough.

She saw the leaping excitement on his face and something in hers answered.

Their hands came together.

"Something else I envy in the living," she murmured.

His grip on her fingers tightened, amazed that she didn't pull away. "Tell me."

Her eyes were dark. They were not the shifting, mutable shades of Daphne's, but the tenderness in them he had never seen from either woman.

"They can love."

Her lips were soft and her breath warm. At first she received him tentatively, passively. Not at all like Gladys, who had wound herself all around him, hands roving and legs pulling him tight against her. Daphne instead hung back, analyzing as she went, much as she had scrutinized Gladys' clothes and body. Ben had patience, though. When she did not object he grew bolder, folding her in his arms and kissing her harder. Her mouth parted slightly. He felt her yield against him.

He had never been one to divorce mind and body. Even in college, where everyone around him hooked up casually, alcohol supplying whatever the night's partner lacked in looks or charisma, Ben hadn't done so more than a couple times. A spark of physical attraction was seldom enough. He required some sort of bond—some affection, a connection. For him to make out as he had with Gladys over the past week had been uncharacteristic. A rebellious experiment born of Courtney's faithlessness.

As he kissed Daphne, he could not hide from himself a growing disappointment.

Because he felt nothing.

He expected, with that strange, unseen, intermittent telepathy between them, that a physical connection would be almost over-whelming. That every sense—including his new one—would light up. Instead—

Releasing her suddenly, he drew back frowning. Was it that there was too much Gladys? That Daphne's appeal was so dependent on her physical appearance that, without it, it left him cold? It wasn't like Gladys was unattractive, God knew.

But she wasn't Daphne.

Hell, thought Ben. Am I really that shallow? Or is it shallow to think of a person as a whole: body, mind, spirit? With Daphne I love the whole, the entirety. —Love?

The word had come to him naturally, without forethought. *Love?*

"*Benjamin,*" Daphne-Gladys plucked at his sleeve to recapture his attention. "*I have displeased you. Perhaps you find my inexperience repellent.*"

"No, of course not," he responded automatically. "This is just a little disturbing. I mean, I don't have a firm handle on what's going on here." At her puzzled look he stumbled on. "Who—how—I mean—who gets to decide who uses Gladys' body? And when?"

Her gaze dropped. "*You would prefer she return?*"

"I didn't say that." He shook his head. "All I know is that it's hard to get my mind around two people in one. Looking like one and seeming like another. And no matter what I prefer, she will come back, eventually. Where will you go when she does?"

"*Back.*"

Back to her slog through the desert of time, he supposed that meant. "Would I see you again? As your old self?"

She didn't answer but merely sighed. There was a scrambling and skittering behind him, and Ben turned to see one squirrel chasing another in circles up a nearby fir. His eye followed them up the trunk until branches hid them and only their squeaks and chatters gave them away. Though impressive for a fir, the tree's highest branches only extended some few yards above Grand Daddy's lowest. They must have stood fairly close together before the redwood began its long lean away.

"*She comes,*" said Daphne-Gladys after another moment.

"Huh? Already? Can you tell her to give us another minute?"

Urgently, she clutched at his wrist. "*Don't forget me, Benjamin! If you care for me, call me to you again. Come for me—help me—*"

With a groan, she slumped to the forest floor, her encumbering hold preventing him from catching her.

~~~

"Euuugh," said Gladys. She rolled onto her back. "Good God."

Ben leaned over her. It was definitely her. If the silky voice hadn't given it away, the cross expression would have.

"What the hell just happened? I have mud on me," she complained.

"You had an episode," he said.

Leaping up, she brushed off her pants, plucked needles from her hair and glared at him. "That must have been amusing for you. And *you* have lipstick on you. Care to explain that?"

"Wow," said Ben. Guiltily he rubbed at his mouth with the end of his sleeve. "This is a tough one. It was a mutual decision, though."

Her slanting brows drew even closer together. "So that's it, is it? I have these 'episodes,' and you take advantage of them? It's not even enough that you're all over me every chance you get—even though there's supposedly 'nothing going on'—but then you try to cop a feel when I'm not myself? Literally *not myself*?" Her voice rose to a squeak and she punctuated each accusation with a hard index finger to the sternum.

"Now just hang on. First off, Gladys, I haven't been 'all over you every chance I get'—whatever we've done was as much you as me—"

"Another 'mutual decision' you mean," she hissed.

"—And I wasn't aware that either one of us was looking for something more," he continued, "so it's kind of unreasonable of you to get mad when I put it like that. Not to mention that I was deliberately blowing it off *to protect you*, remember?"

"Don't raise your voice at me!"

"Don't raise my voice? What the hell, Gladys! You're the one they can hear all the way to Eureka!"

As if on cue, a faint rustling reached their ears, followed by sounds of scrambling over bark.

"The squirrels again," said Ben at a lower volume, forgetting that it had been Daphne-Gladys who heard them earlier.

His companion took a deep, steadying breath. When she spoke again, her voice shook slightly, but it was quieter. "Okay, then. Just for the record, *is* there anything going on between us?"

The forest swallowed her words in a sudden flattening of sound, as if the woods rushed to fill the hush between them. Ben could hear everything near and far: birds, rain, rustling, his own heartbeat. The trees themselves seemed to be listening, waiting on his answer.

Damn. He could say there was absolutely nothing going on and risk pissing her off permanently, or he could say, yes, there was something there, to let her down easy. It was his own fault for messing around with her, heedless of the consequences. Gladys was no drunken frat party acquaintance who would forget him when she sobered up—she was the most prominent resident in the small town where he was stuck for the near future. He should be honest. But if he pissed her off permanently, that would be the end of encounters with Daphne-Gladys, he was sure. And what if Daphne-Gladys was all he got?

His head, quiet most of the morning, began its familiar throbbing. Pressure behind his temples and eyes, tenderness at the back. Must... relax... he thought.

Honest. Be honest, he told himself. But what about Daphne—

Then be minimally dishonest.

He swayed on his feet. "Could we... have this conversation sitting down?"

Gladys made an incredulous face. "I'm the one who just peeled herself off the ground. But fine." She indicated a stump some yards away, decked in the feathery fronds of *Orthodontium gracile*. Ben noticed its seat-like indentation and wondered foggily if that was where young Charlie used to sit and read the journal. There was room for two if they crammed but Gladys opted to stand. Leaning her stomach against the trunk's remains, she plucked individual threads of the moss between her fingernails, a beautician trimming Prince's eyebrows.

"I just got out of a relationship," he said.

She looked skeptical. "How 'just' is 'just'?"

"As in hours before I showed up in Red Gap." He swallowed a sigh. Only wanting to hide his true motives could drag this confession from him. "The reason I left my advisor's project early was that I caught him and my girlfriend together. She was a botanist too. I confronted her and then I got out of Dodge. It was pretty ugly, you can imagine." So ugly, he added inwardly, that I've barely thought of her for the past week.

To his surprise and relief, Gladys' face softened. "Oh, Ben. I'm sorry. That's terrible. I've had a couple of those kinds of relationship-endings myself." She was absently tugging on a fistful of the moss, and when part of it ripped off in her hand she tossed it away. "Then this is a rebound fling."

Inhaling too sharply, he threw himself into a coughing fit. "God, that kills my head," he said when he could speak again. "Gladys— look—I had no business kissing you. I don't know what I want right now. It wasn't fair to you. I have no excuse except that you're very attractive." Not to mention über-willing.

"Okay." She pushed away from Prince's stump and brushed *O. gracile* bits off herself. "You don't know what you want, but you're going to behave yourself now. I'm a big girl. I can deal with that. And this has nothing to do with the fact that you kissed me when I was Daphne."

More coughing. "I—uh—I'm really confused by all that business. Plus, she looks a lot like you. I actually liked kissing just-plain-you a lot better." Which was true, he realized.

Gladys raised an eyebrow but didn't look displeased. "I should probably get you back to the Dryad before you die on me, Mr. Flatterer. Bea would never forgive me." Holding out her hand, she heaved him up, but instead of releasing him, she tucked her arm under his. "You know, we can take this slow."

This *what*? "You mean the hike back down?"

"Don't be thick, Ben," she chided, giving his arm a squeeze. "I mean this relationship."

God, the woman was persistent! Clearly his attempts at sparing her feelings had been too subtle.

They emerged from the Grove and stood where the path widened. Below them on the switchbacks he could see some backpackers holding up a map, tracing a route. The rain had picked up, and Ben felt drops trickling down his collar.

"Gladys." He pulled his arm away as gently as he could. "What I was trying to say in my clumsy way is that I don't think I'm up for a relationship."

"With me." Her voice vibrated dangerously.

"With anyone!" he declared. "I need to take some time. Get my life back together. It wouldn't be right to get involved with you, not when I might be headed out of town for good any day now." It was an outright lie. Even if his health permitted it the very next day, he knew he wouldn't go until he figured out what to do about Daphne.

"You don't have to leave town," said Gladys.

He stared at her. "Of course I do. Eventually. I mean, I'm a registered grad student. I have to show up back at the U sometime, concussion or no concussion. I have responsibilities."

"You just told me your advisor was screwing your girlfriend and that you took off on them and abandoned the project. You really think anyone's holding their breath, waiting for you to show up again?"

"Well—"

"You even think you still have a ... a fellowship to go back to? I'd say it's way more likely that your advisor pulls the plug on your academic career and you have to start over from scratch—without any recommendations from him!"

"What is with you?" he demanded, backing away a step. "You're like listening to a track of my worst fears."

She grabbed the front of his jacket. "I'm sorry. Really, Ben. I don't mean to rub it in. But listen—you don't have to go anytime soon. Some of us have been talking—"

Shaking himself loose, he scowled at her. "Some of who?"

"Some of us: Ray, the Derwents, Joyce, Alice, Clyde, me, others you don't know yet—we thought that, while you were here, we could hire you to do some work for us. Ray was going to come present the idea to you later today."

"*What* idea? What kind of work are you talking about?"

"It was Charlie and Bea who thought of it," Gladys assured him. As she hoped, Ben's thunderous expression dissipated when she named the Derwents. She hurried on. "They thought it would be great to have someone with your expertise put together some information about the Grove for us and Grand Daddy in particular. Make a brochure for us. Come up with a nature-walk spiel. Bea thought your job title could be Tree Champion."

"You're kidding." These must be the "plans for him" Bea kept referring to.

"Why would I be kidding? You're qualified, aren't you? And you owe Charlie for saving your ass out there in the woods."

"Yes, I owe Charlie."

"Exactly. So take the job and you'll be in town for a while."

Tree Champion? Dizziness rocked him.

Gladys caught his arm. "Let's go, big guy. Before you collapse." Propping herself under him, she guided the dazed Ben downward.

At the trailhead she shook open the wheelchair and locked it with her foot. "Don't tell Bea I told you, okay? She wanted it to be a surprise. And for God's sake—pinch your cheeks so you have some color in them. It's been a good morning, right? You made out with Daphne, you scraped me off, and you got a job offer. What more could a guy want?"

A little clarity, Ben thought, as the chair squeaked and rattled its way back to civilization.

He would like to know if the Daphne he made out with was or was not the real deal.

He would like to know why, if Gladys really did consider herself "scraped off," she was humming so cheerfully.

And finally, he would like to know whether Red Gap really ought to hire as their Tree Champion someone who had spent that very morning envisioning its destruction.

CHAPTER 19

Crazy Ladies

Pale October sunlight poured through an unexpected break in the cloud cover, bathing the purple Dryad in an autumnal glow.

As Ben came up the walk, he found himself wondering once more how much of the over-the-top décor was Bea and how much Daphne. With so many more pressing matters to discuss, small talk fell by the wayside.

Charlie had been at work. Orange lights draped the porch railing and columns. Sheaves of corn flanked the door. A patchwork scarecrow sprawled across the swing. Uncarved pumpkins lined the steps. Two new guests stood on the patch of front lawn, admiring. They nodded curiously at Ben as he collapsed the wheelchair and went to prop it against the side of the house.

"Excuse me," one of them said. Her bright green wool sweater clashed electrifyingly with the purple house. "That didn't happen to be Gladys Harrington you were with, did it?"

"It did, yeah."

"Ooh. She's amazing, isn't she? I can't wait to hear her talk. I've read her book four times."

"Yeah," said Ben. "She's got a rich imagination."

He found Bea and Charlie lunching with a guest in the kitchen. Ben's greeting died in his throat when he recognized Carson Keller's thatch of black hair. The filmmaker appeared well-pleased with himself, ensconced as he was between two characters central to Gladys' story, one of Bea's generous sandwiches gripped in his hairy hands.

"You're back, Ben!" Bea exclaimed, half-rising before Ben waved her back into her seat. "You've met Carson Keller, I think?"

"A couple times," Keller said. "He didn't mention me?"

"I know so many famous people in Red Gap they all blur together," said Ben dryly.

"Did you make it up to the Grove all right?" Bea asked. "With his concussion, Carson, I really didn't think he should try the hike on his own, so he called up Gl—"

"I was fine. It was fine," Ben interrupted. *Carson*? "Got a little woozy at the end, but really the best I've felt yet."

"Oh—a good lunch will help, I hope," said Bea, "because some folks are coming over afterward—Mayor Ray, Clyde the veterinarian, Joyce—they want to meet with you."

Ben dug in the fridge for his hostess' bread-and-butter pickles. "What for?" he asked.

"Business idea," said Charlie. "Shouldn't take long."

"It's a surprise," said Bea, clapping her hands together. "I think you'll like it." Charlie must have pressed her foot because she clammed up, still smiling, and refilled Keller's iced tea.

Keller helped himself to a handful of potato chips and crunched away, his contented expression reminding Ben of a cow in particularly rich pasture. "I'm falling under the Red Gap spell, Ben," he said. "I can see why you stay on."

Ben said nothing. He slapped a top crust on his sandwich and joined them at the table.

"We love having Ben here," Bea said fondly. She pushed the basket of chips and the tea pitcher toward him.

Ben looked from Keller to Charlie. "How exactly did you all get acquainted?"

"Familiar story, it sounds like," said Keller. "Charlie rescued me. I went for a morning hike, got a little lost and ended up on this one slope. Then I lost my footing and slid down. Charlie found me limping around on the edge of the woods near the Dryad."

"You got lost in the woods?" Ben repeated. The thought of Keller stumbling around near the Grove that morning was disconcerting, to say the least.

"I'm not much of an outdoorsman," Keller grinned. "Heck. I was probably in shouting distance of town the entire time. Charlie recommended I stick to the trails in the future."

"Prevents erosion," said Charlie.

"Not to mention it's hard to get lost if you stay in plain sight of other people," said Ben. The pitcher rattled against his plate when he replaced it.

"I was in earshot at least, at times," said Keller. He flipped the lid off his sandwich and ground some pepper onto it. His gaze rose calmly to meet Ben's.

Ben felt his chest tighten. Okay, he thought. Bring it.

He turned to the Derwents. "Did Keller tell you he wants to make a movie biography of Gladys?"

"Yep," said Charlie.

"We said we don't know a thing about filmmaking," put in Bea, "but that Gladys Harrington is a popular member of the community and Red Gap is very proud of her." She patted Charlie's arm. "What makes you interested in Gladys as a subject, Carson? Have you done other documentaries about writers?"

Keller shook his head, chewing. He wiped his mouth with his napkin. "She would be my first major undertaking. But her book's becoming a worldwide phenomenon."

"You want to hitch your wagon to a star, of course," said Ben.

"I've done lots of film work, though," Keller continued as if he hadn't heard. "Camera and sound work for my local community access channel. Wedding videos. Corporate training pieces. I made a five-minute short that got picked up by a multiplex to run before their shows. And ten years ago my film school project won a minor award."

Ben hid a smile. Gladys was right, then. Keller was no Ken Burns, no media machine. Just a guy with moonlit ideas of hitting the jackpot.

"An award!" said Bea. "What was that project?"

"A documentary called *Crazy Ladies*," answered Keller. He swished a sip of his tea around, crunching on the ice. "It was a history of some of the female patients at the old Napa State Hospital—you know—the insane asylum. Their archives had some great stuff going back to the 1870s. You okay, Ben?"

Charlie beat on Ben's back until he stopped coughing. "Fine. Fine. All good," Ben gasped.

Keller's face was bland. "I got pretty friendly with one of the facilities guys. He showed me this storeroom full of all kinds of junk—ancient medical equipment, postcards, pictures, patients' things, records. Lots of the old files were supposed to be destroyed, but you know how it goes—it's always somebody else's job, so it doesn't always get done."

Charlie asked the question for Ben. "You know, don't you, that Napa is where Daphne Lindstrom went as a teenager?"

"I do now," said Keller, "but I didn't at the time."

"But isn't that how you got interested in telling Gladys' story?" asked Bea, puzzled. "*Bury Me Not* skips over Justine's time at Napa, but the place is mentioned."

Crunch. Keller downed another few potato chips. "Amazing," he said, wiping his fingertips on the napkin. "Coincidences in life. No, after I discovered the connection, I went back for another visit."

"And did you find anything related to Daphne?" Bea pursued.

"Nothing that could be identified as hers beyond a shadow of a doubt." He shrugged. "That was a dead end. But I did some taping and cataloging for the Gladys story. General background."

"You've already done some taping?" Bea looked horrified.

"Sure I have. I'm making this movie. It just remains to be seen whether it'll be an authorized biography or unauthorized." He shrugged. "Who knows? Unauthorized might even be better for publicity."

An awkward silence fell. Clearly the Derwents were aware of Gladys' opposition to Keller's project and had no wish to be on bad terms with their neighbor. Ben, for his part, could have told them the damage was already done, considering how Gladys responded to his own interactions.

Sensing the shift in mood, Keller sat back with a sigh, patting his stomach. "Well, that was a sandwich every bit as tasty as the one I had down at the Lazy Lumberjack. I thank you, Bea and Charlie. Hope you don't mind, but, while I'm here, could I take a quick peek into the Green Room?"

"Not to film it," said Bea firmly.

"No, no. No filming. Just as a fan of the book and history lover. You know—with that *Crazy Ladies* connection."

Bea's mouth compressed. "Ben's staying in the Green Room now."

"It's all right," said Ben. He pushed his plate away. "A quick look. I'll take you up, Keller."

~~~~~

When the door shut behind them, Ben leaned against it, crossing his arms. "Okay, what's the deal? You were wandering the woods this morning 'in earshot'?"

Keller smiled, his gaze traveling over the furniture and wallpaper of the Green Room. He ran fingers across the rich wainscoting, pulled aside the sheers to inspect the view. "Lovely, lovely," he said. "You know, back in those days, so many people got put away when modern anti-depressants would have done the trick."

Ben bristled. Keller knew nothing of the real Daphne, by his own admission, and Ben had no desire to discuss her with him.

"'Acute melancholia' they used to call it," Keller continued. He peered in the dresser-top looking glass and made a vain attempt to smooth down his springy black hair. "No call for institutionalization in our day and age. Not like some other kinds of mental illness."

"Okay," said Ben. He reached for the brass door knob. If Keller was going to be evasive or mysterious, Ben was not interested.

Swiftly the man was beside him, pushing the door shut again. "Hold up there, Ben. I think what I have to say will interest you, after your morning conversation with Gladys Harrington."

"A conversation which was meant to be private."

"Can I help it if you two are shouting at the top of your lungs?"

"How close were you? Were you eavesdropping?"

"Geez, Ben, it wasn't like I needed a wiretap." He considered Ben's grim expression and relented slightly. "Okay, look—I've laid my cards on the table. Yes, I'm curious about the woman. But I was at a respectful distance. The only bits I caught were the ones anyone on the trails would have heard."

Ben frowned. Pushing Keller aside, he retrieved the bottle of ibuprofen from the dresser and shook two into his palm. "I'm warning you, Keller. Keep your distance. The lady's been pretty clear that she wants you gone. This is borderline harassment." He popped the pills dry. Rubbed the back of his neck. "I'm not gonna help you. She's a friend, okay? I have to take her side."

Keller nodded slowly, not taking his eyes of Ben. "Got it. I understand. But actually I wasn't asking for your help. I meant to help you."

"Help me what?"

"To warn you that you should be careful with Ms. Harrington."

A short laugh escaped Ben. "Excuse me? Dude—I'm not the one

stalking her."

Keller scratched his head, weighing his words. "That visit I mentioned downstairs. Where I went back to Napa State Hospital—"

"Yeah—the backstory," Ben interrupted.

"It wasn't for backstory on Daphne Lindstrom."

"So you said. There weren't any traces of Daphne there. You went for backstory on Gladys."

Keller caught his breath. He looked searchingly at Ben. "You already know, then."

"Know *what*?" Ben demanded impatiently. "That you wanna make a Gladys movie? Yes. That a Gladys movie is really a *Bury Me Not* movie? I figured that out. You got some footage on the grounds; you panned some old pictures. You need help with the voiceover or something? 'From 1889 to 1890, Daphne Chase Lindstrom was a patient of the Napa State Asylum for the Insane—'"

"Daphne Lindstrom wasn't the patient I went back for," Keller said sharply. "I went back because I found out Gladys had been there."

"—Gladys?" Ben felt the edge of the bed behind his thighs. He reached for the bedrail to steady himself. "Meaning what? She's a novelist. She needs to do research, too." The gears ground in his head. "I don't know what you're getting at. Unless…unless you think there was no trace of Daphne Lindstrom there because Gladys got there first?" He thought of the Red Gap Historical Society archives. Had the historian in her been too sorely tempted? Had she ransacked the Napa hospital records for every scrap of Daphne, leaving nothing behind? He could picture her methods: donning the red knit top and twining herself around the friendly facilities guy.

"Yes, Gladys had already been there," said Keller. "But not as a researcher. Not first and foremost, though she may have done some of that to occupy herself. Probably the kernel for *Bury Me Not* came from her time at Napa because she rooted around in the same junk room I did. But if she did, it was in her free time. *Between* her therapy sessions and treatments, if you get what I'm saying."

Ben's mouth fell open.

"She would have had plenty of time for hobbies," Keller mused. "Because Gladys Harrington was a mental patient at the Napa State Hospital for twenty-seven months."

CHAPTER 20

Consensus

"They're here, Ben," called Bea's voice from the kitchen. "It's the unofficial council meeting I told you about."

An instant before her head appeared around the office door, Ben closed the Wikipedia window he'd been poring over.

"More email?" she asked.

"Mmm. I printed a few things. Hope it's okay."

She was already gone, but he heard her throw over her shoulder, "Naturally."

Natural, it was not.

Retrieving the hard copies from the printer, Ben fanned out the pages. *Schizophrenia. Mental Illness. Dissociative Identity Disorder.* He folded the papers carefully to fit in his pocket. He would study them later, although passages had already burnt themselves into memory: "…wide fluctuations across time…can vary from severe impairment in daily functioning to normal or high abilities…" "Multiple mannerisms, attitudes and beliefs which are not similar to each other." "Distortion or loss of subjective time." "…Possibly related to childhood trauma…"

If Keller was to be believed, in her teens, Gladys Harrington had been diagnosed with DID at the Napa State Hospital. Multiple personalities, accompanied by symptoms resembling schizophrenia and mood disorder. It couldn't be true. On the other hand, what motivation would Keller have to lie, when Gladys could so easily deny it and have it confirmed by the hospital?

Twenty-seven months. How was it even possible to spend so long in a place like that at such a vulnerable age and then be deemed cured? Or even functional enough to be released? That she *was* functional was clear, fifteen or twenty years onward—as far as he knew, only he had witnessed her breakdowns.

Mannerisms, attitudes and beliefs which are not similar to each other. No kidding. Like believing a turn-of-the-century ghost inhabits you from time to time?

Distortion or loss of subjective time. Check.

Possibly related to childhood trauma…

What was that Gladys had said about a girl going missing in her neighborhood? A playmate? She'd turned up dead, and Gladys had found her. That kind of experience would certainly freak a kid out, but send her to the mental hospital for years—?

"Ben!" he heard Bea call again, causing him to jump.

Double-checking that he left no incriminating evidence, Ben hurried to join them.

～～～

As advertised, several prominent townspeople were gathered in the Dryad parlor. Mayor Ray was helping himself to coffee from the urn; Joyce looked askance at the various delicate chairs before perching uncomfortably on the fancy-pants crimson sofa, while Clyde the veterinarian sprawled in the matching chair. Two others, whom Bea introduced as Alice, the owner of Etta's, and Rube the mechanic, shook hands with him. Charlie passed a tray of cookies.

"All right, then," growled Ray. "Let's call this meeting to order." His caterpillar brows inched together as he consulted a paper in his hand.

"Looks like we've got everyone present except Gladys—"

"She said she had a conference call she couldn't miss, but she approves," put in Alice, a round little rumpled woman with faded blonde hair.

"Fine," said Ray. "Have a seat, Ben."

The only vacant spot was on the sofa next to Joyce. Ben glanced at Bea, standing in the doorway, but she indicated that he should take it. Fixing a smile on his face, he did, uncomfortably aware of Joyce's meaty thigh pressing his.

Ray cleared his throat. "All right, then," he said again. "Ben—sorry to be all formal about this, but we're a small town and we do things democratically, so we wanted as many of us present as possible. We represent the unofficial town council and chamber of commerce." He frowned at his paper. Cleared his throat once more and began reading, "Over the past decade, the town of Red Gap has experienced a growth rate in revenue of 225%, with 215% of that growth following on the publication of resident Gladys Harrington's acclaimed novel *Bury Me N—*"

"Can we skip down?" Joyce broke in. "I'm expecting a slew of check-ins at 3:00 and Doris gets flustered when she has to do it by herself."

"—*Bury Me Not*," continued Ray in a louder voice. "All available accommodations in town report occupancy levels approaching or exceeding 75% over the past twelve-month period. As a council we have met several times to discuss ways to sustain these numbers and possibly increase them. Even without measures being taken, the possibility of pending foreign-language translations and even a movie adaptation guarantee high interest levels for the next several years—"

"Good garden party, Ray," interrupted Clyde, "The movie'll be in theaters before you finish reading that thing. Ben doesn't need to know all this stuff. Plus, he's addled. The facts and figures aren't gonna stay in his head."

Ben, while resenting the imputation, was relieved to see Ray stuff his paper away and cut to the chase. "All right, then. Look here, Ben. Seeing as you have found your way to our town through serendipity, and seeing as your health and freedom from other present obligations gives you this certain window of availability—"

"We want to offer you a job," said Joyce, pushing harder on his leg with her own as she leaned closer. Coffee breath engulfed him.

"A job?" echoed Ben. He hoped he looked surprised enough. What with Keller's appearance at lunch and the bombshell he subsequently dropped, Ben had not had time to craft a graceful refusal.

Bea gave a hop from the doorway. "We've worked it all out. Ben, you're the missing piece in our whole package. We have the accommodations and the restaurants and Gladys herself to do readings. We have the museum and the trails and the Ghost Walk planned, but we don't have a way to capitalize on the nature lovers. Grand Daddy's been mostly ignored all this time because he's the lone old-growth coast redwood for miles—people just drive right by on their way to Prairie Creek or Del Norte or Jedediah Smith—"

"Except for that one fellow who wanted to take a chainsaw to him," interjected Charlie.

"Yes, him," Bea said impatiently. "But we don't want that kind of visitor. Anyhow, now because of *Bury Me Not*, Grand Daddy is getting all kinds of attention, and we'd love to have information we could share with people. All about the redwoods! A brochure, maybe."

"A big display at the museum," said Ray. "We need pictures."

"How 'bout a nature walk to go with the Ghost Walk?" suggested Clyde. "You could design it, Ben, and train us what to point out and how to handle the questions."

"And Ben has been up in the canopy," added Bea. "Hundreds of feet up! Wouldn't that be something? I saw down near Santa Cruz someone entrepreneurial is offering canopy tours!"

"Wait wait wait," said Ben, sitting forward. He felt sweat spring to his palms and armpits. They hushed immediately, eager to see what he had to say. "Umm...let's not get ahead of ourselves. Bea—first off, one tree doesn't equal a canopy. You could never have anything like a canopy tour with just Grand Daddy. It would have to be lower down, between the firs and maybe some of the younger, second-growth redwoods."

"Ohh." Disappointment shadowed her face for a moment. Then, "But what about just a climb up Grand Daddy?"

"No," said Ben. "Absolutely not. Take unskilled tourists on a rope climb over three hundred feet up? No way. I couldn't be responsible for that. The insurance costs alone would be prohibitive."

"But *you* could get up there," said Ray. "*You* could go up there and take lots of pictures and tell us what you find."

Ben didn't answer.

The council resumed at top speed and volume. "So we'll go with the brochure then." "And the nature walk." "And the display at the museum. I'm thinking on each side of that back wall, by the cross-section—" "That's good, that's good. Like a history of the logging and a what-we've-lost kind of thing." "What about a nature-lover's companion guide to *Bury Me Not*?" "Run that by Gladys. She's the book person." "...Some kind of way to advertise that all the proceeds go toward preserving Grand Daddy—"

"What do you mean, 'preserving Grand Daddy'?" Ben jumped in again.

"It's been leaning a long time," said Charlie.

"I noticed."

"Do you think it could be...reinforced?" asked Bea.

"Bea—" Ben took a deep breath. "Have you ever had to clear the yard of branches after a windstorm? Think how heavy those are, and then multiply that exponentially for Grand Daddy. The thing weighs 1000 metric tons, if it's an ounce. You don't just stick sticks under it."

A silence met this declaration. Ben pushed on. "Look. I think it's a beautiful tree. A marvel. I don't blame you for wanting to make the most of it. But, you've got to know, it's just a matter of time till it comes down." He shifted against the pitiless sofa back.

Or just a matter of time till some out-of-his-mind fool takes an axe to the roots, he thought grimly. He could hardly sit in judgment on Gladys' sanity when his own was so questionable. While he might not think Daphne inhabited him, he was certainly convinced she existed. That she could, if she chose, communicate with him visually, audibly and—God help him—telepathically.

Not that she did choose to, lately. Her absence should have reassured him. He was sane. S-a-n-e. Instead, he felt torn with lowness, wild impatience. If he ever lost it completely and massacred Grand Daddy's root mat, it would only be from a desire to win her back. Which would achieve precisely nothing. At the moment he gave Daphne what she wanted, she would be lost to him forever.

He sighed. "You can't prevent some future huge storm from wiping out Grand Daddy," he went on, "but, apart from praying against acts of God, you could at least keep all those tourists a safe distance away. The longest future for a redwood is one with no people in it."

Dismayed, the members of the council looked at each other.

"But—but—" Ray started up after a minute. "If we block off access to the tree, no one would like that."

"No."

"It would be bad for business."

"Probably."

"Then—" Ray's gaze swung to take in the group— "I think we all agree that's not an option. Every other big tourist attraction redwood lets folks go right up to it. They take pictures with it, climb all over the roots—"

"Even drive through them," volunteered Clyde.

Ben shrugged. "All true. Of course, those trees aren't leaning. Not that I think Grand Daddy would give out with no warning. But no contact would probably be safer, for tree and human alike. I'm just giving you my honest opinion."

"But I think you're saying that, ultimately, there's nothing we can do to prolong Grand Daddy's life," said Bea. "Even if we built a giant fence around the Grove and kept everyone away, that wouldn't guarantee that Grand Daddy wouldn't come down anyhow, eventually."

"That's exactly what I'm saying."

"Well, then." She marched over to stand by Charlie's chair and gave his shoulder a squeeze. "I say we make the most of the time we have. Ben, can we commission this work out of you? Maybe as you study the tree you might come up with some other alternatives to lengthen its life."

His leg jiggled nervously. Now for the refusal. Joyce's thigh pursued his. "I don't know about this," he said. "I can't say how long I'll be here."

Ray's brows re-knit themselves. "Suppose we just kept it to the nature walk material, the brochure, and the pictures? The diorama or whatever in the museum could just be another version of the brochure and walk, with maybe a few additional photos blown up, of course. If you worked on it straight, I don't imagine it would take you more than a week or ten days."

"Some of the pictures might take longer," Bea pointed out. "Since Ben might not be up to climbing Grand Daddy yet."

"Ten days to two weeks, then," amended Ray.

"You mean you want pictures from *up in* Grand Daddy?" Ben asked.

"Of course! You say it's a whole undiscovered world up there," said Bea. "And if Grand Daddy is doomed, we should capture that while we can. That is, if you think it's still safe for *you* to go up."

"One person in the tree isn't going to make a difference one way or the other," answered Ben weakly. "But there are already pictures I could get you of other redwood canopies. Intact canopies."

"They wouldn't be Grand Daddy," said Ray. The others nodded

vigorously. "We'd want shots of what's up there and then maybe the view outward from the top. Think you could do that?"

Ben hesitated. The temptation was great. To be the first, the very first, to ascend it. Possibly a paper could come of it: *Residual Effects of Diminished Cover and Isolation on Damaged* Sequoia sempervirens *Crown, 100 Years Later.* A contribution like that might go some way to salvaging his ruined career.

And then there was Daphne.

If Grand Daddy was the source of her continued existence, could she not be found in its reaches, better than any other place? A shiver broke over him. He shut his eyes, though doing so could not shut out the memory of his dream—clinging to the swaying branches of Hightower, the wind whipping him while Daphne clutched his wrist.

"...Ben?" Bea's voice seemed to come from a great distance.

Ben opened his eyes. His face felt hot from his heart's accelerated beating.

"Give the guy a break, Bea," said Clyde. "He did just fall *out* of a tree and nearly bust his head open." Rising, he strode over to apply his fingers to Ben's wrist.

Ben shook him off. "I'm good. Sorry. No—that's not it. I'm not afraid of climbing again."

"What, then," demanded Mayor Ray. "Is it the money? Seems like you've been running up a significant tab during your stay here: there's the room and board, the doctor's bills, the car tow—"

"Ray Holtz," snapped Bea.

"It's true, isn't it?" Ray persevered. "You're a graduate student, Ben. I imagine you're not exactly rolling in cash. Do this little project for us, and we'll call it all square. Probably still have enough for a little honorarium on top."

"It's not the money," said Ben.

"Then what is it?"

How on earth could he explain? *I can't take the job because half of*

me keeps thinking how I can destroy the damned thing. Because your local
ghost wants me to, and I'm not sure how long I can deny her.

Impossible.

Completely nuts.

Instead of employing him, the good townspeople should commit him. Ben smothered a mirthless laugh. Yeah—maybe Gladys could still pull some strings at Napa State Hospital. Get him a nice room.

"I—uh—don't have a camera or any equipment."

"You make a list," said Ray. "Anything we can't rustle up among us we can have Rube pick up in Eureka."

Rube stopped picking at his blackened cuticles long enough to nod at Ben. "If I can't jury rig it," he said in his soft voice.

"Then it's a deal," pronounced Ray, over Bea's objections to jury-rigging. Putting down his coffee mug emphatically, he went to shake Ben's hand. "Red Gap, it looks like we have ourselves a Tree Champion!"

~~~~~~

As the town councilmen were taking their leave some time later, Joyce managed to corner him in the mud room where he'd gone to fetch the coats.

"I'm glad you'll be sticking around awhile," she said, struggling to catch at the second sleeve of her nylon windbreaker after pulling on the first. Ben obligingly put down the other garments to assist her. "You're certainly looking better than the last time I saw you." Her hand brushed his.

Quickly he retrieved the armload of coats. "Thanks. Feel better too."

She lowered her voice, but the reproach in it was still discernable. "You been spending lots of time with Gladys, but I never did get a chance to finish telling you my own theory on Daphne Lindstrom."

"You didn't, no," he said, ignoring the Gladys bit. "It's been on my mind. I'd like to hear it."

Placated by his obvious sincerity, she pushed the mud room door closed. "Okay, then. It's this way. Remember how Albert Turner worked for Pall Lindstrom? For years, starting when he was still in grade school. Albert was the errand boy, the messenger. He probably saw Lindstrom the most and talked to him the most out of anyone. Then there's the fact that he rose to take Lindstrom's place after the man left Red Gap. I think it points to a special relationship between 'em. The Lindstroms didn't have any children of their own, you know. I suspect Pall felt fatherly toward him."

"Daphne liked him too," said Ben without thinking. *This Albert Turner is a favorite with her.*

Joyce's bleary gaze sharpened considerably, and she left off her contemplation of his chest and neck. "Why do you say that? She did. What do you know?"

"Oh—uh—maybe it was something I saw at the museum. The schoolroom picture or something," he fumbled. "I don't recall exactly."

She deflated. "Oh. No. That's Shane Derwent in the picture with Daphne. Albert was younger than she was by a good five-plus years."

"Right," said Ben. "I remember now." He tried to get her back on track. "So Lindstrom cared for Albert."

"I'm sure of it," said Joyce. "But anyway, I think that's why Albert's ghost is angry—because of his special relationship with Pall Lindstrom. He's mad that everyone thinks Pall killed his own wife."

"And that's why he shakes the bed in that one room?" said Ben, unable to keep the skeptical note from creeping in. "Wouldn't he be better served letting someone know who the real murderer is?"

"Don't you get it—he doesn't want to do that because it would hurt the other person he loves. I mean Daphne."

"Huh?" said Ben.

"Daphne Lindstrom murdered herself," declared Joyce. "She was a suicide, Ben. Albert can't reveal that bit of the story without hurting her reputation. Daphne Lindstrom was no better than she should be, but that doesn't mean Albert wants to expose her. He just wishes everyone knew the murderer wasn't Pall Lindstrom, his father figure."

Ben was conscious of the blood leaving his extremities. The pile of outerwear felt suddenly heavy in his arms.

Daphne a suicide?

He hated the idea. It had been posed to him before, of course, but he had dismissed it from his mind. *That* alternative was admissable only before he knew her. Before she meant anything to him.

But he had to admit it was not out of the question. He thought of her reticence when he asked about her death. The obvious evidence of her depression when alive, from her obsession with the poem to Pall Lindstrom's worries about her spirits.

No.

It was not impossible—it was not even implausible—but he would almost rather think anything now than that she had done herself violence.

Joyce misread Ben's silence and outward calm. "Oh, what would you know," she said disgustedly. "I guess like everybody else you buy Gladys' story."

"I didn't say that."

"Even if you don't, you don't care," she sniffed. "I can see that. All you care about is your trees, I suppose, Mr. Tree Champion. But if you only knew how many millions of people are just dead convinced that it's Pall! Then you'd understand why Albert's ghost is so upset. Gladys raking in the dough while an innocent man's reputation is ruined."

Ben wasn't so sure about the dough, but he got the point. Moreover, he had no further desire to hear Joyce's disturbing theories. "That *would* be upsetting," he said. He patted the heap of outerwear in his arm. "I'd better distribute these. But, Joyce—peace. Next time Albert acts up, you tell him that I believe him. I don't know who did it either, but the two of you have me convinced. It was anyone but Pall Lindstrom."

His pen scratched over the notepad. Digital camera. Rope. Helmet. Jumar ascenders. Descenders. Extra carabiners. Clyde's crossbow. Fishing line. Climber's saddle.

"Can I get some help with this, Ben?"

Ben looked up from his seat on the porch swing beside the stuffed scarecrow. Charlie had backed his truck up to the house, the bed full up with pumpkins.

"Sure thing, Charlie." He lay the notepad aside. "Where do you want them?"

The proprietor ran both hands through his flyaway white hair. "Hope I got enough. Bea likes to line both sides of the driveway with them, all the way down to the mailbox."

"Any which way? Big to small? Alternating?"

"Any which way."

The pumpkins were shiny and slick with mist, white or orange or angry blood-red, a few of them lopsided oblongs like heads of comic-book villains. Loading his arms with them, Ben started at one end of the semicircular driveway and Charlie the other, arranging, rearranging and spacing them out until they met near the apex.

With a satisfied grunt Charlie rolled the final one into place—a genetic monster that in other circumstances would have garnered the blue ribbon at a county fair—and the two men stepped back to admire the overall effect.

"Too many white ones in a row, you think?" asked Ben, pointing.

"Hmm," said Charlie. "Don't like them myself, but Bea said to get every color. How about we break up that run of them and alternate with some of—"

The rest of his decorating suggestion was lost when a distant cry rent the air—frightened, sudden, breaking off sharply.

He and Ben turned in the direction of the sound.

"—The hell?" said Charlie when silence fell again. Nothing more reached their ears until Charlie made a movement toward the trees. Before he had taken two steps, he and Ben picked up the scattered sounds of someone's frantic approach. Sliding, tripping, squelching on mulch.

The man burst from the forest just where the path of tree rounds faded inward. Where Ben had first spotted Daphne Lindstrom.

It was Carson Keller.

The filmmaker's thick hair flopped chaotically, his eyes bugged. While Charlie and Ben stood frozen with surprised recognition, Keller stumbled across the patch of lawn to double over on the walkway, gripping his side and gasping, "Oh, God. Oh, God!"

Ben and Charlie looked at each other, but it was doubtful either one gained much from it. Each was too absorbed in his own response. Charlie remembering his own stricken flight from the woods forty years earlier, and Ben—well, he could hardly imagine what expression he wore, but he guessed it wasn't pleasant. Not if it reflected the surge of suspicion and possessiveness flooding him. What else could frighten a grown man, shrieking, out of the forest? Or rather, *who* else?

Keller's panting was the only sound.

Charlie gripped his shoulder. "Calm down, man. It's okay now. What's wrong?"

Keller's panicked eyes darted from Charlie's face to Ben's to the woods and around again, his mouth still forming the words *Oh, God.*

Ben, too, scrutinized the evergreens crowding the house. He saw only the dark trunks, the greenish-gray light filtering through the branches, the fog gathering strength. He did not see what he wanted to see.

There was no trailing white gown, no tumble of hair, no lightly-stepping slipper over the forest floor.

Show yourself, he commanded silently. Show yourself, damn you!

You think this will work? You think a guy like him can do anything for you?

There was no audible answer—nor did any thoughts not his own flash through his head.

Only this: almost imperceptible pressure against his chest. Her hand.

He knew.

And a flash of hazel eyes.

They were gone the next instant.

CHAPTER 21

Root of the Matter

"You want to come inside, Keller?" asked Charlie. "Have something hot to drink?"

They watched the color gradually return to his face as he sat on the porch step gripping two big fistfuls of hair. He shook his head. "No. God, no. This is embarrassing. I don't need any more witnesses."

"You may have some anyhow," growled Ben. He jerked his chin in the direction of the driveway, where some of the returning guests stopped to admire the new decorations.

Keller glanced up, taken aback by Ben's tone. "You both are taking this pretty calmly. Doesn't either one of you want to know what the hell my problem is?"

"What the hell's your problem?" said Ben.

"Not here," Charlie warned. He led them around the side of the house, digging in the pocket of his overalls for the key to the shed. He shoved aside the lawnmower, wheelbarrow, wet-dry vac, two garbage cans, and an ice-cream maker to reach folding chairs which shrieked with disuse when opened.

Keller collapsed into his. "You gotta give me credit: even after getting lost this morning, I went back into the woods."

"And found your way out," said Ben. "Pretty quickly, too."

"I stayed on the trails this time. Went to the Grove," said Keller. He crossed his arms tight over his chest. "Thought I'd check a few things out."

"How were they looking?" asked Ben dryly. He'd bet his flimsy wheelchair that Keller revisited the scene of Ben's encounter with Gladys.

Keller had the same thought, apparently, because he wouldn't meet his eyes. "I met someone there, in the Grove."

His listeners said nothing.

"A...a woman. I don't know how long she'd been there. I was—er—on my hands and knees looking at something, and then I heard this voice say, 'You also know much of the forest.' Scared the hell out of me, I don't mind saying, because I thought I was alone. I jumped up, and it was this woman in this—I don't know—it looked like an old-fashioned wedding dress or something. She was weird-looking. The light played on her funny. If I was filming I would say I forgot the color conversion filter because she was too pale and bluish and..."

Charlie looked at Ben. Ben was examining tools on the peg-board wall. He unhooked the mattock and hefted it from one hand to the other, testing its weight. He clearly had no intention of adding to the discussion.

"So," said Charlie, "you saw the woman and came tearing back down to the Dryad?"

Keller sat up straighter. Uncrossed his arms. "I hope I have a little more backbone than that. No. I was startled, but I'm a guy who can handle unusual situations. I said to the lady, 'I'm learning my way around.' And she came closer to me and I saw she'd been crying, and she said, 'Perhaps you are he. The one who can help.' I didn't like her so near because she didn't seem to breathe or blink and her eyes were intense, not to mention I've read *Bury Me Not* and done my research on this town and I had a guess who she was. I started to back away.

Maybe I said something about going and getting some more people to help her. That's when she looked me dead in the eye. 'None of them can help. None of them choose to. I have done with them.' She took another step toward me and I backed up again, but there was this giant stump behind me blocking my escape and that was when I panicked. I had to get away. I—I—she was in the way, so I shoved her in the chest as hard as I could and took off—Jesus, Platt! Watch out!"

Ben retrieved the pruners he had dropped, the blades of which had grazed Keller's mop of hair. Speech returned with difficulty. "She said she was done with everyone else, and then you ... *shoved her in the chest?*"

"She was blocking the way," retorted Keller. "Are you kidding me? I see a ghost—someone who died a hundred years ago—and you're worried that I got a little rough? I say if you're still around a century later, you're clearly not fragile." He turned on Charlie. "That's what it was, right? The ghost? That's what I saw?"

Charlie mulled this over. "Sounds like maybe."

Keller leaped to his feet, punching the air with his fists. "I saw it! I saw a *ghost*! I saw *the* ghost!" Panting, he scraped his hair back from his forehead. A sheen of sweat glazed his skin. The next moment he paled, sinking back onto the chair.

"God almighty. I saw it. I'm going crazy. You two aren't even freaking out. This whole town is crazy." Keller whistled, shaking his head. "Unbelievable. I thought it was a load of bull. Tourist crock. But now—you musta slipped something in my sandwich at lunch. I don't know what to think. One thing I do know: it scared the hell out of me, but I'll be ready next time. Forget Gladys Harrington—imagine the movie you could make about this! A genuine haunting. I wonder if it's possible to catch it on film. The trick would be getting it to appear. Maybe if you set up some kind of stationary camera and just let it run and run. Or maybe you could lure it out with promises of help—"

Ben hooked the pruners back on their peg. "I need more aspirin."

He strode past Keller, his hip knocking the back of the chair. When he threw the shed door open, a gust of cold, moist air swept in, sending a swirl of dead needles skittering across the concrete.

"Where's he going?" he heard Keller demand. "This conversation wasn't interesting enough for him? I *saw* the damned ghost." And then, just before the door cut off his voice: "But that's it, isn't it? He's seen it too. That's what's wrong with him. Ben saw it too."

~~~~~

"It." *It*?

This is the guy you pick? fumed Ben. The one who calls you "it"? You pick a guy like Keller because you "have done" with everyone else?

He flung aside the curtains in the Green Room, his hands on the glass, his lower body pressed to the sill. Daphne, damn you, talk to me.

She must be getting desperate in her old age. Throwing over Charlie and now Ben in the space of a week. Hitting up any idiot she found in the woods who could hear or see her.

He rested his forehead against the cold panes.

You've hit a new low, Platt, he told himself. Jealous because the local ghost chose someone else to haunt. Had he imagined it—that he and Daphne made a connection? That she felt something for him as well? He remembered her light teasing, the feel of her fingertips against the back of his hand, the whisper of them in his hair. Charlie never mentioned Daphne trying to touch him. Would she have tried it with Keller?

And then in the yard—the hand on his chest. "What were you trying to tell me?" he murmured, his breath fogging the glass. Was that good-bye? An apology? A warning?

He sifted through his mind for anything that was not him, but there was nothing. No trace of her voice, no shared vision.

"I'm sorry I cursed at you," Ben muttered. "If you heard that. It might have happened more than once." Reaching up, he rubbed the window pane with his sleeve for a clear view of the yard. He pictured their first encounter there, the downpour, the darkness which swallowed all but her glowing form.

Silently his lips moved. He recited what he remembered of her poem. A couple phrases came easily enough now, but they dissolved in empty air. They were no magic incantation, no summons. The conifers bordering the lawn huddled gray-green and secretive.

Daphne.

Please.

Shutting his eyes, Ben envisioned the wrought-iron bench. *You are a friend, Benjamin Platt.* If I'm a friend, he argued, why won't you answer me? You wanted one thing out of me, I said I couldn't give it to you, and now you're gone. What kind of friend are *you*?

A handful of raindrops pattered the glass. Ben's head rocked upward, imagining in it, for one hopeful second, the tap of fingernails. The swift movement brought its attendant wave of vertigo, but when it passed, he saw nothing but the breeze-blown course of the drops and the sway of the branches which cast them. He turned from the window in disgust.

It was only when he threw himself in the armchair and heard a distinct crunching sound that he remembered the papers hastily stuffed in his back pocket that morning. Poor Gladys. He had forgotten all about her and her mental travails. Daphne's supposed possession of Gladys could never compete with the real Daphne's appearances—how much less so when most or all of Daphne-Gladys could be attributed to the latter's split-personality spells, drug-induced delusions, or pure acting? The discovery of Gladys' history of mental illness relieved him, rather. Whatever was going on, he at least wasn't imagining it. Gladys might not be in her right mind when she had her "episodes," but neither was she in Daphne's. No wonder he could kiss her and feel nothing. Beyond vindicating his doubts and lack of emotional connection to her—in whatever guise—it also explained her volatility, why she was horny half the time and pissed off the other. If Gladys' level of "impairment" experienced "wide fluctuations across time," this must be what a peak looked like.

Ben smoothed the sheets out on his knee and stared at them, unseeing.

One thing was certain: there was no one he could talk to about Gladys' history. Gladys least of all. Keller's disclosure would go no further. Why he deemed it necessary to let Ben in on the secret was puzzling. Was it just the sympathy of one man for another—he couldn't bear to let Ben be taken in—or was it something more sinister? A threat, perhaps: I have discovered this much about her. Cooperate or be exposed yourself. Yet the most shocking thing about Ben—that he had communicated with a ghost—was now no more than Keller had done himself. He was safe there.

What more had Keller seen and heard? Ben replayed the Grove scene in his mind, this time imagining Keller hidden from view, eavesdropping. There was Ben's inspection of the roots. Then the discussion of Grand Daddy. Then—well, Ben had wanted so badly to talk to Daphne again that he had *used* Gladys—there was no other word for it. He had done what he could to coax a Daphne performance from her and succeeded. Somehow the words of the Rossetti poem provoked a breakdown.

Ben's train of thought jarred to a halt.

The poem.

How could he have remembered the words—no, *heard the words*—in the Grove, if even just a few minutes ago they eluded him again? It wasn't like the damned thing was *The Iliad*, but he never had a head for poetry. "'My life is like a faded leaf,'" Ben muttered. "'My life is like a frozen thing'... something about sap of spring... Jesus..." He didn't know the words. He didn't have it memorized.

He could only conclude the words came to him earlier because he really had heard something. Someone had been speaking to him.

He had assumed, of course, that the telepathy he shared was with Gladys in that moment. But if Daphne-Gladys was truly, in actuality, *Gladys*-Gladys, that was out of the question. Which meant the real Daphne must also have been present. Present, and speaking to him. Had she, in fact, been answering his summons?

Think, Ben, think.

There had been those impressions—the listening, holding her breath. Not Gladys after all. Daphne. She had been there with them— yes—he had felt her presence, her attention. Until—

The computer print-outs slipped to the floor, unheeded. Ben leaned forward with a groan, covering his face with his hands.

Daphne had been there, invisibly, up until his question.

Why do you choose to use Gladys?

That surge of electric anger he perceived—good God. He assumed it issued from the woman before him, that she objected to his tact-lessness. But it must have come from Daphne herself, furious at his mistake. From that moment on—yes—from that moment on, her invisible presence was gone. Withdrawn.

Ben couldn't say he blamed her. He wouldn't especially want Glad-ys running around impersonating him either, deliberately or not. Did that explain all of Daphne's anger, or could there have been—hope flickered through him—a touch of jealousy in it?

The beating of rain on the roof and windows swelled to a crescen-do, but Ben barely noticed. He yanked his fleece and jacket off the curving coat-rack hooks. Rummaged in his duffel bag for a baseball cap and his head lamp. He would need new batteries.

"Are you headed out again, Ben? It's nearly dinner," said Bea when she saw him grab the key to the shed.

"There's something I need to check out while I'm thinking about it," he answered, heading to the mud room for his boots. "I may be a while. Just save me a plate, please."

Guilt pursued him as he made his slow way to the Grove,

squelching through the sodden mulch. Because of the late hour and the heavy rain, the trails were empty, which was just as well since he had to take frequent breaks. It wasn't only the lingering effects of injury and illness—Ben was loaded down with a shovel, a mattock and a small lantern. Bea watched him go with concern, and Ben palmed her off with some feeble explanation about wanting to track the angle of Grand Daddy's lean as they entered the rainiest season.

He had something else entirely in mind.

The battery lantern didn't cast light very far, but it was enough. He would switch on his head lamp when he started digging.

The Grove waited for him, hushed and still. There was no sound but the rain, and even it was muted and filtered by its contact with a thousand porous surfaces. Where Ben stood, sheltered by the crown of Grand Daddy and his lesser attendants the Douglas firs, the rain might almost not have been. He let the tools drop to the forest floor. Set the lantern on the ground. Sank against the trunk to gather his strength.

If he expected her to show, simply by virtue of his return, alone, he was disappointed.

Ben didn't bother with words. Although he doubted Keller would be eager to return here so soon after his recent scare, there was no need to take chances.

He lay his head back slowly. Reached out with his mind. He pictured the seismographs he had seen, the pen zigzagging across the drum of smoked paper, tuned to capture the tiniest oscillations.

Daphne. Are you here?

There was something. It shot across his nerve endings and was gone. But it left a trace, a shadowy negative. He saw…was it…huckleberry bushes? And ferns brushed aside.

His eyes scanned the Grove, seeking a match. The details were too few. Huckleberries and ferns in a redwood forest were a dime a dozen, though the particular arrangement he had seen evaded him.

After a few minutes' frustration, Ben tried again.

Daphne. If it's Gladys you're upset about, I can explain. The cliché made him grimace, but it didn't matter anyway. She wasn't listening. Not that he could tell.

Sighing, he hoisted the shovel over his shoulder, grabbing the mattock and lantern in his other hand. "Ben Platt, Tree Champion," he said aloud. "Here goes nothing."

Grand Daddy's roots might be thin as filaments, twenty-five or thirty yards from the tree, and they might be just under the surface, but tapestry was the word for them. Carpet. Mat. Not to mention how they were tangled up with everything else under the first foot of soil. Rocks, decaying matter, roots from every other living plant, from fir tree to fern. Ben turned the soil with the shovel and then hacked at the roots with the axe head, using the adze end to free obstructions. After half an hour sweat was running down his back and his body screamed in protest. Not surprising, considering the only exercise he'd had in two weeks was a couple leisurely hikes, helping Charlie yank out the garden, and a few minutes of lightweight pumpkin-lifting.

He rested on the shovel, breathing deeply, trying to ignore the increasing throb of his head and the tendency of the forest to lurch and spin around him after each burst of effort. Really, he'd had dumb ideas before, but this one surpassed all. It had taken a falling *tree* to cut through the Dyerville Giant's root mat—one concussed and fever-weakened man armed with a mattock didn't have a hope in hell. What he really needed was a monster sod-cutter, but he couldn't quite picture getting Ray's approval on that one.

It wasn't working anyhow. If Daphne wasn't going to come even when Ben did what she wanted, she wasn't coming at all. He should just give up and go home. Come up with another plan, like turning the tables on Keller by tailing *him* around.

Another few feet. Then he would fill the dirt back in and leave it for tomorrow. Or never.

Grunting, Ben swung the mattock over his head, wincing as it bit into the ground and sent shock waves through him. The slender roots gave way beneath the blade, but there were thousands of them. He struck again. And again. Swing. Jolt. Pull free. Swing. Jolt. Pull free.

As he found a rhythm, he thought he might just tackle one more patch. To the base of the nearest fir, say.

Fatigue made him careless. He was two-thirds of the way to his goal when his left foot skidded over a slick patch of moss. The mattock wheeled from his hands, revolving like a track-and-field hammer, its handle taking out the lantern. In an instant, the light went out. Ben slammed down on his side, his head narrowly missing a coconut-sized rock chucked aside earlier, the impact sending both baseball cap and headlamp flying.

For a solid minute he was too disoriented to move. He lay, eyes screwed shut, as the predictable dizziness and nausea washed over him and then receded. Tentatively, he flexed his fingers and toes. Nothing seemed broken, thank God. Except Charlie's lantern. But at least he wouldn't have to crawl back to the Dryad, once more in need of Bea's nursing and a day in bed.

In fact, Ben thought, he was beginning to feel…fine. Better than fine. He rubbed his thumbs along his palms. The blisters formed by the swing of the mattock had ceased to exist. They were gone, his skin as smooth as if they never were.

He was, he realized, perfect and well.

Ben's eyes snapped open.

CHAPTER 22

Emptied

The Grove was no longer dark.

A glow had stolen over it, brighter and steadier than the battery lantern.

Ben launched to his feet, knowing he could do so with impunity and afraid she would vanish again before he could see her.

But there she stood. His elusive, maddening ghost. Like a man in the desert who stumbles on an oasis, his eye traveled over her, afraid that thirst and yearning had brought her into being and that she would fade away the moment he mistook her for reality. But, no. There was her thick, waving hair, pinned up and back. Her long white gown. The flawless moonstone of her skin. And those eyes. They were green now, bright as grass in full sun.

"I don't know how I ever thought Gladys could be you," he said, when he was able. "Except that I wanted her to, and she wanted her to."

"*Tell me why you wished for such a thing.*"

At the sound of her voice, he smiled. Half in joy, half in relief. He must look like hell, covered in mud and debris, but Daphne didn't appear to notice. Her smile answered his. He felt the urge to grab her hands as he had Gladys' but refrained.

"Because we're connected," he began hesitantly, "We both know it. You can…keep me out, but it's there all the same. I've been a little crazy since you said good-bye to me. I've been a little crazy since I first saw you. When Gladys had her spells—I—I was a willing participant. Because I wanted to be with you."

Laughing, he shook his head. The conversation was weird. On one level were the words, and, on another, everything else. Impressions, undercurrents, emotions assailing him and crackling like electricity around him. Some were his, some hers. He picked out gladness, relief, understanding, confession—the wisp of jealousy, its fragility belying its strength—and something else…mourning?

"I cannot offer what she offers," Daphne said. In an instant, she dropped the curtain between them and the atmosphere cleared.

"No," Ben protested, reaching for her. "Don't shut me out." Daphne retreated one small step before his hand dropped. "I won't touch you," he said unwillingly, "but please explain."

"Benjamin, I am not like you. Once I was, but no longer."

Yes, yes, he knew this. He was passing through her world, and so on. His impatience must have been evident because the corners of her mouth curled upward in a rueful smile. *"I mean not simply the obvious, that you are alive and I am something other. I mean that what you want is impossible. We cannot be together."*

"Well, why not?" he countered. "Just for a time? I'm not asking you for forever." If she would only agree to the present, he would deal with the future later. "All I'm asking is that you not decide before we've even tried."

He saw her ring glint as she clenched her fists. *"I tell you it cannot be. Do not tempt me, Benjamin."*

"Can't be…because you want to be…freed? I guess I understand. A hundred years—more—is a long time to hang around." On the other hand, if the damned tree might hang on another century, what was so terrible about spending a couple years with him?

"A hundred years," repeated Ben. "You've seen people come and go." A flare of jealousy darted through him as he thought of the generations of Derwent men. Generations of their obsession with her. An obsession, he assumed, not unmixed with attraction. Impossible that it couldn't be. Had the feelings been mutual?

"You don't even remember their names," Ben said, "but every one of them got longer than a couple weeks."

The vivid green of her irises dimmed. *"What do you accuse me of?"*

He hardly knew. But the pent-up frustration of the past several days—no—of the one-sidedness of their entire relationship spilled out. "Of using me! Of using everyone! What is this? I didn't know you existed until you scared the hell out of me in that tree. Then I'm laid up here with my injuries and you come knocking. You come wanting my help. Like you've wanted everyone's help. But if I say I can't give it to you, then you're gone. Sorry, Ben, for turning your life upside-down. And, no, we can't talk about it, even though I'm supposedly your 'friend.' I mean, what the hell is that about? You've got this history of driving people to—to—*despair*—and you don't care what happens to them—to us—if we can't do what you ask. If we won't do what you ask. God, Daphne! Charlie was the only sane one. Deciding to ignore you, to let you work your voodoo on whoever you wanted, but not on him."

If he hoped dimly for an apology, he was disappointed. Whatever chemical-metaphysical combination fueled her unearthly glow, it kicked it up a notch. He almost had to squint to look at her, even more so as she closed the distance between them.

"Are you not at complete liberty to do as you please? To choose, as Charlie has done, whether you will engage with me or not? Has not every single one of these 'people' you refer to enjoyed the same rights? I have asked for their aid, yes—perhaps in my despair I was more persistent than some might have wished—can you not understand how few possibilities have been open to me? But they—these 'people'—have ever been free to do as

they pleased. *To answer, to ignore, to engage, to flee, while my bondage continues without end. Is that torture not enough to secure my pardon, if I have done you or others wrong?"*

The blaze of her anger fed his. "You call us 'free'? I should only speak for myself, but from what little time I've known you, I'm guessing those others weren't any more free than I am once you got a hold of them. How free am I after you've haunted me? Made me doubt my sanity, caused me physical injury, made me consider doing things I would never have done in a million years—" here Ben kicked at the shovel planted in the ground, which gave a resounding clang, "—you've invaded my *mind*, for God's sake—"

"'Invaded,' indeed! Have you not been calling to me for days? You welcomed those very 'invasions'—"

"Of course I did! Haven't I said? But I couldn't help it. That's what I meant. I meant it's your fault in the first place. Don't give me this bullshit about how free I am."

Her mouth trembled. For a second Ben thought she might cry, but then, to his utter amazement, Daphne blossomed into her vivid smile. *"... Bullshit'?"*

He paused. Wavered.

No, he was not going to pretend everything was fine. It might have been only hearing such an unlikely word on her lips, but he felt some of his wrath leaking away.

"Sorry about that. It means ... uh ... nonsense."

"I worked out that much," Daphne answered dryly. *"In effect, you say my words are just that much humbug."* She gave a snap of her fingers.

Ben struggled to keep to the point. "Honestly, Daphne, how can you say I'm free? You think if I left Red Gap tomorrow I'd be free? That you wouldn't still haunt me, even if I never saw you or spoke to you again? You think any of those men were less bound than you, when they had to run off or drink themselves dead or see you every day for forty years and pretend they saw nothing? Charlie's the only one who's survived you, and I don't know if I'm half the man he is."

She didn't answer.

He repressed a sigh, moved to retrieve the shovel. "Look at what I was doing." Scooping up the disarranged soil and mulch, he tossed it back over the severed roots. "It made me so wild that you tried to talk to Keller today. I couldn't stand it. So here I was, doing exactly what I said I'd never do, just to get you to talk to me."

Still she said nothing, holding herself immobile as marble while he worked. It was a crap job, half-assed for sure—Ben would have to hope the distance of the sloppy dirt heap from Grand Daddy would protect it from notice. He had neither the time nor inclination to do better.

Only when he planted the shovel upright and came back with the mattock and cracked lantern did he look straight at her again.

Two tears coursed down her pale cheeks, silent and steady. They were not the first, as the wetness of her skin showed, though she had made no sound. No gulping sobs and dripping nose for Daphne Lindstrom. Maybe those were symptoms of physical unwellness which could not touch her.

"Oh, God," said Ben. Had she looked this way when Keller saw her, and the man shoved her away in terror? Ben felt bad, rather. Guilty. God knew she couldn't help being caught in endless limbo, nor for getting over-focused on it. Not any more than she could be blamed for her eerie beauty or his own—or others'—reaction to it. She wanted to be done with it all, and damn the consequences. He could understand that. If he weren't such a heel.

"Hey," he said gently. "Daphne."

"F-forgive me, Benjamin."

"For what? For choosing me? Abandoning me? For making me think I had to do this?" He threw down the tools. His hand stretched halfway toward her and then dropped to his side. "Hey. Look at me. I'm my own person. You're right. Every choice has been mine. Including this one. That was…cowardly…of me to pin it on you."

"*No. Forgive me that I cannot give you what you want.*"

"You keep saying that. Do you mean that you can't give me time?"

She shook her head. "*That, indeed, I can give you, Benjamin.*"

"But you won't, then." He tried to absorb this. "You don't want to be together because you want so badly to be finished."

New tears brimmed over. "*Benjamin, with you I believe the time would not hang so heavily upon me. With you I would not begrudge a lengthened stay here.*"

He felt weight drop from his shoulders as elation rushed through him. She did care for him. She must! Suddenly it didn't matter if she made no sense, if he had betrayed his own values for her. Or if he was one in a long line of men who had been willing to do so. It didn't matter if she might have felt the same, said the same, to every Derwent man from that day to this. Not if, right now, her heart was his.

Ben couldn't help himself. He reached for her then, his hands closing on her upper arms, lightning firing the length of his body as he felt the solidness of hers in his grasp. Daphne made a soft, gasping sound, her eyes locking with his. He thought he would drown in their wheeling shades.

"Yes," said Ben. "Let me in."

She did. The curtain between them flew up. He braced himself against the tide of thought and emotion, planting his feet instinctively, though it was not the kind of onslaught that could be met that way. He saw the ferns again, the huckleberries. Then he was looking down on—on himself and Gladys, lip-locked at the foot of Grand Daddy. A stab. The wisp of jealousy, here and gone. And then all was Daphne. The whole world. Wistful, hungry with love and longing. The force of her feelings buffeted him. *My dearest. I cannot—forgive me.* A vision of their lips meeting, and Ben could not say if the vision was hers or his own, but he bent his head to hers and kissed her.

The world shifted. The planet. He felt the lurch but didn't care. All that mattered was the warmth of her mouth, the smell and taste of her. She was forest and earth and rain, with a note of lemon woven through, the scent of the redwoods. He pressed her body so tightly to his that he felt the bones of her corset through her layers of organdy and lace, and his own jersey and fleece and Gore-Tex. He must be crushing her. Reluctantly, after a time, he loosed his hold, only to find Daphne's hands in his hair, pulling him closer again. *Love.*

For an age they clung to each other. His mouth moved to her jaw, the tender underside of her chin, her neck. His fingers buried themselves in her curls and he felt the waves loosen and tumble down, sweeping past her waist.

Forgive me, Benjamin.

Her lips found his again and parted in welcome. She sighed, her arms tightening around his neck, her breath mingling with his. So caught up was he that he ignored the second heave of the ground beneath him. And the third, merely stumbling to regain his balance. Only when the ringing building in his ears threatened to drown out all else did he raise his head to find his feet unsteady and gravity bearing down irresistibly. He reeled, his weight falling full against her. Daphne cried out as she staggered back. Her hands scrabbled at the sides of his slick jacket to hold him up, but in vain. He collapsed.

"*Benjamin!*" She dropped to her knees beside him, pressing her hand to his heart and then withdrawing it the next instant. Her breathing shallow, she bent over him. He felt tears splashing on his face but could not lift his hand to comfort her.

"U-u-uhh." His voice wheezed out. What the hell was wrong with him?

She hushed him, weeping, rocking back and forth on her heels, her skirts spilling every direction.

Mustering his strength, he groped for her hand, but the second his fingers brushed hers, she backed away, shaking her head. "*No,*

Benjamin. No more. Oh, forgive me, my love. I was too selfish. I could not help myself. I thought only of me."

If he had been able, he would have laughed. Forgive her for this? After all he had accused her of, she felt guilty for the best thing that had yet happened to him?

Bizarre, though. He felt as if every calorie of energy had been squeezed from him. There was no pain—he still felt completely intact, from his head to his formerly-blistered palms—but he could not sit up or speak to save his life. The ringing in his ears, which he now realized was inside his head and not from without, grew louder. When he tried to think his thoughts into Daphne's head, he only grew confused, shouted down.

"Yes," Daphne was saying. "Did I not warn you that you would be weakened by your time with me?" Her voice faded in and out, and to his muddled perceptions it lost its ordinary clarity, as if it were running through a modifier. "But even in that I deceived you, my love, because I was too weak. I did not tell you it was my touch that would deplete you. I would not have you fear me. It was my touch that connected us, but at a cost to you. Forgive me, Benjamin."

Her touch.

That first brush of her fingers across his knuckles, the back of his hand. He had gone down that time—spent the night in the yard—but he had attributed that to his weakened state, the concussion, the fever coming on.

Yes, it was after that encounter that he first heard her voice in his head. At the museum. Her wry little comment about Nell Holloway. A connection forged.

And the second time, at the bench. He remembered every nerve-ending kindling when she rested her hand on his forearm, when she brushed his hair with fingertips light as butterflies. I slept for twelve hours straight after that, Ben thought.

You did.

And the seeing inside your head? That was new.

In answer she gave him a picture: his hand clutching her upper arm, the puffed sleeve crushed in his grip.

Ah.

God—what would kissing the woman do?

He was fading. Sleep pressed his eyelids. He made another effort: You touched me first.

A silent laugh, bruised with apology. *You extract another confession from me. It was not merely your charm—I remarked your reaction to me. I sought to influence you by every means possible.*

Witch. Ben managed a watery grin. Did you know the bond it would make?

There was a hesitation, an evasion. Then, reluctantly, *I knew of the bond. I had made them before.*

Even half-comatose he was aware of unpleasant stirrings. He gave her the picture: his lips on hers, his hands in her hair, her stranglehold on his neck. It was a question.

She shrank back. *Once only. He… suffered. I vowed I should never again endanger him or… another… so.*

He could feel the moisture from the ground seeping through his jeans and hair. If he had had the energy, he might have tried to hide the next thought from her: Was it Shane Derwent?

Daphne pondered this, her gaze fixed on the trees. *Perhaps. The names grow dim, as you know. My forbearance was to no avail. Though we never touched again, he faded away. Drank himself to inebriation and early death.*

In all truth, Ben didn't give a damn what happened to Shane Derwent. Not only had the man gone and married someone else, breaking young Daphne's heart—if Pall Lindstrom's journal was to be believed—but then he had carried on with her even after marriage, until his jealousy overpowered him and he murdered her.

"No." Daphne spoke aloud. "*You do malign him.*"

She didn't need to read his thoughts to sense his skepticism. *"What became of me was my own doing. He never harmed me. Yet following my death, the power to harm was all mine, as you now see, Benjamin."*

He didn't. He knew only that the peace of sleep beckoned. Ah, well. At least if she lived another hundred years, long after she had forgotten Ben's name she would still defend his reputation.

Daphne found little humor in this observation.

He heard her light tread moving away, but he had already half drifted off. The last thing he remembered was his headlamp reappearing. She clicked it on, laid it on his chest.

Rest now. I will never forget you.

⌇

What happened next was blurry. Ben awoke to find Daphne gone and other voices penetrating the woolly haze. Charlie. Clyde, maybe.

Arms lifted him. He struggled to find his feet but ended up propped up on either side until they reached the bend in the trail where the wheelchair waited. His head lolled on his chest as they rattled and creaked back to the Dryad.

"…Doing with those tools out there?" Clyde asked. "Digging something?"

Charlie's mumbled response escaped Ben.

"Well, you're gonna have to call my brother-in-law in Eureka again or drive him over. There's something seriously wrong with this guy… fell and banged his head again?"

More mumbling. Ben's foot slid off the plate and dragged along the ground until Clyde noticed and stuffed it back on.

"On your head be it, then, Derwent. I still say he could use an MRI. Though, if he doesn't have any medical insurance, he'll have to be Tree Champion for a decade to pay *that* off."

Unconsciousness reached cloudy limbs to draw Ben back.

Daphne?

With his last ounce of wakefulness, he opened his mind, threw the doors wide.

Huckleberry. Evergreen huckleberry... *Vaccinium ovatum*, by the looks of the deep red shoots and glossy leaves. And the sword ferns again. Wind and swaying. The sharp dart of raindrops trickling down her neck.

She sat with her legs tucked to her chest, her forehead resting against her knees.

I myself have done this.

CHAPTER 23

Elusive

Late October in the North Coast Mountains.

It rained steadily, making up in consistency what it lacked in force. The ground grew saturated underfoot; the streams ran full, dumping into the Yoak. The water level rose, covering the first rows of boulders Ben had spotted from the Overhang. Record rainfall, the people of Red Gap noted. Which, in such a perpetually damp climate, was really saying something.

The Dryad continued to hum with activity, and, as Halloween approached, every place in town reported no vacancies. The ramshackle, barebones rooms above Etta's even found occupants—penniless college students on a lark.

Despite the mud and muck, devoted *Bury Me Not* fans continued to slog up the trails, making the soggy round from the Grove to the Overhang back to town. Mayor Ray led the inaugural, lantern-lit Ghost Walk, which met with such popular response that additional tours were added. Over at the Come On Inn, Albert Turner shook the haunted bed from time to time. Even the legendary headless lumberjack made isolated appearances. One afternoon two women came screaming into the Blind Bard having spotted him through the streaky windows of the mill. On another occasion he scared the daylights out of Emma when she was out back of Etta's, dumping the trash. It was Carson Keller who finally exposed Clyde and Rube in cahoots. One early morning when Keller was headed to the Grove for another day of filming, he came upon them re-stuffing the lumberjack's oversized flannel shirt, the ceaseless rain having threatened to make him not only headless but also shapeless. But by that time Keller was enough of a town familiar that he revealed the secret to no one who probably didn't already have suspicions.

Of Daphne Lindstrom, however, there was not a whisper.

When Ben was well enough to sit up, Bea propped him in a back parlor, that the curious guests could resume their tours of the Green Room. But none of them reported anything unusual. No heartbeat in the wainscoting, no slender hand on the rain-glazed window, no glimpse of a trailing white gown through the same.

If Keller saw her again, he never mentioned it, though the couple times Ben had seen him, Keller looked at him with an unreadable expression.

Despite Clyde the veterinarian's misgivings, Ben neither died nor suffered crippling brain damage after his most recent physical breakdown in the woods. Indeed, Clyde could find nothing new wrong with him, no reason why Red Gap's Tree Champion had to spend a solid ten days in bed. Ben's former injuries, from his concussion to his persistent cough, continued to heal, albeit at a snail's pace, as if every ounce of his energy had been diverted to simple maintenance.

"I'd say he's a mite scrambled," Clyde reported to Charlie and Bea over coffee one morning, "but he was already *that*. Half the time I was talking to him, he didn't seem to be listening, but he told me he's fine, fine, fine."

The crease appeared between Bea's eyebrows that was more frequent nowadays. "You don't think it could be mono, then?"

"He's got no symptoms, Beatrice. And we didn't know him before he knocked his head, so we don't even know if this absent-minded-ness is just who Ben Platt *is*. You wanna hear my educated guess—I'm thinking he might be having his quarter-life crisis."

"His what-the-crisis?" growled Charlie.

"Quarter-life crisis. Carolyn was yammering on about it to me the other night because her baby brother is going through one. Jeremy keeps getting degree after degree because he can't figure out what he wants to be. First he's pre-med, then he's pre-law, then he wants to be a vet like me, then he thinks maybe seminary. I told her folks the way to help him make up his mind is to cut him off. Make the boy earn a living. Now here's this Ben—he's already in between things, then we offer him this job and say we're gonna pay his bills here, and next thing you know he's laid up for more'n a week."

"You saying he's lazy?" asked Charlie.

"Ben is not lazy," said Bea.

"I'm saying he's got a good situation here. Maybe too good. We have to make sure he isn't taking advantage of it. I've talked to Ray, and he agrees. We got to give that boy some deadlines."

⁓

If Clyde or the others had known how constantly Ben's mind was working, rather than being relieved, they might have become even more concerned. True, nothing appeared to be going on from the outside: he slept, he stared out the window, he scratched a few notes, he fiddled with the new climbing saddle Ray ordered him, working it between his hands to break it in.

Internally—well, that was another story.

After his rescue from the woods, Ben slept for twenty hours straight. When he finally awoke, starving and still spent, he discovered he was no longer alone.

It was not that she spoke to him more—Daphne said nothing. It was the awareness of her, the bond between them. A faint mournfulness at the edges of his consciousness that had nothing to do with his own feelings. He was, on the contrary, elated. A little punchy.

When he was recovered enough to be deliberate about it, he probed at the edges of their connection, figuratively knocking at the door. She could still shut him out when she chose, but it required much more effort. As if she were just on the other side, her full weight against the barrier to keep it in place. And he surprised her more often. Bursting into her head with no warning. He caught further glimpses of the Grove, the Dryad from the woods—one time he even saw Keller in conversation with Gladys near the Overhang. And more than a few times he saw the familiar setting of the huckleberry bushes and ferns.

Is it your secret hideaway? he asked when he found himself there again. This place? And *where* is it?

Gently but firmly, she shoved him back out of her mind.

I'll figure it out, he told her.

She didn't answer, but he felt her caution, her refusal.

"What's with you, Sweetheart?" Ben murmured aloud. "You're stuck with me now. May as well talk to me."

All too present was Gladys. She took to coming by daily, armed with ironic gifts of flowers and cards for the "convalescent."

One morning it was an armful of unseasonal gladioli. Another, a vase of purple lisianthus in the clutch of a teddy bear.

"You shouldn't have," said Ben.

"You're the talk of the town, you know," replied Gladys. "Or at least of the locals. As much as any live person can be."

"Meaning what?"

"Meaning you've successfully puzzled and frustrated us." She perched the vase on an already-overcrowded occasional table and detached the obnoxious stuffed animal. "Everyone wonders if it really was an accident that brought you here. And why you're injured and sick so often. They debate whether or not you're getting worse. Or if you're hiding out from someone or something."

Ben scowled at her. "I'm not doing this on purpose. And you already know my story."

"Some of it." She wiggled the teddy bear's paw at him.

"All the interesting bits," he rejoined. It wasn't like she was the soul of transparency.

Gladys set the bear down. "I do try to stick up for you," she shrugged. "Not that you need me. Bea turns into this total lioness whenever someone dares to express doubts. But I'm warning you—if you can at all manage it—I'd advise you to crank out some work and crank it out soon."

"I've made some notes."

She held out her hand and he stuffed a sheaf of papers in it.

"What do you know," Gladys said, some minutes later. "These could actually work."

"You sound surprised."

"I am. Most people write like they just learned last week. I was afraid hiring you meant a giant, unpaid ghostwriting job for me, but other than getting rid of all your technical terms I don't think I'll have to do too much."

By technical terms, he supposed she meant the Latin scientific names. It wasn't worth arguing about. He changed the subject. "How's your screenplay adaptation coming?"

She made a whuffling sound with her lips and tossed the brochure draft on the floor. "It's not, really. I'm discovering screenwriting is not my forté. In fact, I've been hitting Carson Keller up for tips."

Ben stared. "Are you kidding me? I thought you considered him the spawn of Satan."

To his amazement, she gave a girlish giggle and looked away. "Yeah, well, he might not be so bad after all. It turns out he's changed direction with his filmmaking plans and chosen something more to my liking."

Although he waited for her to continue, she merely smirked at him in a way he suspected he was supposed to find winning. He sighed inwardly. "I take it he's not planning to do your life story anymore, then."

"Nope—now it's Daphne's," she declared, smacking the armrest of her chair in triumph. "Why cover me when there's someone so much more exciting around? Oh, come on! What's your problem? This is great news. Now, instead of spying on me, we'll just do a couple interviews with questions we agree on beforehand. It's perfect. The rest of the time he's off in the woods with all his equipment—though this might be a ten-year project because he seems to spend most of his time trying to fend off the elements—"

Ben was waving his hands to interrupt her by this point. "What's he doing in the woods? Shouldn't he be at the museum digging through the archives?"

Gladys cocked her head at him, considering. She had taken him by surprise, but Ben made an effort at a poker face. He did one mental sweep—shut an inner door because he didn't want Daphne catching any of his agitation.

They heard the phone ring in the office and Bea's swift footsteps across the kitchen floor.

Hitching her chair closer to his, Gladys resumed. "Not that kind of life story. I should have said, Keller wants to do Daphne's *afterlife* story. He's gone all *Blair Witch Project* on us. You saw that one, right? Where these film students go to check out these murders and get picked off—the movie itself is based on the 'footage' recovered after they're all dead."

"He wants to make a *horror* movie about Daphne?" Ben tried to keep a steady voice. The guy was unbelievable! He shoved her in the chest and now wanted to depict her as some woodsy nemesis?

Gladys was still watching him. "You don't like the idea? I thought it was fabulous. He saw the ghost, you know. She scared the crap out of him, and now he's a believer."

A mercenary believer, thought Ben. "You seem to know a lot about what's going on with Keller."

"I do," she said simply. "The world kept on spinning as you lay dying, after all."

If Ben were a conceited man, he would think her newfound delight in needling him sprung from his rejection of her. Apart from batting her eyes at him, she was all business today. No rubbing up against him, no allusions to past intimacies. He wondered how Keller's and Gladys' unlikely alliance had come about—had it involved the red knit top?

"So he's set up cameras in the Grove? Does he honestly think he can capture her on film, when so few people have actually seen her?"

"Cameras, a recorder. He wanted to do a whole bit inside the Dryad and the Green Room especially, but Bea put the kybosh on that. She also nixed interviewing Charlie. She's sweet about it, of course, but Keller is a little frustrated."

"So what's happened?" Ben prodded. "Has he…captured anything?"

Gladys looked as if she might like to draw out the suspense further, but something in Ben's expression made her change her mind. She shrugged. "Not a thing. Not one teeny, tiny little thing. If he hadn't seen her himself I think he would've packed up and skipped town days ago."

He couldn't help a sigh of relief. "Maybe he'll give up soon anyhow. If there's nothing to be seen, there's nothing to be seen." And Ben would make sure there was nothing to be seen, if he had to hound Daphne ceaselessly to ensure it. "If he can't get any footage, he can't make a movie. No one will want to watch him interview himself. And besides Keller, no one but Charlie, me, and you have seen her. I'm betting Charlie doesn't want to be in his movie any more than I do."

She had risen from her chair to retrieve Ben's notes. Patting the stack neat, she laid it on a side table. Watching her studied movements, Ben felt a prickle between his shoulders.

"But you've agreed to be interviewed, of course," he said.

She gave a mock sigh. "The price of freedom, alas."

"And you're famous enough that that would probably be enough," Ben continued. His hands balled into fists. "Does he think you've seen her, or does he know that you—you—"

That caught her off guard. She whirled on him, eyes narrowed. "That I have episodes? No, he doesn't know. Nor will he."

"How can you be so sure?"

"Unless I've completely misjudged you, I'm betting on the fact that you're not going to tell him, Benjamin Platt!"

God—what *was* he going to tell her? That Carson Keller knew about her history at Napa State Hospital? No way. If he told her that, she would know that he himself knew.

What was Keller's plan? Did he really want to make a ghost documentary, or had he just found a clever way around the author's objections?

"That day at the Grove—" Ben began haltingly, "—the day of your last episode when I—uh—when we kissed and then had that argument—I found out later that Keller spent that morning wandering around in the woods. Charlie 'rescued' him and invited him in for a sandwich. Keller said he was lost, but I don't know how much he overheard. He said it wasn't eavesdropping because we were being so loud."

Gladys caught her breath but said nothing.

"All I'm saying is not to take any of Keller's assurances at face value," said Ben. "He says he's making a ghost story now about Daphne—fine. But that doesn't mean he isn't still hoping to come at you from a different angle."

He saw the motion of her throat as she swallowed, turning her head to the window. "I ought to be flattered, I guess. Whichever way you slice it—*Bury Me Not*, Daphne's ghost—Keller's interested in me."

"That he is."

Resuming her seat, she folded her hands in her lap. "He's an ugly man, isn't he? Fascinating and ugly."

"I don't know about fascinating or ugly," said Ben warily. "He's hairy, I'll give you that. And new. I know you like new people."

"You're being generous," she sighed. "But you're right. He may not be fascinating. Though I suspect he genuinely *is* ugly. Not all men can be handsome and talented like yourself. You may be sickly and lazy—people are divided on that—but everyone agrees you're good-looking."

His mouth twisted. If he was sickly, it wasn't his fault. He couldn't say he was glad to hear the bantering note return to his companion's voice, either.

He said it without thinking, letting that inner door fall open again: You see what I have to put up with.

She was there this time. Faint, musing. He no sooner registered her presence than he bolted up in his seat.

"Jesus, Ben! Are you okay?" Gladys laid a concerned hand on his arm. "You're all covered in goosebumps."

"Foot fell asleep," he said, fumbling hastily for a lie that wouldn't add to his "sickly" reputation.

Daphne was retreating.

Don't go! Wait. Talk to me. He shut his eyes. Was she upset to find him with Gladys? Jealous? He rifled through the array of impressions.

No. She was neither. What then?

His shoulders sagged as he fell back against the chair, oblivious to Gladys' hand now clutching his own.

There was the shade of mournfulness he recognized, staining all. The regret. The tenderness. The woman really had some crazy idea of renouncing him. How the two of them could ever be together he had no clue, but parting was equally impossible. Unthinkable. Spend the rest of their lives having to shut each other out?

Ben sat at the window meditating long after he convinced Gladys to go.

Of all the images he had of Daphne, the one that most occupied him was the lovely girl, high atop the redwood, the one who clung to his wrist as the world fell around them. Tossed by wind, shrouded in fog. As remote from humanity and her earthbound incarnations as the isolated tree which shared her fate.

CHAPTER 24

The Ascent

Ben hadn't counted on an audience.

But in the time it took him to recover his strength and to gather the required tree-climbing equipment, anticipation among the town councilmen peaked. Word from them spread to the tourists, meaning that he was peppered with questions at the Dryad breakfast table and whenever he set foot in town. When? How? Could they watch? Was it safe? Could he teach them? Could they try it? What was the highest up he'd ever been? Had he ever fallen? Did he think Grand Daddy would turn out to be the tallest tree in the world? What did he think was up there? Even Bea begged him not to make the attempt until after nine a.m., so that she could leave the guests' breakfast dishes in the sink and come up to watch.

Now there looked to be at least fifty people thronging the Grove. They jostled to be closest to Grand Daddy, apart from those who, choosing vantage over proximity, scaled the nearby stumps. Carson Keller himself must have arrived at the crack of dawn to set up shop: his angled lights beamed strategically at the base of the tree while he perched on the remnant of Good Witch, aiming his handheld camera at Ben. Ben wondered if Keller had been sick himself—his clothes hung off him and dark smudges beneath his eyes discolored his cheeks. Gladys occupied his canvas director's chair, her legs crossed and ankle swinging jauntily.

"Make way!" bellowed Mayor Ray. The man even had a whistle, which, to his credit, he gave only feeble peeps on, as if knowing outright blasts would be a bridge too far. The crowd parted respectfully for Ben and the Derwents, closing in again when they eked through.

"Wow," Ben said, dropping his armload of gear, "the rain didn't keep anyone away."

"If we waited for dry weather, we'd be waiting a long time," said Clyde, shouldering his way to the front. He cradled his precious crossbow the way some women might carry a purse dog.

While Ben had mapped out and led the Hightower ascent for the U's project team—a nerve-wracking experience because he wanted to impress his advisor and justify himself to his peers—he found he was hardly less on edge before this larger gathering of complete neophytes.

For one thing, the hordes were trampling the delicate flora, and he spotted more than one person trying to strip off a souvenir from Grand Daddy's fibrous bark. For another, everyone wanted a clear view and pushed inward on the circle. When Ben hunkered down to dig the reel of fishing line from his pack, Joyce's crotch came even with his face.

"Uh—I'm gonna need a little room here," Ben told Ray. "Actually, a lot more room."

His breath came faster. He rocked off his heels, sinking onto his backpack, his hands tight on the reel. Around him he saw feet and knees swaying, stamping, surging. Joyce's crotch approaching and retreating. He heard the mayor now putting the whistle to full-lunged use. "Back up! Ben needs everyone to back up! Give the man some room to work! You there—make way."

"Can he get up on one of the stumps so we can all see him, then?" demanded one woman.

"Only if he wants to," retorted Ray. "This is an expert tree-climber here, and we can't be telling him how to do his business. Back up—back up!"

"Ben—do you feel okay?" Bea's voice came to him, tinny and distant beneath the roar of his heartbeat. "Is it your head?"

It wasn't, for once.

He tugged on the strap of his helmet, trying to concentrate. To fend off the waves suddenly breaking over him. No, it wasn't his head or his health. Nor was it just his own nerves.

It was that, all at once, Daphne was with him. And she was beside herself.

She had her full weight against the door between them—that had been the case since her brief appearance during Gladys' last visit—but such was her state that she could not prevent spillover. Fear leaked through. Distress. Outrage.

He could get no mental picture of her, but he hardly needed one. He had never seen or sensed her like this before. And despite her emotional condition, he could not help his own heart from leaping with joy. He had missed her.

Shhhh....shhhh, darling. Ben might even have said this aloud, but fortunately nothing could be heard over all the ambient noise. Is it the crowd that bothers you? They're a pain in the ass, I grant.

You must make them go.

Now he was truly smiling. He had not heard her voice, even in his head, since she left him prostrate on this very spot.

Why?

They press so. I beg you, Benjamin.

Both Clyde and Bea were leaning over him now, concerned. Clyde went for Ben's pulse again, God bless him, and Ben dragged himself reluctantly back to the moment. "I'm good. I'm good," he told them. "Give me a second. And some air." They obeyed instantly, joining Ray's efforts to shoo people further away.

He returned to the matter at hand. They only want to watch, love.

No one will come up with me. I won't let them. I'll be alone. And you'll be there, won't you? Waiting.

He felt her hesitate. Then another throb. He caught fear, regret—a trace of longing.

We cannot be together. I tried to tell you.

Because you think you would harm me.

Because I do harm you, Benjamin. Your long recovery bears witness to this. You must go.

Go where?

Away.

You're giving me up?

I have given you up.

You'll have no one to help you, if I go.

Perhaps the damage you already inflicted will avail me. The rest, as you say, I must trust to time and patience.

Ben rose to his feet, registering the eager hush that fell around him. He sent out his own pulse of anger. Tell me this, then, Daphne—if you've thrown me over, why have you still been in my head? Close at hand?

In response there was a swell of shame. He could almost see color wash her pale cheeks.

I feared you would not survive. I tried to stay away. But I am … weak. That is the reason you must leave. Leave Red Gap entirely. You, Benjamin, must weaken the bond I so foolishly made.

Like hell, thought Ben, purely to himself. He wasn't going anywhere. Spinning out a couple yards of the fishing line, he reached for Clyde's crossbow. A challenging whistle rose to his lips: the Marine's Hymn.

And if I don't?

Her shame evaporated, replaced by indignation at his casual manner. He nearly saw her that time—a flash of eyes. And then Daphne gave him a picture. Aloft, on high, she was looking down at a couple locked in an embrace. Ben caught the wink of metal and a sweep of colored silk and memory supplied the rest: it was his first kiss with Gladys, when she climbed into his lap in the wheelchair. There was a rustle to his left, a snapping. He felt the rough bark slide beneath his hands, and then—he released. The branch plunged to earth.

Ben paused mid-whistle.

So that was her, then, the little vixen.

He should have known, since the woman was responsible for every single injury he'd sustained over the past few weeks. His eyes swept the crowd, almost expecting to see that white-gowned figure among them. He didn't, but a slow grin spread across his face.

That the best you can do, lady?

Bring it.

<hr />

"Okay, I'm gonna need everyone to back up," Ben called. "Way up. The first thing I'll be doing today is trying to shoot this fishing line over one of Grand Daddy's branches. If I can do that, I'll use it to pull the climbing rope up and over. But everyone has to stay clear. The line has a weight on it that I don't want knocking anyone, and some of the smaller branches that can't support weight are sure to come down. Really, you all should be wearing helmets. If you see something falling, yell 'headache!' and get clear."

His speech alarmed the onlookers sufficiently that the clearing around him expanded. Those on the fringes even stood exactly over where he'd been hacking the redwood's root mat. Daphne should appreciate that. He certainly did. Destruction of evidence.

Ben circled round to Grand Daddy's leaning side. Easily 120 to 150 feet to the lowest sturdy branch, but Clyde's Excalibur looked up to the task. He sucked in his breath. Here went nothing.

Nothing, indeed. Ben's first shot sailed into the gray heights, snagged over an epicormic spray and, when he tugged sharply on the line, yanked the whole thing clean out. The ineffectual branch crashed down—shrieks and gasps drowning out his shouted "Headache!"—pelting those closest with rebounding twigs and bark.

That did the trick. The tide around Grand Daddy's base sucked back magically. Only the helmeted Ray, Clyde and Charlie remained anywhere close to Ben.

He scouted through binoculars before his second attempt. Ray nudged him a couple times, pointing at likely branches and offering suggestions until Clyde shut him up.

The second shot raced upward, tracing a perfect, narrow arc over the branch jutting from northeast of Grand Daddy's steepest tilt. Cheers broke out as Ben caught at the weighted end of the line.

He handed Clyde back his crossbow (which the veterinarian held proudly above his head to renewed cheers) to concentrate on attaching the smooth blue arborist rope to the fishing line. Once they were knotted together, Ben patiently reeled in the fishing line, drawing the rope up the long climb, over the branch, and back to the ground. He suppressed a grin when this, too, met with applause. Eat your heart out, Gladys Harrington.

A tiny seed cone plummeted from the tree's upper reaches, bouncing off Ben's helmet with the force of a squirrel landing on his head.

"Pride goeth before destruction, and a haughty spirit before a fall."

Ben glanced upward, laughed aloud. Admit it, woman—you're impressed.

As if he were leading botany section to a class of undergraduates, Ben talked his audience through the next steps: tying the bowline knot to which he would hook in; draping the long tail of the stop knot over his right hand, coiling it four times over his thumb to construct the Blake's hitch, the sliding friction knot that would allow him to ascend and descend if he were not using a Jumar ascender; he demonstrated how to make footloops and don the climbing saddle; how a three-way carabiner worked, hooking the saddle to the rope; the description and operation of mechanical ascenders. And like an undergraduate class, they shouted out questions, made him tie and re-tie the knots, define his terms. Ben knew their own hands were itching for rope—he didn't envy them having to stay earthbound when he would get to disappear into the redwood's crown, scale the roof of the world.

Keller, in particular—Ben could see the gears moving in his head. When he descended later, he would have to bring the rope with him. He was not going to be responsible for any covert attempts by the filmmaker to get aerial footage. Come to think of it, he would probably need to shoot the line up every time he wanted to climb and take it down every night, or else some yahoo was sure to give it a try on his own and find death hurtling toward him at terminal velocity.

With this in mind, he made one last speech before he began his ascent. "Uh—I've been doing this for years. Which means it might look straightforward, but I wouldn't recommend you just get out and try it. Seriously—take it from a guy who just fell thirty-five feet from a Doug fir a couple weeks ago, and who's only here by the grace of God to tell you about it—tree-climbing can be dangerous. Even deadly. It's almost impossible to survive a fall from the redline—fifty feet up or so—so don't just try this on your own unless you really want to crater out."

He checked his pack one more time before hoisting it on his shoulders: camera, extra rope, tape measure, folding saw to cut off dead branches, water bottle, protein bars, headlamp, descenders, fleece, gloves, spade, plastic bags and jars for soil and plant samples. Ray shoved a walkie-talkie in. "In case you need to communicate with us on the ground."

Ben nodded. He slid his feet into the rope loops and grabbed hold of the ascender. He took a deep breath, hoping he wouldn't have to take too many breaks on the way to that first branch. That would only be the start of it—he would be less than halfway to the spire of Grand Daddy—but at least the upper climb would be out of eyewitness view.

If he needed to sit on the damned branch and take an hour to recover before tossing up the next climbing rope, that would be completely his own business. Or—well—his own business and Daphne's.

His fans broke out in another smattering of applause when Ben worked his way to a level above their heads, twirling slowly on the ropes. Cameras clicked; flashes went off. Gladys wasn't kidding when she said not a lot happened in this town.

"This might be the highlight for you all," he called down. "I plan on spending most of the day in the tree, and you won't be able to see anything, apart from the occasional widowmaker pitching down 300+ feet to spear you like a shish kabob, but I promise I'll have pictures and tell you all about it." Now, go on—*git*, he added to himself.

No one budged.

Sighing, Ben shook out his arms and reached for the ascender again. Let the full-body workout begin. Tuck his legs. Click the trigger. Slide the ascender up the rope. Bring his other hand to meet it. Slip the trigger. Pull up with his arms while he tucked with his legs. Two feet gained. Repeat.

The upturned faces shrank as he climbed. Once, when one foot slipped from its loop, causing him to break rhythm and spin on the rope like a trapeze artist, a collective gasp rose to him, but for the most part he ascended into increasing silence. There was birdsong, the tapping of needles in the breeze, the sound of his labored breath, but these were soothing.

The last he heard of his spectators, the last he saw of them, was their enthusiastic response when he gained the targeted branch. Whistles, foot-stomping, cheers, applause. Ben waved sheepishly, too spent for much else. Then he swung his legs up and around the branch, found a firm seat and took a look around him.

At the lowest point of Grand Daddy's crown, Ben found himself still in the thick of neighboring trees, all those which had benefited from the logging of the Grove a century earlier: younger redwoods, firs, hemlock, Sitka spruce. The fall of the titans opened up worlds of space and sunlight to the upstarts, and they thrived. Despite the efforts of the hundred-year-old redwoods to catch up, however, the ancient Grand Daddy continued to preside over all.

As for the crown itself, it was a glorious mess. Typical of his kind, Grand Daddy had long ago given over vertical growth for lateral, most of the branches just above Ben's vantage having sprouted new vertical stems of their own—new trunks, in effect. With horizontal arms growing in turn from these vertical stems, these reiterations mirrored the original trunk-and-branch architecture. So thick did this mirror forest-in-the-sky grow not twenty feet above him that Ben thought he could free climb after ascending just one more rope. Two at the most.

He was eager. Impatient. It would be easy to make a mistake now. Not only did the rich world of the canopy await him, Daphne Lindstrom awaited him as well. With that sixth sense that joined them, Ben knew he drew closer to her, to a place where she could not shut him out. Why this would be, or what this meant he did not know, but he would soon. Her very silent trembling revealed as much. She feared his approach. Dreaded it. Welcomed it.

He checked for traps above: fragile epicormic branches, dead wood suspended and waiting to give way, insect nests, poison ivy. Weighing the coil of rope in his hand, he considered. While he knew his own infinitesimal weight had no impact on the massive tree, both the angle of lean and the sway would increase as he climbed. Dangling over certain death would be disconcerting, to say the least.

His first few throws succeeded only in getting tangled in intermediate stubs of dead wood. Each time he rewound the rope he sent showers of needles, twigs, and some larger branches cascading to the forest floor. Judging from the shrieks and scuttling sounds that carried to him, there was still a numerous crowd below, but they had been warned.

With the detritus thus cleared out, Ben's fifth attempt not only cleared the target branch, but the weighted end of the blue rope swung exactly back to him. He was in business. He pocketed the ascender this time. Without everyone staring at him, he wanted to do this one old school. Bowline knot. Blake's Hitch. Twenty more feet. Start a new rope and go again.

When he climbed to a height above the surrounding trees, he entered the densest section of Grand Daddy's crown. The trunk-and-branch reiterations were so many here that, if he hadn't known better, he might have thought himself in a forest stand, rather than hundreds of feet in space. But this forest stand boasted features uniquely its own: limbs and trunks grown back toward each other, fused, for strength. With the centuries the wood almost flowed together, forming bridges and buttresses linking its iterations. Grand Daddy, strengthening its core, growing relentlessly and indefatigably. As if the Grove, long lost, had been transported to the sky. Here and there Ben spotted a war wound—a dead trunk or hollows carved by past fires—but they had to be sought out. Everywhere he looked there was green. Not just the green of the redwood's needles, but the green of every other living organism making its home in the tree's reaches. Clumps of sword and licorice ferns springing from dark soil deposits and bursting from cracks in the bark. Masses of salal, studded with the swollen blue sepals that resembled berries. Gray-green hairy manzanita, *Arctostaphylus columbiana*, straddling the more exposed areas. There was even, rising from a pocket of soil, a California bay laurel tree. In the far distance, past the wooded rises and falls, stretching charcoal-gray to the horizon—the Pacific.

Eden, he thought. Eden in the rain.

Ben unhooked his carabiner. Life was so thick here he didn't think a clear space could even be found to fall through. He wound the rope carefully around the branch and struggled out of his pack. He would take a few pictures now, not only because that was the purported reason for his ascent, but also to give Daphne time to compose herself.

He pictured her trapped in the same small room with him, shrinking back against the walls to avoid contact. She was cornered. Would she hide? Flee? Attack?

A burst of static nearly caused him to drop the camera. It issued from the depths of his pack. "Ben? Ben?" came Mayor Ray's voice. "Everything all right up there, over?"

Rolling his eyes, Ben ferreted out the walkie-talkie and crushed the push-to-talk button. "Everything's A-OK. Over."

"Good to hear. Have you reached the top yet, over?"

"Negative. I'm in the heart of the canopy, taking pictures. For safety reasons, this is going to be a short conversation, over."

"Roger that. Contact us if you need anything. We'll be taking it in shifts to guard the down rope—make sure nobody tries anything funny. Over."

"Thanks, Ray. I appreciate it. Over and out."

~~~~~~

The day was mild for the season, the drizzle tolerable, except for when a gust would cause the dripping foliage to empty its contents on Ben. Stowing the walkie-talkie, he pulled his second fleece on. The ground crew was taken care of, he'd caught his breath from the climb, he had every picture he wanted from this vantage point—Daphne would have to forgive him for exploring.

Once more he received the impression of the cramped room. A heartbeat that was not his sped in his chest.

"Daphne," murmured Ben. He hoped speaking aloud would calm her.

"*You must come no further.*" Her voice rang out, half-commanding, half-pleading.

"Look—I understand. You're afraid of harming me. Believe me—I have no intention of touching you when I'm 300 feet off the ground. Even I can see the danger in that. Could I see you, though?"

She didn't reply. The wind dumped another splattering of drops on him. Enough of that. He shrugged back into his pack. "Ready or not, here I come."

He sensed a scrambling on her part. A yielding.

"*On your own head be it, then.*"

Ben grinned. "Amen."

As he expected, Grand Daddy's lean and sway accentuated at this altitude. Ben stuck to the uphill side, weaving his way between the closely-packed trunk iterations, careful of slippery patches. "This is amazing up here! Beautiful. I don't know if I've ever seen a crown structure this... prolific. Parts of it are even dry—the rain can't get through. Some of these soil pockets are crazy deep. I've got to measure them. And the flora—there's almost more growing up here than on the ground—"

Something of his enthusiasm must have infected her. "*You are not the only climber. Nor the only explorer.*" An unexpected note in her voice took him a moment to identify. Was it...pride?

"Of course not," he responded. He shook a branch above him to loosen any debris. Finding a foothold, he began working his way to the next level. "But I'm the first one up Grand Daddy. In my field you get points for being the first to climb a wild tree—an unclimbed tree." Hoisting himself to a sitting position he paused for reconnaissance. "Usually you get to name it, but—alas—you robbed me of that privilege."

"*You are not first to climb this tree, Benjamin.*"

He laughed at her insistence. "First *alive* person, then. Hate to break it to you, hon—it doesn't count if you're some half-disembodied ghost who doesn't have to obey the laws of nature. Speaking of disembodiment, would it be too much to ask to have this conversation face-to-face?"

"*My fate amuses you?*"

"I'm in stitches." He clicked another few shots: a clouded salamander, mats of leather fern, a pair of varied thrushes. "Seriously—you're not coming out? I would enjoy my triumph that much more if you could reflect my gloating back to me."

For the first time, he heard her laugh. The rich, delighted warmth of it made him want to hear it again. *"I doubt even Grand Daddy's generous limbs could hold both my poor self and your monstrous self-satisfaction."*

"Oh, so my self-satisfaction is 'monstrous,' is it?" He rubbed the leaves of the shrub brushing against his leg. They were dark green and glossy, leathery, springing from deep red shoots. *Vaccinium ovatum.* Evergreen Huckleberry. Dozens of the bushes inhabited this level of the canopy, crowding more thickly as he worked his way inward to the main trunk. His eye followed the unbroken stretch, noting where clusters of sword ferns punctuated it. Ben's heart did a funny flop. Huckleberry and ferns. He had seen this combination before—many times. If only in his mind's eye.

He strove to keep his voice casual as he picked and struggled and climbed his way through. "If there isn't room for you *and* my monstrous self-satisfaction, Daphne, it's only because of those enormous sleeves of yours. Have you thought how many bolls of cotton gave their lives for those things?"

This time her laugh echoed so close to him that he tried to spin on the spot and catch sight of her, only to have his pack overbalance him. Stumbling backward, Ben crashed through a curtain of hanging festoon plant and landed inelegantly but comfortably atop a deep soil mat.

Daphne's laugh broke off.

Ben blinked. His eyes made a slow examination of his surroundings. He was in the curving hollow of a burned-out trunk, open at the top but sheltered on the sides by its walls. The only entrance was through the curtain of festoon stems because what used to be an opening on the downhill side was now choked with huckleberry bushes and ferns.

Unbuckling his pack, he pushed it away with his boot so that he could move more easily. This was it, then. If he was not mistaken, that view which had so often presented itself through Daphne's eyes—yes.

He edged around the walls inch by inch on his hands and backside, waiting for that moment where the reality would overlay the memory in a perfect fit.

Another inch, another inch. And—

Something bit into the palm of his left hand and Ben jerked away, cussing. Finding his skin unbroken, he leaned over to pluck from the soil the offending cone or bark or whatever it was.

It was a hard little bit of brownish-white. Like dirty ivory.

Frowning, he leaned even closer to squint at it. Some exotic beetle's carapace?

He tapped it. No response. Dead, then. Or inorganic.

Ben dug his fingers into the moist soil to free it, raking through the decomposed remains of year upon year of redwood foliage, bark, litter. Whatever it was, there were more of them.

He had just transferred some of the sorted bits to his chest pocket for later inspection when his questing hand encountered something oddly familiar in the mulch. It was round, hard, smooth. A piece of metal.

Ben froze, staring without seeing as he rotated it in his fingers.

His stomach lurched. Surged up to choke his throat.

He launched himself back through the festoon barely in time, as his gut heaved and he lost that morning's breakfast.

Oh, God.

Oh, God.

It took him a very long time to open his fist and look at what he had found. He did not need the witness of his eyes to recognize it, after all. Because he had seen it so many times before—in photographs and in the flesh, as it were—that he would and did know it blindfolded.

But there it lay. Its luster hardly dulled with dirt or moisture or the passing of those many, many years. The wide gold wedding band of Daphne Lindstrom.

CHAPTER 25

All Her Sins Remembered

If this was her ring, then those curious little knobbly bits that he'd sifted out of the dirt—

He rinsed his mouth with water from his Klean Kanteen. Spat it over the edge to join his earlier effusions. If any of that mess had made it all the way to the forest floor, it would at least guarantee that even the diehards would clear out.

Taking a deep breath, he switched on his headlamp and fished the bits from his pocket. Yes. Of course. He had not known them out of context, but who could blame him? He was a botanist, not an anatomist. And of all human bones, those of the hand had to be the hardest to reconstruct.

They were tiny. A fingertip, maybe. Some carpals. He swallowed with difficulty.

She came from nowhere.

One minute he was alone with the handful of bones and gold ring, and the next he looked up to find her standing before the curtain of festoon. Involuntarily, his gaze dropped to her left hand, half expecting to find it missing, but she was whole, down to the gleaming band on her fourth finger.

She lifted that arm now, turning it slowly, a faint line appearing between her brows. Lowering it again, she looked at him.

"You found me."

Ben stared, uncomprehending. "I—I—yes—I think I did. I mean—" He looked at the bones again. He had no idea what to do with them. He had no idea what to do, period. "...I don't understand," he said. "What are these—what were *you* doing up here? How did these get here?"

"I climbed."

If she were to tell him she had flown, it would hardly make less sense to him.

"You mean you brought your...body...or your bones up here after you were dead."

To his amazement, she laughed. This was getting to be a habit with her. *"No, Benjamin. I was very much alive. My death, such as it was, came afterward. Did I not say you were not the first to climb this tree?"*

She knelt down, careful to avoid physical contact, but the unseen bond between them crackled, flowed, expanded. He felt her pride, her delight in seeing him, not unmixed with sorrow at this weakness. At the same time, she was reading him. *"You are...confused...and, I do believe...revolted."*

Ben made an apologetic face. "It's not you. Well—it is, I guess. I've never handled human remains before. You might have warned me, instead of letting me root around in there."

"How very odd," she answered. *"I thought I made myself quite clear when I bid you come no further."*

"It wouldn't have hurt to be more specific."

"Ah. I see. Perhaps, 'Come no further, lest you find yourself digging up my corpse'?"

He felt his insides settling gradually, in response to her teasing, matter-of-fact tone.

"Or, let me see—" she pointed at her ring. *"'Come no further,*

especially if you be a grave robber.'"

He replaced the delicate bones in the soil where he had found them. Laid the ring gently on top. "A simple, 'Enter this place over my dead body,' would have done."

Daphne gave a small gasp. She raised her left hand once more, this time rotating her wrist and flexing her fingers. "*Oh! I feel it now.*"

"What?"

"*My hand.*" She fluttered it. "*It was so curious. Those—pieces—you had—while you held them I had no sensation in my hand or wrist. As if they were mere phantom limbs. Extraordinary.*"

Extraordinarily disturbing. As if he needed reminders that he communed with a ghost. And one who apparently still bore an active connection to her relics? Those many times he had seen her, sitting in exactly that spot—Ben suppressed a shudder. He had no wish to touch her bones again. Rising to his feet, he gestured to the *de facto* grave. "I beg your pardon, madam. I believe this is your seat."

Rising as well, Daphne sparkled up at him, alive and whole. "*Not my seat only, sir, but in truth my entirety.*"

The space was small. Ben meant to edge his way around her, but the sight of her glowing countenance halted him. Whoever she was, *what*ever she was, there was no denying his attraction to her. They swayed toward each other. He saw the shades of hazel and brown pinwheeling in those eyes of hers before his gaze fell to her parted lips.

The words formed on them. "*Benjamin—we must not.*"

He shook his head. "Right. Okay."

Bones. Bones, Dude! You were just fiddling with her carpals and a phalange or two, and now you want to—

He backed up. They traded places as carefully as strangers in an intricate dance. "Okay," he said again. "So much for my revulsion. Maybe now we could tackle my confusion. What on earth do you mean you climbed up here?"

"*Precisely that.*" She scrutinized the walls of the burned-out hollow, tracing them upward to where they rimmed the gray portion of sky. "*The memories come more readily to me here.*"

Here, where she left her brain.

He didn't know if she caught that, but, judging by a quirk of her mouth, he suspected she had.

"*I spent much of my childhood up in trees. Smaller ones, naturally. I grieved when I grew too old for the short skirts that made climbing possible. Out of sympathy, my mother delayed the change as long as she could, but Red Gap is a provincial place. The townspeople gossiped of my wild ways, and in the end she bowed to them, for my own sake, as she told me.*"

Ben shifted. There was just enough room for him to stretch his legs alongside her flowing skirts. "Did you climb by yourself?"

"*Sometimes. Not always. Often Shane would accompany me. But he was several years older. Well before I donned long skirts, Shane was already working. He was a strong young man, proud of what he could do for the Company. We had a falling out.*"

"I'll bet you did. It never pays to be ahead of your time. Poor guy didn't know that, if he just waited a hundred more years, you would find all his tree-felling skills irresistible."

Daphne regarded him with mock severity. "*Shane was never a faller. His first job was greasing the skids for the logs to slide along. But from the time he was fifteen he became a bucker, removing the limbs from the fallen trees and then sawing the trees into logs. Although, where the old redwoods were concerned, the buckers broke them in chunks. Logs would have been so enormous as to be unmanageable.*" A shadow crossed her face. Ben caught the memory, faint and dark though it was: a team of oxen—perhaps a dozen strong—dragging a massive piece of forest behind them, bound by a chain.

The chain—

"Daphne, Charlie said you chained yourself to Grand Daddy when you heard the lumber company bought the Grove."

She nodded, her chin rising defiantly. "*I did.*"

"Did Shane help you?"

A fierce negative. *"We were not then on speaking terms. It was my own foolish, fruitless plan, conceived shortly after I performed the ceremony binding me to the Grove. The ceremony which, to my lasting surprise, has proven so effective."*

There was a moment's silence. Her sojourn at the Napa State Asylum lay ahead—not a topic he wanted to bring up, even if he hadn't felt the turbulent currents of her mood jostling him. Would it be more painful for her to speak of it or to pass over it?

Before he could decide, he saw a wide, unpaved avenue lined with trees which terminated in an impressive brick and stone edifice, four stories in height and capped by a steeply-pitched slate roof. Cream-colored stone outlined each of the narrow windows, of which there were many. The building was perfectly symmetrical. Ben spied, through the trees, two wings flanking the central structure, each crowned by several round-roofed towers roughly two-thirds the height of the main, quadrangular one. A short flight of steps nearly as wide as the avenue led to a trio of pointed archways, through which, he imagined, many entered but few departed. The Asylum looked, and was, the very picture of a Victorian institution.

"For its time, it was not so terrible a place," she said, to his surprise. *"It was built according to a novel plan that proposed the benefits of cultivated grounds and pleasant views, sunlight, proper ventilation. The severe patients were housed on a floor completely separate from mine. Once I was judged not to be a danger to myself or others, I was permitted the free use of the grounds and could spend the half of each day abroad, wandering the fields or assisting in the garden or piggery."*

"The what?" said Ben.

"Piggery." She smiled at him. *"Where the hogs were kept."*

"You don't say."

Between them the air hummed, rippling back and forth. *You make me happy, Benjamin. I have not felt so for ever so long.*

His insides gave a funny twist, but he answered aloud, keeping his tone light, "Another reason to quit telling me to go away, then."

The tip of her slippered foot was just visible beneath the spill of her gown. Ben found his eyes wandering to it repeatedly. The amount of clothing she wore! Daphne wasn't the only one to regret her long skirts. He wondered if he would ever see her legs. Though, judging from the effect it was having on him, there was something to be said for mystery and modesty. Before he even realized he was reaching for it, her foot disappeared back under the yards of fabric.

He stuffed his hands in his pockets.

"Well, how did you get out of this model institution?" he asked. "By being a model patient, or"—remembering Gladys' theory—"by making up to the doctor?"

"*Dr. Reed?*" Daphne's eyes were round with astonishment. "*Making up to Dr. Reed? That bilious man with walrus whiskers like Arthur!*"

"Arthur who?" Ben asked, batting away the clod of dirt she tossed at him.

"*Why, President Arthur, of course,*" she exclaimed, blushing. "*That is, he was President when I was a child.*" She pelted him with another clod. "*How ungentlemanly of you to call attention to my advanced age.*"

"Can I help it if you're old? And stop chucking your remains at me—I just got over my revulsion."

"*You!*" she shrieked, renewing her assault. More dirt was followed by fistfuls of huckleberry leaves, shreds of fern. Laughing, Ben dodged some, fended off others. He lunged for his backpack and held it up as a shield before throwing it down again to catch at her flying wrists.

"*Benjamin—no—*" Daphne struggled to pull away, horrified. "*You mustn't—what if you're too weak to climb down?*"

"I'll take a chance," he said shortly, pinning her arms by her sides. "Kiss me. Just once."

"*I won't,*" she insisted. Tears started to her eyes. "*For your own sake. Let go of me.*"

"Stop twisting like that," said Ben. "It only makes me have to hang on harder. Just a short kiss. A peck. Then I can collapse here for the rest of the day and you can finish telling your story. Come on, love." He grinned at her. "That way, if I fall asleep before you're done, you can blame it on your deathly effect."

He felt her relenting and released her directly to show his good faith. And he only meant to give her the one peck, but when he saw her tears spill over he couldn't help kissing them away. Daphne murmured her protest, retreating a step, but Ben pursued her, putting out his arms on either side and leaning into the hollowed-out wall to imprison her. He found her mouth screwed tightly shut, poised for a quick jab of a kiss, but the thought no longer appealed to him. Tenderly he touched his lips to hers, whispering her name, coaxing her. The circle of his arms contracted. With a sigh that was nearly a sob, Daphne's mouth relaxed and she drew a shaking breath. They kissed. For one instant she pressed against him.

The tree swayed. There was a deep groan, as Grand Daddy flexed in the wind, the sound of air colliding with solid wood and then trickling through the thousands of leaves and needles in the crown.

Ben pulled back, smiling down at her. "Was that inside my head or out?"

He saw the desire in her eyes darken into concern. "*The wind, only, but next it will be you, I fear.*"

"Mmm." He slumped against the bark wall, sliding downward to a sitting position. "I think you may be right."

Daphne bit her lip. Scooted as far from him as their close quarters permitted.

He shut his eyes to rest them, just for a minute, while her anxious thoughts whirled around him. "Stop worrying," he chided. "You're drowning me. That was completely worth it. I'll be fine in a while. Go—go on with your story—you were telling me how you won over the handsome Dr. Reed."

"*Perhaps if you ate something?*" Daphne suggested.

"Mmm."

He listened to her unzipping and zipping and rummaging through his pack. When he cracked his eyelids, she was holding up a protein bar by the corner of its wrapper, inspecting it dubiously. "That'll do," grunted Ben. "Could you rip the corner open? Thanks."

She tossed it to him. "*Enjoy.*"

"And one more thing—wanna come a little closer? I'm helpless now, I promise. Couldn't throw myself at you if I tried. Of course"—he flicked a twig at her—"if you wanted to throw yourself at me, I'd be powerless to stop you."

Daphne only shook her head. The mournfulness was upon her again. "*You make light of it, Benjamin, but I see that each time the consequences grow more extreme. I have never before ventured to repeat this experiment. What if one time my actions should prove fatal to you?*"

"If the choice is between you dropping tree branches on my head or killing me with kindness, I vote for kindness."

She made no answer, refusing to be teased out of her mood. In a movement he recognized, she hugged her knees to her body, resting her head on them, her gaze fixed on the curtain of plant stems swaying in the entrance.

Ben focused on getting a piece of the peanut bar into his mouth. Honestly, he was rather alarmingly wiped out. Not only did he not want to think about how he was going to manage the descent—he didn't want Daphne thinking about it either. "Go on, then," he prodded. "Tell me how you got out of Napa."

"*My father came for me,*" she continued at last. "*He grew weary of the letters from the asylum—the sameness of them. He declared that, if I could see reason again, he should bring me home, even if he had to… bribe… the hospital with a large donation. But Dr. Reed had no objection. The asylum had grown crowded; he was not sorry to be quit of a patient so relatively quiet as I. And I—I promised my father there should be no* more of my nonsense. I would be an obedient daughter. Apart from a daily constitutional, my life would be circumscribed by the boundaries of home and school and church.

"My grove was a wretched shock. If you could have seen it then, as it first appeared to me—nothing remained but Grand Daddy. Good Witch lay butchered; the rest were gone, leaving behind discarded limbs, stripped bark, bleeding stumps. The undergrowth had all been burnt for easy passage. Moreover, the peace of the place was destroyed. From daybreak to sundown was cacophony. All those shouting men and the saws going back and forth, back and forth. The oxen bellowing." Daphne's hands twisted in her skirts.

Images flickered. Ben saw a young man high atop a fallen tree, axe in hand, calling to another and pointing. His button-down shirt was soaked with sweat and his sleeves rolled up to reveal a powerful build. He turned suddenly, shock washing over his face. Then he scrambled to remove his hat—

Shane? asked Ben.

Daphne nodded, her gaze far away.

"So powerful was my grief that it was months before I recalled my childish bonding ceremony or realized its continued hold on me. But when I did, I found myself drawn there anew. I was too late to save the other trees, but I could protect Grand Daddy."

Another gust buffeted the redwood, with its attendant groan and cracking, its rattling and sway. Ben stiffened, braced himself automatically, not that it would do any good.

His movement drew her attention, and she reached toward him, stopping short. Her smile was rueful. "It used to terrify me, how much the tree bent in the wind. Terrify and thrill me at once. Then, as the years passed, I imagined Grand Daddy taunted me with it. He held out the possibility of his death and my freedom, only to snatch it away as my hopes rose."

"Yeah, well, I have to admit it's not my favorite part about being in the canopy." He crumpled the empty protein bar wrapper. "Distract me. Keep going. What did Shane Derwent think of you marrying Pall Lindstrom?"

"*By the time I married, Shane had been wed himself for nearly a month! To a girl we had used to disdain in our school days for her timidity and aversion to dirtying her clothes. His was a—a—necessary wedding. You see, Shane and I had fought again… that day you saw just now. I accused him of heartlessness—that he would participate in the Grove's destruction. He said he did it for me. He hoped to save money, enough to marry me and take us far from Red Gap—why do you smile?*"

"Nothing, nothing. Go on." Gladys Harrington had stuffed *Bury Me Not* so full with her elaborate, overheated imaginings that Ben supposed it would have been impossible for her not to guess a *few* things correctly.

"*When I declared I would never marry a man who broke my heart and called it love, we parted with sharp words. I suspect that was when he took up with Margaret. There was talk in town—reports of drunkenness and loose behavior. I longed to discover the truth of these, but my pride prevented me. It was not until he was injured some months later that I flew to him and confessed how dearly I regarded him. But by then it was too late. Margaret was with child, and he must needs marry her.*"

"So you married Lindstrom," said Ben.

"*I married Lindstrom.*"

He tried to analyze the hesitation in her bearing. There was grief, yes, but it was muted, tinted by regret. Regret for what? For her beloved Shane knocking up some girl? Or for herself, for continuing to love him after he was married?

"*Pall was a good man. A very good man,*" Daphne cut across his thoughts. "*Unfailingly kind to me—devoted. I did not deserve him. Our life was not a happy one, and our unhappiness was my doing. In my selfishness, I thought only of my affections for Shane, for the ruin the lumber company had made of my grove and for my husband's part in it. I began to dream of escape. I dreamed of climbing again, as I had as a girl. It would be*" *my very own secret. One I kept well. Pall encouraged me to walk daily in the woods. He saw how it relieved my sadness. He never knew what I did there. Each day I wondered: what new tree could I conquer? How high could I go?*

"*It was a cumbersome business, even in my lightest of summer clothing. As I grew more bold, I began removing my heavy skirts—climbing in my shirtwaist and bloomers! Then I learned the use of ropes to reach higher places, always being careful to pull them up after me. As you might suspect, these practices only added to my burden of secrecy. On several occasions I was nearly discovered. Men would pass below, on their way to or from the timber fields, as I perched in the branches above them. Rather than give me pause, the dangers forced me higher, further from the chance of detection.*"

Ben marveled at her, torn between admiration and incredulity. "Is that why you finally decided to climb Grand Daddy—to get away from people? It's impossible that you did it—150 feet to the lowest branch! With nothing but rope. How the heck did you pull that off?"

Her face brightened momentarily. "*Can you not guess? Of course not—it could not be done today. But Grand Daddy did not always lean. What you see now happened inch by inch, so slowly that even I could not perceive its progress. When I conceived my plan, it was but five or ten ticks from vertical.*"

"Okay. But that didn't bring the branches any lower. I know for a fact coast redwoods do most of their height growth when they're young, and Grand Daddy is an old, old tree."

Daphne clapped her hands, tucking her legs underneath her and giving a bounce. "*It was the fir.*" She gave him the picture. Ben's mouth popped open. It was the tree up which the squirrels had scurried while he made out with Gladys during her second episode.

"I noticed that one!" he exclaimed. "I even had the same thought, that they must have stood really close together once—"

"*Indeed? I supposed your thoughts otherwise occupied at the time.*" Her tone was wry. She must have glimpsed his memory.

He grinned at her. "So you climbed the fir—"

"I climbed the fir. It required three attempts because I had never been so high. It was frightening. Dizzying. Several times I considered abandoning my mad idea. But on my last venture I reached the highest branches, the ones which interlaced with Grand Daddy's lowest. By then I was breathless and bleeding, my clothes were torn. The bones of my corset cut me in the most painful manner. Once more I was obliged to descend. If scaling the reaches of the Douglas fir proved so daunting, I knew climbing ever so much higher would be too much for me in my state. I needed to make alterations.

"I had enlisted an unwitting partner in my adventures: young Albert Turner."

"Albert Turner—" said Ben, "legendary errand boy and shaker-of-beds!"

He laughed at her mystified expression. "Never mind. I've heard a few things about this Albert. How did he help you?"

"Albert was like a younger brother to me—"

"Younger brother, Joyce," muttered Ben. "Close, but no cigar."

"For months he was my supplier of rope. I told him all manner of preposterous things. I said I needed it for the garden or I wanted to teach the children how to tie sailors' knots or that we might put on a church theatrical of Jonah. Albert never questioned me, or, if he did, he was easily put off with feeble explanations. When I determined to ascend Grand Daddy and wanted to be rid of my constrictive attire, I made further use of him. We were nearly of a size. I stole his shirt and trousers as they hung drying on the line."

The glow which had animated her dimmed. With an impatient gesture, she brushed the tiny droplets of rain from her waving hair. *"Had I but taken Albert in my confidence, how differently my life might have turned out."*

"He might have prevented you climbing the tree?"

She dismissed this. *"He would not have tried, I am certain. But had even one person known my whereabouts, I doubt not that I might have been rescued."*

Her clear gaze, appealing, met his. He did not understand. "You do mean prevented, then. Prevented from carrying out your plan."

Comprehension dawned slowly on her face, and Daphne flushed from the roots of her hair to her high neckline. "*Benjamin—*" her voice rose, "*let us not mistake each other. I did not climb this tree seeking a permanent solution to my situation. I was no suicide.*"

"Well then—then—" he felt his own face heating in response, "—then what the hell *are* you doing up here? Your—body—I mean."

Rising, she paced the walls of their confines, the edge of her train dragging past Ben's foot. She came to a halt before the festoon curtain and thrust her hand through the hanging stems, pulling them to one side to stare out. "*I climbed higher than this place. A great deal higher.*" She spoke as if she expected Ben to contradict her. "*I gave no thought to the danger. Indeed, I cared nothing for it, little imagining the suffering my heedlessness would cause my husband and loved ones. As ever, I thought only of myself. Of my excitement and the glory of my enterprise.*

"*Alas, Grand Daddy was too much for me. My enthusiasm outstripped my abilities.*"

"You weren't able to descend?"

Her mouth twisted in a humorless smile. "*On the contrary, a goodly fifty feet of the descent were accomplished with no difficulties at all. I fell. Much as you did from the fir tree several weeks ago, but without your good fortune.*"

He had one glance at it—a fraction of second—the hurtling, the rush of air past his ears, the sharp collision of solid wood with ankle and breastbone—before it was lost in his own memory of falling. Ben's sharply indrawn breath echoed the remembered one filling his ears.

Silence fell between them, broken only by the soft dripping of water on foliage and the ragged sound of their shared breathing.

Ben hadn't the strength to go to her, even if he could touch her without danger. Instead, he reached for her with his mind. Wrapped around her.

I'm sorry. Was it the final impact that killed you?

I landed on the very rim of this place. Cracked over it like an eggshell on a table's edge. The pain of my broken ribs was very great. One of the bones must have pierced something inside—I could do no more than whisper, not even when, the following day, I heard the voices of searchers far below. I tried to… cry out… to throw things, but to no avail. My body lived another two days, perhaps. Little suspecting my ultimate fate, I spent those days in prayer and repentance, begging the forgiveness of God and of my poor husband.

The wind pressed against the tree, and Grand Daddy once more gave his unearthly groan, followed by the dampened rattle and tap of the greenery. That same current of air drew one of her curls lovingly from its windings with almost perceptible fingers.

She turned back to face him.

My prayers ceased many years ago, Benjamin. Or, they had until I met you. My repentance, however—

My repentance has been long.

CHAPTER 26

Interloper

The buzz of static awoke him.

Ben opened his eyes to find himself in gray, damp twilight. He knew Daphne could not be far because, despite his awkward position curled in the hollowed-out trunk, he felt no stiffness or cramped muscles, no cold. Perfectly well, as always. Unless you counted the odd sensation of being totally sapped of energy.

He felt a little better now. The nap (if four-plus hours could still be counted as a nap) had done him good. He rose shakily to one elbow, redwood needles and other jetsam glued to his cheek by sleep.

"*It's this, Benjamin,*" came Daphne's voice. She stepped over him to enter his field of vision and thrust the walkie-talkie in his face. "*They have been trying to reach you through this box. I fear if you do not respond soon someone will be obliged to come up after you.*"

"Can't have that." Ben took it from her and rubbed his cheek clean against his shoulder. "Hey, there. Ben here. Anyone listening? Over."

"Ben!" squawked Ray. "Jesus God, we been trying to raise you all afternoon. Clyde down here is all rigged up because he volunteered to go up and have a look. You hurt yourself, over?"

"No! Uh—no—tell Clyde not to risk it. Everything's good. I took

my pack off. Lost track of time. I maybe even dozed off for a bit."
Ben ran out of breath, and when he released the button, Ray was all
a-sputter.

"—Off? Did you say you 'dozed off'? [Static]—dreds of feet off
the ground? [Static]—crazier than I thought!"

"I was hooked in the whole time," lied Ben, "but the crown is so
dense where I'm at it would be nearly impossible to fall." His eyes met
Daphne's. A little higher up would be another matter altogether, he
added, for her hearing only.

"Well, we're relieved to hear it," said Ray, still miffed. "But you better come on down. According to the weather report, there's a front
moving in, and we'd all like to go home and warm up. Over."

An army of people gathered around the down rope was the last
thing Ben wanted, especially if they were cold and grumpy and he
was slow. "Thanks for your vigil. But send everyone home, Ray. Or
tell Charlie to come back if I haven't shown up in an hour. This might
take a while. Over."

After a few more back-and-forths, Ben got his way, assisted by the
threatened cloudburst and the approach of supper time.

"*Can you manage, Benjamin? Have you the energy?*" The questions
which provoked impatience when put by others were welcome from
her lips.

In the waning daylight, her own internal glow shone the more
brightly, and Ben smiled at her in frank admiration. "You'd better come
with me to make sure. I might need some cheering on. How do *you*
get up and down?"

"*I cannot float in air, if that is your question. Rather, I…imagine my
corporeal frame filling a space and there I find myself.*" She stretched out
her arms, brushing the walls of her hollow. "*Once I have physical being,
I move about as you do. Yet, as you know, something is wanting. I seem
··hstantive enough, but few have been able to perceive me.*"

···'t you think, then, that you shouldn't hide out from almost the only guy who can?" Ben teased as he struggled to his feet. Twice Daphne put out a hand to steady him, only to retract it before they touched. He exhaled heavily, leaning against the trunk. "It's down to me, Charlie, and that Carson Keller. You've abandoned Charlie and I forbid you to talk to Keller, so that leaves just me."

"*You 'forbid' me speak to him, do you?*" Daphne said roguishly. "*I've disobeyed men with far more right to command me.*" She hoisted his pack and, after inspecting the system of straps and buckles, fastened it on herself. Ben tended toward the lanky side, but Daphne's corseted frame was positively swimming in the waistbelt.

He took a step toward her, wondering what that waist and those hips would feel like in his grasp. Daphne watched him warily. She held her ground, only twitching when his hands landed not on her body, but on the fabric straps of the waistbelt. He pulled them snug. "Safer that way," he muttered. "Don't want the weight of it throwing off your balance."

His hands were separated from her by three sturdy millimeters of post-consumer recycled PET polyester fabric, but he was reluctant to remove them. On the contrary, he pressed his fingers inward against her. He could feel the boning of her corset. Steel, Good Lord.

"*Benjamin,*" she murmured.

"Why are you wearing this?" he asked, his voice rough. Through the waistbelt he traced one of the ribs. "Did you get to choose? Why not spend eternity in something more practical? You died in Albert Turner's clothes, after all."

"*I—I didn't want to wear men's clothing forever!*" she retorted, as if this should be obvious. "*I chose this gown because it was the loveliest I owned. Do you not care for it?*"

In moments like these, having a mental connection to your true love was a definite handicap. The thought streaked out before he could stop it: she looks like the Gibson Girl from an old-time Coca Cola ad. To his relief and amusement, Daphne took this as an unalloyed compliment. *"Do you really think so?"*

"I think," said Ben in complete honesty, "that you are probably the most beautiful woman I've ever seen."

"Oh."

They stood in silence some moments.

This wasn't getting him any closer to the ground, however. And on top of that, it was frustrating as hell.

Either she shared his sentiments or they registered with her because Daphne backed nimbly out of his hold. *"Come. You must descend now."*

She led the way out through the curtain, picking her way carefully among the tangle of freestanding and fused trunks and branches, turning every few yards to check his progress. When they reached his last rope, she unbuckled his pack and eased the straps off. *"Will it be too much for you to carry? Perhaps you ought to throw it down."*

"I don't think Ray would appreciate me dropping his camera 200 feet," he answered. He took a deep breath, marshaling his strength. The ultralight model couldn't have weighed more than fifteen pounds fully loaded, but to his drained body it felt like a sack of bricks.

Descending the shorter ropes he'd thrown up required some care. Daphne watched as he threaded the bight of rope through the belay device, passed the carabiner through both and hooked the carabiner to his belay loop, squeezing the gate to ensure it was locked. "Better do an auto-block, while I'm at it," he said, "in case you kiss me for luck and I pass out on the descent."

She made a scoffing sound, but Ben saw her satisfaction when he demonstrated the block holding him on the rope. *"Wondrous! Ingenious!"* she breathed. *"I knew only the simplest of knots. If I could not climb without a rope, I must perforce claw my way up and then pray my way down, always dreading a slip of the hands or coming to the end of my strength."*

After a few breaks and the downing of a second protein bar, Ben worked his way to the lowest level of the crown. Beside him, Daphne would wait till he hooked in and began his descent. Then she would vanish and rejoin him on each successive level. He had never witnessed it before, and it pleased him. He alone, of all her past and present... friends? haunted ones? would-be lovers?—he alone had penetrated her secrets.

"It fixes you," he said, the first time she reappeared. "I wondered how you managed, that time I saw you soaked in the rain. And just now your hair was coming undone and you had all kinds of stuff sticking to your dress, but—voilà!—you're all clean and put-together again."

"*I wish I could say the same for you. A hot bath and fresh clothing would do you no end of good.*"

"A shave wouldn't hurt either." He scratched at his chin.

"*Oh, no!*" she exclaimed. "*I like whiskers. A moustache would be so becoming. Have you never considered one?*"

She was serious. He grinned at her. Apparently observing a century's changes in fashions hadn't budged her from preferring her own. "I've never been encouraged to before," Ben said, which was true enough. "Check this out, though—I may not have any whiskers, but if you liked my belay device, this is gonna knock your socks off." From his belt he unclipped the mechanical descender. Flipping open the side plate, Ben let her feed the rope through and click it shut. "This 150 feet will be easier than the other fifty. I just hold the handle in the Descend position and down I go. Piece of cake. I control the speed like so, depending on how far over I pull it. Then to stop, just release—see—and hit it again to lock. My side of the rope to descend, other side to hold."

She made no response and Ben looked up in surprise.

She had ceased to listen. Even to breathe. She held very still, her attention focused elsewhere. When Ben tried to follow her, she shut the door between them emphatically.

"What's the—"

"*Shhhh...you must go now.*"

"Now, wait a second." After their time together—after sharing her story with him and joking and crying and staying with him while he slept—showing him how she got around—she was going to go all mysterious and elusive on him again? "Will you meet me at the bottom, Daphne?"

"*No. No, not now.*"

"Then when will I—"

She began retreating. "*Take care on your descent,*" she interrupted hurriedly. "*Good-bye.*"

In another instant, he was completely alone. It had happened so fast he still had both hands on the descender where he'd been giving his impromptu demonstration.

Was she really gone? Ben waited. He listened. Reached out. But there was no trace of her, not physically and not in his mind.

"*Damn* it," said Ben. "If it wouldn't kill me, I'd put handcuffs on that woman."

~~~

Charlie was waiting at the tree's base on a camp stool, running a piece of bread around the edges of the container he held to mop up the last drops of soup. Apart from the trampled undergrowth and footprints going every which way, there was no sign of anyone else. Keller's light-banks were gone, along with the filmmaker himself, Ray and Clyde.

"What'd you see up there?"

Ben tried to unhitch without falling over exhausted. With Daphne's departure there had been some dizzy moments on the descent, not to mention an overall low feeling that had nothing to do with his body. He drummed up what enthusiasm he could. "You wouldn't believe, Charlie. A whole complete world with its own trees and plants and soil, hundreds of feet up in the sky. It must have been like nothing on earth, when the entire canopy was intact."

Wordlessly Charlie passed the camp stool to Ben and took the rope from his hands, beginning to wind it between the crook of his thumb and his elbow.

"I didn't get to the top," Ben continued. "I stopped about 200 feet up. The heart of the crown. Took lots of pictures, though. Maybe tomorrow I'll go all the way up."

"Don't think there'll be any climbing tomorrow," said Charlie. "With that front coming in. Might not even be any the next few days. Forecast has the lows parked bumper to bumper over the Pacific. Wind advisory, too."

Ben felt a stab of dismay. He bent over his pack to hide his face and stuff gear back in. "Well, if it's not too bad, I'll go up anyhow. I've wasted enough time."

Charlie gave an irritated grunt. "Don't worry about that. I guess that Gladys has been talking to you. You take what time you need and don't hurry things or take chances just because folks have nothing better to do than worry about other people's business."

"Thanks." For a second Ben debated whether or not to say more. It would be a relief to tell someone about Daphne, and with Keller and Charlie his only options it would be Charlie hands-down, but something silenced him.

To his surprise, it was Charlie who brought her up. They were making their careful way down from the Grove, the beam of Charlie's flashlight dancing ahead, revealing a staircase of tree roots here, a fern there, and, once, the unsettling yellow eyes of a raccoon.

"You seen Daphne lately, Ben?"

Ben caught his foot in a trailing vine and stumbled slightly. "I thought talking about her was taboo. Why do you ask?"

"Because Keller was asking me."

Ben caught at Charlie's arm to stop him. They were at the edge of the woods, just beyond the sign marking the trailhead. "Keller asked you if *you* had seen her, or Keller asked you if *I* had seen her?"

"Both."

"What did you tell him?"

"That, no, I hadn't and Bea didn't like me talking about it, and as for you, I suspected you'd been too busy recuperating to do any ghost-sighting."

"Did he…buy it?"

Charlie slapped the coil of arborist rope against his thigh. "There's something going on with that guy. I dunno—maybe it's frustration. You know he's been trying to catch Daphne on film—a dumb idea if I ever heard one—and that's going nowhere. So for a while he was running all over town interviewing people up and down: have they ever seen her? Do they know anyone who has? What family stories do they know about the ghost?" He shook his head in disgust. "You stick a microphone in front of some people and they'll say whatever you want."

"Like what, for example?" Ben asked with some trepidation.

"Oh, you know. That they saw a woman in white leap off the railroad trestle or that you can hear her scream when the wind blows. That sort of thing. And Keller ate it up for a while. But I think he knew you can't make much of a movie with no meat. That's why he wanted to talk to you or me. While you were under the weather, Bea and I held him off—he came by a bunch of times—but now—" Charlie broke off. Clicked his Maglite off-on-off-on in rapid succession.

Ben pictured Bea's adamant protection. "But now what?" he prompted. "He's given up?"

"Now there's something wrong with him," Charlie said again. In the darkness Ben couldn't see his eyes. "He's…I dunno…*agitated* lately. You'll be talking to him, and then he cocks his head like he sees something. Like he hears something. You could hit him with a brick bat and he wouldn't notice 'cause he's not there. Then when he comes to, he's all flustered. Ask the guy what's wrong with him and he changes the subject. I can't really explain it. It's weird. You know what it really reminds me of is—it reminds me of—of—"

He didn't need to finish. Ben remembered another conversation. It seemed like ages ago. "Keller's behavior reminds you of your father's."

Charlie gave one jerk of his chin. Yes.

"It makes no sense," said Ben. He felt his chest tighten. With what, he wasn't quite sure, but it wasn't pleasant. "If Keller was seeing Daphne—talking to Daphne—like … like your father did"—then she would have told me! he thought wildly— "then why would he waste his time doing lame interviews with Red Gap citizens?"

"Maybe she left him alone for awhile," said Charlie. "At first. So he went about his business. But then it ramped up, or something. He probably didn't want to believe his eyes and ears because he thinks he's going crazy, Ben. He thinks maybe it's in his head after all. You remember how upset he was that first time. He thinks he's crazy just like you thought you were crazy. Just like everyone in my family thought they were crazy."

"Well, Keller genuinely *is* crazy," said Ben. God, who wasn't, in this town? He was having a hard time getting his breath. "Because he hasn't seen her again. He might have that first time, but he hasn't since. Whatever he thinks is going on is really truly inside his own head."

Click. Click. Click. Charlie turned the flashlight off-on-off. Click. On. "You sound pretty certain of that." His words hovered in the forest air before sinking into the hush, heavy as the dark clouds rolling over them.

Ben struggled his way through it. Could Daphne possibly be seeking Keller's company as well as his own? It made no sense at all. If she were, what could she gain from it? From him? She could have been trying to scare Keller off, a corner of his brain suggested. But, if that were the case, what would prevent her from telling Ben about it—enlisting his help? Ben had even mentioned Keller up top, during their time together, and she had said nothing.

No. Keller was just plain losing it. Spending too much time interviewing Gladys and having her mental illness begin to affect him. It wasn't unlikely—Ben had doubted his own sanity when Gladys forced her alternate realities on him. Maybe Gladys had had an episode. One so convincing that Keller didn't know which end was up anymore.

And Daphne didn't need Keller now. Not since Ben had shown his willingness to do what she asked. Daphne loved him. She hadn't said it in so many words, of course, but neither had he, and perhaps she was waiting for him to go first. Which he would, he decided, the very next time he saw her.

Ben would have found his own arguments more persuasive if she had not behaved so oddly right before his final descent. Had she been going to Keller then?

The door to him remained closed. The tentative feelers he extended met nothing, not even a sense of her effort to shut him out. It had not been this way when he had lain around the Dryad, recovering. Then, she had been so divided in her desires that she could hardly keep him away.

But Charlie was waiting for a response. Ben's protracted silence probably told him all he needed to know.

"I'm not 100% certain Keller isn't seeing Daphne," Ben conceded at last. The admission in itself gave his doubts new strength. "Look, Charlie. I can't explain. You don't want me to explain."

Charlie exhaled slowly. He squinted upward as the very first drops splashed down on them. "There it is. We better get going. Don't want to track more mud in than need be."

Nodding, Ben made to edge past him, but Charlie put an arm out, slapping Ben in the chest with the coil of rope. "I've said my say already, you know."

"You have." Ben didn't need to ask what he was referring to.

"But I'll say it one more time: you can't help her, Ben."

"Probably not."

"And it can't work out." Charlie crept closer. In the dim, rain-obscured twilight his eyes gleamed. Ben saw another drop track along the plane of his cheek. "People have loved her before. It doesn't change anything except to wreck their lives. You have a life, Ben. I know you think you don't, but you're young. There's nothing wrong yet that can't be fixed. Get your work done here and move on. Don't get sucked in further than you already are."

Ben pushed his arm away. He headed down the trail. "I appreciate your concern," he called without looking back.

"I'm telling you, Ben." Charlie's voice carried to him over the thickening rainfall and the squelch of his own determined footfalls. "She's not like us anymore."

Ben walked faster, his feet beginning to slide and stumble.

"There's no future in it. None at all."

If he got far enough ahead, Ben thought, he wouldn't be able to hear him anymore. But he did. Loud and clear.

"You may as well love the moon."

CHAPTER 27

Lost and Found

"It's ark-building time!" Clyde announced, bursting in through the mud room door without knocking.

"Don't you think of setting foot in here until those boots come off," ordered Bea. "You're a mess, Clyde! What possessed you to be out in this?"

Chastened, the veterinarian retreated briefly and, after much scuffling and scraping and stamping, re-emerged in bare socks. "It's either go out in this or don't go out at all, Beatrice. This is history in the making! Five inches in twenty-four hours! Seven inches in thirty-six! And don't be expecting your afternoon check-ins today because there's been a mudslide clear across the Gap cut-off."

"Oh, no. I hope the morning guests were able to get out."

"Mostly. Ray and Charlie helped re-direct some of them. Ray's talking to the county about getting the plows out, but looks like it'll be a couple days."

Bea groaned. "What a mess. And who'll eat all these cookies?" She gestured at the lemon snaps crowding the counter.

"Always willing to help a friend," said Clyde, stuffing a couple in his mouth. "Hey, where's our local Tree Champion? He left a message this morning about using my bow again. I gotta say you and Charlie were right—the boy isn't lazy. He might be nuts, wanting to go up that tree in all this wind and rain, but he's not lazy."

The words were barely out of his still-chewing mouth when they heard more stamping and scraping from the mud room, and the next moment Ben himself emerged. To Clyde, who hadn't seen him since the ascent, his appearance was a shock, and even Bea found him pale and nervy, his dark eyes darting from one to the other of them.

"What is it, Ben?" she asked, rushing over to grasp his elbow. "Aahh—you're soaked. You better go put dry clothes on and come warm up with some tea."

Ben hardly acknowledged her. "Did you get my message about the bow?" he demanded of Clyde.

Clyde raised his eyebrows. "Sure I did, but you're not needing it today, I imagine."

"I would, if that's okay. Maybe we could swing by your house after I change and get my gear together."

"Ben!" cried Bea. "You can't be thinking—"

"Turns out I got it on me," said Clyde, "if you're out of your mind enough to want to use it on a day like this. Must be the full moon behind all those rainclouds. First it's that Keller saying he wants to learn to shoot it, and then—"

"Keller?" Ben interrupted, his face stony. "What would Keller want to do that for?"

Clyde shrugged, reaching for another octave of lemon snaps. "He invited himself to dinner the other night and seems like we spent the whole time talking about deer hunting. He asked so many questions about it I asked him if he thought I'd make a good star for his next movie. Heh heh! So Keller says, he says he's just always wanted to experience the thrill of the chase and would I mind showing him how it's done. So I said sure. *Not* that I let him shoot anything other than the targets in my side yard, Bea. He didn't do too badly for his first time out, though I'd say those deer aren't in any danger yet."

"Frankly, I don't care one thing about Carson Keller's potential as a hunter," said Bea irritably. She slid the cookies off the cooling rack into a jar before Clyde could filch more. "And I think your time would be better spent down at the cut-off helping Ray and Charlie. And as for you, Ben, you look like you have something else coming on, and rather than climbing that blasted tree, you should probably take a nap."

Bea's—for her—strong language startled both men. Clyde cleared his throat a couple times and Ben ran both hands through his hair. It had grown longer in his weeks here, contributing to his distressed aspect.

"I have to get up there today, Bea," he said gently. "There may not be another chance."

"Why, I'd like to know?" She rapped the metal spatula in her hand on the empty cooling rack. "Seems to me that tree has stood there thousands of years and it can wait another few days until all this rain passes."

"I don't know that it can." His hands were shaking. Abruptly he sank onto a kitchen chair. "It's leaning."

"It's leaned for a hundred years," declared Clyde.

"No," said Ben. "I mean the angle has increased. I've been watching the past two days. With all this rain—the ground is totally saturated. It's giving way everywhere. Part of the trail to the Grove even washed out. I had to break a new one." He slammed a fist on the table. "I've got to do this now!"

Bea stood right in front of him, arms crossed over her stomach, so that he had to look up at her. "Don't be ridiculous, Ben. If Grand Daddy really is like you say, then this is the absolute worst time for you to think of climbing it! Not only is the forecast for more rain and more rain from here to eternity, but the wind is supposed to pick up tonight. You got two hundred feet up; you took some wonderful pictures—we'll all just have to be perfectly satisfied with that."

He could hardly think straight enough to answer her. She hadn't seen the tree with her own eyes—approaching twenty degrees off vertical. She hadn't seen the roots—those damned roots which Ben had done his best to mangle—straining with almost audible creaks when the wind pressed the length of the trunk. She didn't know that Daphne's life was tied to Grand Daddy's, that the end of the redwood's life would signal the end of hers. She didn't know that Ben had gone to the Grove seeking Daphne, calling for her any way he could, battering himself against her silence and fighting the growing fear that she was already past recall.

Was he too late? Had Grand Daddy's roots been sufficiently damaged or so rent from the earth that the tree, though still standing, had already ceased to live?

One thing was clear: he should have kept his mouth shut. Judging from Bea's posture, she didn't intend to let him out of her sight, much less back into the woods armed with Clyde's crossbow. His gaze faltered before hers. "You're right, Bea. I—I guess it was just the excitement of being up in the canopy again. It can—uh—wait a few days for things to calm down. Once the ground drains a little, things would be more stable anyhow."

He didn't think his lie would convince a five-year-old, but Bea breathed a sigh of relief. "Exactly, Ben. There's no need to take foolish risks just to hurry things along."

"But I'll have to finish the job sooner or later," Ben pointed out, in a semblance of his usual joking manner. "Mayor Ray's got me over a barrel. If I don't get that work done, it'll be the financial end of me. That, or he'll hire the headless lumberjack to take me out."

She dismissed this with a wave of her spatula. "Don't let Ray pressure you. He may be mayor, but Red Gap isn't that kind of town. Whatever graft and shady dealings happen in other places, they've been rooted out here. It's not worth anyone's life just to shave a few days off."

At her words, Ben's head snapped up, the wild look back in his eye.

Bea backed up a step, her hand to her heart. "Good heavens! What did I say? Ben, you're worrying me."

"It's nothing." Leaping to his feet, he grabbed her waist and spun her around before planting a loud kiss on her cheek. "You just gave me an idea."

"Oh!" She blushed and gave him a playful push. "Good. Just so long as you're going to be sensible."

"Completely sensible. Starting with changing my clothes and taking a rest." Ben unstoppered the cookie jar and helped himself to a lemon snap. "Whoa, Clyde—you knew what you were about. These are awesome." He slapped the veterinarian on the shoulder. "Thanks for coming by. If Keller's all done with his target practice, think you can leave your bow here a few days?"

"I think it's best to avoid temptation," Bea broke in before Clyde could get any words out. "Clyde, I don't want that thing around. When the weather calms down, Ben can give you a call."

The veterinarian shrugged helplessly at him. "We always do what Bea says around here. But the second she gives the o-kay, the Excalibur's yours."

The familiar swell of panic threatened to swamp his newfound excitement. Ben could manage no more than a nod before he left the kitchen, dragging his feet upstairs to the Green Room. What good was an idea if he couldn't get up Grand Daddy?

Once in his room, he went through a now-familiar routine: he laid a hand against the wainscoting; peered at length out the window at the yard and edge of the woods; took the blue clothbound poetry book from the dresser, letting it fall open to its wonted place. Nothing.

This must be what Pall Lindstrom experienced after she vanished from his life. Blindness and silence. Mystery. Rumors of a rival seeing her. Ben eyed his reflection in the dresser-top mirror. God, he was even starting to look like the guy did post-disappearance, all gaunt and preoccupied.

Rain lashed the window.

He gave one more long look out before yanking the drapes shut. There was nothing he could do now except wait for nightfall. Wait till the Dryad was asleep and then sneak out to brave the elements, crossbow or no crossbow. Stripping off his dampened clothes, he threw himself across the bed and tugged the quilt over him.

He dozed off. Dreamed. He had wound fishing line around a rock. He threw the rock in the air as high as he could, up up up into the reaches of the giant redwood, praying it would hook over a branch. But instead the rock defied physics, floating back down to him as if weightless, breaking apart into a thousand tiny white petals which glowed like shards of moonstone. They fluttered and drifted, catching in his hair and starring his fleece. When he drew his arm closer to investigate, he found they were neither petals nor gemstones nor snowflakes.

They were shreds of lace.

Deliverance came in the form least expected. Ben paused on the landing, taking in the scene below him, where the Derwents, Ray, Clyde, and Rube were deep in conversation with a man in green fatigue pants and a navy blue pullover. *Sheriff* was printed in yellow letters down his arm.

"There he is now," said Ray, catching sight of Ben. "America's Most Wanted."

"What have I done?" asked Ben warily.

"More like what you haven't done!" crowed Clyde.

"It's not bad, Ben. It's good," Bea assured him. She dashed to meet him on the stairs and beckoned. "Come meet Deputy Espinoza."

Deputy Espinoza held out a beefy hand and crushed Ben's in it. "You've been keeping a pretty low profile, young man."

"No, just a normal profile," said Ben, trying to project a casual air.

What could this be about? Did someone see him hacking at Grand Daddy's roots? Would that be the sheriff's jurisdiction or the Bureau of Land Management?

"Seems someone filed a Missing Persons report for you a couple days ago," explained the deputy. "At least we think it's you, if you're Benjamin Wheeler Platt, age 28, height 6'2", weight 180, brown hair, brown eyes, no known scars or tattoos. Last seen driving a blue 1998 Toyota Corolla in the vicinity of Jedediah Smith Redwoods State Park."

Ben's eyes flew to his watch. The 30th. He mouthed a curse word. The project had wrapped two days ago, the very day he ascended Grand Daddy. "No way. Oh, no way. I wasn't thinking. That's me all right. I lost track of the date. How did you find me?"

"Well, the bulletin's all over the county, for one thing. Seems like folks up at the U got a little agitated when they realized you never showed up back there. They said you drove off a few weeks back and you were mighty upset—"

"They should know I was fine. I changed the autoreply on my email," interrupted Ben to forestall another rehash of his embarrassing story.

"They caught that," said Deputy Espinoza, "which was the reason they knew you at least hadn't died on the drive home, but you were still nowhere to be found and neither was the Corolla. You didn't answer phone calls to your home or cell and you didn't answer emails."

"I'm sorry," Ben said. "Really. I'm sorry. I thought the autoreply would do it and then forgot all about it. I didn't mean to get people worried or cause extra work for everyone. How did you find me, anyhow?"

"It was me!" volunteered Ray proudly. "My call got transferred to every department in the county this morning when I tried to get someone to come check out our mudslide and clean it up. It turned out Carla at Public Works was Red Gap's own Carla Nordquist—uh-huh, Liz's stepdaughter—so I was filling her in on all our latest news, and she and I put the pieces together."

"Can you cancel the alert?" Ben asked the deputy, after all the what-a-small-world murmuring died away. "Let everyone know I'm okay?"

"Sure, I can cancel the alert," Espinoza responded. "I could even put in a bit about how you got waylaid to climb some giant redwood, but you might want to contact people and add the personal touch."

Ben's breath caught and he put out a hand. He saw a way to make use of this. "Hang on a second. You're right. I have to fix this myself. Uh—don't bother mentioning my climb, Deputy. Those people at the U, they're kind of redwood fanatics too. I'd—I'd rather tell them myself."

"Will you call, Ben?" asked Bea. "I guess a mass email would be faster, but in this case they would probably appreciate hearing your voice."

"I'll go that one better," Ben said. "Charlie—if I could borrow your pick-up. The weather's no good for climbing now anyhow. I might as well take a day or two and run up to the U. Give them the full story, make peace, that kind of thing."

"Oh, that's a wonderful idea," said Bea as Charlie fished the keys from his pocket. "It's bothered me this whole time that no one knew where you were."

"Really think you're up to driving?" Clyde put in. "With the slide blocking the cut-off, you're gonna need to take the back roads, which'll add at least an hour to the trip, and that's just to Eureka. If you don't mind waiting, I was gonna head that way myself on Thursday."

"No. No," answered Ben hurriedly. "I feel great. And I think I won't wait till then. Bea's right: I've put this off long enough. Let me just throw some stuff together and study the map, and I'll go this afternoon."

～～～

Forty-five minutes later, he was on the road. Deputy Espinoza canceled the APB, and Ben, despite what he'd said earlier, shot a mass email to the department distribution list and a few family members:

Friends and Family, forgive my silence these past few weeks. I left the Canopy Project for personal reasons and have been taking some time to think things over and plan next steps. I apologize again if you have been worried. My health is great, and I have been doing some work for a small town documenting their natural environment. I hope to be in contact with you again soon. For now, email is the best way to reach me. —Ben.

For Lance he added a postscript:

Soongmeister, I haven't returned your Corolla because I hit a deer with it. Long story. It was beyond repair. I plan to reimburse you, but in the meantime, just use my car. Call my housemate for keys. Thanks, man. Sorry again.

Inadequate, yes. Likely just to upset everyone further, possibly. But Ben couldn't focus on that right now.

Right now, his main worry was where to park Charlie's pick-up so that no one would discover it in the next couple days. It helped that Charlie himself would be vehicle-less, since of all people he was most likely to wander the logging roads, trails and stray paths.

Ben inched the truck across a one-lane bridge after checking the convex mirror for oncoming traffic. According to the map, he was within a quarter-mile of the railroad trestle. On foot, that meant roughly a thirty-minute slog through mud and over uneven terrain to the Grove. It might even take him longer, burdened as he was with his climbing gear. His pack was lighter than it could have been: he had had dim visions of stealing Clyde's crossbow from the Dryad mudroom, only to find it already gone. Who knew how long it would take him to get a rope up without it.

He gave a humorless laugh. That was one good thing about Grand

Daddy's increasing lean—it brought the lowest branch that much closer.

Pulling off the road onto the barest suggestion of a shoulder, Ben eased the truck into a dense stand of mixed trees, redwood, fir, hemlock, and pine, springing from ancient woody debris, the dregs of century-old logging efforts. He jumped from the cab, throwing his pack to the ground and hastening to cover the vehicle with whatever moldering branches and detritus he could still detach from the forest floor and fling into the truck bed and over the bumper.

It would have to do. He didn't have time for more effective camouflage. Not if he wanted to reach the Grove before the light was gone. If "light" it could be called, so dim was the sky with ominous clouds and the light but steady, steady rain.

I'm coming Daphne. Hang on.

~~~~~

The saturated ground made for rough trailblazing. Slipping, panting, struggling, weighed down by both his pack and increasing anxiety, Ben saw the thirty minutes stretch into nearly ninety. Truly, it was not a day to be out for a hike. He saw no one. Not even an animal.

At one point he thought himself lost and had to take a laborious detour up a slope to get his bearings. When he finally intersected with the Grove trail, he nearly missed it, hidden as it was by a bank that had given way and sucked down several shrubs and a fallen tree. Blisters formed where his boots rubbed continually.

All this and he still had no idea how he would climb Grand Daddy when he got there.

Ben rested against the fallen tree. It gave off a rich, loamy smell where its roll downward after who-knew-how-many years had exposed surfaces long buried. A beetle picked its delicate way over the lichened bark, weaving between mushroom caps and trailing a line of mites like a teacher and his pupils. The silent, unseen workers of the forest. Over time every bit of the tree would be broken down, its decaying form feeding new life. Fungus, insects, lichens, the sprouts of new trees themselves. New forest from old.

And Daphne—well—if she was gone—

Gone.

If she had ceased to be.

If Grand Daddy fell.

Another hundred years onward, who would know? Death would give way to life. Not her life, no. Not Daphne Lindstrom's. But life all the same.

Ben felt his throat catch. Where was she?

The frantic plan which had driven him, wound tightly as a spring in his gut, began to loosen, to unspiral.

He was too late. The massive bulk of the ancient redwood wrenched upward from its failing roots, degree by degree, but the inevitable fall of the tree would be only a final, dramatic flourish. Already Grand Daddy was dead. A snag. A majestic one, but a snag all the same.

And he, Benjamin Platt, was on a fool's errand.

Not least because he was trying to carry it out in the midst of the worst weather to hit the North Coast Mountains in decades.

If Daphne was dead right now, she would be dead tomorrow. Dead three days from now. Dead, after the chain of storms had passed with their attendant wind. The urgency to reach her, therefore, was senseless. A creation of his own mind.

What but death could explain her utter absence? Every other time she kept her distance she had been unable or unwilling to cut him off completely. He had sensed her just beyond the margins of physical sight. He had forced himself into her consciousness or caught glimpses when she let down her guard. Now there was no guard to let down. There was…nothing.

Ben fingered the waistbelt of his pack, remembering how it had encircled Daphne. He should have stayed with her. Told Ray and the townspeople *something*. Anything, to get them off his back. After her long exile, to leave her by herself when death finally came—

His rapid breath hung in vaporous clouds. Mist enfolding him, blending with the gray, weeping sky that hunched overhead. His head fell back against the moldering log. Everywhere the drops danced across his vision, now rain, now bits of fluttering lace.

He should cut his losses. Head back to the pick-up truck and back to his abandoned life, but instead he found himself clambering up and over the fallen tree. The rotten bark and debris disintegrated under the soles of his boots. One time he slipped, grabbing a handful of tightly-clustered *Hypholoma capnoides*, pretty little mushrooms straight out of a Disney cartoon. Edible, too. Maybe she had once foraged for these.

The Grove was nearly dark. Ben could just discern the wildly leaning Grand Daddy looming. Had the angle increased, or did it just tilt so far now that the imagination played tricks? The gust of wind that assaulted him the next instant was no mental trick, however. Ben found himself pushed several stumbling steps as the blast tore through the younger trees and laid siege to the towering trunk. This time the unsettling groan he had heard in the crown was audible to the very base.

Up. He must get up. How—?

Digging in the pack for the fishing line, he groped around in the limited spotlight thrown by his headlamp. Tie it to a rock? To a stick he could then hurl like a javelin?

Something slapped him in the face. Ben leaped back, thinking it was a bat or a falling branch. It was not.

He turned his light full on it, but it took a few long moments for his mind to make sense of it, it was so unexpected.

Wrapping his fingers around it, he gave a firm tug.

It was a down rope.

Before he could process any of the thousand questions that rushed at him—How? Why? *Who on earth*?—Ben found the whole of his inner landscape instantaneously illuminated, sheet lightning penetrating every corner and recess. His eyes screwed shut instinctively, but it was not that kind of brightness. Another voice cut across his thoughts. Audible or not audible he couldn't say in the confusion, but familiar—yes—and welcome—God, yes!—although the panic in it froze his blood.

Benjamin! she cried. *Quickly!*

CHAPTER 28

Gentlemen's Agreement

"Daphne," he murmured, knowing she could hear him, "—wait for me."

How he made it up so quickly would forever amaze him. Her urgency gave him wings, as did his own relief and joy. She lived still! Ben barely remarked how he swung and spun in the wind or how unorthodox it felt to ascend so far from the trunk, suspended over space and earth by the exaggerated tilt of the tree.

He focused on the technicalities. He would be damned if he blew everything at this point by making a stupid mistake. Tuck. Click. Slide the ascender. Two-hand grip. Lock. Pull up. Tuck. Click. Slide the ascender. Two-hand grip. Lock. Pull up.

As if she knew he could brook no distractions, Daphne absented herself again. Or as much as she could. Another pulse raced beside his own, irregular, now loud, now faint. He did not worry about it. She was alive. He would figure out what was going on when he reached her.

The rope had been looped over an uphill branch. As Ben drew closer, he was able to brace his feet on the trunk and walk. Grand Daddy's diameter narrowed here to about twelve feet. From this point, Ben could crawl and shinny, if need be. With care, he would not need to launch more climbing ropes to reach the densest part of the crown. Whoever placed the rope he just climbed must have reached the same conclusion because he saw nothing but foliage about him.

He unhooked. "Daphne?"

There was no response beyond a ripple of thought. A current without words. She was on edge.

Okay, then. He would have to go find her. No dumb mistakes, he reminded himself.

Ben picked his way carefully into a bizarre and disorienting world. The landmarks he noted in his first ascent were barely recognizable, tipped in a fun-house mirror and stripped by the wind, which had made off with anything not rooted down. And the noise! The redwood's low-level groaning and creaking and rustling were nearly constant, drowning out all else.

He heard it before he saw it, the branch that nearly killed him.

He had struggled upward to the bay laurel and leaned against it, thinking to get his bearings, when a high whistling struck his ears. Turning, he found the six-foot projectile hurtling toward him. It rolled end over end, and Ben leapt away with a cry, limbs wheeling like an action-movie character in an explosion. As he landed, his foot caught the lip of the laurel's soil pocket. Over he went, jarring onto his side, whipping his neck. If not for his climbing helmet, he would probably have sustained a second concussion.

For one long, dizzy moment Ben sprawled across the sloping tree, the friction of the stringy bark enough to hold him. But then, inexorably, gravity began its fatal work, aided by the slick material of his backpack and rain gear. With a wet, rasping, juddering sound, he came loose. He was sliding. Picking up speed—a 175-foot ride toward fatal injury. Scrabbling desperately with outstretched arms he wrenched an epicormic branch loose with one hand—ripped off a raft of bark with the other. A terrified shout filled his ears, a shout he hardly realized came from his own throat. Head spinning, Ben made a reckless effort, flinging himself onto his stomach and digging into the bark with his fingers. His palms burned as the skin tore off. Splinters pierced the underside of his nails. But it worked. He halted his fall—just.

The wind pressed against him, moaning in his ears like a living thing. Sweating and hoarse, Ben squinted up through the rain to see blood running freely down his hands. Given the alternative, it was a beautiful sight.

Weakly he managed to hitch his legs up and stabilize his position. His hands had petrified in gory claws, but with effort he relaxed them. After hugging them to his chest for a moment and spitting every curse word he knew through gritted teeth, Ben set himself to tally up the damage. The wood slivers would have to be removed and his palms bandaged or he would be unable to climb. Only, on close inspection, he couldn't find any wood slivers to extract. They had vanished. As the accompanying pain and burning receded, a slow smile lit his face. Yes. He ran his hands along his pant legs to wipe the blood off. His skin was unbroken.

Before he could look around to thank her, a gravelly voice carried over the wind. "That's right. I thought that might bring you."

It *couldn't* be. But it was.

Incredulous, Ben gaped at the man who emerged above him. None other than Carson Keller, black hair plastered to his forehead, spiked boots dug into Grand Daddy's bark. He had one arm hooked around an upper branch and the other extended to Ben. Not that he was looking at him. Keller's eyes were trained over Ben's shoulder, where Ben knew Daphne must be.

"*Please,*" she whispered to the trespasser. "*This is not the place for you.*"

"You set that rope, Keller?" demanded Ben. He had to holler to be heard above the noise of the storm. "What the hell are you doing up here?"

"Looking for her," Keller ground back. "Looking for you. Both of you. Give me your hand before you slip some more. She won't go far now."

Ben ignored the hairy paw being offered and turned to look at Daphne. She had drawn closer to crouch by his feet, tucking her sweeping white skirts away from him. In this misty light every inch of her glowed, from the aureole of curling hair which the wind teased from its pins, to the shades of her changeable eyes, fixed on him, to her shining fingertips. For a long moment they regarded each other.

Why did you shut me out? Ben asked. I couldn't hear or see or feel you at all. I was so worried that something happened to you. That you—that the tree—

She understood. Shook her head.

Then what about Keller? Have you been talking to him? Did you invite him here?

Her wordless response—astounded, indignant—was immediate. Ben chuckled with relief. Okay, okay. I didn't think you would. But Charlie said he thought Keller was talking to you, and then, when you went all silent on me…

Benjamin, this man—

"You know," interrupted Keller, "it's incredibly rude to talk as if I'm not right here."

Ben was so surprised he almost tumbled from his perch. He whirled on him. "What are you talking about?"

"I'm talking about I can *hear* you, Platt. Both of you. Or at least, I can hear her. And you, when she's listening to you." He ducked as a mass of decaying fern fronds sailed by. "You really want to have this conversation here, where we're liable to get impaled by something, if we aren't blown clean off?"

Ben didn't want to have this conversation anywhere, if it came to that. Whatever Keller was talking about, his mere presence in Grand Daddy's crown was an affront. This was their private place, Ben and

Daphne's, the embodiment of their invisible connection. To find that Keller had invaded the one space—possibly both—sickened Ben.

"*He speaks the truth, Benjamin,*" Daphne said aloud. She did not raise her voice, but it cut through the ambient noise with its usual clarity. He knew from the change in Keller's expression that he heard her too. "*This man has found his way here and we would do well to speak with him.*" Her mournful tone deepened as she said this.

Ben nodded. Fine. But after they heard what Keller had to say, he was rolling up the welcome mat.

Refusing the man's hand, Ben edged past him, working his way back toward the scoop of wind-denuded soil that enclosed the bay laurel. The site was far more exposed than Daphne's hollow, but Ben would sooner be scoured off the tree by a gust than lead Keller there.

Keller gestured at the bushy little tree. "This is fantastic. I mean, you said there was another whole forest up here, but I had no *idea*. My aunt had one of these in her backyard." Ben said nothing, fighting an urge to block Daphne from the filmmaker's view. Sure enough, Keller's gaze returned to her. "And you…here you are again. You're sure one amazing-looking woman. The first time I saw you I was too flustered to get a really good look at you."

"*Sir,*" said Daphne, "*you are impertinent. And your presence here uninvited.*"

Her cool demeanor brought him up short. He flushed an angry red. "Sheez. I meant it as a compliment. Bet you wouldn't have minded if *he* said it." When she didn't reply, he continued, "You can hardly call me an uninvited guest, Mrs. Lindstrom, when you're the one who first approached *me*. I was just minding my own business. Uh—but while I'm here, I hope you don't mind if I—" fumbling in the inner pocket of his jacket, he retrieved a camera.

"No!" shouted Ben. "What the hell is your deal? Put that away. Look—you shouldn't even be up here. Just tell me what you meant about…hearing her, and then you've got to go back down."

Keller hesitated, considering Ben's threatening posture. He tucked the camera back in an outer pocket. "Actually, I don't know how to explain it. I've been pinching myself for days now, thinking I must be asleep because this is all so weird. I didn't think anything about the stories I heard when I came to Red Gap. I was here for Gladys Harrington, you know. It wasn't till she—excuse me—*you* first approached me, Mrs. Lindstrom, that everything went sideways. I was freaked out that day, you know, Platt. It's one thing to hear ghost stories and another to actually meet a ghost, even one as charming as yourself"—here he made a little bow to Daphne—"but once I calmed down I started thinking, well, why not? People have been claiming to see ghosts for centuries. Maybe there was something to it and I should do the public a service and document this one." He sighed expansively and clasped his hairy hands together. "It didn't work though, because my star proved shy. Mrs. Lindstrom, I don't even know if you can be captured on film because you never gave me the opportunity to find out."

He shrugged. "So I kept myself busy with interviews and backstory and learning all I could about the elusive Daphne Lindstrom. When I started—experiencing things—I chalked it up to nerves. I must be obsessing and the lines were blurring."

"What do you mean, 'experiencing things'?" said Ben.

Keller gave him a long look. "Oh. I think you know already. Thoughts would shoot randomly through my head. I would catch glimpses of things—places I didn't recognize. Memories that weren't mine would play. God—I started out thinking I was obsessing, and then that I was losing it altogether! I mean, I'd been interviewing Gladys some, and she told me about her routines when she wrote *Bury Me Not.* How she would sit in the Grove and hold something of Mrs. Lindstrom's and do these 'focusing' exercises, for example. Whatever. We both know Ms. Harrington's history, Ben. I was worried stiff thinking I was going down the mental slippery slope."

Ben's voice was stony. "What changed your mind?"

"I'd have to say it was when I started seeing *you* in my head. A lot. Uh-huh—now I've got your attention. Believe me—you're an interesting guy, Ben, I've told you, but I sure as hell am not obsessed with you. That I do know. If suddenly all these visions of Ben Platt, Tourist and Tree Champion, were busting into my consciousness, I knew there had to be something going on I didn't get. And a couple days ago—when you ascended for the first time—Jesus! That was like a lightning storm."

How was this possible?

Before he thought, Ben turned and caught hold of Daphne's wrist, the covered buttons of her sleeve digging into his palm. How is this even possible?

Thus. She pulled away gently and gave him a scene. It was blurred, watery. Carson Keller in the Grove, backing away, his face stretched with terror. She drew a step closer. Panicked, he looked right and left for escape routes. Then he lowered his head, ran at her like a bull, shoving her out of the way with his arm.

With his arm.

He touched you, said Ben.

He did. Strange that I did not think of it. She gave him a tenuous smile. *My thoughts were more agreeably engaged. Only when you were about to descend did I sense an unwelcome presence.*

"Hold up, hold up," interjected Keller. "Leaving aside for the moment the bit about my 'unwelcome presence'—are you telling me that this happened to me because I touched you?"

"Yes." Ben bit the word off.

"Touching her forged some kind of connection between me and—er—Mrs. Lindstrom?"

"Yes."

"Ahhhhh…"

While Keller sat back on his heels to process this, Ben went on urgently. Was that why you shut me out? You sensed something alien?

"He's talking to a ghost and he calls *me* alien," muttered Keller.

Yes. I had to. I could not even explain, Benjamin, for fear he would overhear. I had to shut my mind completely, to keep him *out.*

I understand. Otherwise you're all right? When I lost you, I feared the worst. The storm—Grand Daddy—the lean has increased—

"So you're saying that everything I saw and everything I heard was for real," continued Keller.

They ignored him. The wind succeeded in loosing Daphne's long hair, which unfurled across her shoulders. *Benjamin, darling, my time draws near.*

"No!" The word broke from him.

You will remember me, won't you? Keep my secrets? Let me rest.

"No," he said again, edging toward her. "Don't talk like that. This isn't the end."

"That ring Ben found," said Keller, "—it was somewhere up here, wasn't it? So much was hitting me that day that it gave me a migraine, but I saw a ring and—I don't know—"

Ben hardly heard him. He wound his hand in the thick waves of Daphne's hair, letting it slide, soft and lush over his skin before he pulled her toward him, cradling the back of her head. He had dreamed of this.

She jerked from his grasp.

He opened his eyes, prepared to see her fear for him and to cajole it away by whatever means possible, but her wild expression drove this from his mind. What is it? Tell me.

That man. He knows about the Hollow. He has gone to find me. Don't let him, Benjamin!

Keller was indeed gone, the noise of his departure muffled by the wind. Feeling panic in his gut, Ben set off in pursuit, scrambling his way up, threading the labyrinth of trunks and limbs, brushing aside the fern outcroppings. He had one advantage: he knew vaguely where he was going, whereas Keller would have to search. Ben also had one disadvantage: his contact with Daphne, brief as it was, rendered him breathless and clumsy. He would have to trust to the crown's density here to prevent any falls. Come to think of it, he had two disadvantages: whenever Daphne disappeared, to reappear again ahead of or above him, remembered injuries seared his hands. Twice he nearly lost his grip.

Through Daphne's eyes, Ben saw Keller standing before the swaying curtain of festoon stems one minute before he came upon him in actuality. By then the intruder had already pushed the curtain aside and entered. When Ben hurled himself through, Keller was on his hands and knees, sifting through the soil.

"Damn you! Leave her alone!" roared Ben, throwing himself at him.

The impact of his body managed to knock Keller onto his side, but not before Ben saw a flash of gold. Daphne's ring.

"Give it back—put it back!"

"Jesus, Platt!" Keller tried to thrust his attacker away.

Sheer adrenaline fueled Ben, but it could not fully overcome Daphne's effect. He was moving through water, flailing uselessly at something large and immoveable as a shipwreck. He twisted and struck and wrestled, but Keller shoved him away time and again before finally losing patience. Balling his fist, Keller reared back and socked Ben in the gut. He went down.

Weird, in more ways than one, to take one right in the sweet spot, have the wind totally knocked out of you, but feel no pain. He heard Daphne's shriek of alarm and hastened to reassure her. *I'm fine—don't worry. Fine, apart from being totally pathetic and zapped of strength because I can't keep my hands off you.*

Benjamin, I can't feel my hand again. He has my—

"Sweet Lord, are these bones?" exclaimed Keller. "*Her* bones?"

Swaying to his feet, Ben unhitched his pack and let it drop off. If he couldn't overpower Keller—and he couldn't in his current state—he would have to outsmart him. He glanced at Daphne. Shut his mind to her. Nodded.

"You found her," Ben said. "The discovery of the century. The mystery of Daphne Lindstrom's disappearance solved. But can you keep a secret?"

Keller stared at him. "Why would I want to? This is the break I've been looking for. Maybe I can't capture her on film—you sure as hell aren't going to cooperate—but I could take her…her…remains down as proof. Do it fast, before this damned tree falls over and everyone finds her." He gave Daphne a shrug that verged on apologetic. "It should be no skin off your back, so to speak. I mean, you're dead. Or something. You've got a body of some kind. You don't need this one." Watching them warily, he worked his camera from his pocket and began snapping pictures, merely darting glances at the screen to make sure he was hitting the general target. When neither Ben nor Daphne protested, he grew bolder, getting down on one knee and brushing the soil aside with his free hand. More carpals and phalanges vanished into his pockets.

Daphne's left hand hung loosely by her side. She hugged her right arm around herself. Ben knew she was feeling sensation recede as Keller dug.

"Of course, you don't know how the bones got up here," Ben pointed out. "That information would be useful to you."

Keller paused. "I'll have to let Gladys' imagination work on that one because I'm guessing you don't plan on telling me."

"We might be able to work out a deal. Say, the story, in exchange for the bones. Daphne tells you what happened and you let her rest in peace."

"What about my proof? What use is a story if I can't prove I found her and that I found her first?"

"Take the ring as proof," suggested Ben. "And you'll have the pictures, besides that."

Carson hesitated in his excavations, frowning. "Well...I guess I could show people the body after the tree comes down."

Ben stiffened. "Good luck with that. Trees this big don't come down nice and neat, all in one piece. Grand Daddy'll probably shatter. And take a swath of forest with him. It might be a job just to get around the root ball itself."

"I might do it anyhow."

Not if Ben didn't move her body first. He pressed his lips together. "What good would it do you—" he persisted, "—a body and no story? And I'm doubting Gladys will help you because, whatever happened to Daphne Lindstrom, it doesn't look like her husband killed her. Gladys won't want to make her book irrelevant. It's a good deal I'm offering you, Keller. The story in exchange for the bones. Permanently. After the tree comes down, if you can still find the body, you can say so, *if* you promise to have it buried. All together. Completely intact. That's the offer, take it or leave it."

"*I beg your pardon.*" Daphne's steely voice broke in. "*Might I be permitted some say in this transaction, considering we bargain over* my *body and* my *story?*"

"Certainly," said Ben, avoiding her furious gaze. "I suppose you could let him have both the story *and* your body." He pointed at Keller's pocket. "I think that's her hand you have in there."

Queasiness washed over Keller's face. He shook it off. Looked squarely at Daphne. "With all due respect, Mrs. Lindstrom, people will have a hard enough time believing my story even with proof. I certainly don't intend on leaving here without any. You can give me the body or you can give me the story. Neither of which does you any good at this stage in your existence, if you don't mind me saying."

"I do *mind you saying,*" she snapped. "*And as for your cold-hearted dealings, Benjamin Wheeler Platt, I consider them a betrayal of the first order!*"

"The bones, Keller," said Ben, nodding at the soil. Keller's mouth worked. He licked his lips. Then he bent over, fishing the bits from his pockets and letting them drop one by one.

After a minute Daphne flexed her fingers, her stormy eyes meeting Ben's. He only dared to give her two short blinks, not trusting their inner dialogue or impressions to be proof against eavesdroppers.

She received the warning, however, and her shoulders relaxed infinitesimally. "*Very well,*" she resumed. "*I find myself overmatched. But I leave you to tell the tale, Benjamin.*"

"Oh, no," he said at once. "It's too long a story, and I might get some details wrong." (Grand Daddy at this pass gave a conveniently frightening groan, accompanied by a volley of sharp cracks.) "You'd better tell him the way you told me—you know—with the mind meld."

Ben could have groaned when the words escaped him. The phrase was unfamiliar enough to Daphne, but Keller's brow furrowed with suspicion. "What are you trying to pull, Platt? Are you making fun of me? This isn't some episode of *Star Trek.*"

"I know, I know. I just called it that because it reminded me of Mr. Spock. The process. But I'm dead serious. Here, Daphne—put your hands on his head and your forehead to his, like you did to me, and tell him the story."

"*I don't want him touching me again!*" she protested. "*Nor so intimately.*"

"You're killing me," growled Ben. "I'm trying to buy you eternal peace. We got your hand back. If I could do the mind thing with him, I would, but I don't have the ability or the *strength.*" The stress he laid on the last word would have been imperceptible, were they not practiced in reading each other.

Bingo. Comprehension.

Daphne closed the distance between her and Keller and laid a firm hand on either side of his head. "*Come closer, sir,*" she murmured.

Keller appeared positively awestruck. He obeyed automatically, his mouth falling open. Cynically, Ben wondered if he had ever before been held by someone so beautiful. Not that it was an experience you grew immune to.

"*Shut your eyes, Mr. Keller, and tell me what you see.*" Daphne drew a measured breath and pressed her forehead to his.

"Uh—uh—" his hand shot out to brace himself against the burned wall of the hollow. "Your skin—you're warm!" (Ben ground his teeth.) "Wow…Uh—this is something! I see—uh—the tree. I'm at the base. There's a girl here—you, Daph—Mrs. Lindstrom, I mean? She has wavy hair and an apron on—"

"*Pinafore,*" whispered Daphne. She shifted, laying the side of her face against his, her mouth close to Keller's ear.

A spasm shook him. His eyes flew open. "Did you feel that? Is the tree going over?"

"*It is the power of the… meld,*" Daphne soothed him. "*Put your arms about my waist and listen.*"

Again he obeyed as if spellbound. "There's a boy. He's teasing you. Showing you a frog." Keller lurched. He tightened his grip on her. "The scene's changing. Now I see a…lumberjack? Is it the same boy—yes—grown up now. Oh, God! He's attacking you! God! He's choking you!"

Ben settled onto his pack, shaking his head, half-amused and half-shocked. He wasn't crazy about seeing Daphne locked in Keller's arms, but more appalling was the tale she was spinning. Throwing Shane Derwent under the bus?

Keller's voice was slowing. He sounded drugged. "You're—you're dead now. The lumberjack is wondering where to hide your body… he looks up…" Keller collapsed against her, as if it were the twentieth straight hour of a dance marathon. She stumbled back but doggedly hung on, leaning her whole weight into him to hold him up. "He's up—in the tree…don't know how…lays your body down…" He trailed off into a guttural groan.

Daphne released him. She twisted from Keller's heavy embrace and let him slump to the ground. His mouth hung open.

"*He will require great effort to shut from my mind now,*" she said.

"I'm sorry," Ben replied. "I couldn't think of another way to make him give your bones back. Or to get rid of him. And right now was when we needed him gone." His laugh was relieved. "Why on earth didn't you tell him the truth? Now he's going to go telling people poor Shane Derwent killed you."

Something flashed in her eyes. "*He was an intruder. I asked his aid, and he treated me as a sideshow spectacle. He had right neither to my body nor to my story. I have been a subject for speculation long enough.*"

"But the Derwents—"

"*Yes.*" Regret rippled outward from her. "*But… I think Keller will say nothing.*"

"Of course he'll say something," Ben objected. "That's why he agreed to put your bones back. The guy's an opportunist and this is his big break!"

"*Perhaps.*" What passed through her mind next was too fleeting for him to make sense of. "*But, again, I think he will say nothing. It was wrong of me to lie so, but if I should be wrong about Keller, the lie cannot harm Shane now.*"

"It's not Shane I'm worried about."

Daphne understood. She smiled at Ben apologetically. "*And I hope Shane is sufficiently removed from Charlie in time that Charlie will not worry overmuch.*"

Ben prodded Keller with his foot and received no response. "Well, I'm sorry I forced you into that situation."

"*No, Benjamin. I am grateful to be whole again. To spend these final moments in one piece.*"

Don't talk like that.

My love, nothing is gained by an avoidance of the truth.

Ben shook his head vehemently. Stripping off his climbing saddle, he set to work loosening the straps. "Auggghh!" he grunted. "Help me pull this on him, Daphne. He weighs as much as a side of beef."

Together they wrestled Keller into the saddle and dragged him, bumping, out of the hollow into a more open spot. If the man woke to find himself not only totally drained but also somewhat scratched and dented—well—at least he was alive. Ben's climbing helmet proved too small for him, so Keller's springy hair would be his sole protection on the descent.

Perhaps we could just roll him off, suggested Daphne mischievously.

If I thought you enjoyed him pawing you like he did, I would, said Ben.

When he found a promising branch to anchor the belay, his hands worked quickly at the figure-eight knots. Keller was wearing the only harness, so Ben found a snug place to position himself. Lowering the unconscious man in high wind was no easy trick. It helped to have Daphne spotting and feeding Ben images. Several times Keller got to swinging slowly, narrowly missing knocking his head against the trunk. At one point he snagged on a small spray of branches, and Ben had to raise him and then drop him rather sharply to break through.

"Add 'whiplash' to the list of injuries," he muttered.

At last he was down. Instantly Ben unhitched and tugged the rope over the anchor, letting the smooth length plummet to earth.

Daphne was beside him. *You should have left that in place, that I might lower you.*

Why would I go down now?

You should descend, Benjamin. It is not safe for you up here.

Not yet.

Benjamin, I will join you below, for as long as I am able. You must go now. Listen to Grand Daddy! Any moment might be the end.

He turned on her. "Not yet! You think I'm just going to go down and wait for you to disappear from existence? When there's still a chance I could save you?"

"*Chance? You have said yourself there is no saving this tree,*" Daphne protested. *"Please, Benjamin. Save yourself for my sake."*

He gave her a memory: their kiss in the Grove.

She put a hand to her lips. *"Yes, I know. But—"*

"If we could be together, would you mind if you went on living?" he pressed.

Mutely, she shook her head. *"But it is impossible. You yourself have said."*

"It may be impossible," he said, "and there may not be time. But I have to try."

Gathering his energy, he braced himself against the swaying branch.

"I have a plan."

CHAPTER 29

One and the Same

He'd never been a fan of Crack the Whip. That grade-school game played at the local roller-skating rink where the chain of children executed fast, unpredictable moves in order to sling off the last person in the sequence. Today was no different.

How far up was he? Three hundred feet? Without dropping a tape measure he couldn't be certain, and really, considering the violent swings when the wind cracked the whip, the margin of error was a good twenty-five feet. Ben had roped himself to a lower branch, but if the elements succeeded in breaking his hold, he would fall at least fifteen feet before being snapped to a halt.

Cautiously, legs straddling the narrow limb beneath him, he double-checked the plastic bag tied to his waist. It sagged with its load of canopy soil. Some rooting compound blended in would have been nice, but at least he could be sure of its fertility. His eyes watered as he screwed them nearly shut. Damn this wind. Taking hold of Charlie's pruners, he inched his way out.

Daphne had been dead against it. *In trying to save me, you will kill yourself.*

"Look—I've thought about this. The only way to extend your life is to extend Grand Daddy's. This tree is a goner. Which means we have to propagate it. Maybe if Grand Daddy lives on genetically, you might too."

"*But the roots will be pulled from the ground. There can be no more fairy rings.*"

"No, there can't. And as I've told you before, at his ripe old age, Grand Daddy doesn't produce seed cones like he used to. Not in number or in—uh—potency. There's a chance one could germinate—a chance—after the tree has decayed into humus, but I'd love to increase the odds."

"*Then what do you propose?*"

"There are a few other possibilities." From his backpack, Ben pulled the folding saw and extended its blade. "You know those lumps that grow on the trunk or the branches sometimes? They look like deformities." Daphne nodded. "They're called burls, and on redwoods you can remove them and put them in a moist environment and hope they root. If they do, you have a genetic clone to transplant."

"*But Benjamin, those burls you speak of—they are enormous!*" She looked askance at the saw.

He grinned. "Are you calling my tool inadequate?"

"*Very much so.*"

"Yeah. You're probably right. But I don't mean to take off one of those bathtub-sized monsters at the base. I'm hoping for a smaller burl or two from a branch up here. Something this little six-inch blade might be able to handle. That's Idea #1. If I don't find any, or if I can't saw them off, then Idea #2 is to get some ripewood cuttings. Root those in a cold frame. "

"*Where would those be?*"

"Oh, a little higher up in the grow zone. Don't worry," he added, when she began to shake her head. "I won't need to go to the top. Just another fifty feet up or so. I want the youngest, vertically-growing ones."

"Without your harness!"

"I never used to use a harness," said Ben vaguely. "I always used to free climb."

"But never under these conditions," Daphne retorted. *"And you forget—I myself have witnessed your free-climbing skills!"*

Giving a dramatic groan, Ben mimicked plunging a knife into his heart, but Daphne ignored him. *"I am not at all convinced by your plan. It endangers your life senselessly, and it seems to me all these methods to… propagate the tree can be carried out after it is on the ground. Perhaps then much more easily."*

He shut the saw with a snap and stood up. "You might be right about the burls. Even if I couldn't get to them—even if I *never* got to them—they would eventually break down and decay. Any seeds left in the humus formed could sprout, possibly. But it would take years and be leaving this to chance. It might be a decade before I saw you again—if I saw you again. And as for the ripewood, remember what you've seen with your own eyes. When redwoods come down, they don't do it intact, and the first things to break off or die are the new shoots, the tender places. Even if some survive the fall, I might not be able to get to them in time. This is already a long shot. I want these things while they're viable."

"And if there is not time—?" She didn't need to finish her sentence. He knew she meant *before the tree falls.*

"It can be done."

Benjamin, who will do all this "propagation" if you die in the process?

Ben paused. Set his shoulders. If that happens, you'll have to give Keller the instructions.

"If that happens, it wouldn't be necessary," Daphne cried aloud. *"I would go with the tree and gladly."*

He didn't want to think about a world without her in it. If he was dead himself, it shouldn't matter, but the thought that she could accept death—welcome it, even—struck him as an ill omen, dooming his enterprise before it had even begun.

"We'll cross that bridge if we come to it," he said.

She reached out and tugged the coil of rope he held. "*Please. Listen to me. What if, instead of the burls, for which you're not equipped, and instead of the cuttings which are too dangerous to obtain, you merely cut off a few small branches right at hand? They could be grafted, could they not? And you descending all the sooner. I could live and you could live. Both of us.*"

"That's a third option," answered Ben, "but the one I like the least. I don't know what it would do to you if I had to graft. The tree would no longer be just Grand Daddy, genetically speaking. It would be the root stock into which it was grafted." He pulled the rope from her gently. "But I'll try all three, if I have time. I'll do anything at this point."

So here he was, with her unwilling blessing, out on a literal limb. He had found and sawed off two burls, a difficult, sloppy job with the folding saw and the tree moving under him. He hoped they weren't mangled beyond use, but it couldn't be helped. He passed them to Daphne for her to bag and drop. The cuttings, for their part, were harder to reach but far easier to remove. This particular branch boasted several promising, upright shoots. He positioned the pruners below where the sprout notched from the branch and clipped. One. He dropped it in the bag. The second cutting sailed away before he could bag it, but the third made it in safely. He passed his sleeve over his eyes and squinted around again. Maybe just a couple more.

Before he could shinny his way to a new branch, the moaning air was rent by a thunderous, multi-layered crash, as if someone had lifted a ten-storey building filled with wooden furniture high above the ground and released it. The enormous percussive force of the sound collided with the wind, smashing Grand Daddy between them. Ben felt the pruners fly from his hand and the bag at his waist tear loose while he spun around the tree limb like a top-heavy ring. When the air released him, he was dangling underneath, clinging for all he was worth.

Daphne's fear for him blazed across his consciousness.

Here. Still here, he managed to tell her, if she could catch that over his pounding heart. It took him another minute to realize it was true. He was still there. The cuttings were gone and the hope of more, but he was alive.

Double-checking that his grip was sure, he lowered himself to the branch below.

It was the Douglas fir. It has fallen. You must descend quickly. Now. I beg you. You see how unstable the ground is.

God, thought Ben. Hope that thing didn't crush Keller. If he isn't under the fir, it probably woke him up, though. To Daphne he added, I'm coming. I can't do any more here.

Who knew where the cuttings had blown too. They might be carried by air currents a quarter mile before they came down. Ben was thrown back on Daphne's suggestion, after all. He would have to get new ones after the redwood was fallen, if any survived their collision with the earth. The odds were dwindling.

He would descend, yes, but there was one more thing to be done. One more step in his weakening plan.

She flew to him when he reached the hollow. Furious, but unwilling to touch him, she kicked dirt on him, hurled greenery. Ben raised an arm to defend himself. "It was fun the other day, but I don't think we have time for this now."

"How dare you be so careless with yourself!" Daphne choked. *"Do you not understand? There is barely a chance these ideas of yours will prolong my existence, but one thing is entirely certain: if you perish in the attempt, we shall never see each other again!"*

"Shhhh … It's okay. I'm okay."

"Stop saying that, Benjamin. I will not rest until you are safely out of the forest—"

"I'm going," he assured her. "Very shortly. You're right that it's too dangerous now. We'll have to go with your plan: I'll come back right after Grand Daddy is on the ground and salvage pieces to propagate."

"*Then don't wait!*" She herded him toward the opening. "*Go now, I beg you.*"

"Just one more thing—no, hear me—I'm taking you with me." Laying down his coil of rope, he rooted through his pack, retrieving a nylon stuff sack and a small shovel. "You know what happens if your bones are separated from each other. If I don't…collect…them all, God knows if I could find them when the tree goes down. You could be spread over hundreds of yards. You could go through another thousand years with no feeling in most of your body. Keller's not going to bury you, whatever he does. He'd probably take whatever he found and turn you into some website or television show or interactive museum display—"

Daphne was shaking her head uncomprehendingly.

Ben zipped his pack up and patted it. "This is going to be uncomfortable for you. Sit down. You'll need to tell me what you feel and don't feel, so I don't miss anything."

"*There isn't time,*" she said, her voice faint.

"Maybe not," he answered, "but there's also no choice."

Helplessly, she obeyed him, tucking her legs to her. Her hands clutched at her skirts, wringing the material.

He took a deep breath. Removed his climbing helmet because the strap felt like it was digging into his chin. This would be uncomfortable for both of them.

Collecting the bones of Daphne's left hand posed no problem, as most of them had been unearthed repeatedly. Ben swallowed hard several times, but he kept everything down. He laid the pieces to the side. He should have stolen Bea's upholstery brush. It would have been a far subtler tool to uncover remains than the shovel. Each time he pierced the soil with the latter, he dreaded both the *tink* of contact and the *crunch* that meant he'd broken something.

He tried to keep Daphne out of his head, but she could read his face easily enough.

"*I'm sorry, Benjamin,*" she murmured when he exhumed a longer, slender bone and went rather greeny-pale. "*I do believe you've found part of my arm. If it were possible, I would do this for you.*"

Not trusting his voice, he only nodded. There's a reason I became a botanist, instead of a medical doctor. *Tink*, went the shovel. Ben threw it down. This was ridiculous. There wasn't time. He needed to get over himself. Pretend they're rocks, he told himself. Cold, dank, oddly-shaped rocks. Rocks.

The rich black soil compressed between his fingers, occasional bits of bark biting like shrapnel. He moved handfuls of the earth, sifting it over his palm to ensure nothing escaped him. Gradually, the pile beside him grew: her left hand and arm; some ear-shaped, scoop-shaped thing ("*My shoulder, I suspect.*"); one delicate swoop, rounded on one end and flattened on the other. A clavicle?

If he could be certain he would encounter nothing but bones, he might have grown inured to the process, but he fought a growing fear that some artifact might have survived, one that would remind him all too forcefully that he handled human remains. A piece of cloth, perhaps. A twist of rope. A hair comb. A crude message that, if his efforts failed, this time nothing of her would remain but such lifeless relics. Nor did he relish the thought of digging up her skull. If he removed it from the soil, she would be unable to speak to him—unable to kiss him (were he in a kissing mood)—until he had reunited it with the rest of her body and buried the total together. He would leave it where it lay, he decided, until the very last.

What Ben did come upon a half hour later, was therefore an even greater shock. He had removed another clavicle and what he suspected were some of Daphne's shattered ribs, when he plunged his fingers once more into the dirt and nearly broke them. Of course, with her so near, there was no pain, only a jarring and the knowledge that they would hurt like hell the second she got far enough away.

"What the…?" Ben shook out his hands and then reached down again. Rather than scoop, he scraped and brushed, brushed and scraped. He felt it before he could see it. The rough, stringy texture of redwood bark.

There was no skull to be found, then. No button from Albert Turner's stolen shirt. No hair pin.

There was nothing but the bark.

Because Grand Daddy had grown around her.

Ben sagged back on his heels, too stunned even to hide it from her.

Over the hundred-plus years, the tree had absorbed her, subsumed her. What did it mean? She would not be moveable—that was certain. Not by him, and not by Carson Keller. The greater danger would be that the bones which were still loose would become permanently separated from the rest of her when the tree fell, thrown who knew how far away and scattered over the forest. Meaning that, if he managed against all odds to clone Grand Daddy and spin out Daphne Lindstrom's existence, it would be a shrunken and deprived continuance. Her left arm, shoulder, collar bones, several ribs completely without sensation and useless to her. He picked up one of the tinier bones in the heap, rubbing it in his palm. Miraculous, really, how something so light, so fragile, could ruin all.

Noiselessly, she approached him. He remembered standing in front of the Dryad with Charlie when Keller came roaring out of the woods and how she had touched him then without touching him—the hand on his chest. This time he felt it brushing against his hair, stroking it. *It's all right. You have done all you could.*

Have I? he shot back. Or have I done nothing? Made things

worse. Royally screwed everything up. Who knows—what if I hacked through some of the fir's roots when I was out there with the mattock. And now it's gone down and ripped up Grand Daddy's root mat—

Come. With her foot she began to push the pile of her bones back into the hole Ben had made. They rattled and thumped across the exposed bark. *Nothing more can be done. We shall… put me back and hope for the best. If the fir has damaged Grand Daddy's roots, it may take no more than one powerful gust to end this. I will bury myself again, and you—you must go.*

Ben didn't move. He felt wetness on his face that had nothing to do with the chilly rain.

The mighty tree creaked. Several nearby limbs cracked, loud as gunshots, and the festoon curtain blew inward, spraying them with drops.

Daphne gave a small sigh as she recovered the use of her chest and left arm. Taking up Ben's discarded shovel, she began refilling the pit. *Take the rope,* she urged him. *Tie yourself in and I will lower you.*

He jerked his chin, shaking off the drops.

The hell with that.

His arm shot out, wrapped around her legs in their flowing skirts and pulled her against him. She stumbled. Toppled over him with a gasp. Before she could recover, Ben rolled on top of her.

"*Have you taken leave of your senses?*" she demanded. Trying to wriggle out from under him, she twisted her face away from his mouth. "*You shall be weakened—rendered unconscious—and I shall not have the strength to save you. Remember how heavy we found Mr. Keller!*"

"I don't care," muttered Ben against her cheek.

"I *care!*" Daphne retorted. She shoved him with all her strength, but to their mutual surprise, he hung on.

Ben took advantage of her amazement to kiss her full on the lips. He clutched her to him, her body soft and strong and vital, breathing her lemony scent and reaching to loosen her hair. He didn't know if it was the desperation of the moment, the adrenaline coursing through him, his hunger for her, but he felt nothing save the tide of excitement—there was no enervation, no fatal weakness.

Suddenly, Daphne ceased to struggle. She did not relax, but rather held herself as if frozen.

It was Ben's turn to be surprised. Had he misread her? He had thought, under the circumstances, she would forgive him a lack of finesse. He pulled back.

Her eyes met his with a glow that almost scorched, but they were not angry. They were…wondering.

Benjamin—how is this that you have strength to resist me?

Actually, if you didn't notice, I've never had the strength to resist you.

She shook off his joke. He watched the hazel stars in her eyes blossom and run together. *You have something of mine in your hand. No, the other one,* she added when he let go of her tumbled hair.

Realization dawned. Ben released her and sat up. He opened his other hand, and the two of them stared at the small six-sided bone, roughly triangular in shape, nestled in his palm. "What is it?" he asked.

"*I don't know.*" She rose on her elbow, waving her left hand thoughtfully, then prodding it with the other. "*But it's something about… here.*" She indicated the base of her palm where it joined the wrist.

"You can still move your hand," he said.

"*Yes.*"

"And feel it, for the most part."

"*… Yes.*"

His closed the precious bone in his fist again. Focused. He recognized his shallow breathing, his flushed cheeks, the ridge of a huckleberry root under his right thigh. He swayed. Shifted his weight to balance again. But it was the movement of the tree, not his own inability to stay upright. And the roaring in his ears was the storm.

He leaned in to her and pressed his mouth to hers for a long moment. Drew back.

She watched him.

"I can touch you," said Ben. His voice shook slightly.

"*So you can.*"

"Daphne—this might be all we have."

Softly, she laid a hand to his cheek. "*You've given up, then?*"

"I don't want to leave you."

"*Not even to save yourself?*"

No. If I go now I might never see you again. My brilliant plan—
She saw his unspoken doubts. *I know, my darling.*

A strangled cry broke from him then, and he crushed her to him,
his mouth finding hers and moving against it as if he could consume
her, swallow her as the tree had, take her into himself. Daphne made a
low sound in her throat. She wrapped her arms around his neck, giving
as good as she got, raising no objection when his hands ran the length
of her back, when he locked his hips against hers.

The damned dress, growled Ben. I can't feel a square inch of you.

"*There's something I must tell you,*" she panted.

"What?" He pulled her on top of him, afraid her corset and his
weight would asphyxiate her. Reaching down, he seized her ankle, felt
his hand slide over silk stocking.

"*I'm a widow.*"

He paused in his explorations to read her. Her face was washed in
pink. Good Lord. She was from the 19th century, after all.

"*I've—I've been a widow for decades now,*" she continued, not meeting his eyes. "*Which is why it is not at all improper for me to appear in
white. But I would not have you suppose that I—that I—*"

It was a trick, getting his class ring off without losing contact with
the all-important carpal, but Ben managed. He slid it onto the ring
finger of her right hand, where it promptly slid off. Her thumb was a
better fit. "Daphne Lindstrom, would you do me the very great honor
of becoming my wife?"

She could not speak, but her glittering eyes and the swell of joy buffeting them both made a response unnecessary.

"You may only be mine for a few hours," said Ben, "but I've loved you from that time you stood outside the Dryad in the rain and smiled up at me and talked smack about my climbing skills."

Laughing, she buried her head against his chest. "*And I have loved you since we sat on the bench together and you offered me your companionship.*"

"No way!" He gave her a little shake. "That's—what—a few days later? Totally not fair. Was it my lack of whiskers? If I don't look like Chester Arthur, I don't get the girl?"

She pinched him playfully. "*You have the girl.*" Another blush suffused her. "*The bride.*"

"'Bride,' you say?" His hand resumed its progress up her leg. Encountered her garter and, above that, the lace hem of her drawers.

"*Wait, Benjamin.*"

He arranged his face in what he hoped was a patient expression but couldn't suppress a groan when she lifted herself off him to kneel by his side.

"*I suspect you are no more willing to descend now than you were a few minutes ago?*" she prodded.

"Less. If this is all we have, I'm not going anywhere."

"*Then I too have a plan, Benjamin. One perhaps equally farfetched and unlikely to avail us.*"

He gave a rueful chuckle. "The best kind. I just hope it's quick. I have my own ideas for how I'd like to spend my last hours."

"*Quick. Yes. It can be.*" She reached for his pack, zipping and unzipping various pockets until she found the folding saw and his Swiss army knife. She waved the latter at him. "*You had this with you when I first saw you.*"

"I thought I'd have to corkscrew a deer to death. Are we celebrating our marriage with champagne?"

With her fingernails she slid out the blade. The tree gave another almighty groan as a gust assailed it. Amidst cracks and splintering sounds, the hollow enclosing them ticked perceptibly another degree downward. Ben's eyes met Daphne's, fear bridging the gap. Not last hours, then. Last minutes.

She thrust the tools at him. *"The choice has been taken from us. You must do this now! Listen carefully: when I am gone, you must saw through Grand Daddy's bark—any place where you can reach the living wood. Then take the knife blade and cut yourself. When it bleeds, press the wound to the tree. Do you understand? Say as I said, 'You shall never fall while I live. I do solemnly bind myself as your protector. My life to yours.' Then you must take a handful of the soil and eat it."*

So many questions boiled suddenly in his head he could barely articulate them. 'Farfetched' didn't begin to describe her so-called plan! Did she possibly think her ceremony could work again? Work for *him*? Had not her own captivity been the result of some unrepeatable quirk in the universe? Could two lives be bound to a tree? And then there was the fact Daphne had abandoned her self-proclaimed role as protector and Grand Daddy was doomed any second—could trees call bullshit?

"Benjamin, don't you see? You will die now, my husband. You cannot survive the fall of the tree. I might—I might—in some fashion, but I would not go on without you. Let us go together or not at all."

He was still shaking his head, dazed. "But where will you be? Why do you want me to do this, and you won't be with me?"

"If I do not go, you will not be able to cut your skin. I will not venture far. You have only to call me back to you. Benjamin!" her voice rose in urgency, *"the tree… balances! Do this instantly!"*

And she was gone.

His ragged breathing and rushing blood filled his ears. Along his fingertips pain stabbed as the punctures left by wood splinters re-opened. His palms burned, the skin scraped raw. Daphne's tiny bone slid from his grasp, plopping soundlessly back into the canopy soil. He could barely bend the fingers he had rammed earlier into Grand Daddy's bark.

Ben tried once, twice, three times to grip the knife, but he could not close his hand on it. Damn it all. Well, it wasn't like he didn't already have plenty of open wounds now, but how the hell would he saw through the redwood's thick stringy bark to get at the living wood?

The burls. The burls he hewed off. The cambium lay exposed there.

Ben stumbled from the hollow like a drunken man, clambering over fused trunks and branches now nearly horizontal. Where—where had he found them?

Daphne helped. *Beyond the clusters of leather fern.*

When he located the spot, he found the skin of his hands red and angry but no longer bleeding. Ben grit his teeth and dragged them along the jagged edge of the burl wound until the blood flowed freely once more. Holy hell, that killed.

He slammed both hands against the exposed wood. "You shall never fall while I live," he muttered. "I do solemnly bind myself as your protector. My life to yours."

Instantly, Daphne reappeared at his side. She was once more immaculate. *The soil now.* The screaming pain in his fingers and palms vanished as if it had never been, and, without thinking, he grasped the hand she extended to him. He had not taken more than two steps before he remembered his dropped talisman, nestled in the soil of the hollow. He remembered, even as the ringing built in his ears and his energy leaked away.

"*Benjamin!*" Daphne felt his collapse—comprehended at once. His buckling knees scarcely contacted the tree before she returned, pressing the fragile source of his immunity into his limp hand. "*And this—*"

In the darkness and rain Ben could barely make out the clump of black soil she held out, but his grip on it was firm again. Don't think. Just do it. He shoved it in his mouth, trying not to breathe as he chewed and crunched. Decomposed redwood foliage and other canopy flora, fungal sporocarps, bugs and their eggs. Ruthlessly, he swallowed. It took a couple goes to get it down but it went.

When he looked up, the deed done, it took a second to find her. She rested against a neighboring trunk. He staggered toward her, lurching from trunk to branch, blinking away rain drops and ducking airborne foliage. They fell in each other's arms.

How long do we have?

Not long. She gave a gentle tug on his neck. *Come to me.*

He needed no further invitation. What was a little dirt in his mouth to a woman who was half-tree herself? Kissing her fiercely, he strained her to him, his hands searching out the feel of her beneath the layers of organdy, lace, boning. The curve from breast to waist to hip, from backside to outer thigh. His healed but bloody hands streaked the white of her gown. And when he felt Daphne's own hand steal under his fleece and his wool shirt, when she laid it timidly but decidedly on the flat of his stomach, he thought if the tree didn't kill him, desire would.

Her head fell back. He felt with his mouth the trembling breath in her throat and the gallop of her heart in her breast. The damned dress! He thrust his hands under her many skirts. There were the silk stockings, clinging to her calves, and the hem of her knee-length drawers. After a brief hesitation, his searching fingers passed under the lace to encounter bare skin. Ben groaned, slamming her hips to his and kissing her so roughly his mouth felt raw and his fingers ached.

Ached?

No.

For another long minute he refused to acknowledge it. Any of it. The burning, growing in his palms. The tenderness in his mouth and throat, as if—as if he had swallowed a good quarter-cup of dirt and bark. Pain should not be thrusting itself on his awareness. Not with her right here. What the hell was happening?

When the reality could no longer be dismissed, Ben loosened his hold just enough to look at her.

Her eyes were closed. She was wan—her otherworldly glow dimmed and flickering.

Panic choked him. "Daphne?" He planted his feet wide to brace himself and lifted her by her shoulders. Her head rolled. "Daphne!"

No sound emerged, although her lips moved. *It is now ... I go.*

"No!" Ben shouted. "Hold on—"

She could no longer raise her arms, but he felt her ghost touch. On his hair, his mouth, his cheek. *The roots pull free. I ... do love you, Benjamin. Perhaps we shall meet again.*

The world was falling. Breaking apart, imploding in a chaos of sound as it teetered over the abyss. They had seconds, only. He took her in his arms, half-falling, half-rolling, back into their hollow. They sank in the yielding earth.

Daphne—Ben urged. Give this to Keller. *Now!* Ben sent the pictures: the burls, the cuttings, climbing over the fallen tree to search for green, unbroken survivors. The water, the rooting compound, the cold frame. Let them take root. Let them live again.

"Did you do it?" he demanded. "Does he have it?"

Just the faint shadow of a smile. *My clever husband.*

And then they were flying. Plunging through space. The air whistled past, rising to a scream. A whole section of the hollow's burnt wall ripped loose, and Ben threw himself across Daphne to protect her. They were riding a rocket, straight into the ground.

One parting flash in her eyes, before their light was extinguished. *Courage.*

CHAPTER 30

The Crater

Life in Red Gap stopped. Mid-sentence, poised, fork or glass in hand, boot halfway off the foot. Bea stood immobilized, holding a cookie sheet so long the heat burned through her oven mitts and she dropped it with a squeak. Gladys Harrington didn't hear the question put to her at the Blind Bard; her interlocutor forgot she was posing one. Mayor Ray halted in directing the bulldozer and the operator just managed to hit the brakes. The frustrated tourist trying to take the back roads out of town looked up from her map, wild-eyed.

It sounded like a freight train colliding with a planet. A deafening, crashing boom that shook houses and rattled bric-a-brac off shelves, followed by ten thousand troops firing pop guns, hurling chopsticks and flapping palm fronds. The fall of the Douglas fir had been audible to those living on the woodland border, but this event eclipsed it entirely. For years, those who heard it would remember exactly where they were and what they were doing. It was Red Gap's very own moon landing, the town's JFK assassination.

Until the rain and wind stopped a full day later, no one dared to venture into the woods, but they knew, simply by turning their eyes to the skyline, that their mighty guardian had fallen.

Carson Keller was the first thing they found before they even reached the Grove. He lay face-down, caked in mud, so weak he could not speak for days. By his side he clutched a plastic bag with two fist-sized knobbly lumps of tree in it, from which he would not be parted. Clyde the veterinarian and later Dr. Stevens from Eureka diagnosed nothing but the usual bangs and scrapes, so the townspeople could only assume Keller had been messing around too near the leaning tree, sensed his danger and attempted to crawl away, fainting with shock and fear.

It was indeed a sight to render them wordless.

The crater left by Grand Daddy's unearthed root ball measured forty-two feet across. That snarl of roots itself towered three storeys above them. Calculations done months later put the tree's height at 347 feet, though the spire had broken off and been thrown another fifteen yards. As for the Douglas fir which preceded it, and whose fall might have accelerated Grand Daddy's, it lay pinned beneath the redwood like a mouse tail under a boot. People hesitated to stand downhill of the trunk—even a hundred feet along it, after you had slashed, hurdled, climbed, and struggled to reach that point, it felt too much like you were a lump of dough about to go under the rolling pin.

Following the tree's demise, tourism crested to a new high. For a brief time, even *Bury Me Not* and Daphne Lindstrom were overshadowed, as news crews, non-book-reading hikers and nature-lovers joined the mix, making off with souvenirs from every easily-reached part of the tree. Charlie's grumblings about the "looky-loos" increased, but, as Bea pointed out, if not for all the people crawling every inch of Red Gap's woods, it might have been months before anyone found Charlie's pick-up.

Months before they realized Ben had gone missing again.

Our News, Our World: Entertainment

7.12.05

Transcript: Kaye Long Interviews Carson Keller

Long: Welcome to another edition of *Our News, Our World: Entertainment.* Today I'm pleased to have with me on the show acclaimed producer, director and filmmaker Carson Keller, whose documentary *Fatal Blow* recently won both the BBYU Critical Choice Award and Grand Prize at the Wild World Documentary Film Festival. Mr. Keller, tell us what your film is about.

Keller: *Fatal Blow* is your classic man-versus-nature story. From the time of Christ, this stand of coast redwoods grew in a pocket of the California Coast Mountains. By 1890, all but one of them had been logged, but that one particular tree hung on and became a symbol of survival, nature triumphing over man's decimation. But then, two thousand years into its life, it fell at the hands of Benjamin Platt, a botany postdoctoral student turned eco-vandal. Platt's lover betrays him, and, as a result, he takes revenge on the redwoods they've both devoted their lives to studying. He strikes a fatal blow.

Long: Fascinating. Let's take a look.

[Video Clip]

[*Studio Keller* logo appears with piano music in background. Scene of redwood forest fades in. Sequence of scenes plays with narrator voiceover: heavily-wooded mountains from the air, a shot from the base of a tree looking up into the crown, various redwood forest flora]

Narrator: They are the giants. Living for thousands of years in the moist, overgrown slopes and crevices of the Northern California mountains. Reaching unimaginable heights. Supporting worlds of their own. But they have always been at our mercy.

[Another sequence of scenes: logger with a chainsaw, cutting through a redwood tree; tree falling; wood being milled; sawmill detritus; furniture showroom.]

[Cuts to still shot of man at the base of a redwood with his back to the camera. His head is tilted back to look up into it. One arm points. The other hangs by his side, holding a crossbow.]

Narrator: *He* was pledged as their protector, but when the redwoods betrayed him, he took his revenge.

[Cut to botanist Dr. Courtney Sherwood in her office. On her desk, a climbing helmet sits atop a stack of paper. In the background hangs a poster of Del Norte Coast Redwoods State Park and a bumper sticker reading "Nature is my church." She taps her fingers on the desk.]

Dr. Sherwood: Did Ben Platt love his work? Yeah. I mean, yeah, he did. But love can be a twisted thing. A destructive thing. It was with Ben.

[Cut to scene of the fallen redwood. People gather near it, dwarfed by it. Some bear candles, as if they are holding a vigil. One woman wipes tears away as she hangs on to her hiking partner. Red Gap mayor Raymond Holtz stands with his hand on one of the up-ended roots. Then he turns to face the camera.]

Mayor Holtz: We were taken in, plain and simple. We nursed a viper to our bosom. [He clears his throat. Looks back at the tree.] We just didn't see this coming.

[Camera zooms in on redwood bark until background is reddish and blurry. The shot jiggles.]

Narrator: The wild earth. Love. Betrayal. Sabotage. Revenge. When life struck at him, he struck back. He struck ... a *Fatal Blow*.

[End Video Clip]

Long: Wow. You certainly found a dramatic, timely topic. Now tell me, Mr. Keller—you say when you first arrived in Red Gap, California, your intention was to make a biographical film about Gladys Harrington, popular author of the *wildly* popular novel *Bury Me Not*, which I love. I've read it twice.

Keller: Absolutely. That's what I was there for. The book was a sensation, after all, and I think I wasn't the only person interested in the mind behind the story.

Long: Truly. How did you change your mind and your topic, then? Take us through the process.

Keller: It was really Ms. Harrington herself who convinced me that more exciting, more compelling material even than *her* was all around me. I mean, I'm sure you know that *Bury Me Not* is loosely based on actual people in Red Gap's history.

Long: The ghost, you mean. There really was a Justine Sauvee.

Keller: [Pause] There was. Her name was Daphne Lindstrom. And like Justine in the book, she disappeared.

Long: Do you yourself hold with the theory in the book—that Justine's husband strangled her and the town covered it up?

Keller: [Clears throat] Well, now, Ms. Harrington would be the first to admit that she's a fiction writer. And as such, I—[clears throat again]—I think she's constructed a very exciting, plausible story. My intent isn't to—uh—uphold or undermine her novel. My movie doesn't really even have anything to do with all that, except that the tree Benjamin Platt sabotaged happens to be the same tree featured in *Bury Me Not*. I'm really more interested in how this person Ben Platt kind of wormed his way into everyone's good graces over the course of a few weeks and then went behind their backs and attacked them where they were most vulnerable. I mean, they had given him the title "Tree Champion"! He was supposed to be documenting their prized redwood.

Long: Yes, and you claim that, along with documenting it—climbing way up into the branches, hundreds of feet off the ground, taking pictures, writing up some verbiage—he also did some things to imperil the tree.

Keller: Yes. Like I said, he had gained everyone's trust. They let him wander the woods at will. Borrow their tools. Borrow their cars. I located an area some twenty-five yards from Grand Daddy (the giant redwood) where Platt was found incapacitated one evening. I had a couple botanists inspect the area after the tragic storm, and they agreed that damage had been done there with some sort of cutting tool. Well, we know for a fact Platt had a mattock and a shovel with him that night.

Long: And why would he do this? He himself was working on a postdoctorate in botany and forestry at Humboldt State University. What would turn a man like that—a tree hugger, basically—into a vandal? An eco-vandal.

Keller: Based on extensive interviews, we know Platt was in pretty sorry shape when he showed up in Red Gap. He had hurt himself in a fall from a tree and sustained a concussion, among other injuries, so he was confused. But he was also very close-lipped about where and what he'd come from. He didn't seem to have people who were close with him. It wasn't long before he began to worry some people. I mean, he started to get obsessed with the town's ghost story. He even went so far as to say he'd *seen* the ghost. *Heard* the ghost. I think he was basically unbalanced, whether by nature or because of his injuries. You take that and you add a messy break-up with his girlfriend—also a botany and forestry postdoc at HSU—and you get a very troubled guy.

Long: This famous town ghost! I'm sure the viewers and I would love to hear more about her. What did Platt claim to have seen?

Keller: [Sighs] A—uh—a figure in white. A woman. Curly brown hair. Dressed in a full-length gown with a short train. Greenish eyes. Basically, she tallies with descriptions of Daphne Lindstrom, the woman who disappeared in 1895.

Long: She was supposed to be very beautiful, wasn't she? Or was that just dramatic embellishment for the novel?

Keller: [Muffled] She was the most beautiful woman I ever—that is—historical sources agree that Daphne Lindstrom was a remarkably attractive woman. And that her ghost—well—was that too.

Long: All right, then. Uh…have other people seen Daphne? Her ghost, rather?

Keller: Yes. Supposedly.

Long: Did *you*, in the course of shooting, did *you* ever see the ghost?

Keller: [Long pause] Possibly. Er—at a great distance. One time, and never again. It's almost impossible to be in an environment like that where you're living breathing eating drinking this story, and not start to imagine things.

Long: [Chuckles] Of course. I bet.

Keller: But I'm not—I've never been the kind of guy who gets the girl.

Long: [Laughs awkwardly] Okay. Well. Why don't we move on, then, and talk about some of the controversy that has arisen from your film? I know there were a few people who refused to be interviewed.

Keller: Yes. Yes. Uh—the couple that owns the bed-and-breakfast where Platt stayed. Mainly them. Them and a few others.

Long: And why is that?

Keller: I think they just want to put it behind them. The couple, I mean. I mean, they, most of all, got the wool pulled over their eyes. Plus, the husband, Charlie Derwent, he's descended from the family Gladys Harrington calls the Davenants in *Bury Me Not*. Between the novel and my documentary and the upcoming film adaptation, there's just been too much publicity. They're private people. They want to stay out of the limelight.

Long: And yet I have a quote from the wife Beatrice Derwent stating that, "*Fatal Blow* is a fiction from start to finish, with no more truth to it than [Gladys Harrington's] novel. Benjamin Platt was a fine young man, completely of sound mind, as we and other witnesses can attest. Furthermore, we had scientific experts examine Carson Keller's claims, and their findings refute his. Dr. Simon Limswick of the California Polytechnic State University has studied the site and concluded that Grand Daddy fell as a result of logging damage done a century earlier, combined with rain-saturated ground, high wind, and the nearly concurrent fall of a nearby Douglas fir, which both lifted up and severed the shallow, fragile root mat of the coast redwood."

Keller: Fine, but my experts found otherwise.

Long: Supposedly this Simon Limswick has teamed up with a Lance Soong—also a recent graduate from the Humboldt State University program—and the two of them will be featured on an upcoming episode of *Nova*, refuting the claims you make in *Fatal Blow*. Soong, a professor himself now, has been especially vocal in protesting what he calls the "character assassination perpetrated against Benjamin Platt in the Humboldt circle."

Keller: I would point out that Professor Edgar Wilson, head of the "Humboldt circle," whom I feature in *Fatal Blow*, is considered the foremost expert on the coast redwood *Sequoia sempervirens* worldwide. *The* expert. He knows his stuff. And he was Platt's former advisor, so in a good position to judge Platt's character. That's all I have to say about that. We agree to disagree.

Long: Okay. Fair enough. Both sides have academics backing them with strong opinions. How about novelist Gladys Harrington? Does she have a take on all this?

Keller: I actually haven't been able to get her reaction. She's been in seclusion.

Long: Your names were connected romantically for a time, weren't they?

Keller: I think she would disagree with you there.

Long: Do you believe the rumors that her "seclusion" stems from a nervous breakdown, brought on by these events?

Keller: Uh…that tree meant a lot to the town. If she *were* to have a nervous breakdown no one could blame her. But—er—no, I think she just needed a little time. And a break from all the questions.

Long: Mm. Okay… So then all that fuss over your allegations barely died down when there was a surprise discovery, right?

Keller: Right.

Long: You wrapped up your interviews, you were in the middle of editing and—blam!—you see this on the news:

[Video Clip]

[Clip from KIEM news broadcast dated 7.11.04. Humboldt County Sheriff's Deputy stands before microphone held by unseen reporter.]

Dep. Espinoza: Over a week ago, a pair of Fourth of July hikers wandered off-trail near Red Gap. While picking huckleberries, they came upon several artifacts in the undergrowth, including a portable folding shovel and a partially-crushed helmet. After further exploration of the area, they located several bones which have since been established as human remains.

Reporter: Has the county been able to confirm the identity of the body?

Espinoza: It was not a complete body. Just a few bones. I am not able to give an official confirmation at this time, no.

Reporter: Can you comment on the rumor that the remains might be those of Benjamin Platt, a visitor to Red Gap who went missing in October of 2003?

Espinoza: I cannot at this time.

Reporter: Was it true that there might be more extensive remains, but they're buried under a mammoth section of the redwood called "Grand Daddy," which fell in October 2003, the very day Platt went missing?

Espinoza: Well, if you know that much, you know the piece of the redwood is bigger than a semi-truck and lies in a crater twelve feet deep. So if there are more remains underneath, I'd like to know how anybody has verified that.

Reporter: What about the recent theory put about by a documentary filmmaker, that Platt sabotaged the tree? Do you believe this possible identification of him clearly in the vicinity lends support to that idea?

Espinoza: That's really outside the purview of this investigation. I have no comment.

[End Video Clip]

Long: What a bolt from the blue! Tell us what happened next.

Keller: Well, the county finally admitted the remains really were Benjamin Platt. You'd think that would settle things—I mean, there he was, kind of caught red-handed after death. He was supposed to be headed back to check in with his university department, the day the tree fell, but there he was. So another lie to people who trusted him. I thought it was kind of poetic justice that the guy goes to undermine the tree, and in the end the tree smashes him.

Long: Again, your critics argue that Platt might have been *in* the tree when it fell, rather than on the ground. For instance, neighbor Clyde Sills spoke with Benjamin Platt that very morning and said Platt wanted to head back up the tree the same day, even though the weather was poor. This is the same Clyde Sills who made several examinations of Platt's health over the few weeks and called him "as sane as the next guy after those first couple days."

Keller: Yes. Well, as I point out in the film, Sills is a great guy and a great *veterinarian*, but those two things don't necessarily qualify him to make medical diagnoses. Platt also asked for the use of Sills' crossbow, to launch a climbing rope into the tree, but didn't get it that day. If Platt climbed the tree, how did he get up there without any way to set a rope? [Shrugs] No way of knowing now. It was not a day for climbing. I think the evidence is pretty persuasive that he snuck into the woods to make sure the tree was going to go over like he hoped, and he got caught out.

Long: A mystery in a mystery.

Keller: Definitely. Even Platt's parents didn't want the tree moved to see if more clues could be found. They just buried the bones they had. They didn't want the spot marked either because they said their son would not have wanted to increase off-trail traffic through the redwoods.

Long: Is it true that investigators found one bone mixed in that did *not* belong to Platt? A much older, more weathered one.

Keller: [Coughing. Takes a sip of water.] Another layer to the mystery. That was never officially verified. I think, if there was anything, they glossed over it. All the found remains were buried together.

Long: So you do not have a theory about that other bone, if there was one?

Keller: I do not.

Long: At any rate, all those twists and turns generated some good publicity for your movie, even if they were something of a headache for you. And speaking of headaches, you managed to make *Fatal Blow* despite suffering severe migraines for the past couple years.

Keller: That's right. It was a challenge. The World Health Organization says that 303 million people worldwide suffer from migraines, but so little is known about the causes and treatment.

Long: Have you suffered from migraines all your life?

Keller: Actually, I got my first one in Red Gap. The same day I got the idea for this movie. I think I might be allergic to redwoods.

Long: [Laughs with him] Too bad, too bad. Maybe you should be donating to migraine research, instead of the—what is it—[Shuffles papers]

Keller: Grand Daddy Legacy Foundation.

Long: That's right. The Grand Daddy Legacy Foundation, which you started, I believe. [Reading] "The mission of the Grand Daddy Legacy Foundation—quite a mouthful—is to propagate genetic clones of the fallen giant, in the hopes of reversing the history of redwood destruction and extending the life of this symbolic tree." Firstly, what does that all mean, and, secondly, have you had any luck so far?

Keller: Considering what this tree has meant to the town of Red Gap, I think it's only fitting that we try to restore it to the community in some sense. A symbolic gift in return for all that redwoods have meant to them and how they have been exploited, from the days of the Red Gap Lumber Company to the wanton destructive act of Ben Platt—

Long: [Interrupts]—Not to mention your own film, which, however consciousness-raising, will probably also threaten them with increased forest traffic.

Keller: Uh—well, maybe you could see it that way.

Long: I don't mean that aggressively. No—I saw your movie, and the first thing I wanted to do was get out there and see Grand Daddy and Red Gap for myself. I include myself as an exploiter. So, okay, how does the Foundation "restore" the tree to the community?

Keller: Well, the Foundation right now has moved to a maintenance mode. I actually got it going almost right after the tree fell. I had scientists collect cuttings (new little branches) and burls (lumps of deformed wood) from the fallen tree. If they survived cultivation, they would hopefully develop into transplantable genetic clones of Grand Daddy.

Long: Any success?

Keller: Not with the cuttings, no. It took pretty long for the area around the tree to become even marginally passable. By the time we got some, they were in sorry shape. Burls were tough, too, because, on a tree as old and huge as Grand Daddy, the burls were also old and huge. But two little ones we had, they survived. Under my supervision, the scientists put them in water and waited for little sprouts and roots to come out. Then they were transplanted that winter in Daphne Lindstrom's Grove and monitored. Well, something went wrong with one of them because we never heard from that one again, but the other— it's taken off. In just 2-½ years it's already ten feet tall. Growing like a weed. We put a fence around it for now to protect it, but eventually it'll be big enough that that won't be necessary.

Long: A happy ending to this tragic story.

Keller: Fingers crossed.

Long: Well, Mr. Keller, thank you for your time, and good luck with the upcoming wider distribution of your film. Once again, that's *Fatal Blow*, a must-see documentary for nature-lovers and fans of *Bury Me Not* alike. Thanks for coming by.

Keller: It's been a pleasure.

2005

No one noticed the ring-bearer had gone missing until the bridal party was assembling in the parlor. Not surprising, really, considering Megan had spilled tea down the front of her wedding dress, and both her twin sister Rachel and her mother Bea were frantically dabbing and spotting cold water on the stain.

"You're a mess, Meg! This is why I only drank water or 7-Up until after all the pictures were taken."

"You really think it's that bad?" said the bride. "Maybe Dad and Brian and Robby could move the arch into the shade."

"Then you'll be knee-deep in mud," her mother pointed out. "It never dries out there." She straightened up, cocking her head to consider. "It'll have to do. Just try to hold your bouquet in front of it. Do it *now*," she commanded, thrusting the armful of pale-pink Heritage roses at her, "because here comes that awful wedding coordinator of yours. What does Robby call her?"

"Ball-Breaker," whispered Megan, giggling. "Because of her initials. But I think she's really Barbara."

The fiercely elegant bottle-blonde swept the room with a glance calculated to freeze everyone into silence. She clapped her hands smartly. "The groomsmen are seating the grandmothers and the quartet is tuning up for the prelude. Is everyone accounted for and lined up? Mrs. Derwent, the groom's brother is standing by to escort you. Where's the flower girl?"

"There, BeBe," squeaked Megan, plastering her bouquet to her chest and pointing at a six-year-old cousin, who was curled up in the wingback looking at picture books.

"Stand up, dear," ordered BeBe. "Your dress will wrinkle. Now you go right after your great-aunt, when the music changes, remember? And the ring-bearer?"

"He *was* right here," said Rachel apologetically. "I gave him part of a granola bar to keep him quiet."

"And then I told him to go wash his hands in the kitchen when he was done," said Bea.

But four-year-old Noah was not in the kitchen. Nor was he in the dining room, office, back parlor, mud room, or any of the unlocked rooms upstairs, the women discovered.

"Maybe he went outside to sit with his mother," suggested Rachel. "I'll take a peek."

"Whatever you do," said BeBe, "don't upset the guests."

Ten minutes later, the frantic matron of honor thought "upset" didn't begin to cover it. The folding chairs on the Dryad's back lawn lay abandoned or up-ended as seekers scrambled over the grounds and into the surrounding woods, hollering as they fanned out. Cousin Samantha, the boy's mother, alternated between sobbing helplessly and tearing around in circles, shrieking for Noah in a manner Rachel thought would surely scare the boy back into his hiding place. Megan had added not only mud splatters to her tea-stained wedding gown, but also a fringe of fir needles. Ray Holtz, former mayor of Red Gap, took it upon himself to raise the alarm with county authorities, while BeBe Gardner was overheard grumbling that four-year-old wedding attendants were not recommended for *exactly* these reasons.

Fully twenty minutes after his absence sent everyone into a frenzy, Noah reappeared. By that time the Dryad had been turned inside out, with any space a four-year-old could possibly squeeze into opened and inspected more than once. Bea's exceptional housecleaning skills passed muster. The sofa cushions and book cases, the cabinets and closets, yielded not a single dust bunny, much less a child. The Dryad's setting received an equal going-over. The shed was unlocked, every car checked, the porch swing cushions raised. Even the cellist's instrument case suffered repeated investigation.

It was Charlie who finally noticed the boy. Noah sat on the wrought-iron bench, calm as he pleased, the same bench he had most certainly not occupied a minute ago and which people had been rushing past nearly the entire time.

So as not to frighten him, Charlie approached as if nothing was amiss. "What's that you got there?" he asked.

Noah looked up from the shiny, pear-shaped metal loop in his hands. "I dunno. The man said if I went and sat here, I could have it."

"Then it's yours, I guess," said Charlie. He sat down beside him. "Did you hear us calling? Your mom's been looking for you."

The boy shrugged. "Maybe."

"Nooooooo-aaaaaaahhhh!" screeched Samantha, running to enfold him in her arms. Word spread quickly among the gathering that the search was off, but the others kept a respectful distance, finding the mother's explosive combination of relief, tears and fury adequate for the occasion. She squeezed him till he protested, her make-up a receded tide of mascara and eyeliner. "Why did you run away like that? Didn't you hear me calling you? Don't ever, ever, ever do that again!"

"Okay," said Noah. "Look what I got. From the man."

Samantha turned her wet, confused gaze on Charlie, who had been trying to edge away. She took the metal loop from Noah. "Got what? This thing from Uncle Charlie?"

"Not from me," said Charlie. "I guess someone else gave it to him to try to get him to go back to us."

She sniffled. "I don't like that. Some weird guy in the woods who doesn't even come himself to return a little boy to his family? What is this, anyway?"

"It's—a—a carabiner," said Charlie. "People use them for rock climbing or—uh—tree climbing."

"He wasn't a weird guy," said the boy stoutly, reaching for his present. "He was nice. The lady said he better hurry up and get me back, but he said fifteen more seconds wouldn't hurt. He showed me how to open the gate, see?" He unlocked the carabiner for them.

"There was a lady with him, and *she* didn't even walk you back?" demanded his mother. Her eyes scanned the woods beyond, as if she expected this unfeeling couple to be picnicking carelessly by the side of the path.

"Then the man said did I know that metal bench right outside the edge of the grass, under the trees, by the purple house? And I said yes, I was staying at the purple house. And he said that's what he thought. And he said, if I would go back to that bench and sit, he'd leave this car—carbonator for me there."

"Well—that was nice of him, I suppose," Samantha conceded stiffly. "I'm still mad at you, though. Anything could have happened to you! You could've gotten lost. Or fallen down and gotten hurt. How far into the woods did you go, anyhow?"

"Unner the fence."

"What fence?"

"The one around the tree."

"Oh, hey," Charlie spoke up. "Whenever you see a fence, that means you stay on your side and whatever's inside the fence stays on *its* side. That particular fence was put up to protect that tree until it's bigger and stronger."

"You should tell that to the lady, then," protested Noah. "When I was inside the fence, she was too." His smooth brow furrowed. "I don't know how she fit unner the fence. Or got back out. Her dress was big like Aunt Megan's."

"—Was it—was it white, like Aunt Megan's?" said Charlie.

"Uh-huh."

"Are you all right, Uncle Charlie?" Samantha asked.

"What did the lady look like?" said Charlie.

"She was pretty, with lots of big curly hair and eyes that were smiley."

"And the man? What did he look like?"

"I dunno."

"Short or tall?"

"Tall. Real tall."

"Fat like me, or kinda skinny?"

"Lots skinnier'n you."

"Noah!" laughed Samantha.

"Yellow hair or black or brown?"

Noah thought about this. "Brown. But it had some gray in it like old men like you, Uncle Charlie. But he wasn't old."

"What is it, Uncle Charlie?" Samantha said again. "Do you know these people?"

He was staring over Noah's head, back into the thick stand of trees. Redwoods and firs. Dusky and silent in their mysterious solidarity.

A few languorous notes from the wedding musicians sounded, shimmering in the September sun before stretching and mellowing as they entered the forest.

Charlie stood up. "It's nothing," he said. But he was smiling now. "We got a wedding to go to!"

Samantha took Noah's hand to march him back to the house, darting apologetic glances right and left and throwing out explanations. She didn't hear Charlie's muttered comment behind her.

Maybe no one did.

He said again, "It's nothing."

He threw one last glance over his shoulder. Nodded once, though anyone looking the same direction would say there was nothing to be seen in the gray-green shadows. "Nothing. Except I never did think I'd see either one of those two. Not ever again."

Acknowledgements:

Thanks once more to my long-suffering critique group who bore with my swings from "No, I'm not ready to send you any yet" to "Hurry up! Hurry up! Why haven't you finished?" Sorry this one was so scary for you, Lucia.

Nancy Brose helpfully answered random forestry questions. Any remaining errors or—worse—vast swaths of redwood ignorance are entirely my own fault.

I appreciate the creativity and support of the wonderful folks at Gorham Printing, especially Kathy Campbell, the fabulous designer, and Kathleen Shaputis who embodies promptness and encouragement.

And finally, thank you to Scott, who thought Ben should see a doctor, and my children for their input on the cover and the many times I asked them to go play outside or "keep it down." Love you all.

Reading Group Guide:

1. If you were producing a film version of *Everliving*, whom would you cast in the roles?

2. To whom does the title refer?

3. The epigraph from Ovid's *Metamorphoses* comes from the story of Apollo and Daphne. What connections can you draw between the mythological tale and Daphne Lindstrom's story?

4. In what way is Daphne similar to Gladys' book character Justine Sauvee? In what ways is she different? How close is Justine's relationship with "Shep" to Daphne's with Shane? How much of a connection do you think Gladys had to Daphne?

5. At one point Ben thinks Daphne "looks like the Gibson Girl from an old-time Coca Cola ad." In what ways did Daphne fit the feminine conventions of her time? In what ways did she struggle against them? Can you think of other stories where 19th-century women were committed for being "unfeminine"?

6. What is the role of history and story in the novel? How many different histories/stories are recorded? How do characters use those histories to understand the present?

7. Why do you think Carson Keller does not reveal the story Daphne gives him? Why do you think he implicates Ben?

8. Who do you think was ultimately responsible for what happened to Grand Daddy?

9. What other ghost stories or "paranormal romances" have you read? How does this book compare?

10. What was most surprising to you, in reading about the lives of redwood trees?